THE FAMILY INHERITANCE

FIONA LOWE

PRAISE FOR FIONA LOWE

"A gripping tale about greed, the price paid for ill-placed trust and the lessons that come with having it and losing it all ... Ultimately, **The Money Club** is about hope." — *Weekend Australian*

'**A Family of Strangers** is a glorious, heart-warming tapestry of a novel.' —*The Herald Sun*

'Rich, thought-provoking, and extremely absorbing, **A Home Like Ours** is yet another incredible read from the very talented Fiona Lowe.' —*Better Reading*

'An insightful, warm and engaging story, **A Home Like Ours** is another fabulous novel from award-winning Australian author Fiona Lowe.' —*Book'd Out*

'Fiona Lowe's ability to create atmosphere and tension and real relationship dynamics is a gift.'
—*Sally Hepworth, bestselling author of The Mother-in-Law, on **Home Fires.***

'Part-Liane Moriarty, part-Jodi Picoult, **Just an Ordinary Family** is a compelling drama about a seemingly 'ordinary' family that implodes after a domino effect of lies, betrayals, disappointments and regrets ... set to be the next Big Little Lies.' —*Mamamia*

'Lowe weaves character development and complexity with stunning finesse ... this story is not a light read, but it is one that proved difficult to put down.' —*GLAM Adelaide* on ***Just an Ordinary Family***

'Fiona Lowe is the undisputed queen of Australian small-town fiction ... a moving character-driven tale that steadily draws you into its thrall.' —*Canberra Weekly* on ***Just an Ordinary Family***

'A complex story that seamlessly intertwines many story lines. It is full of interesting characters that reveal more and more as the story progresses. It is raw, incredibly engaging and reads beautifully.' —*The Big Book Club on* ***The Family Inheritance*** (previously published as *Birthright*)

'Distinctly Australian with its power to evoke grit and tenderness, joy and bleakness, tragedy and comedy, all at once.'
—*Better Reading* on ***The Family Inheritance*** (previously published as *Birthright*)

'Lowe is a master at painting believable characters with heart and soul that contribute to creating such an addictive read.'
—*The Weekly Times* on ***The Family Inheritance*** (previously published as *Birthright*)

'A sweeping Australian novel of lost love and tangled family secrets.' —
Australian Country on ***Daughter of Mine***

ALSO BY FIONA LOWE

Daughter of Mine

The Family Inheritance

(*PREVIOUSLY PUBLISHED AS* *BIRTHRIGHT*)

Home Fires

Just an Ordinary Family

A Home Like Ours

A Family of Strangers

The Money Club

The Accident

Thank you for buying

The Family Inheritance

(*PREVIOUSLY PUBLISHED AS* *BIRTHRIGHT*)

For a free novella, ***Summer of Mine***; the prequel of **Daughter of Mine**, please join my VIP Readers newsletter. You'll also be the first to hear about new releases, book sales, competitions and giveaways. Register at

fionalowe.com

Did you know BookBub has a new release alert? You can check out the latest deals and get an email when I release my next book by following me at

www.bookbub.com/authors/fiona-lowe

THE FAMILY INHERITANCE
PREVIOUSLY PUBLISHED AS BIRTHRIGHT

First Published by Harlequin Australia in 2018
This revised UK edition published in 2022 by Fiona Lowe

The Family Inheritance
ISBN 978-0-6456187-1-6

Cover Design by Barton Lowe

Published by Fiona Lowe

To the men in my life—my father, my husband and my sons—who taught me that the love and support of a good man eases life's load.

No legacy is so rich as honesty—William Shakespeare

Where there's a will, there's a relative—Roger Karshner

CHAPTER ONE

'It's Sunday morning on Australia's radio show.'

The twang of a banjo exploded in Sarah's ears, hauling her aggressively and abruptly out of a deliciously deep sleep. Worse than that, it imploded a wondrous dream of a place where she floated peacefully, bathing in all its wonder. A place no one expected her to juggle the transport logistics of bread and cheese, solve staffing issues, find missing wallets/keys/phones/items of school uniforms/homework —in fact, no one was asking her to do anything at all. It was her definition of bliss.

She lay momentarily stunned, her heart pounding and her mind struggling to compute more than *No! Too early! Go away!* The realisation it was Mother's Day dribbled into her consciousness more slowly, before jabbing her like the sharp end of stick.

Stupid, stupid, stupid. Why didn't you check the alarm last night?

She'd shared her life with Alex for twenty-two years and she was intimate with the fact that eighty per cent of the time he forgot to switch off the six-day-a-week radio alarm on Saturday night. So here she was awake in the dark at 6.30 am on Mother's Day. Fabulous! The temptation to wallow in a seductive bath of 'why today of all days?'

tugged at her, but martyrdom wasn't a coat that fit. All her life she'd been a problem solver, a fixer—a woman who got things done. Sure, she was awake ridiculously early on a day that was technically 'her day', when sleeping in was an essential part of the manual, but was it an opportunity? Carpe diem and all that jazz? She smiled. This year, they only had one kid at home and she'd bet Gus wouldn't be up this early, giving her and Alex plenty of time to celebrate.

Rolling over, she moved to spoon her husband. Her arms touched warm but empty sheets just as Alex's feet hit the floor with their usual thump. A streak of cool air zoomed in under the duvet, skating up her spine. She sat up in the dark.

'You're going for a ride?'

The sound of lycra snapping against skin answered her. She worked at not sighing out loud and actively bit off the words, 'It's Mother's Day'. There was no point uttering them.

When the children were little, Alex had helped them make her breakfast in bed but the moment they'd become teenagers he'd stepped back, saying, 'She's your mother, not mine.' Apparently, Mother's Day had never got close to an event for the Hadfield family. Sarah tried to take the same hands-off approach to Father's Day but she was hopeless; each year she found herself reminding the kids it was coming up, cajoling each of them into making a card, and she always arranged a family outing.

'Go back to sleep,' Alex said, his early-morning voice raspy.

The yellow light from his bedside lamp penetrated her closed eyelids, turning everything orange. 'Argh.' She pulled the duvet over her head.

'Sorry.'

The light snapped off and as if that was their cue, the dawn chorus of raucous cockatoos screeched as loudly and as stridently as a fire siren. She flinched; the sound mocking her for entertaining thoughts of sleeping in. Alex silently patted her shoulder and she sleepily raised her head for a kiss. She missed and her cheek hit his shoulder as his hair brushed her forehead. Oh well. At least they were still trying after two decades together. It was more than could be said for many of their peers.

Over the last few years, there'd been a cascade of divorces in Mingunyah. The domino effect had started after Bianca Russo drank too much red wine at a Rotary dinner, grabbed the microphone and announced to the room she was leaving her husband. More marriages went on to fail, and each time Sarah heard of another separation she found herself examining her own marriage. Alex didn't seem to need the same reflection. Their discussion on the night of Bianca's bombshell was a case in point.

'You know what this means?' Alex's coffee-coloured eyes had shone with the same enthusiasm that had captured her heart two decades earlier.

'That yet another marriage of people our age has hit the wall?'

A momentary look of remorse crossed his face. 'Yeah, that part's sad. But their land abuts the farm. We could build a fourth dairy. Milk another two thousand goats and secure our milk supply. This is the next step in taking our cheese beyond Victoria.'

It was a tempting idea, one that would free them up from relying on other milk suppliers. 'They may not want to sell.'

'Oh, I think they will. Ed paid top dollar for that place and it's heavily geared. There's no way Bianca will get her share of the marriage assets without them selling. And we'll be waiting in the wings with an offer they can't refuse.'

'Look out, Australia,' she teased, 'Mingunyah Cheese is coming.'

'We're not stopping at Australia. Think of the foodies living on the West Coast of the US. They'll fall over themselves to get their hands on our healthy, organic cheese.'

As always, his excitement was both terrifying and infectious. 'I always knew life with you wouldn't be boring.'

'Damn straight.' He'd grinned and kissed her again before demonstrating exactly how exciting and exhilarating life with him could be.

Back then, they'd thought the goal of entering the American

market was the ultimate prize, but they'd been wrong—China was the crowning glory. They'd opened an office there and now exported their marinated goat's cheese and sheep's yoghurt. It was beyond their wildest dreams and recently, with a middle management structure firmly in place, they finally had time to explore interests outside of the business. Sarah was yet to get out from under her workload and family commitments but Alex had committed to cycling.

He was a cycling store's dream come true, from his state-of-the-art Italian, full carbon-fibre bike with its lights, computer and little solar panel for charging his phone, to his gloves for every season and booties with heated insoles. Given that winter mornings were below zero, it made sense. Sarah didn't begrudge him the thousands of dollars he'd spent on getting kitted out—it wasn't as if they couldn't afford it. In fact their bakery benefitted from cycling tourists and skiers, selling them, among other things, marinated fruit muffins nicknamed turbo buns.

Like every other morning, Sarah lay in bed listening to the familiar sounds of cycling shoes clicking into cleats, the gentle whirr of tyres, and the clunk of gears changing until they faded into the distance. Now fully awake, she ran through her options. She could stay in bed and wait for Gus to wake, remember it was Mother's Day and give her breakfast in bed. The only flaw with that plan was that, without his father or younger sister in the house, the chances of Gus waking before ten and remembering the significance of the day were slim.

Always practical, Sarah got up and, alone in the kitchen on Mother's Day, made herself coffee and baked a cake.

A rather sad and pathetic-looking cake.

Sarah cocked her head to the left and studied the offering. She couldn't believe her no-fail chocolate cake had sunk on her. But then again, nothing was going according to plan so far and it wasn't even ten yet. Grabbing dark chocolate from the pantry and cream from the fridge, she went into fix-it mode just as she had the week before when her sister-in-law Anita had texted, *Doubt our plan to run away for a spa day on Mother's Day will fly. Margaret will want family lunch*

Sarah had immediately texted back, *Riverbend 12.00*

Why had she done that? Sure, she'd hosted Mother's Day for her mother for years, but now that Anita and Cameron were living in Mingunyah, her lovely sister-in-law, who was a stellar cook, had probably been about to offer to host lunch herself. Anita's mother had died before she'd married Cameron, so although Mother's Day was a bittersweet day for her, Anita had never known the inherent problem of the day—being a daughter and a mother.

For years Sarah juggled trying to have her own day as well as making sure her mother felt special too. More than once it had culminated in hot tears and chest-crushing frustration. After one particularly disappointing year, she'd pretty much accepted that until her mother was no longer with them, expecting to have Mother's Day exclusively for herself was both unrealistic and angst-inducing. Since then, Sarah kept breakfast for herself—although this year even that seemed in peril—and devoted the rest of the day to being a dutiful daughter. Her brother, Cameron, was a dutiful son on the occasions it suited him. Their younger sister, Ellie, was unfamiliar with any aspects of the term 'dutiful'.

Sarah absently licked the spatula dripping with the remnants of the melted chocolate and fervently hoped her emergency cake ministrations wouldn't send anyone into a sugar coma.

'Happy Mother's Day, Mum.' Gus, her gangly, almost seventeen-year-old son ambled over, wrapped his arms around her and gave her a hug. 'Bit hard to give you brekkie in bed when you're already up.'

She resisted glancing pointedly at the clock. 'True, but I'll happily eat it with you at the kitchen table.'

He scratched his head and opened the fridge, staring into it as if willing whatever it was he was looking for to levitate from the shelf and float into his hand.

'Are there any croissants?'

'Did you buy any?'

He looked sheepish as he closed the fridge door. 'Where's Dad? Is he in town?'

Sarah gave in and checked the clock, surprised to see it was ten thirty. 'He was riding to Gravitt's Lookout. I thought he'd be back by now.'

'I'll call him and get him to buy some.'

Sarah did the calculations in her head and knew that wasn't going to work. 'How about you toast me some of our fruit loaf and slather it in butter? Then be my kitchenhand so we're ready when the hordes descend.'

Gus grinned. 'I'll even make you a cup of tea.'

'You're my favourite middle child.'

He rolled his eyes. 'One day Finn and I are going to get you to admit you like Emma best.'

'Only on Mother's Day,' she quipped, tousling his chestnut hair as if he was seven. 'And only because she remembers the croissants.'

Of her three children, Gus was the sportiest and yet he was also the most reserved. A talented footballer and skier, he was the quiet one among his friends, often surrounded by noise and girls— hugging, squealing girls. Sarah noticed that other boys with similar skills always carried themselves with an air of confidence—a certain swagger—but the moment Gus walked off the footy field or hung up his skis, he seemed to retreat into himself just a little. This bothered her but whenever she mentioned it to Alex, he'd sigh and give her a look that inferred she was worrying over nothing.

'That kid,' he'd say, pride lighting up his face, 'has the world at his feet. If he plays his cards right, he'll end up playing footy in the AFL.'

'Mum?'

'Hmm?' Sarah was on her knees with her head in the fridge playing Tetris to make room for the cake. The buzz muffled Gus's words but she thought she heard 'play'.

At yesterday's match, Gus took a spectacular flying leap and cleanly marked the ball. Slowly running in, taking his time, he kicked the winning goal right on the siren. Not only did the entire team slap his back, the crowd slapped Alex's. Her husband glowed with as much pride as if the ball had come off his own boot.

Carefully sliding the cake onto the middle shelf, Sarah rose and closed the fridge door, pleased Gus was mentioning the moment. He generally underplayed his achievements. 'It was an impressive play, darling. Your coach was beside himself.'

'Yeah.' Gus's hand gripped the handle of the kettle. 'He was.'

Sarah heard resignation instead of pride and gave him her full attention. 'Isn't that a good thing?'

He dropped his gaze, concentrating on pouring boiling water over the tea leaves. She waited for him to say more but his large hands fumbled with the tea cosy.

'Gus?'

'G'day, mate.' Alex appeared in the kitchen, sweaty and red cheeked. 'Everyone at the café's talking about your mark. Old Daryl Cotter said it reminded him of your grandfather.'

Confusion crossed Gus's face. 'Grandpa didn't play footy.'

'He's talking about my dad.' Sarah was sure she must have told Gus at some point over the years that her father had played for the Mingunyah Tigers. If she hadn't, then her mother certainly would have said something. Mind you, her father's playing days finished not long after he married Margaret so footy hadn't really been part of their shared life. Come to think of it, her father had never talked about footy much at all. His only nod to his time on the team was a dusty framed photo that hung off a rusty nail over his workbench in the shed. The fit young player staring out at her with a roguish glint in his eyes had always seemed a totally different person from the man who was her father. He'd been older and greyer, and the roguish glint had been replaced by a businessman's preoccupied stare.

'Ask Gran about it at lunch. She's probably still got some photos.'

'Photos?' Alex snorted. 'Her entire house is a shrine to Kevin.'

A ripple of irritation ran along Sarah's veins and she tried to shake it off. After all, there was no good reason for it—Alex was right. Decades after her father's death, her mother still kept many of his things on display, but the football memorabilia was not part of the collection.

A memory came to her—clear and bright—tumbling her back to

when she was eleven. Determined to avoid her mother and her demands that she 'clean up that tip of a room', Sarah was hiding in the shed. Looking for something to pass the time, she went exploring and, under a faded old green tarp, she discovered a pile of dust-covered boxes. It was the equivalent of finding lost treasure. One was filled with tarnished football trophies, all engraved with her father's name. Inspired, she rummaged about in the old biscuit tin he kept on his workbench and, among the tins of dubbin and boot polish, she found the Silvo. Listening to Wham on her Walkman, she spent an enjoyable hour polishing the trophies and bringing them back to their former glory. When she was satisfied that they couldn't shine any brighter, she ran into the house waving the gleaming cups.

'Look, Mum!' she said proudly.

Her mother's face rapidly stiffened into hard and sharp lines. '*That's* what you've been doing instead of cleaning your room? Take those straight back to where you found them.'

'Why? You've got Cameron's tennis trophies on the mantelpiece, so why not Dad's?'

'Do. As. You're. Told.' Margret ground out the words as if Sarah was being excruciatingly difficult and trying her patience to breaking point. 'Or do you want to feel the sting of the wooden spoon?' Having recently experienced a series of run-ins with that spoon, Sarah reluctantly trudged back to the shed. Her submission to her mother's request, however, wasn't enough to stop the simmer of resentment swelling in her chest.

'It's not fair,' she complained to her father as she sat on the end of his workbench after tea.

His hazel eyes held only resignation. 'They don't fit with your mother's decor.'

'Neither do Cam's!' An unfamiliar hot spot burned in her chest and she rubbed it.

Her father marked the wood he was measuring with his flat red carpenter's pencil. 'It's a rule that mothers display their son's trophies.'

'Then wives should have to display their husband's trophies.'

He laughed and stuck the pencil behind his ear in his familiar and reassuring way. 'It doesn't work that way, blossom.'

'I'll keep them in my room then,' she said indignantly, confused by her father's acceptance of what she clearly saw as a double standard.

'Tell you what. How about I teach you how to make a cabinet for them? We can mount it on this wall.' He pointed to a gap between two tool boards.

They'd spent a few happy weekends making the cabinet. With infinite patience, her father had taught her how to accurately measure timber and mitre corners and the art of a bevel edge. For a time, she'd taken great delight in polishing the glass and dusting the trophies. When puberty hit, she'd lost interest in carpentry, the trophies and hanging out in her father's shed.

The memory faded, pushed out by Sarah's sudden realisation that it had been decades since she last thought about that special time with her father. What had happened to the cabinet and its contents?

Gus placed the buttered fruit toast and a cup of tea on the table before pulling out a chair for her with a flourish. 'Here you go, Mum.'

Gus's timing was terrible. The clock was ticking down fast and she still needed to peel potatoes, make a berry sauce and set the table before the family arrived. Overriding the urge to keep working while she ate, Sarah made herself sit down and appreciate his efforts. She picked up the warm, fragrant toast and remembered that Alex's arrival had interrupted their previous conversation. 'Gus, what were you telling me when I had my head in the fridge?'

But Gus was asking his father about his average speed up the mountain on the morning's ride. Alex held his bike computer in his palm and they bent over the device—one chestnut head and one jet black sexily streaked with grey—studying the numbers. Sarah smiled. Boys and their toys.

Her mobile rang.

'Happy Mother's Day.'

'Finn!' Her heart rolled and she grinned at the sound of her eldest child's voice. She still remembered the moment the midwife laid baby

Finn in her arms and the rush of love thundering through her with such overwhelming intensity it would have buckled her legs if she'd been standing. Eighteen years later, her baby was doing his first semester at Melbourne University and studying agriculture. By stalking Facebook, Sarah had gleaned that more partying took place than studying. 'You remembered. Thank you.'

'Of course, I remembered,' he said smugly. 'I even sent a card.'

'Did you?' She'd cleared the post office box the day before. 'It hasn't arrived yet.'

'Oh, I only posted it last night,' he said easily. 'Appreciate the effort, Mother dearest. Cards are so old school. Everyone laughed at me when I said we had to walk past a letterbox on the way to the party. All my mates are messaging or Snapchatting their mothers.'

She laughed. 'In that case, I'm honoured. Thank you very much. I'll enjoy reading it when I get it.'

'I didn't say I wrote anything,' Finn teased. Voices in the background called his name. 'I gotta go, Mum. Love ya.'

His duty done, the line went dead and disappointment socked her. She'd wanted to ask Finn about his lectures, about college and if he'd got the results back on the essay he'd been struggling to finish. Alex laughed at something Gus said and a shot of anger—white and hot—flashed behind her eyes. *It's supposed to be my day. My breakfast at least.*

'Alex, get in the shower,' she said more snappishly than she intended. 'Everyone's arriving at twelve and I need your help. And Gus, start peeling those potatoes.'

Resignation slumped Gus's shoulders but he walked to the island bench without a word.

Alex's eyes flashed the colour of burned butter. 'I'm not one of the kids, Sarah.'

But you've just spent two hours playing. 'No. Sorry.' She wasn't sorry—she only said it because she didn't have time to argue right now. 'I'd really appreciate it if you could take a shower and set up the ping-pong table for Noah.'

'Ellie's coming?'

'Maybe. She said she was, but you know Ellie. It's anyone's guess if she actually turns up. I really don't understand why she finds making a decision and sticking to it so difficult.' Her younger sister was a mystery to Sarah.

Alex gave his only-child shrug, the one he'd perfected over the years. He brought it out as a silent comment on her family, but it spoke very loudly. As much as the shrug annoyed her, Sarah was often secretly jealous of Alex's only-child status and the fact he was blessed with largely uninterested parents. Alex didn't have to spend his Father's Day cooking for Ray.

Miaow! For goodness' sake, what was wrong with her today? It wasn't like she'd never hosted Mother's Day before. This was the eighteenth time, although it was the first occasion all her siblings would be together since—God! When was the last time they'd all been under the same roof on Mother's Day?

She sipped her tea, reassuring herself that Anita would arrive early to help. They'd open champagne and be quietly buzzed before Margaret strode through the front door in a cloud of perfume and took centre stage. Before Cameron and Ellie got around to sparring. Before Ava threw a tantrum because Chloe and Noah were ignoring her. She quickly reminded herself that these were just blips on what would be a happy day.

Sarah loved her mother and when it was just the two of them together, she enjoyed her company and her wit. No one told a story about the foibles of Mingunyah's residents better than Margaret. Although she was spry at seventy-six, Sarah was conscious that her mother moved a little more slowly these days and arthritis made fine-motor movements tricky. Over the last three years, Sarah had developed a habit of dropping in to Mill House each weekday for a quick hello. Her mother usually had a job waiting for her. This suited Sarah as she didn't want her mother climbing ladders, changing light bulbs and risking breaking her hip. Although her mother didn't make a fuss of thanking her—that had never been Margaret's way—Sarah knew she appreciated her care and concern. But on days like today, when the family gathered en masse, Margaret leaned into the role of the matriarch with gusto, and Sarah found that champagne always helped.

Alex's mobile rang. 'Phil,' he said in what everyone in the family recognised as his boss voice.

Sarah and Gus stopped what they were doing and looked at him. That voice on a Sunday never boded well.

'Shit. When? Have you ...?' Alex was listening intently and nodding. 'I'll be right over.' His face was grim as he cut the call but his eyes lit up with the excitement of a challenge. It was the same light that had twinkled in his eyes the night he'd proposed to her.

'There's a problem at dairy two's processing plant. If we don't get it fixed, we'll lose a day's production.'

'Dairy two?' Sarah's stomach lurched. 'That's the shipment for Beijing. The truck's got to leave for Melbourne by three tomorrow to make the plane.'

'Exactly.'

'We could draw off dairy three to fill the order. It would mean telling Coles we'll be short this week but—'

Alex nodded. 'It's a good back-up plan but let's just wait and see. I might be able to fix it.' His experience as a mechanical engineer often saved them. 'It probably means I'm going to miss lunch.'

Sarah wished he'd try harder to look disappointed. 'Remember to ring your mother,' she called as he departed for the shower. 'I better ring mine,' she said absently to Gus, picking up the phone.

'Why? Gran will be here in two hours.'

'You know she likes a sense of occasion. She likes to be called on her birthday, Christmas and Mother's Day even if I'm seeing her later in the day. While I'm talking to her, I'll ask her about the football photos.'

'You're not going to get like Gran when you're old, are you?'

She waved Gus quiet as her mother answered. 'Happy Mother's Day,' Sarah chirped in a sing-song voice.

'Who's speaking?' Margaret asked cantankerously.

Sarah tried not to sigh at this game that had started in her childhood when Margaret insisted the first thing they ever said on the phone was their name. 'It's Sarah.'

'Sarah? What are you doing at the police station?'

'I'm not at the police station, Mum. I'm calling you from Riverbend.'

'Someone's stolen my car.'

'From the garage?' Horror streaked through Sarah at the brazen theft. That sort of thing didn't happen in Mingunyah. 'How? When?'

'If I knew that, it wouldn't be stolen, would it?'

'Have you rung the police?'

'No,' her mother said imperiously, as if Sarah was a little bit slow. 'I was trying to call the police when you rang. Now you're tying up the line.'

I called to wish you happy Mother's Day! Sarah reminded herself that her mother was stressed, which was why she sounded rude. 'Do you want me to come over?' *Hello? Bad idea. You've got ten people coming for lunch.* 'Actually, Mum,' she hastily amended, 'I've got a better idea. Call Cameron. He can drive you to the police station then bring you here for lunch.'

'I can't ask him to do that. Your brother's a very busy man.'

And I'm a very busy woman. Sarah drew in a long breath and blew it out slowly, because she was never going to win *that* competition. 'It's Sunday, Mum. It's Mother's Day. I'm sure Cameron's got the time and he'll be happy to help.'

At least one of those statements was correct.

Anita was propped up on pillows and balancing a tray on her knees as her two youngest daughters bounced on the bed.

'Do you like the flower, Mummy?' Ava asked. 'I chose it.'

'Open your present, Mummy,' Chloe demanded. 'I chose it.'

Ava put her hands on her hips. 'I chose the present.'

'You both chose the present,' Cameron said, lifting his eyebrows in a 'here we go again' tilt. 'And *I* cooked the pancakes.'

'Open your present,' the girls chorused.

'She'll open it after she's eaten breakfast. Come on, shoo. Leave Mummy to eat her breakfast in peace.'

Ava pouted. 'Aw, but I want her to open it now.'

Cameron clapped his hands and the noise echoed around the room like a gunshot. 'Kitchen. Now. Or you won't get to see her open her present at all.'

Surprisingly, the girls obeyed, running from the room.

Anita sighed as she took in the slightly charred pancakes and the rapidly cooling coffee. She didn't even want to think about the state of her kitchen. 'I'm sure I need a champagne and orange.'

'Plenty of time for that,' Cameron said, giving her a kiss. 'We don't want the girls telling the family you were on the slops at breakfast.'

'It's Mother's Day. Sarah will approve.'

He flashed her a look. 'Mum won't.'

Anita wasn't certain Margaret approved of her, full stop. She'd been part of Cameron's life for fifteen years now and there were still moments when her mother-in-law's grey eyes took on a decidedly steely hue. Naively, Anita thought that giving Margaret four grandchildren would have helped things along, but apparently the lack of a grandson was a mark against her. That riled, given that gender determination was solely Cameron's domain. Still, ever since they'd moved to Mingunyah, Cameron was intent on not upsetting his mother. As Margaret had generously paid for Phoebe's full-size cello and they were hoping she'd buy Ruby's new dressage saddle, Anita didn't wish to upset her either.

'It's a shame we're not hosting Mother's Day this year,' Cameron said as he stole a piece of pancake from her plate.

His mild censure prickled. 'We've been through this. I was leading up to offering and suddenly Sarah had it all organised.' If Anita were honest, it was a relief to have a weekend off. For months she'd spent almost every weekend helping Cameron establish Prestige Country Properties by cooking and hosting lunches and dinners for clients he wanted to schmooze and impress. 'I'll tell Sarah today that she's off the hook for next year and we'll host.'

'Good. By the way, what am I giving Mum for Mother's Day?'

Anita pointed to a pretty gift bag on her dressing table. 'Her favourite perfume and a silver-framed photo of you and the girls on the beach at Mallacoota this summer.'

'Perfect.'

'I thought so. I've wrapped both boxes. All you need to do is sign the card.'

'What would I do without you?' He leaned in and kissed her on the lips. 'Hmm. Maple syrup.' His grey eyes twinkled. 'Shame the girls are home.'

'Not all of them.' Sadness fluttered over Anita like a cape. This was her first Mother's Day without all her daughters at home.

'The older girls are loving school, Annie,' Cameron said with resigned weariness. 'It was the right decision.'

Anita wanted to agree with him but a tiny part of her held back. She was the product of a poverty-stricken high school in the far-flung northern suburbs of Melbourne. Not once had she entertained the thought of her daughters attending boarding school but then again, she'd never anticipated Cameron's push to move the family back to his childhood town either. Although, unlike her childhood, his had been happy. It was the death of his father that changed the course of his adult life and tainted his love of the town to the point he didn't even mention Mingunyah early in their relationship.

It took until their four-month dating anniversary before Cameron casually mentioned growing up in the country. The news stunned Anita because Cameron oozed urbane smoothness and nothing about him said country roots. She'd assumed he'd grown up feeling out of place and run from Mingunyah—like she'd run from Coolaroo—the first chance he got and never looked back. It was only after they'd announced their engagement that he finally took her to meet his mother and elder sister. That weekend challenged every idea Anita held about country people.

It was a jolt to realise that, unlike her, Cameron didn't leave home and reinvent himself, he'd just left home. The second bombshell exploded after a very formal family dinner party, where Anita needed to closely observe which fork was used for which course before picking up her own. After Cameron drank one glass of whiskey too many, they retired to the guest room, where he'd paced back and forth before kicking a chair and growling, 'The family business was stolen from me.' The bitterness in his tone gripped her like the bruising press of fingers against her throat. Rattled and wanting to help, she'd asked what had happened but instead of telling her, he'd drained the cut-crystal glass of its expensive amber fluid, and given her a dark, grim smile.

'Water under the bridge.' He'd patted the mattress of the four-poster bed and grinned at her sloppily. 'Now, wife-to-be, come and make me feel better.'

They'd fallen into a pattern of only visiting Mingunyah at Christmas, Easter and on their way to and from the ski fields until four years earlier, when the seeds of change were unwittingly sown: the big girls became horse mad. Sarah suggested they join the Mingunyah pony club and ride with their cousin, Emma. She'd also recommended a trusted horse broker. The girls were ecstatic. Cameron not at all.

'Jesus! My sister's unbelievable. She might have money to burn but we don't. Do you have any idea how much it costs to keep two horses? Forget hay. We'll just feed them hundred-dollar bills.'

Anita, who considered Sarah to be the sister she'd never had, immediately defended her. 'Sarah knows the girls love riding. She just wants to help.'

'Help?' Cameron snorted. 'If she wants to help, she can buy the bloody horses.'

Eventually worn down by Ruby and Phoebe's incessant campaign to join the pony club, Cameron begrudgingly accepted Sarah's offer of free agistment at Riverbend.

Visits to Mingunyah increased. Anita preferred staying with

Sarah, where the older cousins entertained the little girls and she got a rest, but Cameron insisted on staying with his mother: 'There's more room at Mill House.'

Yes, but there's Margaret. Staying with her mother-in-law didn't come close to relaxing.

Despite the increased frequency of visits to Mingunyah, Cameron always arrived back at their Glen Iris home saying expansively, 'You gotta love the smell of the city after all that fresh air and horse shit.'

So, on a seemingly ordinary Thursday evening when Cameron dropped his briefcase at the door, tugged at his tie and slumped onto a chair, his life-changing words were a bolt from the blue.

'I'm sick to death of Melbourne. The traffic's a nightmare. The pollution's giving me headaches and the noise never bloody stops.'

Suddenly Cameron was waxing lyrical about waking up to the sounds of bellbirds and the bush. He was sick of 'working his arse off' for other people. He craved a challenge.

Worried, Anita bought a book titled *Navigating the Male Midlife Crisis*. The prologue alone terrified her and she didn't read any further, telling herself that Cameron was *nothing* like the self-absorbed men described in the first ten pages. She quickly gifted the book to a friend and it was a relief to banish it from the house.

Three months later, Cameron announced, 'Mum's not getting any younger. It would be nice for her if we were closer. Nicer for the girls too.'

This was both a surprising and dubious point. Margaret lost interest in the girls soon after they dutifully kissed her hello and she'd admired or criticised their outfits. The older girls garnered more attention because Phoebe played the cello beautifully and Ruby had a 'perfect seat', which continued to win her a clutch of eventing ribbons. Margaret showed scant interest in the little girls unless she was saying, 'Be quiet', or telling them a story about her glory days.

Unease pitched her stomach. 'When you say closer ...'

'I want us to move to Mingunyah.'

But we've just finished renovating the house. The first house she'd ever considered a home. With a shaking hand, she poured him a drink. 'The big girls are teenagers. It's a tricky age to change schools and we'll never find a cello teacher the calibre of—'

'They don't need to change schools. They can board.' His eyes glittered with enthusiasm. 'It's an investment in their education and, equally important, in the school network. Since the girls started there, I've sold six significant properties and all those commissions came through the parent network.' Excitement vibrated off him and he leaned in close. 'All those games of golf I've played, all your ladies' lunches, sets of tennis, your cooking classes, not to mention the cocktail and dinner parties we've thrown, have paid off.

'Adam and Liane Doherty have just bought Clearwater out on the old Mingunyah Track. Where the Dohertys go, the McKenzies follow. When Ricky Taranto and Sunny Chen got wind of their interest, both asked me about listings in the district. Believe me, once those two stake a claim in the valley, the floodgates will open. Soon anyone worth knowing will have a place there. It's the perfect time to go out on my own.'

His confidence rattled her deep-seated need for security, but the reality was, her security was tied unalterably to Cameron. He'd plucked her from a grimy and vulnerable lifestyle, showered her with love and surrounded her with the sort of financial comfort she'd only ever dreamed about. Although his comfort level with debt was greater than hers, she trusted him implicitly. 'If you think it's the best way forward ...'

'Hell yes!' He slapped his thigh. 'Mingunyah's finally taking off and we need to be part of it. Look at Alex and Sarah. They're raking it in. That fucking cheese of theirs is a licence to print money. Even their sourdough bread that was just something they did for cheese tastings has its own identity. Christ! It's on the menu of every restaurant and café within two hundred K.' He drained his shiraz. 'We deserve this opportunity, baby girl. We're owed it.'

So they'd moved to Mingunyah. It had thrown her life into disarray for months.

Margaret was ecstatic to have Cameron close again. The little girls transitioned to Mingunyah Primary without a skipping a beat and the big girls loved boarding at St Cuthbert's. As the parents of boarders, Cameron and Anita met a lot of expat and international parents at school functions. Apparently, Australians living in the crowded cities of Asia waxed lyrical about their homeland's wide open spaces and Asians wanted to diversify their investments. Both groups had the disposable income to buy a plot of eucalyptus-scented paradise. As Cameron kept saying, 'It's win-win, baby girl.'

Not quite. Anita missed her elder daughters more then she let on and she pined for her lost in-home cooking business.

The unexpected treat of the move was her closer friendship with Sarah. Her sister-in-law went out of her way to introduce Anita to people as well as welcoming her into her book group. It was an eclectic group of strong-minded women and more than once, Anita had felt out of her depth intellectually and spiritually. She was, however, always the best dressed. That was something she didn't understand about Sarah. If Cameron was to be believed, and Anita had no reason to doubt him, Sarah and Alex were falling off their wallets, yet Sarah often looked as if she was wearing her gardening clothes. If Anita had Sarah's disposable income, she'd never bargain hunt for designer clothes and shoes again.

The phone rang. 'The girls!' She almost upended the breakfast tray in her eagerness to answer it.

'I doubt it,' Cameron said. 'They always call on your mobile.'

'Hello,' she said breathlessly, ignoring her husband's authoritative tone.

'Oh. It's you.' Margaret's haughty disappointment hit like a bucket of icy water.

'Happy Mother's Day, Margaret,' Anita said with forced brightness, remembering the cello and the anticipated saddle.

'I want to talk to Cameron.'

And happy Mother's Day to you too, Anita. 'Of course. I'll pass you over.' She thrust the phone at Cameron and whispered, 'Your mother.'

'Mum,' Cameron said jovially. 'I was just about to ring you. Happy Mother's Day.'

As Anita took a sip of her coffee and tried not to wince at the bitter taste, she watched Cameron frown. She wondered what Margaret was saying.

'Surely Sarah—' He lifted the phone from his ear and Anita heard her mother-in-law's usually well-modulated voice hit an unintelligible screech. 'I can hear you're upset, Mum. Yes, Sarah should have—' He sighed. 'I understand. Yes, of course. No, it's no problem.' He pressed the off button and threw the handset onto the bed. 'Shit.'

'What?'

'Mum reckons her car's been stolen.'

'God. That's awful.'

'Yeah. And apparently, Sarah wasn't very sympathetic. Now Mum's in a state.'

'To be fair, Sarah's hosting lunch,' Anita said, setting aside the tray and throwing back the covers.

'Yeah, well it means I have to go over and sort out the mess. Hell, it will probably take all morning and I'd planned to—' He threw her a doleful look. 'Sorry. I won't have time to clean up the kitchen. The girls will help.'

If he was suggesting their five-and seven-year-old daughters help, then she knew the kitchen was a disaster. 'There's pancake batter on the floor, isn't there?'

He leaned down and kissed her on the mouth. 'Love you.'

Oh yeah. Happy Mother's Day, Anita.

Ellie breathed a sigh of relief as the car thudded over the first cattle grid, heralding their arrival at Riverbend. The car was making a knocking noise and despite a lack of flashing warning lights, she wasn't totally convinced the engine wouldn't suddenly seize. Today was not the day to break down, not that any day was good for that sort of inconvenience. But Sarah was still pissy with her for not coming to their mother's birthday two months ago and, going by the regular reminder texts her elder sister had started sending at noon the day before, not even death was an acceptable excuse for missing this year's Mother's Day lunch.

You know how Mum loves it when we're all under the same roof.

When that text arrived, Ellie was very tempted to type back, *Does she though?* But she didn't want to have that particular conversation so she went with the less controversial, *I'll try to be there.*

Sarah's reply had been instantaneous. *Noah always enjoys being with his cousins.*

Ellie had nothing she could use to dispute that. Noah adored his older cousins with the sort of hero worship narcissists dreamed about and he loved playing with Ava and Chloe. The problem for Ellie was that no matter how great Noah's enjoyment, it wasn't enough to offset the discomfort she experienced whenever she was in the bosom of her family. Like a bad case of hives, there was little she could do to reduce her reaction to her mother and siblings, so, in the way of anyone with allergic tendencies, she avoided the irritants as much as possible. When she had no choice but to be in the presence of her family, she used alcohol instead of antihistamines.

With Cameron's return to Mingunyah, the family-gathering goal posts seemed to have shifted. Over the last year, invitations had increased exponentially, which put her in a tricky situation. After all, there were only so many excuses a girl could use to refuse to attend.

'Yay!' Noah cheered from the back seat as the *thud-thud-thud* of tyres on iron bars stopped and the crunch of rubber on gravel took its place. 'We're here. That took for*ever*.'

'Hardly,' Ellie said, smiling at him through the rear-view mirror. But then again, her seven-year-old found sitting still a challenge. His little body constantly vibrated with energy, wriggling and writhing in anticipation, and his tight black curls—so at odds with his almond-shaped eyes—bounced wildly. She wished her enthusiasm for the day was a tenth of his.

In the years before Noah, when she was living and working in Thailand, the Land of Smiles offered up the perfect excuse for her not to attend family functions: distance. Ellie held fond memories of that time and they weren't restricted to living in a tropical climate among a mostly Buddhist population. Ellie wasn't naive enough to believe that anything stays the same forever and she was intimate with the fact that life changed whether you wanted it to or not. And eight years ago, her pregnancy had raised more than one dilemma for her. Although living away from Australia gave her freedom from family, she wasn't a natural risk-taker and it made sense to err on the side of caution. So she'd returned to Australia to give birth in a midwife-run birth centre with a world-class hospital across the hall. It had seemed a safer bet than having a baby in rural Thailand, close to the border with Myanmar.

She and Noah settled in Sydney, although that decision had little to do with the magnificent harbour or the pulsing nightlife, and more to do with it being the first city the plane touched on Australian soil. That and it wasn't Victoria. Sydney, however, had proved to be an expensive city for a single woman with a child and despite sharing the cost of housing with others, Ellie reached a point where she could no longer ignore the fact her bank balance spent more time going backwards than forward. Being unable to afford all the things the city offered those with a medium to large disposable income threw up the stark and unrelenting question: what's the point of living here?

The year before Noah commenced school, Ellie started looking for a job in rural New South Wales. The limited choice of jobs quickly dictated she widen her search and, still determined to avoid Victoria, she'd looked at South Australia, Queensland and Western Australia. As she'd scrolled past an advertisement with a logo of a house sketched with a heart in the place of a window, eleven words snagged her gaze: *Valley View Neighbourhood House seeks mentor for recently arrived Burmese community.*

Surely it was a different Valley View from the town thirty minutes down the road from Mingunyah? The two towns were so similar they were hard to tell apart, but it was unwise to mention that to a local. Mingunyah deplored Valley View for its underhand tactics in securing the shire offices a hundred and fifty years ago and Valley View hated that the only high school in the district was in Mingunyah. The rivalry always spilled over at the footy, where blood was invariably shed on the oval and then again post match, when girlfriends and wives were seduced by opposing sides.

When Ellie was growing up, one of the most cosmopolitan things in a mainly Anglo Saxon town was the espresso machine Gino Cilauro's grandfather had imported in 1965 for the then equally eccentric and worryingly foreign pizza-pie shop. By the time Ellie was thirteen and spending school-holiday nights at Tony's, they'd dropped 'pie' from the name but there was still a hint of the word in the shadow on the old sign. The second cosmopolitan thing to hit town was the black-market trade of homemade dips Con Papadopoulos sold from his greengrocer's shop. Not many of the meat-and-potato-trained palates welcomed the eggplant, yoghurt and garlic combinations but she'd adored the strong flavours scooped onto pita bread. Her mother had been less enthusiastic: 'No boy is ever going to kiss you after eating that!'

Ellie had thought this a good thing and enthusiastically shovelled more dip into her mouth.

On closer reading of the job advertisement, it became clear the town was her Valley View. Her mind boggled that Burmese refugees now lived there.

If her pregnancy had been a fork in the road of her life, so was this job. When she combined her experience in Thailand with growing up in Mingunyah, the position was tailor-made for her. There was just one significant drawback—Valley View's proximity to Mingunyah. Ellie had tried to walk away from the siren call of the job, but it became impossible. The scope of it was something she could sink her teeth into and really make a difference. She applied, rationalising that it was pointless to worry about being so close to Mingunyah when her application may not even be considered. The board offered her the job at the end of a video-link interview.

After a sleepless night and as the early dawn light splashed against a hazy city sky, she conceded that staying away from Mingunyah was in her and Noah's worst interests. So they moved into a share house on the eastern edge of Valley View, primarily because Mingunyah lay to the west. A day after she unpacked the last box, she telephoned her mother.

'I suppose you think you can just move back into your old room.'

Not even if I was destitute. 'We're living in the old Guthrie place on the outskirts of Valley View.'

'Why on earth do you have to live in a commune?'

Ellie chose to laugh; it was that or say something that would inevitably cause Sarah to telephone and berate her.

'Actually, Mum, it's more of a collective.'

Really, it was just four women sharing a rambling old weatherboard farmhouse. Wendy, a yoga instructor and home healthcare worker, liked to decorate the front veranda with Tibetan Buddhist prayer flags to detract from the peeling paintwork. Rachel, the high school art teacher, extended her art to include the hanging of thirty teapots from the branches of the fragrant peppercorn tree by the gate; it meant visitors found the house far more easily than peering for the RMB number. Grace, whose paid job was in town planning at the shire offices, worked hard at resurrecting the old orchard, coaxing cherries, apples, quinces and almonds from the lichen-covered trees, as well as planting an enormous vegetable garden. She'd knocked together a stall out of old crates and palings and sold produce at the farm gate, mostly on an honesty system. Noah and Wendy's daughter, Bree, loved helping Grace in the garden. They also manned the stall on the weekends until they got bored, which was generally after about fifteen minutes. Ellie ran chooks and her border collie, Splotch, rounded them up, along with the two sheep that kept the grass under control.

It was hard to believe two years had passed since they'd moved in.

Ellie swivelled in the driver's seat and faced her son. 'You ready to open some gates for me?'

'Yeah! Gus showed me how.' Noah unbuckled his seat belt. 'I have to close them too, Mum. Uncle Alex will go mental if the goats escape.'

He sounded just like his cousin and Ellie thought of her brother-in-law. Alex wasn't really the type to 'go mental' but then again, she'd never let any of his prize stock wander onto the highway. It sounded like Gus may have and, as a result, learned that his usually reasonable father had his limits—limits that stretched a lot further than his mother's.

Noah's hand reached for the door handle.

'Sit!' she yelled and Splotch, who was sitting quietly on the seat, gave her a doleful look. 'You know the rules. You stay sitting until the car stops. Then you can open the door.'

'Yeah. But, it's almost stopped.'

'And if you fall out you'll be stopped forever,' she said, trying not to shudder. 'If you want to open and shut the gates, you follow the rules. Otherwise you'll be inside the car watching me do it.'

Noah grimaced as if he wanted to argue the unfairness of the conditions but he sat back. She stopped the car a few metres from the gate and pulled on the handbrake.

'Now, Mum? Please.'

She glanced down the track, saw a plume of dust and a vehicle barrelling towards them. 'Okay, but don't open it until the other car's stopped.'

Noah was out the door in an instant, his running feet somewhat impeded by the slurping grip of muddy ground. He climbed onto the gate and gave her a wave while he waited.

A slither of guilt wound through her. Noah loved Riverbend and often asked to visit, but as much as Ellie wanted to acquiesce, she could never fully shake off the feeling that Sarah felt awkward and uncomfortable in her presence. Every time Ellie convinced herself she was imagining it, Sarah said or did something ambiguous that brought the feeling rushing back. Ellie had no such confusion with Cameron—

he openly disapproved of her and her life choices. So much for the theory that the youngest child was always indulged, never judged and always forgiven by fond elder siblings. Then again, the Jamieson family had always done things differently.

As the on-coming vehicle came closer, she made out two distinctive white cylinders extending over the roof of the cab. Tradie's ute. Surprise tangled with the financial implications. Calling out a tradie on a Sunday wasn't going to be cheap. Ellie wondered what had happened to precipitate it.

The vehicle slowed then stopped and Noah waved enthusiastically at the driver.

A broad-shouldered man of medium height got out of the ute, his hat casting a shadow over his features. The constant low buzz of anxiety that lived inside Ellie—the high-alert warning that was all about Noah's safety—kicked up a notch. She pushed open the door, swung her boot-clad feet onto the damp track and strode for the gate.

'G'day, mate.' She heard the driver's voice before she reached Noah. 'Do you need a hand?'

'I can do it,' Noah called out. 'I know how.'

'Good on ya.' The tone was laconic and wry. 'I could have done with your help a couple of hours ago.'

'I'll close it too,' Noah added proudly. Her son was generally keen to help but just lately she'd noticed he was particularly eager to help men.

Ellie reached the gate and gripped the top turn, positioning herself between Noah and the unknown man. Keeping her head down, she kept walking, taking the gate with her.

'Mum!' Noah's furious objection laced the word. 'You said you'd stay in the car.'

Glancing around, she eyed a grassy tussock with deep grooves created by the pressure of the bottom of the gate. She kicked it. 'I thought it might get stuck on this.'

Noah shot her a sceptical look as the tradie said, 'Eleanor?'

The surprise and pleasure in the man's voice stilled her. Noah took the chance to gleefully push the gate to the full extent of its hinges.

The man wore filthy jeans and a navy blue polar fleece that featured an embroidered logo on the left side of his chest. It was a clever design of two similar shapes—the right side was an orange flame and the left a blue water droplet—and was ringed by the words, 'Mingunyah Plumbing Heating & Cooling Specialists'. As Ellie stared at him blankly, he pulled off his battered hat. Muddy blond hair that badly needed a cut fell across a high forehead and dark lashes ringed bright blue eyes that squinted into the noon sun. Eyes that were studying her.

Sweat pooled under her arms as he scrutinised her. It had been a long time since a man had looked at her like that, which was exactly how she liked it. The urge to grab Noah's hand and run back to the car engulfed her as fast as the flames of a bushfire.

'Ellie Jamieson, right?'

Before she'd decided if she was going to admit to being herself, Noah said, 'That's my mum's name. I'm Noah.'

'Pleased to meet you, Noah. I'm Luke.' Deep lines arrowed around his smiling mouth and eyes—lines that spoke of a life lived outdoors—and he stuck out his hand to Ellie. 'Luke Sorenson. Mingunyah Primary.' She must have looked baffled because he added quickly, 'We had Mrs Pye in Grade Six. She made us run the perimeter of the playground every morning.'

Ellie had a sudden flash of a boy with white-blond hair racing past her before turning, running backwards and taunting her that she ran like a girl. She'd beaten him enough times to keep things competitive. A laugh bubbled up at the memory; a laugh that surprised her.

'Do you still run backwards, Luke?'

He gave a self-deprecating shrug. 'I'm a boundary umpire. What about you?'

'She chases me,' Noah said. 'She can't catch me, but.'

'You look pretty fast,' Luke said in the easy manner of someone familiar with children. He turned back to Ellie. 'The school had its hundred and fiftieth a couple of years back. Mrs Pye came and a dozen of us did the run for her. Didn't see you there.'

'No.'

He rubbed his stubbled jaw thoughtfully. 'Didn't you head off to some swanky Melbourne boarding school?'

'Scholarship,' she lied with perfected ease. It was so much easier than the truth.

'You back for a visit then?'

'It's Mother's Day,' Noah chipped in. 'Sarah told Mum we had to come cos it's Gran's special day and she deserves it but Mum said it's her special day too and—'

'Noah! That's enough.' Ellie hastily cut off her son before he quoted her less than optimal opinion about today's lunch to this virtual stranger. It was a quote from a rant she'd made to Wendy when she'd been certain Noah was watching television, but apparently not. 'Mr Sorenson isn't interested in that.' Except going on the glint in Luke's oddly hypnotic blue eyes, he looked far too interested. 'He needs to get back to his family for Mother's Day and you need to close the gate after him.'

Luke's gaze rested on Ellie and she realised it still held the same teasing playfulness it had all those years ago. Back then it made her squirm with a feeling that lurched between delight and determination. Now it just made her squirm with unease. She deliberately looked over his left shoulder. 'We're late.'

'And I need more supplies for the job.' Luke jammed his hat onto his head. 'Noah, don't move, mate. I want to see you when I drive through the gate. Good to see you again, Ellie.' He walked to the ute without glancing back.

As Ellie trudged to her car, she felt her shoulders fall from up round her ears. She hadn't been aware that they'd risen.

CHAPTER TWO

MARGARET PINNED the diamond brooch on the lapel of her navy woollen coat before looking in her cheval mirror and checking it was straight. She'd worn the spray brooch with its scroll design for forty-four years, not caring that for twenty of those it had been considered old-fashioned. Diamonds never went out of style and now, with vintage fashion all the rage, her granddaughters adored the brooch. They always made a fuss whenever she wore it, and so they should. It wasn't just a beautiful piece of jewellery worth a lot of money, it represented a lot of hard work—hers. She'd earned every single one of the 123 baguette-cut and twelve brilliant-cut diamonds. The day the brooch became hers was still etched in her mind—far more vividly than anything she'd done yesterday...

Cameron's arrival ten months after Sarah's was as swift as Sarah's had been agonisingly slow. In the time it took for Kevin to deliver her into the care of the midwife, park the Fairlane and walk back inside the hospital, her son was born. The following day, Kevin's father, George, visited her. He came alone and outside of the rigidly enforced visiting hours, a fact that hadn't surprised her. Not even the dragon charge sister could resist George's charm. When he unexpectedly walked into her private room, her first reaction was one of wide-eyed surprise immediately followed by disappointment. The least she'd expected from her father-in-law was flowers—and not just any flowers. Certainly not the common pink-edged cream carnations that every other woman in maternity had received. No, she deserved a massive bouquet of white roses for what she'd just done.

Quickly buttoning her matinee jacket, she sat up higher in the bed. 'Hello, George.'

He gave a silent nod and pulled up a chair. She was about to say, 'Have you seen the baby?' when he said gruffly, 'This is for you.' Pulling an old blue velvet jewellery case out of his jacket pocket, he pushed it into her hands.

Hopeful anticipation quickly pushed aside astonishment and her fingers shook, fumbling with the ornate brass latch. She finally managed to open the box and gasped in delighted relief—it was exactly what she wanted to see. The ornate diamond brooch George had given his wife, Enid, on their tenth wedding anniversary was nestled in luxurious cream silk. Margaret knew it well; her relationship with the brooch had started long before her relationship with Kevin.

The first time she'd been captivated by its tantalising sparkle was at a library fundraiser, where it had glinted on the lapel of Enid's fur-trimmed coat. It was Margaret's second week in Mingunyah after accepting the job as teacher-librarian at the high school and at age twenty-six, she'd never been so close to such an expensive brooch outside of a jewellery store. Nor had she met a woman who wore such a valuable item with so much casual style.

'This old thing?' Enid had said in response to Margaret's compliment. 'I'm glad you like it.'

'Like' was the understatement of the century. Margaret had coveted the brooch from that moment.

'Oh, George.' The wonder that it was finally hers danced through her fingertips as she lightly stroked the diamonds. 'Thank you.'

Never a demonstrative man, her father-in-law cleared his throat and gave her shoulder a gentle squeeze. 'I always knew you'd be good for this family, Maggie. You rescued us.'

With difficulty, she dragged her gaze away from the hypnotic brooch and looked at him. 'You've always been good to me.'

And he had been—so much so that George was the only person she ever allowed to call her Maggie. Early on, Kevin had tried once or twice, but he soon learned she only responded to Margaret. But her admiration for her father-in-law was established before her marriage to Kevin, starting a few months after Enid's death.

She and Kevin had been seeing each other for over a year but her goal of getting his ring onto her finger was proving elusive. She'd tried everything she could think of: listening to him talk about the sawmill and agreeing with his grievances even if she disagreed; watching him play endless games of football and enduring the monotonous post-game parties where Kevin was always absorbed in analysing the game with Gary Longmuir and Pete Cooper. Many parties were spent warding off the attentions of a few of his mates and their drunken pickup lines: 'I wouldn't ignore you, darlin'. I'd show you a good time.' She imagined they probably would, but instant gratification wasn't something she invested in. Her eye was on the long game—the future.

At the six-month mark and starting to despair, she'd tweaked the traditional advice of 'the way to a man's heart is through his stomach' by serving Kevin chicken and veal Kiev and chocolate soufflé before dishing herself up on a platter. Kevin savoured the meal before savouring her, sending her hopes soaring. But while Kevin hadn't sought to end things with her after that meal, he hadn't shown any signs of taking the next step either and with her twenty-eighth birthday having come and gone, she was at a loss as to what to try next. The idea of kissing one of Kevin's mates to startle him into a claim of ownership was starting to look like a viable option.

When she accepted an unexpected invitation from George to dine at Mill House, she was struck by a thought the moment she stepped into its high-ceilinged Georgian hallway: Was she pursuing the wrong Jamieson? Surrounded by impeccable decor and obvious wealth, the idea of marrying a rich man thirty-five years her senior suddenly became something worth considering.

Over a meal of beef Wellington cooked by George's housekeeper and accompanied by a bottle of Penfold's Grange, he eventually said, 'My son's a fool for not snapping you up.'

Her meat-laden fork stalled halfway to her mouth. It took a moment for her brain to recover from its momentary shock and kick up a gear.

While she weighed up the best way to respond, George continued, 'I, on the other hand, always get what I want.'

'I imagine you do,' she purred, unwilling to burn any bridges lest George was expressing interest in her.

'Do you want him?'

His directness stunned her. Of course she wanted the handsome heir to the biggest employer in town, but things between her and Kevin were travelling at a snail's pace and had been for some time. Was saying 'Yes, I want Kevin' the right answer if George's motive in asking her here tonight was because he was interested in her? She kept her cards close.

'All I want is to make this family happy again.'

'Good. We're in agreement then. It's what Enid would have wanted too. My darling wife spent the last eight years waiting for Kevin to marry and make her a grandmother.' His voice quavered slightly. 'That bastard cancer took her too early.'

The haze in Margaret's mind cleared. George's intentions had nothing to do with pursuing her. Tonight was all about her and Kevin. 'There's nothing I want more than to be Kevin's wife but—' She leaned forward, opening her palms and aiming for a gesture of conflicted understanding. 'He's still grieving for his mother.'

'Life goes on. My son needs a wife and an heir to get him back on track,' George said decisively. 'Leave it with me.'

Her heart rate picked up, filling her with hope, but she tried to quell its expectations. 'Leave what exactly to you?'

'Everything.' He poured her a whiskey and raised his glass to hers with a wink. 'I promise you'll be walking down the aisle of St Mary's before the year is out.'

True to his word—and two days after her twenty-ninth birthday—that was exactly what she did. Wearing a cream, pure silk wedding gown with exquisite hand-embroidered scalloping and seven thousand seed pearls, she glided along the blue carpet on George's arm in front of the who's who of Mingunyah and the surrounding district. He placed her hand in Kevin's as he stood nervously in a pale blue tuxedo next to his best man, Gary Longmuir. Mark 'Tiger' Ralston, the groomsman and one of a group of men she'd toyed with kissing to make Kevin jealous, gave her a big wink. Margaret liked Tiger a lot more than Gary. Gary was too serious and Kevin valued his opinion a little more than Margaret would have liked.

The squawk of a cockatoo brought Margaret back to the present and she gave the brooch a fond pat. The action made something niggle in the back of her mind—something Cameron had said to her recently. Was it about the brooch? It wasn't like Cameron to notice jewellery, unlike that wife of his, who did enough noticing for the both of them. The annoying niggle burrowed in, demanding to be answered. What on earth had he said?

How long since you had the setting checked on your brooch, Mum? Cameron's voice came back to her, soothing the prickling need to remember. *It would be heart-breaking if one of the diamonds fell out.*

It would be. Her hand rose unbidden to her mouth as an even worse scenario occurred to her. What if it got stolen like the lemons on her tree that had all suddenly vanished? As soon as she saw Cameron she'd insist he take the brooch to Melbourne this week and have Abe Rubenstein's son check it and value it for insurance purposes. The Rubensteins had cared for the Jamiesons' jewellery for decades and she wouldn't trust anyone else with the task. Although part of her would love to see the look on Derek Lung's face if she took it into Mingunyah Jewellery. The man sold the occasional diamond solitaire engagement ring but most of his sales consisted of costume jewellery and watches. She doubted he'd ever held anything like the brooch.

She checked her watch. It was time to leave for Sarah's. Irritation zipped through her as she searched for her car keys. It was Mother's Day! Surely one of her children should have offered to drive her? Why had Sarah and Alex moved out to Riverbend? After all, when they started out as cheese makers in the old factory, they bought their milk with no intentions of ever farming themselves. Margaret clearly recalled the first time she met Alex. He told her most emphatically that his father and grandfather struggled for years on the farm, which was why he chose to study engineering. So much for that malarkey. Riverbend was a good half-hour drive out of town and the last stretch was a minor road full of potholes and corrugations. She had much preferred it when her daughter lived three streets away and was available whenever Margaret telephoned.

A car horn sounded long and loud, making Margaret jump. It was probably that dreadful Hamish Makin visiting his mother. That boy had been a difficult child and now he was an obnoxious adult. If she'd known a decade ago that subdividing the land surrounding Mill House would mean noisy neighbours, she might have changed her mind. She peered through the lace curtains, expecting to see a bright blue Holden complete with a spoiler and dual chrome exhausts, but gasped in confused delight and surprise. Rushing to the front door, she pulled it open and waved as Cameron got out of the car.

'Hello, dear,' she said presenting her cheek for a kiss. 'Why on earth are you driving my car?'

'Got any more of that merlot?'

Sarah turned from stacking the dishwasher to see Cameron standing in the kitchen, glancing around expectantly, empty wine glass in hand. It was that tricky period at a formal lunch when the table had been cleared after the main meal but dessert and coffee were yet to be served. Twenty minutes earlier, Cameron had emptied the second bottle of wine into his glass so his question was really more along the lines of a statement: I'm sure you have another bottle of that very expensive wine I'm enjoying so let's open it.

Cameron liked to drink the wine Alex served, and it wasn't as if they couldn't afford to offer wines from the high end of the range, but Cameron rarely brought a bottle to add to their cellar. She knew this about him—had known it for a long time—but today, for some reason, it irked her. She had plans for the third bottle of merlot and it involved her, Alex and the couch.

'I'm making coffee,' she said, hoping he'd take the hint.

'After this morning's fun and games, I'd prefer to stick to wine.' Cameron smiled as he spied the unopened bottle in the butler's pantry. In three strides, he was holding the bottle in his beefy hand. Sarah heard the seal crack, and then the *glug-glug* of the velvet liquid swirling into the deep bowl of the glass. She had a sudden poignant memory of the days when red wine came corked and all it took to stymie greedy guests was hiding the corkscrew.

'Oh, thank God. You've got more wine.' Ellie appeared in the kitchen and extended her glass. 'If I have to hear one more time how embarrassed my mother is about my housing situation, I need to be blotto.'

'So how is life with the lesbians?' Cameron asked, filling her glass.

'I imagine the same as life with the heterosexuals,' Ellie said equably as Sarah flinched at Cameron's question.

Like most things about her younger sister's life, Ellie's sexuality was a mystery to her—one they'd never discussed. Ellie had never openly said she was gay but then again, she'd never said she was straight either. It didn't help that she dressed in baggy T-shirts in summer, oversized flannel shirts and vests in winter, wore jeans on cold days, knee-length shorts on warm days and work boots no matter what the season. When Sarah considered that, apart from the occasional smear of gloss on her lips, Ellie's face was never touched by makeup, that she drove an old Subaru station wagon and she was vegetarian, the evidence seemed pretty conclusive— right up until it wasn't. Sarah always got stuck on the facts that Ellie had never introduced a woman to the family—or a man, for that matter—she wore her eye-stopping blonde, curly hair long and she always waxed her legs.

And then there was Noah.

Sarah had read enough to know that Noah's existence didn't mean Ellie was straight. But it struck her as odd that Ellie would choose to use Thai donor semen, so she was reasonably confident Noah had been conceived naturally. Of course the window of opportunity to ask the question was long past. It had got lost in the stunned surprise of Ellie's out-of-the-blue phone call telling Sarah that not only was she unexpectedly in Sydney, Sarah was an auntie. Her spoiled and self-indulgent baby sister had once again managed to shock her.

The most recent Ellie thunderbolt was her decision to return to the valley, but she supposed that was old news now. Despite Ellie living closer than she had in decades, Sarah felt as removed from her life as she had when Ellie was living overseas. But it had been longer than that. The truth was that the last time Sarah felt close to Ellie and relaxed in her company was the summer before her wedding to Alex, when she'd taught her little sister to wax her legs.

Sarah quickly capped the merlot bottle in a vain attempt to save some wine for Alex and steered the conversation away from sexuality. 'Talking about Mum, does Graeme Aitkens have any idea who took her car for a joyride?'

When Cameron arrived at Riverbend House with their mother, Margaret had breezed in, taking centre stage on the couch and accepting her gifts with the graciousness of the Queen before mentioning she was quite thirsty. Sarah, busy playing hostess and keenly feeling Alex's absence, had appreciated Anita's suggestion that Cameron help Gus organise the drinks. It turned out to be a stroke of genius, because apparently, her brother was the only member of the family capable of mixing a Bloody Mary to their mother's exacting standards.

'Sergeant Plod reckons it was opportunistic kids.' Cameron sipped the wine. 'He reckons Mum must have left the keyless remote in the car.'

Sarah shook her head. 'Mum wouldn't do that. She's always had a thing about security. Remember how Dad used to tease her about being a city chick? He'd say that leaving everything unlocked was the only Mingunyah tradition Mum didn't adopt. God, how many times growing up did we get into trouble for leaving our bedroom windows open when we left the house?'

'I never lock my windows,' Ellie said absently, her gaze fixed on the trampoline outside.

'You don't have anything worth stealing,' Cameron said.

'I have my Tibetan chimes.'

Sarah glanced at her sister, trying to work out if she was being serious or just winding up Cameron. She could never tell and she wished she could, because joining forces with Ellie and pushing their brother's buttons was her sort of fun. As much as Sarah loved Anita—they shared the sort of relationship she'd never come close to achieving with Ellie—they couldn't bond over teasing Cameron. To her knowledge, Anita didn't tease him. Sarah found this a little odd, because she teased Alex a lot. More than once she'd wondered if this lack on Anita's part had something to do with the seven-year age gap in the marriage or with the slightly disconcerting thought that Anita worshipped Cameron for marrying her.

'And so many thieves are going to bother to lift brass chimes,' Cameron responded predictably before turning to Sarah. 'It's a bit hard to argue hard-core theft when the car was parked in the IGA parking lot without a scratch on it. When I asked the good sergeant to run fingerprints, he told me I'd been watching too much American television. As far as he's concerned, the car's back where it belongs, end of story.'

'Is there a chance Mum's forgetting things?' Ellie asked.

'No,' Cameron said firmly in his 'I'm the brother and I know best' voice.

A slight stiffness rippled across Ellie's shoulders. 'She's already told me twice today that Lindsay Bolt visited her last week after seeing a blue porcelain cat worth two thousand dollars identical to Mum's on *Antique Roadshow*.'

'She probably thought you didn't hear her the first time when you were distracted by Noah's enthusiastic assault on the chips.' Noah had leaped onto the bowl as if he'd not eaten the salty treats since the last time he'd visited. Mind you, that was a distinct possibility. Sarah knew Ellie's parenting veered from being super strict with some things and incredibly lax with others.

'Sarah and I see more of her than you do,' Cameron added pompously. 'We'd have noticed if there was something wrong.'

'I'm not worried about her memory,' Sarah said, 'but I do worry she's determined to stay in the house. It's too big for her. I think it might be time for her to sell and downsize. I'm going to take her to look at the new townhouses they're building on the old saleyard site. Two of her friends have already put down deposits.'

'Mum doesn't need to move. Rita Bosco comes once a week to clean,' Cameron said.

'It's not just the housework. It's the garden too. Alex, Gus and I spent last Sunday doing a massive prune and clean up. Moving would solve that, but in the meantime, I was thinking of getting a quote from a gardener. Ellie, do you have a Burmese man or woman who'd be interested in some work?'

Cameron looked sceptical. 'You know what Mum's like. Do you really think she'll be happy having an Asian gardener when her father was tortured by one?'

'Oh, for God's sake,' Ellie snapped. 'The Burmese aren't Japanese and Mum, for all her faults, isn't racist. Her grandson's half Thai and she shows as much interest in Noah as she does in Ava and Chloe.'

Sarah decided it wasn't politic to mention that in comparison to the doting interest Margaret had lavished on Finn, Gus and Emma when they were little, the attention she gave the younger grandchildren was negligible. It was almost as if she'd used up all her grand mothering energy by the time they arrived. But that aside, she had no idea what

Cameron was on about. 'Mum hasn't got a problem with the Japanese. She and Dad visited Tokyo, remember?'

'I just think it's better if someone in the family does the garden,' Cameron said firmly. 'What about Gus?'

'What about me?' Gus ambled in through the back door with Noah standing on his feet and Ava hanging off his back like a monkey.

'I've got a job for you,' Cameron said in a magnanimous tone. 'Mowing Gran's lawns and weeding her garden.'

'Oh.' Gus looked underwhelmed.

'It's fifteen dollars an hour. Cash in hand, mate.'

'Thanks for thinking of me, Uncle Cam, but Dad pays twenty-two. I think I'll stick to milking sheep and goats and sticking cheese into jars of olive oil.'

'Giddy up, Gus!' Ava commanded. Her cousin whinnied like a horse, turned and headed back outside.

Ellie laughed. 'Looks like you'll have to up your rates, Cameron, or do it yourself for free like Alex and Sarah.'

'I'm busy establishing a new business. Unlike some people, I don't get weekends off.'

'We could draw up a roster,' Sarah suggested before Ellie made a crack about working for the man and the constant seeking of profits over people. 'Between us, we can keep the garden under control until she sells.'

'Mum's never mentioned to me that she wants to sell the house,' Cameron said. 'It sounds like you're badgering her into it.'

A jet of anger shot along Sarah's veins, not dissimilar to those she'd experienced as a child when Cameron falsely accused her of something. 'I'm not badgering her. I'm discussing options.'

'If she'd wanted to move, she'd have done it years ago,' Cameron huffed. 'It's not like she's only just started living there alone. Dad's been dead for twenty-six years.'

'Being on her own isn't the issue!' She pulled back, softening her tone to try to get him onside. 'She's not keeping up with the garden.'

'Well, I suppose I could possibly commit to helping once every couple of months but definitely not when Phoebe and Ruby are home competing and I'm flat out towing a horse float to every gymkhana within a hundred K.'

'They might be happy to work for fifteen dollars an hour,' Ellie said wryly.

A red flush crawled up Cameron's neck. 'Just wait until Noah's a teenager and you're driving all over the country for his passion.'

'What about you, Ellie?' Sarah asked, trying to keep them on track and away from lunging at each other's throats. 'How much garden time can you spare?'

'I think Mum should employ someone. It's not like she can't afford it.'

'True, but she doesn't spend money easily.' The words were out before Sarah realised she'd spoken them.

Ellie's sparkling, pool-blue eyes opened wide as if she couldn't believe what she'd just heard. A throaty laugh bubbled out of her and tears trickled down her face. 'Oh, it was worth coming today just to hear that.'

'And I thought you came to see us,' Sarah said, locking onto offence to block her guilt over the uncharitable comment about her mother.

'I for one appreciate our mother's fiscal prudency and investment savvy.' Cameron shot Ellie a combative look. 'I doubt you'll say no to a six-figure inheritance.'

'Actually, I'd rather she spent her money making her life easier now than passing it on to me.'

'Spoken by the woman who's already benefitted from a big chunk of change.'

'Cameron,' Sarah cautioned as she scooped coffee into the plunger. *Alex, please come home now and distract everyone with a story of how you rescued the cheese.* She checked the clock: 3.35. She'd expected to have heard from him by now.

'What are you on about?' Ellie asked, clearly perplexed.

'Don't give me the innocent act. Sarah and I went to Mingunyah High but that wasn't good enough for Princess Ellie. You badgered

Mum and made her life miserable until she had no choice but to give in and send you to MLC.'

Ellie's mouth tightened. 'I believe you got three years at Mannix College when you were at Monash Uni.'

'It didn't come close. Your education cost fifty times what ours did and gave you opportunities we never had. But have you used any of them or the networking it offered you? I don't think so. How many courses have you started? Three?' He ticked them off on his fingers. 'Four, if you don't count the tarot cards and aura-reading class. Did you ever finish any of them? I don't think so.'

Ellie's nostrils flared. 'If it bothers you so much, brother dear, why don't we pro rata what was spent on my boarding and your college fees. If we do that we'll both owe Sarah money from our inheritance, because she lived in a share house in Carlton.'

'Shut up, both of you! It's disgusting, talking as if Mum's money is already yours. Mum's always kept the contents of her will private, so for all we know, she might be leaving everything to the hospital. Inheritance is a gift not a right, and our mother is still very much alive, thank you very much. And she's waiting for dessert.' Her hand shook as she poured boiling water over the ground coffee.

'Hey! Why am I being lumped in with being a baddie? It was Cam who brought up the subject and took a crack at me.' Ellie set down her wine glass. 'I'm going outside to jump on the trampoline with Noah.'

The moment the back door slammed, Sarah sighed. 'Thanks for imploding a happy family gathering, Cam.'

'What? Why am I in trouble for saying something we've both thought for years? It was time it was said. She's had privileges you and I were denied and she's wasted every single one of them.' He looked out the window, watching Ellie holding Noah's hands and jumping high. 'I mean look at her! Her car's on the verge of dying, she's renting a room in a house that's been a thorn in the side of the shire for years, her clothes look like she buys them from the op shop and Noah, the poor kid, has no male role models. What the hell is she doing with her life?'

Although Sarah had said similar things to Alex over the years, agreeing with Cameron didn't come naturally. 'Noah has you, Alex, Gus and Finn. I believe the new PE teacher at his school is a man.'

Cameron rolled his eyes. 'It's almost impossible to be a role model when we see the kid less than three times a year.'

'Perhaps if you didn't bait her quite so much, she'd come more often.'

'Jesus. I need some fresh air.' He strode out of the kitchen, making a beeline for the French doors and the veranda.

Alone in the kitchen on Mother's Day. Again. Sarah arranged the cheeses on the board, unwrapping her favourite—their blue vein cheese. Eighteen years ago, this cheese had launched their business. Back then their goal was to become known as the cheese makers of an Australian-styled version of the famous French Roquefort. For five years, it had been their signature cheese but once they'd introduced their goat's cheese marinated in herb-infused olive oil, it quickly outpaced sales of the sheep's milk blue to the point they had to reassess the demand. It was the first business decision she and Alex had disagreed on and he'd accused her of letting sentimentality get in the way of sound business sense: 'The figures never lie, Sarah.' She'd hated that he was right and, as the cheese making had been her idea, letting go of the blue had been like severing a part of herself. Now it was only made in small batches and sold as a boutique cheese in the café.

Anita walked into the kitchen, her petite frame bustling with energy. 'How can I help?'

'It would be great if you could hull the strawberries. If we surround the cake with them, it might draw attention away from the fact it's totally uneven.'

'I can do that.'

'Thanks. Everyone *else* seems to have disappeared on me.'

'Are you okay? You sound a bit upset.'

'Sorry. I've been feeling a bit Jekyll and Hyde all day. Probably because I missed my sleep-in or I'm premenstrual.' Her periods had been all over the place lately and she didn't even want to think about what that might mean. 'Oh, what the hell.' She grabbed a bottle of vintage champagne out of the fridge, popped the cork and poured them both a glass. 'Happy Mother's Day.'

'Happy Mother's Day.' Anita smiled as she sipped, enjoying the dry and tangy flavour. 'Next year, I'll host and you can bring the champagne. No arguments.'

'You're on. You don't fancy doing Christmas too, do you?'

'Just let me run it past Cameron. You know how men like to be consulted about these things.'

Sarah didn't know any such thing. She was the front-end controller of their domestic lives and the coordinator of the family calendar. She told Alex the date and time of family functions and he turned up and served the drinks. For some reason, the idea of Anita telling Cameron that she'd asked them to host Christmas rankled. It gave Cameron the power to say no. As she and Cameron had been in competition all their lives, giving him the advantage didn't sit right at all.

'I'm kidding,' Sarah said lightly. 'Of course we'll have Christmas here. It makes sense. Mum dislikes change and we've got the pool so it's best for the kids.'

Anita's forehead wrinkled slightly. 'Well, if you're sure.'

'Absolutely.'

'Have you heard from Emma today?'

'Not yet. She'll only just be waking up to Sunday in France, so hopefully I'll get a call soon. I hope Alex is back by then.'

'You'll feel better after you talk to Emma. I know I felt a lot happier after chatting with Phoebe and Ruby. Did Gus—'

'Sarah? Oh, there you are.' Margaret shot a disapproving look at the two of them leaning against the island bench, drinking. 'I'm glad you're enjoying yourselves. Meanwhile, you've left me sitting alone in the dining room.'

'I've only been gone a couple of minutes, Margaret,' Anita said apologetically. 'I came in to help Sarah. We'll call everyone to come back and sit down.'

Margaret looked at the platters. 'Cake and cheese? Is that all you're serving? People will go home hungry.'

Sarah's hand tightened around the stem of her glass despite having anticipated and prepared for Margaret's reaction. Her mother's sweet tooth was legendary. When her parents had hosted dinner parties, there'd always been two desserts to choose from and, on extra-special occasions, three. If she was ever asked to name the desserts of her childhood, she'd answer chocolate ripple cake, brandy Alexander pie and chocolate mousse. All of them featured alcohol and lashings of cream. Today's offerings were a compromise to accommodate everyone's tastes and waistlines.

'I've also got your favourite truffles.'

Margaret's critical demeanour faded and she smiled. 'Your father bought me those.'

'I remember. He ordered them from the Australia Arcade in Melbourne and when they arrived in their beautiful tin, Cam and I would beg you to let us have one.'

Her mother laughed, a tinkling, girlish sound, and she leaned in conspiratorially. 'Sometimes, I ate them all myself.'

Sarah remembered that too.

CHAPTER THREE

SARAH SAT on the couch with her feet resting on the ottoman, a glass of merlot in her hand and a plate of cheese, biscuits and grapes balanced on her lap. It was six o'clock and apart from the gentle swish of the dishwasher, the house was quiet. She toyed with the idea of watching a movie or finding something on the PVR but she hoped Alex would be walking through the door any minute. He'd been gone for hours, which wasn't unusual but even so, she'd left a message on his phone. She knew he never replied when he was consumed by a crisis but she'd expected him to have called by now.

She thought about rousing herself and driving down to the dairy but she'd been on her feet for almost twelve hours and the idea seemed like far too much effort. She sipped her wine. Whatever the problem was, Alex's lack of contact meant they hadn't lost any milk. If production had been affected, he would have summoned her to the office hours ago to make apologising and soothing phone calls to customers and to adjust the invoices.

'I'm starving.' Gus slumped onto the couch next to her. 'Those kids work me harder than coach does at training. What's for dinner?'

'Whatever's in the fridge that takes your fancy.'

'So, you're not cooking?' Surprise wrinkled his handsome face, reminding her of Alex in his younger days.

She loved her husband and sons dearly, but sometimes she wondered at their expectation that she was the sole solution to all their wants and needs. 'Angus George Jamieson, I've got two words for you: Mother's Day.'

'I thought Mother's Day only lasted until lunchtime.'

'That's April Fool's Day.'

'Oh, yeah.' His hand snuck out to grab a biscuit and cheese.

She slapped it lightly. 'Get your own.'

He sighed and rested his body against hers as his head dropped onto her shoulder. She closed her eyes, savouring contentment. Almost seventeen-year-old sons lurched between the needs of their seven-year-old selves—loving nothing more than a cuddle from their mum—and the distance demanded by their almost-adult selves.

'Mum?'

She leaned her cheek against his hair and forgave him that it no longer held the sweet scent of a little boy. 'Yes.'

'You know how school's doing *Sweet Charity* this year?'

Gus lived and breathed footy and skiing, and Finn hated being the centre of attention, which left Emma as the only child involved in the drama productions. As her daughter was in France, Sarah hadn't taken much notice of what was happening on the arts front this year. 'No.'

'Yeah. Three shows. It opens in two weeks.'

She suppressed a woot of delight. This year she had a get-out-of-jail-free card. No being roped into making costumes, painting sets, doing hair and makeup and propping up a stressed-out drama teacher. 'I'm enjoying my year off from all the theatrics on and off stage.'

'About that ...' Gus shifted on the couch. 'I'm in it.'

Sarah's eyes flew open and she sat forward so she could see his face, checking his expression to make sure she'd correctly heard his softly spoken words. 'You're in it? As in working backstage? Doing the lights?'

He shook his head. 'I'm Oscar.'

'Oscar?' It had been years since she'd seen the 1960s-set musical and all she could remember about it were the songs 'Hey Big Spender' and 'Rhythm of Life'.

'I'm one of Charity's love interests. Anyway, I told Mrs Lipton you'd help like you always do. She needs you at school tomorrow at four.'

Sarah stared at Gus as a dozen half-formed thoughts bounced off each other. 'Wow. That's ... big news. Well, not the bit about me helping Mrs Lipton, although some more notice would have been nice.' Then enthusiasm won out over surprise and she smiled. 'I can't believe you auditioned. Do you have a song?'

He dipped his head as he always did when he didn't know if he should be proud or humble. 'Two.'

Her heart swelled at this unexpected event. For years she'd listened to Gus sing in the shower but he'd never shown any interest in singing in public. When he'd started high school and she suggested he join the choir, he'd rolled his eyes at her.

Moving the cheese plate to safety, she hugged him. 'Congratulations, sweetheart. This is exciting. I'll try to get everyone to come. Perhaps Finn can drive Phoebe and Ruby home that weekend and then the whole family can see it. Oh ...' Her enthusiasm dimmed slightly. 'Emma will miss it.'

'What's Emma going to miss?' Alex fell onto the couch beside Gus. Grey shadows hovered under his eyes and grease stained his shirt and hands.

'Tell your dad,' Sarah prompted.

'Tell me what? I hope it's good news, because I've had a shit of a day. A water pipe burst—'

'Alex.' Sarah cut him off, knowing if she didn't, he'd talk about work and Gus's news would get lost. They juggled keeping the business and their home life separate, struggling constantly and frequently failing completely. Although Sarah insisted they all eat dinner together each night, there were too many occasions when, despite their best intentions, she and Alex were so busy discussing a business problem or a new idea they didn't notice that the kids had upped and left the table. 'Go on, Gus.'

Gus hesitated.

Alex sighed. 'Come on, champ. All I want is a shower and food so spit it out.'

'I auditioned for the school musical. I've got a lead.'

Alex frowned. 'That's after the footy season, right?'

'No. It's two weeks away.' Gus chewed his lip. 'I'll have to miss the match against Kyabram.'

'Bloody hell, Gus. That's an important match.' Alex pressed his fingers into his temples as if he couldn't believe what he was hearing. 'If there's one thing a man doesn't do, it's let his mates down. Bruce will have your guts for garters.'

'Coach is always on about teamwork, a fair go and giving people a chance, but he never subs me off. Cooper McFarlane and Rory Stefanovic are keen. They deserve a go. They can play.'

'The talent scouts aren't driving up from Melbourne to see Cooper and Rory. How's it going to look when you don't play because you want to bloody sing?'

'It's *one* match, Dad,' Gus said belligerently, rising to his feet.

'Yeah. And a really important one.' Alex stood too, slightly shorter than his middle child. 'God, what were you thinking? You've had other years when you could have done drama. Less important years. Why the hell choose this one?'

'Alex,' Sarah warned. 'Let's all take a deep breath. I'm sure Gus weighed everything up before he auditioned.'

'Seriously, Sarah?' Alex snorted. 'What sixteen-year-old boy thinks and weighs up options?' His eyes narrowed. 'Okay, mate. Who's the girl?'

Gus met his father's steely gaze. 'There's more than one girl in the show, Dad.'

For a moment, Alex's face lost its tension and he laughed as if he was remembering his own adolescence. He gripped Gus's shoulder.

'There's always going to be a girl, mate. Your job's to focus on what's important to you, not her.'

Sarah startled, surprised by Alex's blunt and selfish advice. It went against everything she believed about their relationship. 'Relationships are a two-way street, Gus, give and take on both sides. I think what your father means is no one should ask you to give up your dream and take on theirs.'

Alex grunted. 'I'm quite capable of explaining what I mean.'

'I'm not doing the show because of some girl. No one forced me to do this, okay, so get off my back.' Gus turned and strode out of the room.

'Christ. What the hell's got into him?' Alex sat down hard and shoved a biscuit and cheese into his mouth.

'I know it's a surprise but I think it's good he's exploring something outside of sport. All the parenting advice says kids shouldn't be pigeon-holed too early.'

'That only applies if the kid doesn't have talent in anything. Gus does and his timing's lousy. If Bruce cracks the shits, and I'm pretty sure he will, Gus won't play in the firsts again this year.' Alex pulled his phone out of his pocket. 'I'll call him.'

Sarah put her hand on his arm. 'Let Gus talk to him first. Besides, tonight's not a good time.'

Alex looked at her blankly.

Oh, for the love of God. 'Mother's Day.'

'Oh yeah.' He slid the phone back into his pocket. 'How'd lunch go?'

'Good. Only a couple of flesh wounds.'

'Ellie and Cam?'

'Yep.' She reached for the merlot bottle and poured him a glass. 'I managed to save this for you.'

'Thanks.' His head fell back as he swished the wine around his mouth, savouring the complex flavours.

'So? I'm assuming you saved the day?'

'Yes and no. Jack Forster put a fucking backhoe through the water main and no one thought to turn off the power before the dairy flooded. Not only did the milk get contaminated, the conveyor belt got fritzed.'

'We lost a third of today's milk?' That was a disaster. 'Alex! Why didn't you call me?'

This time it was Alex's hand that shot out and clamped on her arm. 'It's okay. Luke Sorenson came out and fixed the pipe. I rang the emergency number at Randall's and the part we need for the conveyor belt should arrive by noon tomorrow.'

'And that's all good but nothing's been done about the orders. I'll have to go into the office now and adjust the paperwork. I need to call Coles and—'

'It's sorted,' he said wearily, shoving the last of the cheese into his mouth.

'How?' She couldn't imagine Alex would have done it. Not only had he been flat out dealing with the mechanics of the disaster, their financial software package annoyed and frustrated him.

His eyes were closed again. 'Kelly did it.'

Kelly? Kelly Bamfield was their mousy office manager and although she was extremely good at her job, she didn't work weekends. None of the office staff did and it was rare for either Sarah or Alex to call them in out of hours; the two of them could handle all aspects of billing, staffing, payroll, marketing and customer relations because they'd done it all themselves in the years before they could afford staff. Why had Alex asked Kelly to come in and deal with it? It didn't make a lot of sense unless—

A warm feeling glowed in her chest, quickly filling her with the joy and security of being cherished. She smiled at Alex's uncharacteristically generous gesture, relishing the significance of what he'd done.

Nudging him gently, she said, 'You gave me a Mother's Day present.'

His brow creased and then he opened his eyes, looking straight at her. For a moment, their rich brown depths—normally so full of energy—were eerily still. Then he blinked. 'Happy Mother's Day.'

'Thank you.' She leaned in to kiss him on the lips but he turned his head before she reached him and her lips grazed his stubbled cheeks. She laughed. 'We're misfiring today.'

'Today?'

'Remember? This morning I went to kiss you goodbye before your ride, and I missed your mouth and got your shoulder.'

He didn't show any signs he recalled it or found it amusing.

'Are you okay?'

He rubbed his face. 'I'm just tired and filthy. Besides, if I snuggle up with you now, you'll only complain I stink.'

She couldn't deny that. 'Fair enough. Go grab a shower and I'll make you something to eat. There's Ellie's share of the lamb.'

'Sounds good.'

She watched him leave and as she rose from the couch, it occurred to her that the day was finishing exactly as it started—her alone in the kitchen on Mother's Day.

'Have a good day,' Anita called to the girls' backs as they ran towards their friends on the school's play equipment.

When she'd first arrived in Mingunyah, her busy Melbourne life had come to a screaming halt, replaced by something that was foreign and yet came with moments of disconcerting familiarity. Mingunyah school mornings were the same organised chaos of getting the girls up, fed and out the door but her drive to school in gridlock traffic and the challenge of parallel parking the SUV was replaced by walking to school with the girls and Fudge, their one-year-old chocolate labrador. But the ease and familiarity of chatting in the school grounds with the other parents—ninety-eight per cent mothers—that she'd worked so hard to achieve in Melbourne had vanished. Once again, she was the newcomer—the person who needed to prove herself worthy of being included in established groups.

Anita was far too familiar with that routine. Some of her earliest memories were of the narrow and assessing gazes of kindergarten girls confident in their power as a group. They were the social gatekeepers and little Anita Jankovic, in her hand-me-down clothes, never made the cut. Over the years, she'd learned that most adult women didn't outgrow that fast assessment and back in Melbourne, it had taken three years of sucking up and moments of humiliation to prove to the Botox Babes, the powerbrokers of the neighbourhood and the school's social hierarchy, that she was worthy of belonging. It had also involved abandoning all traces of her childhood and writing a new script for where she'd grown up and gone to school. Fortunately for her, none of the women had grown up in the outer northern suburbs, let alone set a foot there, so no one questioned her recreated past. Those social gatekeepers were the reason Anita never stepped out of the house without her hair blow waved, her face immaculately made up and her clothes and accessories carefully coordinated. From yummy-mummy gym wear to her little black dress, and with all the gradients of smart casual wear in between, adult Anita was no longer side-lined on appearance by the elite groups she sought to enter.

Just like at the older girls' private Melbourne school, the Mingunyah Primary schoolyard had distinct clusters of mothers. The Pony Club Mothers dressed beautifully in boutique country-style clothes—quilted jackets, Liberty-print blouses, knee-high leather boots —that oozed money and style. The PCM were at ease in their own company, confident in their social standing and not in need of new members. This came as a rude shock to Anita, because she'd assumed that her married name and Phoebe and Ruby's involvement in pony club meant the group would open and welcome her. Despite her Melbourne sophistication and fashion style, the PCM had initially been slow to show any overtures of friendship.

The Sustainability Sisters were the mothers who dressed in natural fibres, religiously composted, recycled, reused, swapped, bartered and zealously judged everyone on where they fell on the rubbish-free scale. They ran the school's kitchen garden and cooking program. Anita had both interest and skill in that arena, but her self-imposed dress code meant the SS were hesitant to open their group to her. Although Anita recycled paper and plastics and attempted to pack 'nude food' in the girls' lunch boxes, she knew her occasional lapses and her makeup choices were possibly considered heresy to this group. She did think, though, that she'd made a connection with Tam, whose yoga class Anita attended at the Mechanics' Institute.

The working mothers fell into two groups. The first arrived at school prior to Anita, dropping their children off at the before-school care program because their job started early. The second group arrived at the gate wearing their work uniform—anything from the royal blue IGA shirt and navy pants to green hospital scrubs. They did a hug, kiss and run at the gate. The only times Anita met the working mothers was at school talks, weekend working bees, the concert and the fundraising trivia night. They were a fun but disparate group who each had barely enough time to spend with her husband, her kids and the housework, let alone finding any spare minutes to get to know Anita.

Then there was a group Anita had mentally tagged 'the battlers'. Some would say it was a label only a well-educated, upper-middleclass, latte-drinking, sauv blanc–sipping person would give but Anita knew she had the right to use the word. Growing up, Anita had lived that life. The battlers were not so much a group as a ragtag mix of parents who always arrived at the gate just after the bell accompanied by their school-age children dressed in an approximation of the uniform. The women frequently looked exhausted and worn down by life despite their uplifting tattooed quotes. Their skin was often tinged with a grey pallor and pulled hard and tight across their cheekbones, making them look older than their years. The men didn't look exhausted but their demeanour ranged from angry to resigned and utterly unapproachable.

After the school children disappeared inside, this group would release the younger siblings from strollers. As the kids raced to the play equipment, the parents would light up cigarettes and draw in the smoke with a hunger known only to the starving. Bliss came on the outward breath, followed by sheer relief. Anita always pulled her gaze away from that first puff lest the temptation to go over and pluck the smoke out of someone's mouth overwhelmed her. It may have been years since she smoked, but she missed it far more than she missed her mother. Invariably, the vice principal came over and politely but firmly reminded everyone that smoking in the school grounds wasn't permitted and the group would decamp across the road to the public park. Anita hadn't entertained a single thought of seeking entry into their group. Why undo twenty years of hard work by going backwards?

Over the course of the past year, Anita had slowly and determinedly made inroads with the Pony Club Mothers. Her first foray was inviting them for morning tea using the Cancer Council's 'Biggest Morning Tea' to serve two purposes: raise funds for cancer research and prove she had the class and style demanded by the group. Of course, serving Moët & Chandon helped. When Cameron's brows had risen at the sight of the expensive but empty bottles in the recycling bin, she'd said, 'Business expense. I'm befriending the wives of the men who run this town.'

'I've taught you well, baby girl. Just make sure you give me the receipt for tax purposes.'

'Anita!'

She swung around to see one of the PCM mothers marching towards her across the schoolyard with the precision of a targeted missile. 'Morning, Jess.'

'Love that colour on you. Can I ask a favour? Could you possibly pick up Mia for me this afternoon? I've got an appointment in Albury and I might not get back until six.'

'Of course. No problem at all. Ava and Chloe will be thrilled.'

'I thought they might be. Mia's exceptional with the younger children and she takes her buddy responsibilities very seriously.' Jess dropped her head in close and said quietly and conspiratorially, 'I plan to remind the staff about that next year when they're selecting school captains.'

Anita smiled with relief. It may have taken a year but she'd finally come full circle and all her hard work networking was finally paying off. This conversation was identical to the ones she'd had in Melbourne with the other school mothers. It made an idea flicker. The immaculately dressed woman in front of her wielded a lot of social power. Could Jess's request to collect Mia after school be an opportunity?

'You'll be tired tonight after all that driving. Do you need dinner? I could make you a family-sized lasagne.'

In Melbourne, Anita had established a small in-home business, Cooked By a Friend. She'd targeted two demographics—one was time poor and the other time rich, but both had large disposable incomes.

'Oh, I couldn't possibly ask you do to that.'

Anita gave a calculated shrug. 'You're not asking. I'm offering. It's no problem. Really. It's what I used to do back in Melbourne.'

'Cook for friends?'

'Cook for clients. I menu plan, shop and cook for busy people in their home. I also taught one-on-one and group cooking classes. But my offer of the lasagne is a gift for a busy friend.' A gift she hoped would pay off with word-of-mouth recommendations. Although Anita knew the Mingunyah client pool was limited, with the right contacts, she hoped she might just be able to get three or four regular clients. She'd missed working.

'I had no idea you'd worked in Melbourne,' Jess said as though having a job was a novel idea. 'If your lasagne's as good as those yoyos you brought to the cake stall, I'd be a fool to say no.' She blew a kiss to Mia as the bell rang. 'I'd better go. I'll call you if anything changes but otherwise I'll see you just before six.'

'I'll have your lasagne, salad and garlic bread ready and waiting.' Anita waved to Ava and Chloe before exiting the schoolyard and turning left in the direction of the butcher.

John Dalton greeted her before the tinkle of the bell fell silent and both of her feet were inside the shop. 'Mornin', Anita. That husband of yours got you cooking for a crowd again?'

Anita enjoyed this aspect of country living. Although she'd used a dedicated butcher in Melbourne, that shop employed a lot of staff and she was just another well-dressed woman in a sea of many. 'Actually, John, I'm cooking for a friend. I need your best beef and pork mince.'

'No worries, love.'

After she'd answered questions about the children—John had a grandchild in the same class as Ava—and listened to a new story about Cameron throwing sawdust around the shop as a kid, she left with her white paper–wrapped parcels stowed in her basket. She was just passing the Mingunyah Cheese and Bakery Café, which was part of Sarah and Alex's business empire, when she heard someone call her name. Turning, she saw Sarah alighting from her car and walking briskly towards her.

'God, I need coffee,' Sarah said emphatically, looking frazzled and wearing mismatched earrings. 'First Gus announced at breakfast that he needed his white shirt for assembly this morning. I found it languishing in his dirty-laundry basket where he'd put it on Friday, complete with a tomato sauce stain on the front. I despair of that boy ever conquering thinking ahead. I'd just raided Finn's wardrobe and found him an old shirt when Alex came in from his ride and asked why I was still at Riverbend when I had a meeting in town with a supplier at eight thirty. I won't tell you the words I used or what I said to him about setting up meetings for me and not telling me about them. I rushed out the door and while I was driving through the mobile dead zone, the supplier must have called to reschedule because the moment I hit the eighty K sign, my phone beeped. And just to complete my morning, Mum's called, complaining that Rita's doing too much polishing of furniture and reorganising of knick-knacks instead of cleaning the bathrooms properly. She wants me to find her a new cleaner. I love my family, but right now I feel squished between teenagers' demands, forgetful husbands and my mother. They're doing my head in.'

'You really do need coffee,' Anita said sympathetically, thinking how lucky she was to have daughters. The older girls were born organised and the little girls showed a similar skillset, whereas Finn and Gus seemed to require a lot of micromanaging. 'I wonder why Margaret's not happy with Rita? I've used her a few times to help before some of Cameron's client weekends and I thought she did a great job.'

'I have no idea. Right up until this phone call Mum's always sung her praises. Anyway, sorting out that mess is my next job, but coffee first. So how about you? Got time for a coffee?'

'Sure, but just a quick one. I've got a job today.'

'A job?' Sarah's hand paused on the café's door. 'I didn't know you were looking for one.'

'Neither did I.' Anita laughed a little self-consciously as she followed Sarah into the shop. 'It's surprised me too.'

'Two lattes to go please, Mel,' Sarah called to the barista.

During Anita's first weeks living in Mingunyah, she'd insisted on paying for her own coffee but Sarah wouldn't let her. When Anita told Cameron that accepting the free coffee made her feel uncomfortable, he'd laughed.

'It's one coffee a week. Besides, she's family.'

Anita, who had no family and very limited contact with distant cousins, was baffled. 'How does her being family equate with free coffee?'

'It would be ill-mannered of her to expect you to pay, because that would be adding to her profits. Plus, you paying embarrasses her about her wealth and upsets her that you've rejected her hospitality. It's why I always drink their wine when they offer it.'

'So, you're saying I'm doing Sarah a favour by letting her buy me coffee?'

'Exactly.'

Not wanting to upset her sister-in-law, Anita took Cameron's advice and ceased trying to pay. And although Anita had intended to donate each saved four dollars to the CFA tin on the counter by the cash register, she hadn't quite got around to it.

While they waited for their coffee, Sarah asked, 'So, what's this job?'

'It's not so much a job as a first step. I'm thinking of restarting Cooked By a Friend, so I offered to make one of the influential school mums a lasagne.'

'Good for you. You're welcome to put some flyers on the café's noticeboard.'

'Thanks, Sarah. I appreciate your support.'

'No problem. In fact, show me a menu and I'll order some meals for the freezer.'

Anita was aghast. 'I can't sell you meals.'

'Why not?'

'Because you're family.'

'What's that got to do with anything? The way I see it, you make ready-made meals and I'm a wife, mother, daughter and businesswoman working more than full time. Hell, I'm your perfect customer.' Sarah passed Anita her coffee before taking a sip of her own with the fervour of an addict.

Once they were outside, Sarah continued, 'I'm sick to death of coming up with dinner ideas, not to mention cooking. I ask Alex and Gus what they want to eat and they say, "I don't mind. Whatever you want." They think they're being obliging but they're just passing the buck. More than once I've had to actively work at not yelling, "I want you to plan the menu, buy the food and cook it." Lately, it seems like I've been cooking all my life. I want a break. Or at least have someone else make some of the decisions for me.'

For the second time in a week, Anita wondered if something was going on with her usually upbeat sister-in-law. 'I'll make you a lasagne.'

'Thank you, but I'm paying for it and another four meals. Seriously, Anita. Put me on your books for five meals a week and email me a menu. I'll fire it back to you by the end of the day.'

A thrill shot through Anita at landing a big ongoing order on her first day but it was immediately tempered by memories of growing up. She'd learned the hard way that there was no such thing as a free lunch. Everything came at a price. 'I don't need charity, Sarah. I only want your order if it's genuine.'

'Oh, it's genuine all right,' Sarah said with feeling. 'Think of it as your contribution to the harmony of the Hadfields' family life. Cooked By a Friend, or in this case, a sister, couldn't have come at a better time.'

All of Anita's anxiety drained away. Pulling out her phone, she brought up her calendar. 'What day suits for me to come to Riverbend to cook the meals?'

'Any week day.'

'How about Friday this week but Tuesdays after that?'

'Done! Now, I've got to love you and leave you. I'm off to look at some grout in Mum's bathroom.' She gave Anita a quick kiss and crossed the road to her car.

Anita was stirring bolognaise sauce when Cameron arrived home looking for lunch. He caught her around the waist, spun her, bent down low and kissed her.

'Something smells fantastic.'

She welcomed his mouth against hers, thankful for the decision all those years ago to allow her new friends at the city childcare centre where she'd worked to drag her to the upmarket bar to celebrate her birthday. When she'd met Cameron, her determined journey away from the fringe 'burbs and their stench of struggle had already begun, but he'd fast-tracked things for her. He'd been her guide and continued to be. Her gratitude never wavered.

'It's lasagne.'

'My favourite.'

'It's not for us.' He gave an exaggerated sigh and she laughed. 'Okay, I'll make an extra for us but this one's special. It's part of my plan to relaunch Cooked By a Friend and ...' She couldn't contain a squeal of glee. 'I've already got a five-meal-a-week customer.'

'I always knew your lasagne was magic,' he teased before sobering. 'Cooked By a Friend? I thought you were letting that slide because country women wouldn't consider letting someone else cook for them?'

'I've missed the business more than I expected and perhaps I was wrong about country women. The first time I talked about Cooked By a Friend, I got a client.'

There were two very good reasons why she didn't mention that the customer was Sarah. One, it was unlikely her sister-in-law truly represented the town, although there was a small but definite pocket of wealth in Mingunyah that Anita planned to mine, and two, it was impossible to anticipate Cameron's reaction to anything that involved Sarah. Whether it was because Sarah was the eldest by a bare ten months and they'd landed up in the same class at school a few times or if it was something else entirely, Cameron blew hot and cold with his elder sister. But this was Anita's business, so the transaction was between her and Sarah and had nothing to do with him.

'I think there's a niche market in Mingunyah. Hopefully, today's just the start.'

'Maybe.' Cameron sounded sceptical. 'I can't imagine Mingunyah having as many clients as you'd like. It's a shame this kitchen doesn't lend itself to cooking classes.'

She bit her lip, not wanting to revisit that disappointment all over again. Finding a house in Mingunyah that suited all their needs had been an enormous challenge and, as Cameron liked to tell people, they'd compromised. In truth, Anita had compromised. In Melbourne, they'd modified the kitchen in the Glen Iris house to both satisfy commercial kitchen regulations and include the installation of a mirror above the island bench so she could teach larger classes. Her current kitchen didn't come close to accommodating four people, let alone twelve.

'I don't think the Mingunyah version of Cooked By a Friend is going to have cooking classes.'

Cameron seated himself expectantly at the kitchen table as if lunch was going to magically materialise in front of him. 'But your cooking classes made the money.'

He was right; her classes had proved so popular that she'd established a waiting list. Her success lay in running themed classes, which guaranteed return custom. Watching *MasterChef*, *My Kitchen Rules* and numerous professional cooking shows, along with reading *Epicure* and *Delicious Magazine*, kept her abreast of what was hot and what was not.

'True, but the classes catered to city women with time on their hands. Aren't country women supposed to be great cooks? I'm not sure they'll have the same appeal here.'

'Perhaps not to women born and bred here, but I think there's a market for you.'

Anita ladled roasted pumpkin and tomato soup into two bowls. 'Which market's that?'

'The cycling widows.'

She thought of Alex's intensive cycling training program that saw him out on the road seven days a week. 'Do you mean women like Sarah?'

He shook his head. 'No. Not Mingunyah women or even the weekenders. I mean the Melbourne women whose husbands come here to ride. I've seen them in the antique shop, the bookstore and the cafés, killing time. They're your niche. Fill their day by touring them around the farmers' market, introduce them to local produce, bang on about global miles, seasonal food, farm freshness and all that bullshit, then teach them to cook something. They'll eat it up.'

The microwave beeped. Anita stared at him. 'That's a brilliant idea.'

'I know.' He glanced around. 'Sarah given you any bread recently?'

Anita opened the breadbox and placed a seed-encrusted rustic sourdough baguette on the breadboard before slipping the knife underneath it. Cameron leaned over and grabbed it off the bench as Anita delivered the bowls to the table.

'I'll talk to Sarah about using their products in my cooking class recipes.' Despite Sarah saying there was nothing charitable about her meal order, being able to advertise Mingunyah Bread and Cheese made her feel less in Sarah's debt. 'We can give each other some promo.'

'They don't need the promo, Annie.' Cameron sawed into the bread with a determination greater than the task required. 'Have you seen the number of followers they've got on Facebook and Instagram, gushing about their products?'

'But I need their promotion,' Anita said, stirring some of Sarah and Alex's sheep's yoghurt into her soup. 'They've got a fan base of foodies. If I can tap into that ...'

'Clever girl.'

A tingle of pride shot along her spine at his praise. 'There's just one fatal flaw to this brilliant plan. Our kitchen's too small for classes. Even if we hadn't maxed out our renovation budget, there's no physical space to extend. We'd have to build a whole new kitchen in a different space and that will cost a fortune. I'd be starting so far in the red it wouldn't be worth it.'

Cameron chewed on the hunk of bread he'd dipped into the soup and stared off into the distance. Anita knew this was his 'thinking' stare.

'What?'

'Shush.'

She knew better than to rush him so she sipped her soup, enjoying the deep, smoky flavour that came about by accident when her hand slipped on the spice packet. Instead of half a teaspoon of smoky paprika landing on the bright orange surface, more than two tablespoons plopped in. It had turned into a useful mistake—one she'd be repeating.

'What's your ideal group size?' Cameron finally asked.

'I guess six to ten, if we're aiming for a boutique experience.'

'So, we need someone with a larger kitchen.'

'Cam, I can't just ask someone if I can take over their kitchen every Saturday or Sunday.'

'I know.' A smile full of ideas stole across his face. 'But this isn't just someone.'

Anita thought of Sarah's beautiful French provincial–style kitchen with its decorative corbels, fluted pilasters and the moulded chimney breast with a pressed metal splashback. All of it showcased the shiny black five-burner stove with its two ovens. Not to mention the acres of polished wooden benches, the vast number of cupboards and built-in wine rack. It had been featured in *Country Living* magazine, complete with its signature white clock, wicker baskets overflowing with freshly picked vegetables and a row of shiny copper pots; the envy of all cooks. A stab of jealousy caught her and it wasn't just limited to the kitchen; Sarah's renovations had been devoid of any real budgetary constraints. To add insult to injury, just this morning Sarah had told her she was sick to death of cooking.

Although Riverbend's kitchen would suit her perfectly and Sarah was supportive, Anita said, 'There's no way I can ask Sarah.'

'Not Sarah,' Cameron said. 'Besides, Riverbend's too far away. The women you're targeting are in stuck in Mingunyah for the weekend. The venue needs to be in town and walking distance from the market.'

'The church hall?'

'Mill House.'

She laughed. 'Stop teasing me.'

'I'm not.' He set down his spoon and leaned forward. 'Think about it, Annie. It's a huge kitchen. It's got rustic charm that matches a weekend in the country. You can tailor your themes around that. Old-fashioned country food with new twists. Use the Aga. I know Mum hasn't cooked on it in years but it's still connected. We can get someone in to check the flue.'

Despite her mother-in-law's joy at Cameron's return to Mingunyah, Anita felt the emotion hadn't fully extended to her and the little girls. 'What makes you think Margaret will agree to me using her kitchen?'

'Well, she doesn't use it much herself.'

'It doesn't follow that she'll let me impose.'

'She might be very supportive of the idea if it's a way of staying in the house.'

'I don't understand.'

'Sarah's got a bee in her bonnet about Mill House being too big for Mum. She's badgering her to downsize. Mum rang me this morning, spitting chips. Despite telling Sarah she wasn't interested in moving into a new townhouse, sister dear insisted on driving her out to look at one.' Cameron flicked a piece of bread around the bowl with practised accuracy, wiping it clean. 'It's more about her needs than Mum's. Sarah just wants to make her life easier. She was complaining on Mother's Day about helping Mum with the garden.'

Usually Anita defended Sarah to Cameron but this time she found herself agreeing. 'She's been complaining about a few things lately, including hosting Christmas. I offered but she immediately refused.'

Cameron rolled his eyes. 'My sister the martyr. And really, what's she got to whinge about? Mum doesn't want to sell up and move and why should she? Mill House has been in the Jamieson family since 1870 and, with one exception, it's always been left to the eldest son.'

Anita sat up a bit straighter, not quite believing this never-before disclosed piece of history. 'Are you saying Margaret has willed you— us —the house?'

His mouth tightened. 'Put it this way: I'm in the process of finding out.'

'Oh, Cam,' she said sympathetically. She could never forget the three occasions over the years when he'd got thoroughly sozzled and cried about the loss of the family business. 'Try not to get your hopes up. You know Margaret's ignored tradition before, so why would she follow an archaic inheritance system for the house? Besides, it would exclude Sarah and Ellie.'

'Mum's got other investments.'

'Worth as much as the house?'

'I've got a very strong suspicion she's worth a lot more than she lets on.' He tapped his fingers on the table. 'Let's work this out. You'll need the use of the kitchen, the dining room and the downstairs powder room. That's three rooms to rent.'

'Rent?' She heard the squeak in her voice. She'd never needed to factor in rent before. One of the reasons she'd started Cooked By a Friend was because the setup costs were negligible. Debt had cast a dark shadow over her childhood and the thought of borrowing money against a fledgling business and risking insolvency terrified her. 'How much will that cost?'

'Don't panic, baby girl.' He squeezed her hand. 'I'm talking a peppercorn rent. I'll negotiate it with Mum. How about as part of the deal, you make her a couple of meals a week for her freezer? That way we can tell Sarah that Mum has a cleaner and a cook. Sister will relax and more importantly, when she knows you're using Mill House for your business, she'll stop pushing to sell it.'

A flutter of disquiet rippled her stomach. 'I don't want this plan to upset anyone, especially Margaret and Sarah.'

Cameron waved away her concerns. 'It won't. If anything, it solves far more problems than it creates. I'll talk to Mum this afternoon.'

Her growing excitement that the cooking school might again be a reality was momentarily tempered. 'I guess if she says no, I can always contact the CWA. Not that a squat, 1960s cream brick building oozes the sort of character or charm I want to sell our concept.'

Cameron stood up and pulled her to her feet, his expression full of confidence. 'Have you ever known my mother to say no to me?'

She smiled and kissed him.

CHAPTER FOUR

'Hi, Alex, it's Ellie.' The sound of bleating goats floated down the line, making her smile despite her nervousness.

'Hey, Ellie. How are things?'

'Not bad.' Ellie liked her brother-in-law. Alex was uncomplicated, kind and smart as a whip and if she was ever put in a position where she was asked to choose, she'd pick Alex over Cameron any day. 'Noah and I were sorry to miss you on Mother's Day.'

'Yeah. Lesson learned. Never let a moron operate a back hoe.'

She laughed lightly as her fingers tangled nervously in the office phone cord. 'I'll remember that.'

'You after Sarah? Your call's come through to my mobile.' She licked her lips.

'Actually, it was you I wanted to speak to.'

There was a slight pause and Ellie imagined the cogs of Alex's mighty mind turning. She didn't usually call Sarah, let alone him. 'Righto. Fire away.'

She drew in a breath and let Ellie-the-professional speak. 'I've got three Burmese families keen to move to Valley View and join their extended families. They've been guaranteed jobs at the abattoir when a vacancy comes up but so far they've waited six months. I've just spoken with Ken Havers. He says unless someone unexpectedly leaves, they'll be waiting another six months to fill two retirement positions.'

'I sat next to Ken at a business breakfast last month,' Alex said. 'He can't remember ever having such a stable workforce and says that inviting the Burmese to come and work for him was his best idea yet.'

'He's done an amazing job. Valley View's reaping the rewards of his pragmatism and philanthropy. The Burmese come from small mountain villages so they love living here in the valley. They enjoy fishing, growing vegetables, running choo—'

'How many jobs are you chasing, Ellie?'

She smiled, appreciating how Alex always cut through the bullshit. 'Ideally six. Minimum three. If it helps, one of the men, Hi Loo, has some experience with goats.'

'Bet he's never milked two thousand of them and that's only one dairy.'

'Probably not, but he's keen to work.' She heard the rumble of a tractor and Alex saying, 'Over there,' before his voice came back to her at normal volume.

'The roster's short on milkers and we need another farmhand. I reckon we could take two full time and possibly some casuals in dispatch.'

'That's fantastic, Alex. Thank you.'

'Don't thank me too soon. Milking starts pretty bloody early. Do they have transport from Valley View to get out here?'

She jotted 'community bus?' on her notepad. 'Leave it with me. I'll sort something out.'

'All new employees start on three months' probation but going on Ken's experience, I'm not anticipating any problems.'

'Hopefully not. Listen, Alex, I've found it's really useful to talk with existing staff before the refugees start work. You know, explain a bit about where they've come from and why they're refugees. Hose down any concerns that they're taking local jobs and answer questions, that sort of thing. It helps with the settling-in process. When can I come out and do that?'

'You need to set everything up with Sarah. She'll confirm the exact number of jobs we can offer.'

Bugger. 'Okay. I'll call her tomorrow after you've filled her in.'

'Call her now. She's in the office. Why didn't you go straight to her?'

'I thought you did the staffing.' The lie slid off her tongue. 'My bad. Thanks for your help, Alex. I really appreciate it.'

'No worries. Catch ya later.'

The line went dead and Ellie set the receiver back in the cradle, staring at it. *Crap!* The whole point of ringing Alex was to avoid talking to Sarah. Conversations with Alex were straightforward and easy. Conversations with Sarah were like wading through muddy waters, knowing that dangers lurked beneath the surface but being clueless as to exactly what those dangers were and when they were going to strike. Ellie was acutely aware of Sarah's silent disapproval of her and how she lived her life, she just wasn't certain why Sarah bothered wasting any energy on it.

Her mother's disapproval she understood; Ellie hadn't toed the Jamieson family line, she'd caused 'problems'. Added to that was her lack of a Y chromosome. It didn't take a qualified analyst to notice that Margaret preferred men to women and always had. Even at seventy-six, her mother glowed when a man entered the room, which contrasted starkly with her behaviour at an all-female event. Cameron had benefitted from this character trait. He was the golden boy, and Ellie imagined that Sarah had grown up in the shadow cast by his crown's glow. It left her elder sister holding the position of firstborn but without the usual entitlements. Whenever Ellie observed her family together, as she had on Mother's Day, she found herself wondering if Sarah was aware that she'd spent her life seeking their mother's approval.

Perhaps *that* was the source of Sarah's disapproval of Ellie— siding with Margaret?

She supposed it made an odd sort of sense, although it didn't account for Cameron's critical opinion of her. His attack on Mother's Day about the cost of her education had been as bitter as it was unexpected. Both Cameron and Sarah had left home to start their adult lives when Ellie was still a child so she had little experience of usual sibling antics. Her brother and sister were more like adults who'd played minor roles in her life. She had fleeting memories of them returning home for their father's funeral, but that week had been surreal. Although Sarah stayed at Mill House for longer than Cameron after the funeral, the most solid recollections Ellie had of doing sisterly things with Sarah was the week before her sister's wedding.

As the youngest bridesmaid, Ellie had gloried in all the preparations but nothing had prepared her for the thrill she got when she'd looked at herself in her mother's cheval mirror. A beautiful stranger wearing a full-length royal blue gown stared back at her, golden hair swept up, eyes wide and bright and lips touched with a hint of pink lipstick. It was a moment free of doubt. She was beautiful — stunning, even—and she'd squealed with the joy of it. It was during the wedding reception that she'd become aware for the first time how she could command attention without opening her mouth. People's gazes stalled on her. Women gushed over how pretty she was, boys got tongue-tied and seemed in awe of her and men spoke to her as an equal and cut in to dance. She'd floated through the evening on a sea of compliments, and vowed *never* to return to being the kid she was the day before the wedding.

By the time Ellie truly needed a big sister, Sarah was married and living overseas.

She picked up the phone again but her fingers stalled on the number pad. It would be politic to drive to Riverbend and visit Sarah, and with any other employer Ellie would have chosen the face-to-face meeting without hesitation. But with Sarah, that meant small talk and opportunities for her sister to ask questions about Noah. On the surface, those questions sounded like interest, but they always came with a subtext: *I've got three children and vastly more parenting experience. Do you have any idea what you're doing?*

She groaned. Visiting Sarah was a necessary goodwill gesture to help ensure future job placements. She had no choice but to take one for the team. To facilitate a long-awaited Burmese family reunion she needed to have contact with her own family. The irony wasn't lost on her.

Her mobile buzzed and she read the word 'School' as it lit up the screen. Her scalp prickled.

'Ellie Jamieson.'

'Hey, Ellie, it's Karen Lecke. Noah's complaining of stomach pains. I tried the "go lie in the sickbay and get bored" trick but I think he's got the bug that's going around. Can you come and get him?'

Ellie stifled a groan, thinking about all the work she had to get through today. Then again, Noah being sick totally solved her dilemma about Sarah, giving her the perfect excuse to telephone her sister. It would be one call of the many she'd now have to make from home while Noah was tucked up on the couch.

'Sure, Karen. I'll leave now.'

'Okay, mate,' Ellie said to a rather pale Noah as they pulled up in their driveway. 'Go inside and put on your jammies.'

Noah slid out of the car without his usual bounce and trudged to the back door, shoulders slumped. Ellie unloaded the green enviro bag filled with bottles of electrolyte solution, Panadol and hand sanitiser. According to the pharmacy assistant, half the town was down with this bug and she and the rest of the household could live without it.

She'd just slung Noah's backpack over her shoulder when he called out, 'Mum! Look!'

She hurried up the steps to the closed-in veranda. Water was pouring out from under the door. 'Oh, jeez.' Did someone leave a tap on? She struggled to open the swollen door and a wall of water gushed over their feet.

'Cool!' Noah said, suddenly sparking up.

'Where's it coming from?' she asked, talking more to herself than to Noah.

'I'll find it. I can do it.'

Before she could stop him, he'd ducked into the house and was tramping through the water in his school shoes.

'Take off your shoes!'

He only had two pairs and her bank balance didn't need them falling apart from water damage. Slipping off her boots and socks, she waded inside and walked into the bathroom. Like the kitchen, it had been tacked onto the old farmhouse long after the initial construction. The kitchen dated back to the thirties but the bathroom was slightly more modern. It was part of the enclosed veranda that once doubled as a bedroom. The first thing she looked for was a running tap—it wouldn't be the first time that Bree forgot to turn it off after cleaning her teeth. The basin, shower and bath taps were all shut off and, thankfully, the toilet wasn't overflowing. She whipped open the cupboard containing the ageing hot-water service. It had been dripping a lot lately, but despite that it was sitting on its concrete block above the flood line. Clearly, it wasn't the culprit.

'Mum!'

Ellie found Noah and the burst pipe in the kitchen. 'Oh God. I should have turned off the water.'

'I can do it.'

'No. You stay here and don't touch anything.'

She splashed her way to the back door, ninety-nine per cent certain that the entire contents of the water tank were now inside the house.

After switching off the pump and shutting off the tank, she returned to find Noah floating a plastic toy boat and Splotch helping things along by bumping it with his nose. The last thing she needed on top of five centimetres of water in the house was a muddy dog.

'Splotch. Out!'

The border collie raised his head, a hurt look in his big brown eyes.

'Now!' She pointed to the door.

After a quick and ever-hopeful glance at Noah, Splotch padded slowly away.

The chill of the water numbed her feet and Ellie tried not to let the mess overwhelm her. 'Towels,' she said weakly. 'I'll get some towels.' But even as she said it, she knew towels weren't the answer.

'I'm gonna be sick.' The flush of excitement generated by discovering the flood had faded, leaving Noah's face ashen.

'Here.' She grabbed a plastic bowl off the sink and shoved it under his chin as he heaved. She rubbed his little back and mumbled soothing words, noticing the water was deeper on one side of the kitchen than the other. She smiled. It was the first time she gave thanks for sagging foundations and a DIY extension. They may not have any running water but with the lean-to lower than the rest of the house, she was hopeful the flood was confined to the back section of the house.

After tucking Noah into bed with a vomit bucket, a bell, electrolyte solution in his drink bottle and a talking book, she rang Heather Guthrie, the owner of the house, to explain the situation.

Heather, who always spoke to her tenants in an 'I'm a very busy woman' voice, sighed. 'And you're sure that's the problem?'

Ellie tried not to grind her teeth. The only time she mourned the fact she couldn't afford to buy her own home was when she needed to convince a landlord there was a problem that was seriously interfering with her quiet enjoyment of the property. 'I can message you a photo of the water. Of course you're welcome to come over and see for yourself.'

'I'll make some calls.'

'We'll need a water delivery.'

'Tenants are financially responsible for water.'

Pressure built behind Ellie's eyes and she worked on keeping her voice calm. 'The only reason I've run out of water is because the—' *your!* '—pipe burst.'

'Yes. And if you let me get off the phone, I'll arrange for that to be fixed.'

Don't say it. Do. Not. Say. It. 'Great. Thanks, Heather.' She pressed end call, closed the door between the kitchen and the hall and yelled, 'Bitch! Bitch! Bitch!'

She messaged Wendy, Rachel and Grace a photo. They replied they were sorry but were tied up at work. Could she cope on her own for a few hours?

Could she? Like so many other times in her life, she had no real choice but to do just that. Wading onto the veranda, she propped the door open with a brick, allowing free passage for the water to flow outside. Then, after pulling on her boots, she made her way to the garden shed. Grabbing a broom and a leaf shovel, she carried them back to the house and set about sweeping out the water, pausing only to check on Noah when the ache in her shoulders burned too hot to be ignored.

After an hour, all her muscles burned, as did her throat. Desperate for a cup of tea, she checked the kettle. 'Of course you're empty.' She picked it up and, with an irrational spark of hopefulness, took it out to the tank. Tapping the rungs, she listened for the responding echoes and determined that the water level was so low it was probably full of giardia just waiting to make her sick for months on end. Back in the house, she bypassed Grace's wine supply—not that she wasn't sorely tempted but it wasn't yet noon—and checked the fridge, regretting her 'no carbonated drinks except for parties' rule. They had finished the orange juice at breakfast. *Bugger.*

The honk of a horn made her jump and she slammed the fridge shut, fully expecting Noah to call out, startled from sleep. The fact he didn't wake was indicative of how unwell he was and how much his body needed the rest. To prevent another horn toot, she ran outside. A ute was parked behind her car. The windscreen was tinted and she couldn't make out if the person inside was male or female, but the plumber had arrived. *Okay, Heather, I take back one of those bitches.*

She waved and as she got closer, the driver's door opened and she saw a familiar logo. A moment later, Luke Sorenson stepped out.

'I heard you need a plumber.' His grin was friendly, familiar and somewhat disconcerting.

'You heard right. A burst pipe in the kitchen. I've shut off the water.'

He nodded. 'Good. Probably saved you some mess.'

'Oh, I don't know.' She indicated the water line on her jeans. 'I think I arrived home much the same time as the tank completely emptied.'

'I got here as soon as I could.'

'I thought Helen would have called someone from Valley View.'

'For you, she called the best.' His smile was the teasing one of their childhood but before she could roll her eyes or say, 'Yeah, right,' he added, 'I'm working on some spec homes she's building. Bit surprised you're living here.'

She bristled with indignation. Was he inferring the house wasn't good enough? Or was it a shot at Rachel and Grace? Or was she just being overly sensitive? *Settle.* She took the safer road.

'It's a great old house.'

'You're not wrong there. I just assumed since you came back to the valley, you'd be living in Mingunyah.' The inquiring rise of his brows added, *Where your family lives.*

'It makes more sense to live where my job is,' she said quickly. 'Carbon footprint, cost of fuel and all that.'

'So how long have you been back?'

'A couple of years.'

Startled, his head snapped forward and he blinked. The comical action made him look like an emu. 'How did you keep that so quiet? Poison the grapevine?'

'I guess I'm just not that interesting.'

'You're a Jamieson.'

'Not in Valley View. Here I'm just Ellie from the neighbourhood house.'

'I seriously doubt that.' He leaned into the cab before handing her a takeaway coffee cup stamped with the words Valley View Café and capped with a black lid. 'Thought you might need this. I wasn't sure what you drank so I took a punt on a flat white.'

She stared at it, not quite able to believe it was real. 'You brought me coffee?'

'If you're more of a tea drinker, I've got a thermos of hot water and a tea bag.' He glanced at the prayer flags and a V carved into the bridge of his nose. 'Nothing herbal, though. Sorry.'

'Don't be sorry. Coffee's amazing.' She took a tentative sip to test the temperature and followed up with a deliciously big swallow. 'Thank you.'

This time his smile swirled a dimple into his cheek. 'All part of the service. Want to show me the way?'

'Sorry?' Her mind was absorbed by the warmth and thirst-quenching qualities of the coffee and nothing at all to do with that dimple.

He laughed. 'Wow, you really did need that drink. Going by the lean on the front door, I'm guessing we enter round the back?'

'We do. I'm not sure when that door last opened but I'm thinking at least a decade ago. This way. My little boy—'

'Noah, right?'

'Yes.' It surprised her that Luke Sorenson remembered her kid's name. 'He's got gastro and he's asleep so—'

'Poor kid,' he said, dropping his volume. 'There's a lot of it about. I'll do my best to be quiet but plumbing can be noisy.'

She recalled how easily he'd spoken to Noah at the farm gate and found herself checking his left hand for a wedding band before remembering that for tradies, a ring was often an OH&S hazard.

She was about to ask him if he had kids when they reached the kitchen and Luke gave a low whistle.

'Things are a bit damp,' he said, squatting down and fingering the flaking pipe. 'At least it wasn't sewage.'

She shuddered at the thought. 'Is that plumber psychology to make me feel better before you hit me with the bad news?'

As he swung on his haunches to look at her, a shaft of sunshine caught his hair, lighting it up like a white flare on a dark night. 'Is it working?'

Something about his expression and the tone of his voice made her face heat in a way it hadn't done in years. She hid behind the coffee cup and drained the contents.

'How bad is it?'

'The pipe's cactus.'

'But you can replace it?'

'Technically.' He pushed to his feet in one fluid movement before walking into the bathroom.

She followed, trying not to notice the way his blue work pants moved across his behind, leaving little to the imagination. She wasn't a woman who covertly checked out men. Hell, she didn't check men out period. 'That doesn't sound very reassuring.'

He studied the rust stains on the porcelain and grimaced. 'I need to get under the house.'

'Really?' She shuddered again, only this time it was because of spiders and rats. And snakes. Although technically if there were snakes there wouldn't be many rats but still ...

He laughed at her expression. 'It's okay, Ellie. You don't have to come under the house with me.'

He sidled past her and she instinctively stepped back. She'd been giving men a wide berth for years. Anything to minimise the chance of an accidental touch—or otherwise—down to zero. But, used to sharing the bathroom with just a seven-year-old rather than a broad-shouldered plumber, she miscalculated her position. The backs of her knees slammed into the edge of the bath and buckled. She toppled backwards.

'Oh!' Flinging out an arm to balance herself, she grabbed thin air. For a second she teetered—that moment between a semblance of balance and crashing awkwardly to the ground.

Luke's hands shot out, wrapping themselves firmly around her upper arms and grasping her tightly. His fingers dug painfully into her skin. The quick grab stalled her fall, but the impetus of it shot her forward until she was tilting into him. *No!* She jerked, throwing her head and shoulders back, desperately trying to stop herself from crashing into his chest.

His arms locked and she swayed. 'Whoa! Steady, Ellie. I've got you.'

And that was the problem. His hands clenched so tightly around her arms they may as well have been steel bands. Panic rose and eddied through her, drying her mouth to desert conditions and flipping her heart rate into the red zone.

He bent his knees and suddenly his clear blue eyes came into focus. 'You okay? I thought we were both going to end up in the tub. That or your head was going to break my jaw.'

'Sorry.' But she wasn't sorry at all. She only said the word because she needed to reassure him so he'd let her go. 'I need to sit down.' He lowered her onto the bath's edge and the moment he let her go, she crossed her arms in relief. She rubbed where his fingers had been.

'Hell, did I hurt you? Sorry. I was trying to help.'

She heard contrition in his voice and saw consternation in his expression. She didn't want to care that her reaction was bothering him. She didn't want to have to reassure him, especially when she was busy battling to find her centre of calm, but despite that, she mustered up a weak smile. 'It's fine. Just a tender spot.'

'Sorry.'

'A few bruises are better than a concussion. Thank you.'

'You're really pale. Are you sure you're feeling okay?'

'Yes!' It came out too loud and too abrupt but his solicitude was disconcerting. She much preferred flippant Luke and wished he'd replied to her thanks with something like 'That's how I roll.'

'Right then.' He rubbed the back of his neck as if it was causing him pain. 'I better get under the house and take a squiz.'

She stayed seated, not risking standing again until after Luke left.

'I'll be in the kitchen when you resurface.' *A large room with plenty of space to put between us.*

Ten minutes later, Ellie was busy pulling things out of the bottom of the pantry and checking for water damage when she heard the rumble of Luke's voice outside talking to someone. Peering through the window, she recognised Wendy's cropped black hair and went to join them.

'Hi, Ellie.' Wendy gave her a wan smile. 'Luke was just explaining things to me.'

Luke, who looked like he was wearing a hundred years' worth of dust and had filthy grey cobwebs hanging off him, gave her a professional nod. 'It's not looking good. Not surprisingly, all the pipes are shot. The pipe to the septic's so thin it could go at any time.'

'So you'll replace them all?'

'I'd love to, but Helen's not keen to spend any money on the house.'

'Well, there's a surprise,' Ellie said tartly. 'But she's conceded we need a new pipe in the kitchen and one to the septic, right?'

'She's pushing for a repair.'

Umbrage simmered in Ellie's gut. 'But—'

'Read this.' Wendy put a letter into her hand. 'It was in the PO box this morning.'

Ellie unfolded the page and noted it was from Helen and dated the day before. As she scanned the printed words, her heart sank. 'It's an eviction notice.'

Wendy nodded. 'And because the lease has been month-by-month for a year now, it's totally within her rights. Apparently, she's sold part of the farm to VicRoads for the road widening.'

Ellie turned and gazed at the old orchard behind the house. Trees planted in straight lines decades ago by people now long buried spread their gnarly, lichen-covered limbs towards the sky. An unexpected pain gripped her. 'Does it include the fruit trees?'

'Probably. Helen might have grown up on the farm and called it home, but she loves money more than happy memories.'

'Home doesn't necessarily mean happy.' The blunt words slipped out before Ellie realised she'd spoken.

'Exactly, sister,' Wendy said emphatically. 'And you're preaching to the choir.'

Luke was silent but his questioning gaze was fixed firmly on Ellie. There was something unnerving about the way he looked at her—as if he was seeking answers to unknown questions. The uncomfortable feeling she'd experienced in the bathroom rushed back. She'd spent years trying to be as inconspicuous as possible, and she hated it when people gave her a second glance, let alone studied her. Pulling the sleeves of her hoodie over her hands, she gave in to the urge to disappear behind the baggy top. If only she could bury her face in the material too.

More than anything, she wanted to banish Luke's gaze. The only way to do that was to cover her gaffe and shift his attention far away from her. 'I'm sad Helen's sold this place but I'm hardly surprised. Everyone in the district knows old man Guthrie used to hit first and asked questions later.'

'Bastard,' Wendy muttered.

'Yeah,' Luke agreed, looking contemplatively at the fruit trees. 'Scary bastard. He always carried a shotgun.'

'So, Luke.' Ellie forced herself to look at him. 'We're still here for a bit longer and we need water. How soon can you fix the pipe?'

'Mum, you'll be pleased to know the claws on your brooch have all been checked and repaired. There's no danger of any diamonds falling out.'

Margaret smiled at her son as he flipped the jewellery box open. She was dazzled by the brightness. 'Heavens! They're sparkling.'

Cameron laughed. 'Rudi put them in the sonicator to give them a new lease of life. And you'll love that they're worth more than the last time they were valued. I rang your insurance company and sent them a copy of the valuation so you're all sorted. They'll post you a copy of the updated policy.'

'Thank you dear,' she said, still admiring the brooch. 'I'm surprised they let you do that.' Who was her insurance company?

'That's the beauty of the power of attorney, Mum. Like I explained to you, it's not just in case you get sick and, God help me, I hope you don't. The good thing is, it lets me ease your load with things like the insurance. It's little things like that lawyers charge for.'

'I'm lucky to have such a thoughtful a son who takes care of his mother.' She patted his hand before offering him a slice of cake with his tea.

Cameron's arrival was unexpected and it was fortunate she'd found three slices of passionfruit sponge in the fridge. It was a surprise to see them sitting neatly on a plate, covered in cling wrap, and she assumed they must be leftovers from yesterday's bridge afternoon, although that was a little strange. For over twenty years, when it was her turn to provide afternoon tea, she'd always served scones. But she must have sensed he was coming, as Cameron had a soft spot for cake.

'You look after me so well, darling. Your sisters could take a leaf out of your book.'

Cameron nodded and sighed. 'Another up side of Anita renting the kitchen on Saturdays is Sarah will have to back off about this downsizing nonsense.'

Margaret had no idea what he was talking about, but the thought of leaving her house filled her with an all-encompassing dread. 'I'm not selling Mill House,' she said shrilly. 'I won't.'

'And you don't have to, Mum,' Cameron said soothingly, his handsome face full of understanding. Sitting directly opposite her at the table and wearing a beautifully tailored suit, he looked and sounded exactly like Kevin ...

'And you don't have to, Margaret,' Kevin said wearily, tearing at the knot of his tie. 'It was just a suggestion. I just thought you might enjoy going out.'

It was their first Friday night in Mingunyah as a married couple.

They'd honeymooned on tropical Hayman Island, where Margaret luxuriated in watching and touching her fit and good-looking husband. On the beach, she'd noticed she wasn't the only person to openly stare at his naked chest but she was the only one with the right to touch him. To slather coconut oil all over his skin and feel the play of muscles underneath it. To use her hands and mouth on him until he was hard. To lower herself over him and feel him bucking underneath her. To have him solely to herself. Every moment of it was worth the long, long wait.

Returning to Mingunyah tanned and relaxed, Margaret intended to be the sort of wife whose opinions were both respected and sought by her husband. She had no intention of continuing to exist on the side-lines of Kevin's life like she had during their protracted courtship.

'I enjoy going out, Kevin, and if Gary was dating someone it would be a great idea. But sitting listening to the two of you talk football tactics and statistics all evening isn't exactly my idea of fun.'

He frowned as if this was news to him but instead of saying, 'But that's what you've done for two years,' he said, 'What about inviting one of your single friends?'

Somehow, he had failed to notice that Margaret didn't have any single girlfriends. Arriving in Mingunyah single at twenty-six— almost over the hill in 1970s marriage terms—it had been a strategic tactic to only befriend young married women. After all, why add to the competition? And married women wanted nothing more than to match up their single friends so everyone could be as happy as they were. Her bridesmaids, Sylvia and Louise, were both married and a perfect example of this phenomena. Margaret had met Louise first and had subsequently befriended Sylvia when Louise said that Sylvia's family and the Jamiesons were very close. So close that the town always expected Sylvia and Kevin to marry. One night about two months into the friendship, Margaret mentioned this and Sylvia had laughed uproariously.

'Me marry Kevin? God, no! It would be like marrying my brother.' As she sucked the martini olive off the toothpick, a calculating look had entered her hazel eyes. 'But you know what? You'd be a perfect match for Kevin.'

'No,' Margaret had demurred coyly before widening her eyes and glancing over the rim of her glass. 'Do you really think so?'

'Oh, yes.' Sylvia clapped her hands in delight. 'I'll throw a dinner party and invite him. I've been dying to use the fondue set I got for a wedding present.'

Now Margaret stepped in close to Kevin and started undoing his tie. 'Darling, all my friends are married just like we are. We're now part of the young Mingunyah marrieds and we should be spending our weekends with other couples. Besides, tonight's our first Friday night in our new home and I thought it would be fun to stay in.'

Her fingers disposed of his tie and started on the buttons of his shirt. 'And you're playing footy with Gary tomorrow so you'll have hours with him. I'm definitely not the sort of wife who expects you to come straight home after the match either. Stay and enjoy a couple of beers with him, talking stats and facts before you come home at seven to Chateaubriand and me.'

She ran her hands up his chest and kissed him long and hard until a low groan crossed his lips. 'That sounds fair, doesn't it?'

He dropped his forehead onto hers. 'Very fair.'

'Excellent.' She had other plans for their marriage—plans that included banishing football from their lives—but now was not the time to mention them. Some things needed to be finessed. 'Darling, go and get changed for dinner and then make me a Bloody Mary and tell me all about your day.'

'... Mum?'

Margaret startled and blinked, bringing Cameron's face back into focus.

'You were a million miles away.'

She smiled at him as her memories continued screening in the back of her mind. 'I was thinking about your father. You look so much like him. So handsome. Before he was stolen from us so suddenly, we had a lot of happy years in this house.'

'I love the old place too, Mum. It's not just full of my childhood memories, but of you, Dad and Grandpa. Dad used to say if the walls could talk, the Jamieson secrets would whisper long and loud. Remember when I tricked Sarah into thinking the house was haunted?'

A ripple of irritation ran through her. 'I remember your sister breaking a vase and you cutting holes in one of my best sheets.'

Cameron grinned and gave her a wink. 'But you still love me.'

Margaret laughed, her old annoyance fading under a rush of love. Her mind located the black-and-white film reel of the day Cameron was born. 'I've never forgotten the moment I first held you in my arms. You gazed up at me and I gave you my heart in a way I'd never given it to anyone before. I was the mother of a son and every woman should know that pleasure.' She snapped out of her reverie and fixed her gaze on Cameron. 'The Jamieson line can't stop with you. Someone told me there's a diet Anita can go on so you can have a son.'

'A fifth-generation Jamieson living in Mill House?'

She smiled just thinking about it. 'Exactly.'

He leaned forward. 'Mum, I know how much you love this house. I'll do whatever it takes to help you stay here.'

'Thank you, darling. Ellie doesn't care and Sarah—'

'Doesn't understand you like I do. The only reason she wants you to move somewhere smaller is to make her life easier. Put you somewhere so she doesn't have to visit you every day. I mean how hard is it to help a little now and then with the garden? Hell, you spent years caring for us.'

'I did, didn't I.' Vindication grew like ivy, sucking and clinging to the disappointment she experienced when she thought about her daughters. Sarah's begrudging help. Ellie's abandonment.

'I virtually raised Ellie single-handedly but I never got any thanks. Not that a mother expects—'

'Even so ...' Cameron's voice trailed off, validating all of Margaret's thoughts.

'Sometimes I think you're the only one of my children who understands me.'

'I try my best.' Cameron licked cream off his fingers. 'I was thinking, now that you've given me power of attorney, it's probably an idea to tell me where you keep your will. You know. Just in case.'

She refilled his tea cup. 'You don't have to worry about that. My will's safe with Robert.'

'Robert's been dead for three years, Mum.'

'Tsk.' She knew that, but the space where the name of her solicitor should sit was blank. 'You know who I mean. Robert's son.'

Cameron frowned. 'Dan Horton? Really? I thought you'd changed solicitors. I know Sarah likes him but I'm not sure that's enough to recommend him.'

'It's true, Dan does suffer from being a little too much like his mother.' Margaret sat a little straighter as pride ran up her spine. She'd always outshone mousy and wimpy Mary Horton. 'But I've always thought Dan got enough of Robert's mettle and business savvy to compensate. Besides, our connection with the Hortons dates back to your great-great-grandfather. For as long as there's been a Jamieson in the valley, the Hortons have been our solicitors.'

'Still ...' Cameron turned his cup on its saucer. 'I bet Dan's charging you an arm and a leg for the pleasure.'

Was he? Unease skittled through Margaret. It wasn't just her will Dan was looking after but her investment portfolio too. The last few statements she'd received had so many figures that she'd got a headache trying to work out which payments corresponded to which services. Rattled, she'd shoved the bewildering paperwork into the filing cabinet. 'Nonsense. I'm a valued customer. Your father and I were very good friends with Robert and after Kevin died, Robert—'

'Yeah, I know,' Cameron said tightly. 'Robert saved everything except the mill.'

Margaret pursed her lips at the old chestnut, frustrated at Cameron's inability to let it go even after all these years. 'I know you were disappointed about the sale of the mill but as much as I loved your father, it was in a parlous financial position when he died and bleeding money. Without Robert's intervention, we could have lost everything, including the house. Instead, he made me a lot of money.'

'But as you just said, bland Dan isn't Robert. You're depending on him to make your money work for you, which is fine if you're happy and confident in his skills ...'

Her unease morphed into a sharp shard of worry. 'What are you saying? Have you heard something about Dan?'

Cameron shrugged. 'All I'm saying is once a firm believes they've got you for life, they see you as an easy target to charge you exorbitant fees for doing not very much. If Dan's new Merc is anything to go by, I'd say he enjoys spending money as much as his vapid mother.' He sipped his tea. 'All I want is for you to be confident in Dan. If you've got concerns, I suppose I could carve out some time and take a look at the figures. You know, just to make sure he's doing his best by you and not ripping you off to pay for his new toys.'

Her mouth dried. Robert had always complained about Mary's voracious spending. What if Dan was taking advantage of her to pay for his lifestyle? He'd always been a mummy's boy and nothing would make Mary happier than for Dan to be skimming money off the top of Margaret's investments. She wanted reassurance but Cameron was busy with his new business and being a modern hands-on father, despite that wife of his not working.

'You're got far too much on your plate as it is.'

Cameron leaned forward, picked up her hand and folded it in his. 'Mum. I'm never too busy for you.'

CHAPTER FIVE

Sarah sprayed Sophie Fotina's hair with half a can of hairspray, reinforcing the 1960s beehive that most of the girls in the cast of *Sweet Charity* sported. 'There you go, Soph. You look fantastic. Break a leg.'

'Thanks, Mrs Hadfield.'

Sarah dropped the round hairbrush into the large pocket of her apron that contained bobby pins, blue eye shadow, pancake stage makeup, a long-handled comb and hair ties, among other things. She'd been part of the Mingunyah High School production's hair and makeup rodeo before and having everything she needed on her person made the job more efficient. She glanced around. Thankfully no one else was waiting to be turned into a hippie or a stripper, which meant she had just enough time to dash out and collect her mother and be back before curtain. Grabbing her bag, she jogged to the car. Two days earlier she'd explained to Margaret that she was a parent helper before the show and that afterwards she'd be tied up chatting to other parents and waiting for Gus. 'It's probably easier all round if you drive yourself, Mum. It's not far and that way you can go straight home and avoid the foyer crush.'

But despite the short distance between Mill House and the high school, and the fact that her mother often drove herself an extra kilometre to the bowling club for dinner, her suggestion had been met with judgemental dissatisfaction. 'It will be cold and dark. And that gravel pit of a carpark is a long way from the auditorium.'

She'd had a point—the surface was a little uneven. The spectre of her mother lying with a broken hip haunted Sarah. 'How about I ask Alex or Cameron to pick you up?'

'They're both very busy. If you want me to see Gus's play, you have to take me.'

Now Sarah parked the car outside Mill House and ran up the path. She pressed the old brass doorbell before quickly shoving her hands into her coat pockets to protect them from the pricking chill of the icy air. Margaret answered the door with her hair set and her face made up but still in her bathrobe.

'Mum!' Sarah wailed, her heart sinking. She'd asked her mother to be ready for 7.15. 'We'll miss the start!'

Her mother pursed her lips. 'Don't take that tone with me, young lady.'

'Sorry, Mum.' *Why are you apologising? You're not twelve.* But she didn't have time to analyse old habits; she needed to get her mother dressed and out the door. Rushing upstairs to the bedroom, she stopped short in surprise. Her mother's bed was piled high with frocks—a veritable fashion history of gowns from the seventies to the new millennium.

Sarah recognised the royal blue, pink and green check Thai silk gown Margaret had worn to the opening of *The Phantom of the Opera* in Melbourne in 1990. Peeking out from under it was the heavily beaded bodice of her Mother of the Groom frock for Cameron and Anita's wedding. One dress was pulled from its protective plastic; a silver and black lurex gown Margaret sewed in the seventies from a Vogue pattern. As a little girl, Sarah had adored that dress, believing Margaret to be even more elegant than the model on the pattern envelope. It was one of the last frocks Sarah recalled her mother making. By the eighties, the sewing machine was mothballed and Margaret regularly went to Melbourne on shopping sprees.

During her teenage years, Sarah loved the run-up to the Spring Racing Carnival when her mother's shopping expeditions took on epic proportions. On the four significant racing days in Cup Week, 'the frock' was only one part of a very strategic ensemble where hat, gloves, shoes, earrings, bracelet, necklace and handbag all played equal roles. As part of Margaret's preparation for Derby Day, Cup Day and Oaks Day, she gave the family an annual fashion parade, inviting opinions and comments. Sarah, always in awe of her mother's taste and style, could never find anything to criticise and 1988 had been no different ...

'Your hat's wrong,' Cameron said bluntly. 'It looks stupid.'

'Shut up, Cam.' Sarah flashed a triumphant look at her mother. 'Don't listen to him, Mum. You look perfect.'

'There's no such thing as perfect, Sarah.' Margaret fiddled with her hat. 'There're always ways to improve, and your brother's right. I need to tilt this further forward.'

While her mother busied herself with the hat and her father took a familiar blue and gold box out of his pocket, Cameron gave Sarah the finger. She gave it straight back.

'Here's something that might help complete the outfit,' her father said in the same wry tone he used every November.

Margaret's grey eyes lit up the way they always did when she was given a gift. 'Oh, Kevin,' she breathed, fingering the jewellery. 'How did you know?'

Most years her father laughed, but this year he said, 'I know the rules of this game, Margaret, and many others.'

Her mother, gazing lovingly at the heavy sterling silver chain, didn't seem to have heard him as her response was her standard, 'Please fasten it around my neck.'

It wasn't until the Cup Week after her father's death, when Cameron produced a familiar blue box, that Sarah had discovered her mother's spring carnival preparation always included a visit to Rubensteins Jewellers. Margaret chose the item of jewellery she wanted and gave instructions on when and to whom the necklace or earrings were to be delivered.

Sarah gave herself a shake and refocused. Handing her mother a cream silk blouse that hung neatly in front of a pair of black tailored pants with a matching jacket, she said, 'I'm thrilled you're finally having a clear out, Mum.'

'What?' Margaret's arthritic fingers struggled with the blouse's fine pearl buttons.

Sarah stopped herself from reaching out to help. History taught her it would only slow things down—Margaret hated anyone touching her clothes. 'Donating your old clothes. Kerry at the op shop will be beside herself with that haul.'

'The op shop?' Margaret gasped as she snatched the trousers from Sarah's hand. 'Don't you dare take my clothes to the op shop.'

Sarah didn't have time to argue. 'No, Mum. Of course not. Got your shoes? Good. We have to go.'

Sarah rally-drove the short distance to the school, ignoring her mother's comments about her preference to arrive alive, and dropped Margaret off at the door of the auditorium. As it was now almost show time, the car park was full and Sarah was forced to use the overflow paddock. When she flicked up the handbrake, the dashboard clock displayed 7.27 and her heart raced. She hated being late and she still had to navigate her way across a dark and tussock-filled paddock. Despite using the torch app on her phone, she still managed to sink ankle deep into a puddle. Who needed clean boots anyway?

Wet and muddy, she finally arrived at the theatre just as the doors were closing. Of course, her seat was in the middle of the row and nine people needed to stand to let her pass.

'Sorry. Excuse me. Thank you.' She scuttled along the row, ignoring muttered comments about mud and, just as the house lights went down, slid into her seat next to Alex. She craved an understanding smile and a kiss hello, but all Alex said was, 'You're cutting it fine.'

Frustration boiled. 'You think?'

'Sarah! Hello!'

In the post-performance crush of parents and students, Sarah turned to the voice. Her heart sank. 'Stella.' She forced enthusiasm into her greeting. As much as she disliked the *Mingunyah Herald* journalist, it wasn't worth getting offside. 'How are—'

'Look at you.' Stella's eyes raked her up and down with a look that left Sarah wondering if she'd somehow managed to get mud on her cheek as well as her boots or if she had something green stuck in her teeth. Before Sarah could decide if Stella was complimenting or criticising her, the woman was leaning in. Air kiss one. Air kiss two. Job done. Stella immediately fixed her full attention on Alex. 'Of course, you're looking as handsome as ever, Alex Hadfield.'

Sarah watched Stella's lips push through the air before leaving a bright pink lipstick imprint on Alex's cheek. She'd been watching similar scenarios play out all her married life. She called it the 'Alex Effect'. If she ever put out a range of greeting cards, one would say, 'The woman who marries a handsome man becomes invisible'. It seemed to be one of life's lessons.

Early in her relationship with Alex, episodes like this stroked all of Sarah's insecurities like a bow sliding over strings. But Alex had chosen *her*. And Alex was impervious to flattery. Twenty-two years on, her confidence in their marriage was strong, and bolstered by all they'd achieved together with the business and as a family. These days she derived an element of amusement from the antics women employed to get Alex's attention.

'Alex, you must be so proud of Gus,' Stella cooed.

'We're both proud, Stella,' Sarah jumped in, the current strained relations between Gus and his father front and centre in her mind.

Usually in situations like this, Alex gave her a wink or an eye roll but tonight he grimaced as if he was swallowing his words. The strain rode up his jaw and she saw a muscle twitch, making her glad she'd spoken first. Alex usually had the energy of two men but tonight he looked worn out. Solicitude filled her. On top of a busy work week, he was probably overdoing the cycling, training for the Victorian Three Peaks challenge. Why anyone would want to ride 235 kilometres in thirteen hours was beyond Sarah's comprehension. It sounded like torture. As far as she was concerned, mountains existed to be skied down after a leisurely sit on a ski lift spent admiring their stunning and craggy vistas. But Alex was hell bent on competing so she was supporting his dream. The sooner they got home so he could get some sleep, the better.

Stella's palm pressed against her generous décolletage. 'But what a surprise. I mean, who knew the boy could sing?'

In a town where athletic prowess was king and the arts languished a long way behind, Sarah had her suspicions as to why Gus had spent years focusing on football. If Stella's feigned attempt at surprise was anything to go by, Gus had every reason to have hidden his singing talent for so long.

As if on cue, Stella added, 'It's a brave move in more ways than one.'

Alex laughed at the barb but Sarah heard the tension woven through it. 'I think it's got everything to do with Sophie Fotina being cast as Charity.'

'Ah, young love,' Stella said, throwing a meaningful glance at Alex. 'Oh, to experience that delicious and addictive rush again.'

'I don't know ...' Sarah curled her arm through Alex's, staking a claim now that Stella was openly flirting. 'I can live without all the angst that goes with young love. Besides, like port, there's depth, flavour and a certain comfort in a well-aged love.'

'God, Sarah. We're not old.' Alex pulled his arm away and waved at Gus, who'd just emerged from the dressing rooms in the middle of a crush of students.

Sarah caught the slight lift of Stella's well-shaped brows and the questions in her eyes. *Damn it, Alex. Of all the people to get snippy in front of, why Stella?*

She smiled at the woman. 'Lovely to see you, Stella, but please excuse us. We have to join the rest of the family and congratulate Gus.' She grabbed her husband's hand and pushed through the crowd.

Gus was being hugged and kissed by girls, and hugged and thumped on the back by boys. Today's teenagers were far more emotionally demonstrative than back in her day, but then again, this was a theatre crowd. She was suddenly struck by the similarities between the footballers and the performers; did they realise they celebrated highs in the same way?

'Gus, you were amazing,' she said proudly, giving him a kiss. 'Wasn't he, Alex?'

Alex's dark brows furrowed, giving his handsome features the thunderous look she'd dubbed 'Zeus' year ago. 'Yes.' The word sounded like it had been wrenched out of him.

Gus shrugged. 'It's okay, Dad. I know it's not your thing.'

'That's got nothing to do with it. You did a good job. Sang well. Doesn't change the fact you've let your team and yourself down. Without you on the ground today, Dylan Morton was the standout player. He'll be the one to catch the eye of the scouts, not you.'

'Not here, Alex. Not now,' Sarah muttered, furious at him for spoiling Gus's moment. 'Finn! Over here.' She hailed her eldest son, who was chatting with friends, and glanced around for the rest of the family.

'Well done, Gus, darling.' Margaret presented her cheek for a kiss. 'It took me back to my twenties and the first time I saw *Sweet Charity*. Can someone get me a cup of tea?'

'Gus! Gus!' Noah barrelled into his cousin, hugging him around the hips. 'Why have you got makeup on?'

'Great job, Gus.' Ellie kissed him before explaining to Noah that actors wore makeup because of the bright lights.

'Bro!' Finn put Gus in a head lock and playfully punched him on the arm. 'Never thought I'd see you singing and dancing when you're sober.'

'Shut up,' Gus said good naturedly, but he studiously avoided his parents' gaze.

Sarah's anxiety ratcheted up a notch. The fact Gus wasn't looking at her made her worry that his assurances—'I'm an athlete, Mum, I'm not going to write myself off'—weren't strictly true. She mentally added, *Find time to chat with Gus*, to her never-ending to-do list. Perhaps she could drive him to school one morning this week. One-on-one chats in the car had worked with Finn. She hoped they would be as successful with Gus.

'Oh, Sarah!' Anita arrived next to her. 'You must be bursting with pride. He was fantastic!'

'He was, wasn't he.' Sarah automatically kissed her sister-in-law, loving that Anita's enthusiasm matched her own. It was only as she drew back that she realised far too late that she hadn't greeted Ellie the same way. Turning to Ellie, she said, 'Thank you for coming.'

'Noah was very excited. It's all he's talked about today.'

Sarah, who was still nursing a bruised ego that Ellie had called Alex first about jobs for her Burmese clients, tried unsuccessfully not to take offence at the inference that Ellie hadn't come for the family. 'I hope he enjoyed it.'

'Gus,' Cameron boomed. 'Did I ever tell you that I played Judd in *Oklahoma!* at uni? Your grandfather had a great voice too. Jamieson genes, eh?'

With a pang of nostalgia, Sarah remembered her father's coveted World Record Club collection of Broadway musicals. Did Margaret still have the black vinyl discs in their leather-bound and gold-embossed book? Kevin had loved Rodgers and Hammerstein musicals and he'd played them all, from *Carousel to The Sound of Music*. Her fondest memories weren't his pitch-perfect renditions of 'People Will Say We're in Love' but when he dropped the needle onto 'Shall We Dance' from *The King and I*. He'd grab her hands and spin her around the lounge room until they were both breathless and laughing. Or until her mother said, 'For God's sake, Kevin, turn it down.' Twenty-six years and she still missed his warmth.

'Sport and music, eh.' Cameron slapped his nephew on the back. 'Alex, you sure you had a role in this boy's DNA?'

'He got my good looks.'

'Lucky for him,' Cameron said jovially. 'Then again, you were always prettier than Sarah.'

At the mention of her name, Sarah turned—her brother's voice breaking her reverie. 'Sorry? What?' Her words collided with Gus's.

'Steady on, Uncle Cam.'

She took in Cameron's unusually florid face and Gus's worried expression, and wondered exactly what her brother had just said about her.

'Had a few, Cam?' Alex asked wearily.

'You bet I have. I just sold the Murchison property on Woolscour Lane.' He leaned in and touched his nose. 'You two aren't the only successful business people in town.'

'Congratulations,' Sarah offered against a flinch of resignation. It would be much easier for her to be pleased for her brother if he'd stopped talking at the word 'Lane'. Instead, he'd turned his good news into a competition. But what did she expect? In some ways, she was responsible for their rivalry; it had started the day he was born and been fostered as he grew and consumed vast amounts of their mother's attention.

'Cameron's exactly the sort of businessman this town needs,' Margaret said. 'Someone with some get up and go.'

'Here's your tea, Gran.' Phoebe held out a cup and saucer in one hand and a cupcake-loaded plate in the other.

'Gracious, dear.' Margaret held up her hand like a stop sign. 'It's far too late for tea.'

'Mum,' Gus said. 'Sophie's having a cast party.'

'Where?' Sarah noted that he wasn't actually asking permission to go. The Fotinas owned a cider house. Surely it wasn't going to be there?

'Don't stress, Mum. It's at their house.'

'What time does it finish?'

'I'll make sure he gets home,' Finn said before inhaling a cupcake he'd plucked from his cousin's plate.

'But you can't drink and drive so how will you get—'

'Can we come?' Phoebe and Ruby chorused.

Finn and Gus exchanged a look—one that bothered Sarah because it held an element of protection for their younger cousins. She didn't have to reach very far to assume it was protection from alcohol. Or was it drugs? There'd been an issue with marijuana in Finn's year and she wasn't naive enough to believe it had been completely stomped on.

'Sorry, cuzzies,' Gus said. 'It's just for the people in the play.'

'Finn's not in the play,' Phoebe said indignantly. 'So if—'

'Heavens, look at the time,' Anita said abruptly, finishing her conversation with Ellie and turning to the main group. 'Come on, girls. Gymkhana in the morning.' Kissing Cameron on the cheek, she said, 'See you at home,' before herding her daughters towards the exit.

''Night.' Ellie gave a general wave to everyone. Noah was pressed up against her side, almost asleep on his feet and not keen to walk to the car.

'I'll give Ellie a hand with Noah and then head home,' Alex said quietly in Sarah's ear, sounding much more like his normal self. 'See you there.'

Before Sarah could thank him or kiss him goodbye, Margaret said irritably, 'Why do teenage girls have to squeal like that? I want to go home. I've been ready to leave since the show finished.'

It was exactly as Sarah predicted but she swallowed the *I told you so*. 'I'll take you home, Mum. Just give me a minute to sort out the arrangements with the boys.'

'If it helps, I can drop Mum home,' Cameron offered.

'Oh, Cam, thank you.' Sarah's surprise at his offer tangoed with a flicker of guilt at her earlier uncharitable thoughts. 'That would be a great help.'

'Do I get a choice?' Margaret asked a little testily.

Stay calm. Sometimes, there was very little difference between tired toddlers, teenagers and spent septuagenarians. 'Of course you do. It's totally up to you.'

'Are you sure it's not out of your way, dear?' Margaret asked her son.

'Mum!' Sarah's bottled-up exasperation bubbled over. 'Cam passes Mill House on his way home, whereas I live in the complete opposite direction.'

Margaret sniffed. 'At least one of my children lives close by.'

What on earth? Where was this coming from? She and Alex had moved to Riverbend ten years ago, which, up until Cameron moved back to town, was a hell of a lot closer to Mill House than he or Ellie had been in years.

'Mum, you see as much of me as you did when I lived in town. More, now the kids are older.'

'Come on, Mum.' Cameron took Margaret's arm and shot Sarah a conspiratorial look. 'Let's get you home.'

As they walked away, Sarah looked around for Finn and Gus. As both were over six feet tall, they were usually easy to spot but they were nowhere to be seen. Goddamn it! Her sons had taken advantage of her distraction with Margaret to scarper before she gave Gus a curfew. A spurt of righteous indignation sent her hand into her bag. Digging out her keyless remote, she planned to drive directly to the Fotinas' and give Gus his curfew in person. It would not only embarrass him, which would be the perfect punishment for skipping out on her before all the arrangements were settled, but it would also give her the opportunity to check out the supervision of the party.

'Hello, Sarah.'

Genuine warmth filled her at the sound of the precise and accented voice. She looked up and automatically leaned in for a kiss. 'Edmund. How are you?'

He smiled down at her. 'Very well. And Gus, he was the star tonight.'

Mother pride swept through Sarah and she grinned widely, able to speak the truth to this dear friend. 'I thought so too.'

Edmund had been their first employee and he'd become part of their family; a far more involved uncle to their kids than Cameron. It had been a sad day when Edmund resigned to start Protea, the only fine-dining restaurant in Mingunyah. Three years later, he'd opened a second restaurant. Hibiscus was a seasonal business located on the mountain and catering to the well-heeled ski crowd. Sarah loved that she and Alex had played a small role in his success.

'It was good of you to come to the show.'

He shrugged as if it was no big deal, but Sarah knew it couldn't be easy for him to be in a theatre filled with families watching their children shine. 'It's Gus,' he said simply. 'A man never forgets the terror or the overwhelming joy of delivering a baby.'

She laughed and squeezed his arm, remembering her own terror. 'I'm just glad you were there with me.'

'It was an honour and now I have a godson.'

As they strolled out to the carpark, they chatted about their respective businesses and Edmund's plans for the opening weekend of the ski season. Sarah accepted his invitation to the party at Hibiscus on behalf of herself and Alex, looking forward to being part of the glitz and glamour of the night. 'I guess I'll see you then,' she said, giving him a goodbye hug.

'I'm looking forward to it. Goodnight, Sarah.'

As she clicked her seat belt into position, she remembered her recalcitrant sons. Picking up her phone, she texted Finn. *Your brother needs to be home by one*

Remarkably, a thumbs-up emoji came straight back. It always surprised her when Finn showed signs of being the adult he technically was.

Mothering duties fulfilled, she found herself singing 'Hey Big Spender' and suddenly laughed. Alex fitted the lyrics perfectly. She texted him—*Home soon to show you a good time*—then pressed the ignition button and pointed the car towards home.

Anita held her breath as she pulled a sponge cake from the Aga in the Mill House kitchen. Before she could feature the stove in her cooking classes, she had to conquer it herself and she was confident she almost had it mastered. She touched the centre of the cake lightly and it reassuringly sprang back.

'I don't understand you modern women.' Margaret almost twirled into the kitchen wearing a stunning pink frock with a matching pink and white floral jacket. 'You've got all the mod cons and opportunities and yet you want to turn back time. The first thing I did when we moved into Mill House was buy an electric stove. I told Kevin there was no way I was going to be tied to the kitchen and that cantankerous, wood-eating beast.'

Anita wiped her hands on her vintage 1950s apron and smiled at the cream beast with its simmer plates and two ovens. Despite the steep learning curve, she loved it. Unlike her own childhood kitchen, which hadn't offered any succour, just empty cupboards, she considered it the heartbeat of the house. 'But don't you think there's something about the warmth and cosiness of a kitchen and the aroma of comfort food that says love and family?'

Margaret snorted. 'Not in February.'

'I promise I'll only use it in the cooler months,' Anita added quickly. Although Margaret had agreed to her using the kitchen for classes, Anita was still feeling her way. She didn't want to give her mother-in-law any reason to revoke her permission. Margaret was a strong personality and there'd been a tricky moment a few days earlier when Anita was preparing the kitchen for its inspection by the council's environmental health officer. Margaret had strolled in with a cigarette clamped firmly between her fingers, seated herself at the table and demanded an ashtray and a cup of tea.

Anita went through life avoiding confrontation as much as possible and when she combined that tendency with the awe she always experienced at her mother-in-law's ability to command a room and everyone in it, normally she would have capitulated. But with her yet-to-be-approved kitchen registration at stake and with it her cooking classes, she'd said, 'Um, Margaret. I thought we'd agreed on no smoking in the kitchen?'

Her mother-in-law's grey eyes flashed silver. 'Did we just?'

Stand firm. 'Yes. Cameron discussed it with you. He explained that—'

'Smoking is bad for me. I know.'

Actually, Cameron had explained to Margaret which rooms she could smoke in, but Anita wasn't going to quibble. 'Your health's important to us.'

'Hmph.' Margaret stubbed out the cigarette with a vigorous twist. 'I'm still allowed a Bloody Mary, am I, or are you denying me that pleasure too?'

'Of course you can have a Bloody Mary. Would you like me to make you one?' Anita offered quickly, ignoring the time. 'After all, it's five o'clock somewhere.'

Margaret gave her a long and appraising stare and then, very slowly, her mouth curved into a complicit smile. 'I like the way you think.'

Anita both sighed with relief and silently squealed with joy. Not only had she defused a difficult situation, Margaret had complimented her. That was a first.

Since then, things with Margaret had gone smoothly.

Anita tapped the cake tin and turned the sponge onto the cake rack to cool. 'You look lovely today, Margaret. That outfit's divine.'

'This old thing?' Margaret gave a little twirl. 'You know, I met Hannah Corby once.'

'Did you?' Anita was impressed. She knew all about Hannah Corby—she'd spent the nineties cutting out pictures of models wearing designer clothes from magazines.

'Oh, yes. She was a friend of a friend and we met on a horse ride out to Moke's Hut. The view across the valley was stunning and I suggested she draw inspiration from the varied hues of the high country for a collection. She made me the most divine dress as a thank you.'

'Wow! Do you still have it?'

'Of course. Would you like to see it?'

'I'd love to, but I don't want to hold you up if you're about to go out.'

'I'm not going out. Why on earth would you think that?'

The snappish tone disarmed Anita. 'You're dressed as if you're going out.'

Margaret glanced down and smoothed the front of her frock, her fingers caressing the shantung. 'I like pretty things.'

'So do I.' Anita followed Margaret upstairs but to her surprise, her mother-in-law bypassed her bedroom and walked into another one.

'Ta-dah.' Margaret opened the double wardrobe doors. Inside, there wasn't a spare centimetre of space. The chrome hanging rod bowed in the middle from the weight of the clothes. Hats and hat boxes spilled from the upper shelf and shoes crowded the floor.

'Oh my God.' Anita gasped and her hands shot out involuntarily, desperate to touch everything. 'May I?'

'As long as your hands are clean.'

Anita didn't even care that Margaret sounded like a school teacher talking to a child; she was too busy unhooking coat hangers and gazing at clothes that dated back to the late sixties. She fingered a lemon-coloured fine wool suit.

'I wore that to Government House.'

Anita rehung it and pulled out a pantsuit. 'And this?'

'The opening of the new maternity wing of the Mingunyah Hospital.'

Anita continued pulling out clothes and Margaret told her every occasion she'd worn the outfit.

'What about this dress? The cut is gorgeous and the lacework's beautiful.'

Margaret's hand rose to her throat. 'Kevin's funeral.'

'Oh God.' Anita flashed hot and cold. She hurriedly hung the dress back in the wardrobe. 'I'm sorry. I hope I haven't upset you.'

'Kevin may have died but I wasn't going to be one of those frumpy and blotchy widows. I wore a stylish hat decorated with a black velvet band and a large black rose and, of course, black gloves.' Her eyes sparkled with memories. 'People told me that my elegance helped them with their grief.'

'The right dress is a powerful thing.' Anita thought about how her clothing choices had helped her move far away from her BC— before Cameron—life. 'This is six decades of Australian fashion history. You've got clothes here from Prue Acton, Jenny Kee, Carla Zampatti. It's worth a fortune.'

'Is it?'

'Oh, yes. Vintage clothing is all the rage.'

'Are you saying people would pay good money for my clothes?'

'Yes, but you wouldn't want to sell them, would you?'

Margaret slowly ran her hand along the plastic-covered clothes and then shut the wardrobe doors with a decisive swoosh. 'I don't see why not. I can't wear most of them any more.'

Anita experienced a pang at the thought of the collection being split up. 'The museum might be interested.'

'Pah! I'd rather sell them. How do I go about it?'

'There are a few different ways. On consignment at vintage clothing stores or online.' Anita immediately recalled Sarah saying she'd spent two hours the week before sorting out Margaret's computer issues and had a vision of losing hours doing something similar. 'What if Cam and I set up an eBay account and run it for you? It will be a big job to catalogue all the clothes and photograph them but Sarah might be able to help.'

'No! I don't want Sarah involved. She wants to send my clothes to the op shop.'

The comment hit Anita with the intensity of a slap. 'Over my dead body. These clothes deserve to be loved.'

'Exactly.' Margaret leaned forward and dropped her voice. 'Sarah can't know about our plan. No one can know. This has to be our secret.'

'Yes, of course.' Delight spun through Anita. Not once in fifteen years had Margaret ever confided in her like this. Despite some concerns about how she was going to manage her time juggling the family, Cooked By a Friend and cataloguing Margaret's wardrobe, there was no way was she going to refuse. 'Would it be okay if we moved the clothes to my place? That way I can photograph them when I have time.'

'Hello?' Sarah's voice floated upstairs.

'Shh.' Margaret hurried onto the landing and her imperious voice drifted back into the room. 'Sarah. I was wondering when you were going to arrive.'

'I said eleven.'

'Gracious! Is that the time? Anita, you shouldn't have distracted me.'

As Anita joined Margaret on the landing, she smiled, knowing the criticism was a cover. 'My bad. Hi, Sarah.'

'Let me get my handbag.' Margaret walked down the stairs.

Confusion creased Sarah's forehead. 'I thought we were having morning tea first and testing Anita's cakes.'

'We are.' Anita recalled Margaret telling her very emphatically that she wasn't going out today and yet obviously mother and daughter had an arrangement. More family secrets?

While Margaret went to 'powder her nose'—code for smoking a cigarette—Sarah savoured a cupcake. 'It's official. You've mastered the Aga. When's your first class?'

'The moment I receive my registration. They said it should come through by the end of the week. I've got four people on standby for my first class and one of the recipes I'm teaching is a goat's cheese risotto using your cheese.'

'Great.' Sarah fiddled with the edges of her napkin. 'I still can't believe you're going to teach people to cook here.'

A few weeks earlier, when Anita told Sarah about the cooking school plans, her sister-in-law had seemed pleased, although not overly enthusiastic about the idea. Now Sarah looked pensive and before

Anita could stop herself, she asked, 'Does it bother you that I'm using the kitchen?'

Sarah sucked in her lips. 'It's more that I don't want it to bother Mum.'

Anita didn't want the issue with the kitchen to affect her relationship with Sarah, but at the same time she didn't want Sarah to negatively affect her plans. 'Have you ever known Margaret to agree to anything she didn't approve of?'

Sarah gave a wry laugh. 'You've got a point there. Mum's always been very vocal about her likes and dislikes.'

'Exactly. And we gave her a business plan and answered all her questions. She's had plenty of chances to refuse. It's not like I'm taking advantage of her.'

'I never thought you were,' Sarah said quickly. 'I know you gave up a lot to support Cameron in his move here and I understand your need to run the classes—'

'And this kitchen perfectly showcases country style,' Anita cut in hurriedly, sensing a 'but' and not wanting to hear it.

'Cooking in a historic country house is certainly a niche market.' Sarah glanced around with a practised business eye. 'It's just this is Mum's home and—'

'I promise it's not going to be an imposition. I'm starting slowly and initially the classes will only be on Saturdays when she's playing bowls. Obviously, I'm paying her for the use of the kitchen.' Anita glossed over the fact it wasn't a dollar amount. 'I'm also cooking her some meals and I'm in and out of the house during the week doing prep. I thought that might help you out a bit too. Give you a break from the daily visits? It's just you seem a bit strung out at the moment.'

Sarah's mouth curved into a wan smile. 'I don't mind popping in.'

'You don't mind doing lots of things but when you add them all up, they can drag you down. How about I take over Tuesdays and Thursdays?'

'Are you sure?'

'I probably should have offered ages ago. I know you're worried the house is too big for Margaret, but I've been here every day for two weeks and she's fine.' Anita decided not to mention the uneaten meal she'd found in the dining room. When she'd asked Margaret about it, her mother-in-law had told her she'd felt unwell and rushed to the bathroom, forgetting all about it. 'To be honest, if you want to worry about someone, worry about Ellie.'

Sarah's cup clattered onto her saucer. 'Why? What's wrong?'

'Cameron said he heard on the grapevine that the old Guthrie place is going to be demolished for road widening.'

'Ellie hasn't mentioned anything to me.' When Anita raised her brows at the comment, Sarah gave a strained laugh. 'You're right. When does my little sister ever tell me anything? Hell, she doesn't even ask me for things.'

Anita passed Sarah another cupcake. 'You have every right to feel hurt. She shouldn't have bypassed you and gone to Alex about those jobs. She's lucky you didn't say no.'

'And disadvantage people who've already suffered so much? I couldn't do that just because Ellie's thoughtless when it comes to her own family. She's always been self-centred. I've often wondered how different things might have been if Dad hadn't died when he did. It was bad enough for Cam and me but we'd already left home. Ellie was so young and people felt sorry for her. Combine sympathy with those blonde curls, huge baby-blue eyes, and butter-wouldn't-melt-in-her-mouth smile, and no one was prepared to say no to her. She knew it and she got away with murder.' Sarah sipped her tea. 'I find it really odd that someone with so little regard for her own family works so hard helping others.'

'Perhaps she's appeasing her guilt for what she did to Margaret? For how she treats you now?'

'Who knows. I've almost given up trying to work her out.' Sarah wriggled in her chair as though shaking off uncomfortable thoughts. 'Anyway, I've got more important things to worry about than Ellie.'

'Gus and the football thing?' Anita refilled Sarah's cup. She always listened carefully to her sister-in-law when she talked about her children, their antics and how she managed them. Anita's mothering was instinctive only in as much as she vehemently knew what she didn't want to do. As for the rest, she read parenting books, attended seminars and closely observed women who appeared to have a good relationship with their kids.

'Actually, it's more Alex than Gus. He's taking Gus's three-week suspension from the firsts as a personal insult. I thought he'd be over it by now, but he's still grumpy and out of sorts, stomping around at home and in the office. He's driving the staff mad. The other day he was all bent out of shape about the accounting software. I told Kelly she was a saint to put up with him.'

'That's not like Alex.'

'Actually, he's often grumpy about the accounting software.'

Anita laughed. 'Men. Can't live with them, can't live without them.'

'Right now I could live without Alex behaving worse than my teenagers.' Sarah fiddled with her Russian wedding ring, rolling the bands over each other. 'You know, I expect drama and tantrums from the kids but not from my husband. I don't get it. It's not like he even played footy when he was a kid. Hockey was his sport.'

'Don't be too hard on him.' Anita was always a little bit in awe of Alex, not that she'd ever admit that to Sarah or Cameron. She thought about how Cameron had been happier and more excited about each day since they'd moved to Mingunyah. All that new energy flowed into their marriage. 'Perhaps Alex needs a new project?'

Sarah groaned. 'Don't say that. We've just reached a point in the business where we've got some time to ourselves. Besides, cycling's his new project—he doesn't need another one. He's riding about fourteen hours a week as it is.'

Anita changed tack. 'It sounds like he's got himself organised. What about you? You keep talking about finding something for yourself.'

'I think my project's working with Mum to sort through everything in this house. She's a magpie and there's still stuff here that belonged to

Grandpa. I thought her overflowing wardrobes would be a good place to start.'

Anita's heart raced. Somehow, she managed to swallow her squeak of protest before it exploded across her lips and gave away Margaret's secret. 'That's a bit personal, isn't it? Clothes are more than just material, they're memories. You know she's still got the dress she wore to your father's funeral? How can you expect her to part with that?'

Sarah's head fell back and for a moment she silently gazed at the ceiling. 'I suppose when you put it like that ...'

Anita's anxiety receded slightly but she needed to cement her argument. 'And we both know how stubborn Margaret can be. You've got a better chance of her cooperating if you start on the easy jobs.' Anita tapped her head as a thought occurred to her. 'I know. What about the study? She's probably got tax returns dating back to the day she and Kevin moved in. I doubt she's emotionally bonded to those.'

Sarah shot her a grateful smile. 'And this is why you're more of a sister to me than Ellie's ever been.'

'Ellie's loss is my gain,' Anita said, meaning every word and burying her guilt. After all, biological sisters kept secrets from each other and Ellie was keeping far more than one small secret from Sarah.

CHAPTER SIX

'On behalf of my people, we thank you for opportunity.' Kin Hoo, Valley View's Burmese community leader, pressed his hands together and gave a quick nod of his head to the Mingunyah cheese makers and farm workers seated in the break room. 'Burmese people very happy to work here. Be part of Mingunyah Cheese. Taste very good.'

A ripple of laughter wove around the room.

'I thought you lot were lactose intolerant,' Des Winke called out.

Kin Hoo looked momentarily confused and Ellie said, 'Does milk upset your stomach?'

'Ah!' He nodded his understanding and looked straight at Des, his brown eyes shining. 'But goat milk okay. Better than cow.'

'Blood oath it is, cobber,' Des said proudly.

'Does anyone else have any more questions?' Ellie had already spoken to the group prior to introducing Kin Hoo but it was always good to follow up.

'What about the women?' Susie Faraday asked belligerently. 'Why aren't they being offered any jobs?'

'Many Burmese women are working in Valley View,' Ellie said carefully, wishing to avoid accusations of being sexist. 'We're very grateful the Hadfields can offer employment but it was the families' decision that the men would accept the first four jobs.'

'Women want work too,' Kin Hoo said. 'We hope soon be more jobs.'

'In the run-up to Christmas,' Sarah said, 'we're hoping to be able to offer work to three women. If you'd like to be involved in the orientation and training, Susie, that would be fabulous.'

Ellie glanced at her sister, surprised and impressed at the smooth way she'd handled a possibly explosive situation. Then again, why was she surprised? Sarah was half of a very successful business after all, but Ellie rarely thought of her as anything other than her older and disapproving sister.

'Yeah, I'd like that.' Susie stuck her hands in the pockets of her white coat, the uniform of the cheese workers. 'I reckon it doesn't matter where you're from, what you look like or what language you speak, us women need to stick together.'

The men groaned but most of the other women nodded their support. Ellie smiled directly at Susie. 'That's very true. Thank you. I'm sure the women will appreciate your support. Valley View Neighbourhood House has a Thursday night women's dinner once a month. You're very welcome to come along. On the whole, Valley View's been very welcoming.'

'Mingunyah's better,' one of the men called out.

'Hey, Sarah. What about throwing one of those Friday team lunches at the end of this lot's first week?' another said.

'I'm sure that's possible, Craig.'

Ellie thanked everyone for their time and released a breath as people drifted back to work. Kin Hoo and the other Burmese men left with Alex for a tour of the farm and the dairies.

'That went better than I'd hoped. You have lovely employees.'

'Most of them are great.' Sarah walked over to the coffee machine. 'Do you have time for one?'

'Sure.' She wanted to plead busy and bolt but that would make her look ungrateful when really she was very appreciative of Alex and Sarah's support of the Burmese. 'Any chance of a chai tea?'

Ellie regretted the question the moment the hint of a grimace touched Sarah's lips.

'I thought you'd given up meat but wine and coffee were your vices.'

Ellie gave an overly bright smile. 'They are indeed my vices. It's just lately I've been lying awake staring at the ceiling, so I thought I'd try cutting back.'

'I'm probably overly dependent on my two o'clock coffee but without it I struggle to stay focused for the rest of the afternoon.' Sarah pressed the grinder button on the Italian coffee machine before throwing a tea bag into a mug and adding a small amount of boiling water from a tap. 'This probably falls far short of the wet chai you use.'

Ellie mostly used tea bags but she didn't correct Sarah. She rarely bothered to correct anyone unless it was going to impact badly on her. On most occasions, the incorrect idea provided her with an element of safety; one more defence in keeping people at arm's length. Instead of making small talk while Sarah frothed the milk for their drinks, she wandered over and read the break room's noticeboard. There were ads for free-range eggs, quilting classes, an audition notice for MADS—the Mingunyah Amateur Drama Society—and someone had pinned a bevy of business cards around the edge of the board to form a colourful border.

The bright blue and red logo of Mingunyah Plumbing Heating & Cooling Specialists caught her eye. She instantly thought of Luke presenting her with a coffee and his open and teasing smile. A smile that disarmed her. That concerned her; she prided herself on being immune to smiles and the sharp teeth that so often lay behind them.

'What are you looking at?' Sarah handed her a mug.

'We have the same plumber.'

'I'm surprised you need a plumber if your house is being demolished. By the way, I found out *that* bit of news from Anita who heard it from Cameron. Did you ever intend to tell me?'

The words hit with the sting of a reprimand. 'I didn't tell Cameron and I wasn't deliberately keeping it from you, I just didn't think it was worth mentioning. We tend to communicate by phone and email rather than visiting, and neither of those details will change when I move. You'll still be able to contact me.'

'What if I was driving past and I wanted to drop in?'

Ellie laughed, enjoying the amusement of the absurd.

'What's so funny?' Sarah sounded genuinely mystified as well as snippy.

Too late, Ellie realised her sister hadn't been cracking a joke. 'Sorry.'

'Really?'

'Oh, come on, Sarah. There's no need to sound so pissed off. I thought you were joking. After all, you've never dropped in on me before, so why would you suddenly start now? I mean, how often are you even in Valley View, just driving past?'

Sarah's nostrils flared. 'I don't think it's an unreasonable request for your family to know your new address.'

'Okay. Fine.' Ellie took a big slug of her tea, hoping the spices would magically soothe her.

'Do you have a new address?'

'Not yet.'

'When do you have to be out?'

'The fifteenth.'

'That's not far away.'

The statement didn't seem to require a reply. She continued sipping her tea, all the while planning her exit strategy for the moment she'd drained the mug.

'Ellie, you need to take this seriously.'

A ripple of tension rode across her shoulders and Ellie straightened just a little. It was a familiar feeling—she always experienced it at some point when she spent time with her mother, Cameron or Sarah. 'I am taking it seriously.' A hot and uncomfortable sensation crawled along her skin, mocking her attempt at sounding neutral.

'Are you even looking for a place?' Sarah was like a dog with a bone.

'Yes.'

'You do realise if you can't find somewhere in Valley View, you'll have to consider Mingunyah. Rental accommodation here is scarce too but I suppose Alex and I could—'

'No!' The word shot out loud and sharp—protection against the barrage of unwanted advice.

Sarah startled and the chocolate flecks in her eyes darkened against the hazel. 'No? I haven't even said how I could help.'

You've said enough. Ellie carefully placed her mug on the sink. 'I've got this,' she said, desperately trying to keep the tremble out of her voice.

'Do you really?' Sarah's brows disappeared under her fringe. 'Your track record's hardly stellar. The Guthrie place was barely ideal. Noah—'

'Is my responsibility. Not yours.' She slung her handbag over her shoulder. No way was she going to be beholden to Sarah, or to anyone for that matter. Once you owed someone something, they owned you. 'You don't need to organise anything for me. I'm not your kid sister any more, Sarah. I grew up a long time ago.' *I grew up far earlier than you'll ever know.*

Sarah vibrated with offence. 'Oh, for God's sake, Ellie. Why are you always so touchy? I was only trying to help. That's what families do for each other, although you obviously missed the memo.'

'Help' wasn't a word Ellie associated with her family. Every part of her screamed to run but somehow she managed to take in a deep breath and steady herself. 'I appreciate all your help with the jobs for the Burmese community, but that's all the help I need.' She reached the door. 'I've taken up enough of your time. I'll let you get back to work.' Raising her hand in a quick wave, she stepped through the door and marched across the gravel carpark. In the two minutes it took to get to her car, her heart rate slowed from rib hitting frantic to just plain fast.

Family be damned. She'd live in her car before she moved to Mingunyah.

What the hell was wrong with her sister? Incensed and baffled, Sarah dumped the two mugs in the break room's dishwasher. She needed to debrief, give Alex a blow-by-blow of the conversation she'd just had with Ellie. He'd run it through his dispassionate filter—the one he always reserved for her family—and help her make sense of how a genuine offer of help had been so thoroughly rejected. It both riled and hurt her that Ellie happily asked for and accepted help on behalf of the Burmese community, yet she resolutely snubbed her when the help was for Ellie and Noah.

Picking up her folders, Sarah made her way around the outside of the cheese factory and walked towards the 'office suite'. She smiled at the jokey name that had stuck all those years ago when they'd made the big leap and bought the first demountable. Originally, the office was the kitchen table in the old cheese factory—paperwork and cheese samples fighting for space with Finn's rattles and baby food. When they'd moved to Riverbend, they'd used one of the six bedrooms as a dedicated study. It didn't take long to realise that an 'at home' office was too tempting for her and Alex to 'just quickly check something' over the weekend and lose an hour. Mobile phones and their social media presence were a big enough time sink so the first demountable was their attempt to separate the business from their home life. It was the right decision. Now, with over seventy employees, it made better business sense to have the office located in the middle of things and accessible to everyone.

On the inside, the three demountables looked like any other office space with carpet, pot plants, artwork and work stations. With the strategic use of skylights and three glass sliding doors leading onto a long veranda, there was plenty of natural light. If the weather wasn't too hot or too cold, people took their laptops onto the veranda and worked to a soundtrack of chirping birds and bleating goats, along with a view of the landscaped gardens, the glorious vista of rippling blue mountains and, in winter, snow-capped peaks.

She opened the sliding door closest to her office and automatically glanced at the 'Who's In and Who's Out' whiteboard. As she rubbed out the word 'meeting' from next to her name and wrote 'in office', she noted that the logistics manager had ducked out for school pickup, the sales manager was on the road, the marketing manager was in Melbourne at a seminar and the production manager was in the factory. The only two people marked as 'in' were Kelly and Alex. Dumping her folders on her desk, she walked to his office. Through the glass partition, she saw evidence of Alex: the ever-changing photos of champion cyclists he was currently using as his computer's wallpaper and the curls of steam rising from his coffee mug. Sarah smiled at the bold, black quote printed on it: *Thanks, Dad. I turned out Awesome.* Finn had given it to Alex just before he'd left home to start university.

She was about to text Alex when she heard the low rumble of his voice immediately followed by Kelly's distinctive laugh. She crossed the open space and stopped short. Kelly sat at her desk but instead of peering at her computer screen in her usual myopic way, she was leaning back in her chair with her head tilted up, gazing straight at Alex and listening to him intently. That in itself wasn't a crime. But when the glow in her wide-eyed gaze was combined with a smile that made her face light up in a way Sarah had never seen before, the pose came close to workplace misconduct.

Normally, Sarah would have chalked it up to the 'Alex Effect' except for the fact that Alex's head, with its distinguished salt and pepper hair, was bent close to Kelly's face and his lips were moving. Sarah couldn't hear the words but she clearly saw their effect on Kelly —flushed cheeks and sparkling eyes blazing with lust.

As Alex talked, his hands massaged their office manager's shoulders.

The intimate image burned Sarah's eyes and socked her like a punch to the gut. Air vaporised. Lungs cramped. Blood drained to her feet, leaving her mind reeling. One side of her brain was screaming 'OMG!', while the other half tried rationally decoding the situation—perhaps Kelly had a sore neck? Sarah knew how good Alex was at massage.

'What's going on?' The words felt thick and ungainly in her mouth and she barely recognised the sound of her own voice.

Alex's hands flew to his sides and he leaped back from the chair like it was suddenly spurting flames. Kelly threw herself forward, her hands gripping her desk as she skated the chair in close. Both looked at her, their eyes dark and wild and their faces pale with shock. Sarah caught the 'holy shit' look Kelly threw at Alex. Alex missed it; his gaze was fixed on Sarah.

Emotions swirled in his eyes. First, guilt. It faded fast, replaced by distress and dismay, but they soon vanished until only one emotion remained. Pity.

An uncontrollable and agonised sound left Sarah's mouth, filling the loaded silence. Memories of Mother's Day pummelled her like punches. Alex hadn't asked Kelly to come into work on Mother's Day as a gift for Sarah, he'd asked her so he could spend time alone with her.

'Sarah.' Alex spoke her name gently, invoking the same tone he always used with the kids when they hurt themselves. Only, instead of saying, 'Let me kiss it better,' he said, 'We need to talk.' There was no contrition in his tone.

This can't be happening. This. Isn't. Happening. But Alex's four small words, worth so little in a game of Scrabble, were synonymous with life-changing heartache. Like the splintering of a wooden boat foundering on rocks, the words moaned and groaned in her mind with creaking finality. Loud, long and in painfully slow modulation, they dominated every thought. Her lips felt swollen and her mouth was full of cotton wool trying to choke her. A tremor started in her fingers, spreading quickly and turning her legs to the consistency of jelly, threatening to buckle her knees. Shock rendered her mute. Even if her stunned mind was capable of generating a command, nothing in her body had the ability to obey. All she wanted to do was slide into a heap on the ground, put her hands over her head and rock.

Don't you dare fall to pieces in front of them. Don't let them make you a victim. She summoned strength from God knew where, locked her shaking legs and dragged in a long, deep breath.

'It appears we do indeed need to talk.' The ice in her voice sounded eerily like Margaret. Sarah lifted her chin and looked directly at the other woman. 'Kelly, Alex and I are going home. Unless one of the dairies catches fire or there's a life or death situation, we're not to be disturbed. Take messages. Are you clear on that?'

Kelly glanced at Alex, seeking confirmation, and he gave her a quick nod. 'Yes.' She licked her lips. 'Sarah, we're sorry. If it helps—'

Alex frantically shook his head at her and Kelly stared at her hands.

We? The word screeched around Sarah's head like fingernails dragged down a blackboard before stabbing her multiple times in the heart. She balled her hands into tight fists as if that alone was going to keep her upright and in one piece.

'Alex. We're leaving now.'

'I'll be with you in a minute.'

No way in hell was she leaving him alone with Kelly. 'If you want me to listen to you talk, we leave together. Now.'

'It's okay. You go,' Kelly said quietly, touching his shirt sleeve.

Oh my God! Whatever universe she'd been catapulted into, it was completely wrong. Sarah was the person who got to reassure Alex, not their office manager. The woman Sarah had hired to make their lives easier. Their *employee.*

The irony whipped her and, out of nowhere, she heard her father's wry tone, the one he had used when everything went to shit. *That seemed to go pretty well.*

Sarah didn't know if she wanted to sit, stand, pace or be still. She loved Riverbend and the house to bits and it had always been her oasis, wrapping itself around her with a peaceful welcome whenever she stepped through the door. Not today. Not late on what should have been a perfectly ordinary Friday afternoon. Not when normal had vanished and absolutely nothing between her and Alex was familiar. She'd refused his offer of tea, coffee, juice, water and wine. Her throat was parched but she doubted she could swallow and if she could, she was certain the moment anything hit her stomach it would come straight back up.

'Let's sit down.' Alex extended his arm towards the couch, where she'd snuggled up with him on thousands of evenings over the years, including just two nights ago.

She gagged and the acrid taste of acid scored her throat. 'I can't sit next to you.'

'Jesus, Sarah.' Alex ran his hand through his hair. 'Take the chair then and stop jumping to conclusions.'

Anger bloomed, spreading through her hot and thick like treacle. 'Conclusions? That woman wore adoration in her eyes and you were massaging her neck!'

'That doesn't mean anything's happened.'

'If nothing's happened, why did she apologise?'

'Because she's kind and you were upset.'

'Of course I'm bloody upset!'

Alex winced. 'Look, Sarah. I promise you, nothing's happened between Kelly and me.'

The image of his hands on Kelly's neck and shoulders flashed in her mind like a beacon. She was used to women flirting with Alex but his constant lack of reaction to them had always been a reassuring balm. His touch on Kelly's skin was a massive betrayal.

'You're telling me you haven't had sex?'

Relief filled his face. 'Yes. That's exactly what I'm telling you.'

Yet again, the picture of the two of them burned brightly, starkly at odds with his words. 'Why not?'

'We didn't want to hurt you.'

'Hurt me? Are you serious? If that's your definition of not hurting me, you're an idiot.' Changing her mind about the wine, she sloshed pinot grigio into a glass with a shaking hand. 'Let me get this straight. You haven't had sex with her but you'd like to?'

Haggard lines pulled at his handsome face. 'Sarah.' He sounded as if she was the one being difficult.

'Don't "Sarah" me. I'm trying to make sense of this. I mean, why wouldn't you want to have sex with a woman fifteen years your junior? Hell, her body hasn't popped out three kids and sunk or spread in all the wrong places.'

'You're still an attractive woman.'

His words flailed her. 'Oh, a compliment? Thank you so very much.' She thought about their sex life, which despite twenty-two years of marriage, had always been regular even if there were periods when it was perfunctory and lacked a bit of spontaneity. Recently though, they'd been enjoying a renaissance and things in bed had been great. Her stomach rolled, wine shot to the back of her throat and she felt herself sway.

'Oh God. Have you been having sex with me and imagining I'm her?' *Say no. Please, Alex, say no.*

Alex rubbed his face with his palms but didn't speak.

A silent scream shrieked in her head. She bit down hard on her forefinger, welcoming the pain; needing it to prevent an anguished sound from escaping into the room and declaring her devastation. She gulped more wine.

'Does Kelly want to have sex with you or are you just deluding yourself?'

'She was the one who suggested we wait. She's very considerate of your feelings.'

'Are you fucking *kidding* me?' Sarah screeched. Alex flinched. He hated it when she swore and 'got all emotional'. Over the years, she'd tried hard not to give in to the outer parameters of her feelings and she rarely shouted or cried because she knew it made him excruciatingly uncomfortable. Well, bugger that. 'God, Alex, you should have slept with her.'

'You don't mean that,' he said wearily as if he was dealing with a child who'd just said, 'You're not my friend any more.'

'Oh, but I do.' She pointed her wine glass at him. 'You've thought about having sex with her. You've obviously fantasised about having sex with her. The two of you have talked about it, right?'

'Yes.' He spoke slowly and deliberately. 'But it hasn't actually happened. Surely that counts for something?'

She stared at him, totally lost and disoriented in the maze of his thought processes. 'What does it count for?'

He jerked to his feet. 'I'm trying to do this the right way.'

'The right way?' Hysterical laughter burst out of her. 'Who knew there was a right way to destroy trust and break my heart?' She sobered as her mind grappled with the cascading foundations of a marriage she'd never once doubted. 'You want me to give you absolution because you've kept your wedding vows and nobly abstained from adultery? Except you haven't, Alex. You've been mind-fucking her while you've been using my body.'

'Look, Sarah, I'm sorry.' He opened his hands. 'I didn't want you to find out this way. I've been trying to find a good time to tell you for weeks.'

'Believe me,' she said bitterly, 'there was never going to be a good time to tell me.'

His shoulders fell and he looked diminished in size, no longer the vital man she knew and loved. 'I'm not happy, Sarah.' His softly spoken words fell like granite boulders. 'I haven't been happy for a long time.'

Her heart tore at his pain while her mind valiantly tried to absorb this unexpected news. 'I didn't know.'

'No.'

It was the first thing he'd said to her that hinted at a reason for his uncharacteristic behaviour. 'Why didn't you tell me?' she asked softly. Carefully. Hopefully.

He shrugged. 'Life's busy.'

I'm your wife! Confusion and hurt overrode her sympathy. 'But you told Kelly?'

'She understands me.'

'She *understands* you? And what? After twenty-two years, three children and running a business with you, I don't?'

For the first time since they'd arrived at the house, he looked her straight in the eye. 'At home you treat me like one of the kids.'

'Don't be ridiculous.'

His head tilted and his brows rose as if to say, *I rest my case*. 'I need space, Sarah.'

'Space?' This time she snorted and wine ran up her nose. 'We live on a farm, Alex. You're surrounded by space.'

'I need space from you.'

The words lanced her, ripping through her like a jagged saw leaving no part of her untouched. 'We run a business together, Alex. We have children together. How do we manage all that with *space*?'

'I'll move out,' he said purposefully. Suddenly, he was a man with a plan and his regretful tone vanished. 'We can work the rest out as we go.'

'No!' Agitation rocked her but she didn't know if it stemmed from fear, anger, grief or shock.

'Right now, it's for the best.'

She fought for equilibrium as a revelation burst into her mind, raining down on her with the clarity of crystal. 'Can you hear yourself? You want space. Your wife doesn't understand you. You've taken up cycling. You're contemplating an affair. You're a 47-year-old walking, talking cliché of a midlife crisis.' She reached out her hand and grabbed his arm. 'Alex. Don't throw away everything we've achieved for a hormonal imbalance.'

He shook away her touch. 'Jesus, Sarah. This is exactly why I didn't tell you.'

'I think I'm entitled to make a scene when my husband announces completely out of the blue that he's leaving me for another woman. You've missed a few steps along the way, buddy. What happened to talking to me and trying marriage counselling?'

'Look,' he said crisply, his annoyance sharpening. 'I'm not moving in with Kelly, okay? And I'm not ruling anything out. Just understand that I need some time on my own.'

Time on my own. When had Alex become so selfish? God, how she wished she could ignore everything and everyone and put her own wants first. After all, who in their mid-forties, sandwiched between teenage children and ageing parents and with so many people making demands on them, didn't crave time on their own? The concept of space sounded pretty bloody wonderful.

She hadn't lived with Alex for two decades without becoming intimate with his foibles and strengths. Tenacity, determination and a drive to win was an asset in the business world. In a relationship, not so much. Obviously, he'd made his decision weeks ago and it was pointless standing here arguing and begging until she was blue in the face. It wouldn't change his mind. He wanted space and time alone and he'd take it no matter what she said or did. Every part of her screamed to throw herself at his feet and grip his ankles so he couldn't take a single step towards the door, let alone walk through it. Once Alex moved out of Riverbend, returning became an option, not a rule. But despite knowing that as well as a cop knows the law, she was done prostrating herself. What she did know was that she needed time to process the shock of Alex's bombshell. Time to work out her next move.

'Fine.'

Alex's eyes narrowed, his expression suddenly guarded as if the word was a bomb that was about to explode in his face. 'Fine?'

She drained her glass and swallowed hard. 'You're telling me you want space. I'll give you that space.'

'Thank you.' He sounded grateful and his shoulders straightened.

Sarah squashed an errant flash of guilt that threatened to penetrate her fulminating rage. 'You're welcome. I promise you'll have your space in an hour. That's how long it will take me to pack my clothes.'

'What?' Bewilderment widened his eyes. 'Why are you packing?'

'Because I'm moving back to the old cheese factory.'

'Sarah, you don't have to do that.'

She couldn't decide if he was begging her or being considerate; either way, she didn't care. 'Oh, but I do. You were quite specific that it was *me* you needed space from. Not Gus or the business or Riverbend. So it makes sense that I'm the one to go.' She put down her empty glass. 'Oh, and Alex, if I hear that Kelly has so much as set one foot inside this house, I won't be as understanding as I'm being now. I'll come at you, guns blazing, and hit you with a financial settlement that will jeopardise your share of the business.'

Numb with rage, she stormed out to pack.

CHAPTER SEVEN

Anita had never taken ecstasy, but if it felt only half this energising, she could understand why people were tempted. She rushed into the house, flinging her arms around Cameron's neck and kissing him full on the mouth. 'The class was amazing! I loved every minute of it and it's given me a totally new idea.'

'What's that?'

'One of the women peeked in the dining room and said it was the perfect setting for high tea. And she's right. Margaret's got all that glorious china and the full silver tea service. Of course, along with tea, ribbon sandwiches, macaroons, cupcakes and scones, jam and cream, I'd offer champagne. Oh, Cam, Mill House offers so many possibilities. Thank you for making it happen.'

He gave her an indulgent look as he squeezed her behind. 'You did all the hard work, baby girl.'

She thought about the long hours spent scrubbing down Margaret's greasy kitchen. The accumulated grime surprised her given how fastidious her mother-in-law was with her clothes and the fact Rita came in to clean. It appeared, however, that between cleans, Margaret didn't mop up any spills.

'But without your idea and bringing Margaret on board, I wouldn't have a cooking school.' She glanced around at her own kitchen and noted that Cameron lacked the clean-as-you-go gene just like his mother. 'Where are the girls?'

'Tucked up in bed watching a movie. Between the playground and the footy, they've been on the go all afternoon so I fed them early. You got any food left over from that class? I'm starving.'

'You poor man.' She kissed him again. 'Help me unpack all my containers and then I'll feed you.'

He pulled her in close. 'Is that a promise?'

She giggled. 'Absolutely. I know the way to my man's heart.'

Later, when everything was stowed away, Anita sat on Cameron's lap, sipping celebratory champagne and sharing an enormous slice of chocolate cheesecake. 'One of the women enjoyed today so much she's planning a girls' weekend. She'll book out a class and wants it to include dinner and wines to match each course.'

'I hope you got her number so you can follow up.'

'Of course I did. It's sales one-oh-one and I was taught by the best.'

'Damn straight.' He refilled their glasses. 'Talking sales, I uploaded those photos we took of Mum's clothes. They're live on eBay.'

The spoon paused on its way to Anita's mouth. They'd only photographed ten outfits. 'I thought the plan was we'd photograph everything and then load them up so shoppers can see the full collection.'

Each week night after the girls had gone to bed, she'd written up detailed notes on two outfits before modelling them. Initially, Cameron had been reluctant to give up his evening to take photos, suggesting she wait a few weeks until the big girls were home on their school holidays so they could help, but she'd talked him around. With some guidance from her, he'd got the hang of taking shots from all angles, showcasing the minute details of the clothes. They'd laughed at the serendipity that Anita was the same size Margaret had been when she'd worn the outfits.

'It's not like a physical store, Annie,' Cameron said with a hint of exasperation. 'You don't need to fill it with stock so it doesn't look empty. Shoppers browse using specific keywords. Besides, it will be weeks before we've photographed everything. It makes sense to load the photos in batches. This way we can iron out any bugs and see if Vintage Glamour can generate some money.'

'I think we should stick to the original plan.'

'Let me convince you otherwise.' His hands cupped her waist. 'You know that red evening dress?'

Anita knew exactly which gown he was talking about. It fitted her like a glove, narrowing her waist and lifting her breasts. When she'd seen herself in the mirror, she'd flashed back to her childhood— sitting on the lumpy and fraying couch with her mother and watching re-runs of *Dynasty*. While her mother slowly drank herself into oblivion, Anita lost herself in the show, weaving daydreams about wearing glamorous and expensive gowns just like Joan Collins and Linda Evans. Only in Margaret's dress, she was living the real deal. She'd laughed and twirled, stuck out her boobs and pouted at Cameron, *Dynasty* style.

The moment he'd finished taking the photos, Cameron had peeled the gown off her and buried his face in her breasts. The sex had been unexpectedly intense and afterwards, as they'd both lain on their backs catching their breath, he'd said, 'I think I'm going to enjoy this project after all.'

The memory made her smile. 'You mean the red taffeta with all the ruffles?'

'Yeah. It sold half an hour after I uploaded the details.'

'No way!'

'Way.' He sounded like a teenager and his wide smile made him look like one.

A ripple of consternation snuck in under her elation. 'Damn. I thought I was up to speed with current prices but perhaps we should have sold it by auction.'

'Way ahead of you, baby girl. I've set the rest to sell by auction. The last time I looked, the canary yellow suit and the full-length, black, crushed velvet dress were already over your suggested price.' His grey eyes sparkled. 'Who knew women spent ridiculous amounts of money on old clothes?'

'Vintage designer clothes,' she reminded him with mock sternness. 'Women want a piece of fashion history.' Perhaps she wasn't the only girl who'd used *Dynasty* as an escape from the anxieties of a childhood spent hiding money and being the adult. 'I guess I'll be adding the post office to my list of Monday errands.'

'Not so fast—this is internet shopping. Wait until I've confirmed the payments have gone into the account.'

Excitement skittered and buzzed, making Anita light-headed. Had she finally, after all these years, done something that would impress her mother-in-law? 'I can't wait to tell Margaret.'

Cameron caught her hand and pressed a kiss into the palm. 'I think it will be a much nicer surprise for Mum if we don't say anything now but present her with the money after everything's sold. If we give her a five-figure sum rather than the amount we got for one dress, she'll be a lot more excited. Not to mention grateful for all our hard work.'

Considering his proposal, Anita leaned into him, tucking her head under his chin. 'I really like the idea of Margaret being grateful.'

'So do I.'

'But is it possible?'

His mouth thinned. 'I guess we'll find out.'

Anita's phone beeped with a text but she was warm and cosy with Cameron and lacking the inclination to move.

'Annie? Aren't you going to read it?'

'It's eight o'clock on a Saturday night. I'm tired, off duty and on an at-home date with you.'

'You're a business woman now.' He tipped her off his lap. 'It might be one of your clients from today wanting to make a booking or perhaps they left something at Mill House.'

'Slave driver,' she said without rancour as she walked into the kitchen and picked up her phone. 'It's Sarah.'

Cameron had already stretched out full length on the couch and was reaching for the TV remote. 'If she's inviting us for Alex's birthday, we're in. I happen to know he bought a bottle of 2012 Grange for it and I'm more than keen to taste a seven hundred and fifty dollar bottle of wine on his coin.'

Having swiped the screen while Cameron was talking, Anita now stared uncomprehendingly at the text.

'Annie? Did you hear what I said?'

'I did but ... God, I hope I'm wrong. I think Sarah's left Alex.'

'Bloody hell.' He sat up. 'Did we know that was on the cards?'

'Not at all. Then again, she hasn't exactly been herself lately. She did say a few weeks ago that she wanted a break.'

'A break? In the last eight months, they've been to France and Penang. And what about that private island on the Great Barrier Reef that was eighteen hundred dollars a night?'

Anita didn't care that much about France or Penang but she remembered the pea-green envy that had engulfed her when Sarah told her about the private tropical island. She'd been awed by the photos of turtles laying eggs on the beach, bewitched by the bright colours of the tropical fish, which could be easily seen just by standing on the little pier, and stunned by the clarity and brilliant turquoise blue of the water.

'The other day, Sarah told me Alex was being difficult over the Gus thing, but how is that a reason to leave?'

Cameron grunted. 'You know what Sarah's like. Her opinion's the only one that counts.'

Anita usually thought Sarah very fair. Over the years, she'd often observed her sister-in-law turning herself inside out to see both sides of an argument, but the other day Sarah had been particularly unforgiving of Alex. *I expect drama and tantrums from the kids but not from my husband.*

'I don't understand.'

'Exactly what does the text say?'

'I've moved into the old cheese factory for a bit. Can you come over for some wine while I whine?

'Bugger.' Cameron pressed the remote and the roar of the crowd at the MCG filled the room. 'I guess that's put the kybosh on lunch and the Grange.'

Sarah spent Saturday lurching between a thundering fury tempting her to smash every breakable item within reach, and life-draining despair. When misery hit, it hollowed her out before pumping her full of pain that rendered her inert and barely able to rise off the couch. She wanted to hide inside the old cheese factory flat forever, but two conversations were required. One she wanted to have now—needed to have now, even. The other she wished she could put off forever.

The news she'd moved out of Riverbend twenty-four hours ago was still contained, but she was under no illusions it would stay that way for long; after all, this was Mingunyah. She'd always thought if the town could harness the energy gossip created and use it for good, the shire's carbon footprint would be negligible. The juicy details of her marriage problems would soon be deconstructed in the café, discussed under the radiant warmth of the gas heaters in the chilly barn of Royce's Farm Supplies, on the ramp of the servo while petrol was pumped, and in kitchens and bedrooms throughout the district.

Oh my God, did you hear that Sarah Hadfield's left Alex?

Are you serious? Has she lost her mind? What on earth is she thinking?

And *that* was exactly the thought she read on Anita's face when she opened the door to her sister-in-law. Abandonment twisted Sarah's gut.

'Oh, Sarah.' Anita hugged her hard. The hint of criticism faded, immediately replaced by concern. 'How? Why? What happened?'

Sarah poured them both a glass of sauvignon blanc and took a long, fortifying drink. Although she had no qualms telling Anita about Kelly's play for Alex, she baulked at sharing the shame-inducing retelling of Alex's 'I need space from you'.

'Alex thinks he's in love with Kelly Bamfield.'

'Shit.' Anita's hand flew to her mouth. 'I'm sorry. That was inappropriate.'

Sarah's laugh held a slightly hysterical edge. Her life was falling apart but Anita was apologising for swearing? Then again, Anita was like Margaret in that old-fashioned way of not swearing in public; something Sarah tried to be better at and frequently failed. 'I think it's very appropriate. In fact, I used a far stronger word than that when Alex told me.'

'Did you have any suspicions?'

'None.' She narrowed her gaze, studying Anita's face carefully. 'Why? Have you heard something? Was it already around town before I even knew?'

Anita shook her head. 'The only chatter about you and Alex is Gus throwing his chance at the firsts. It's just, well, lately you haven't been quite yourself, so I thought perhaps you knew something was wrong.'

'It was a bolt from the blue. I didn't know anything until Friday afternoon.'

Anita grimaced and fiddled with the stem of her wine glass. 'What I don't understand is why you've left Riverbend. I mean, isn't that just making it easy for him to be with Kelly?'

The statement gave oxygen to the unsettling thought that had dogged Sarah all day. She refilled her glass, trying not to let her agitation take flight. 'I believe it will make it harder for Alex to be with Kelly.'

Anita looked dubious. 'How?'

'If Alex left Riverbend, he'd have carte blanche to embrace his midlife crisis. I refuse to let him do that.'

Anita pulled in her lips as if she'd sucked on a lemon. 'The thing is, from the outside, it doesn't look like that.'

'What do you mean?'

'You've not only left your husband but you've abandoned your son. Women in town will judge you harshly for that. They'll be sympathetic to Alex.'

'Women in their forties should be congratulating me.' Righteous indignation raised her voice. 'By moving out, I've called bullshit on his "I need space" nonsense. Think of all those deluded women who've supported their husband's midlife crisis, and helped them find an apartment and move out in the hope it will save their marriage. Hardly any of those husbands move back in. Most end up with another woman living in the space the wife set up for them. I refuse to enable Alex to do that to me. He can't just up and leave. He must own his behaviour. He needs to face his familial responsibilities. Me leaving Riverbend forces him to be a full-time father to Gus.'

Anita shifted in her seat. 'Yes, but only you know that.'

Sarah didn't know if she should appreciate Anita's take on the situation or feel betrayed. Anita was family and her friend, and by default she should be in her corner defending her. Then again, her sister-in-law never liked to rock the boat.

'Are you judging me?'

A look of horror streaked across Anita's face. 'No. Not at all. It's just ... if I was in your shoes, I think I'd have let Alex leave.'

Yes, but you never stand up to Cameron. You let him call the shots every single time. Sarah bit down on the belligerent words. 'I've done what's right for me and my marriage. Hopefully.'

'I guess you know Mingunyah better than I do ...'

'This has got nothing to do with Mingunyah.'

'People will have opinions.'

'That horse has already bolted,' Sarah muttered.

'Have you told Margaret?'

'No. I don't want to worry her.' The truth was, Sarah didn't want or need a lecture on the sanctity of marriage. Nor did she wish to be told yet again how her parents had never taken each other for granted. Not that Sarah thought she'd taken Alex for granted.

I'm not happy, Sarah. I haven't been happy for a long time.

'I really don't want to tell anyone.' Her voice wobbled and she gave an almighty sniff.

'No,' Anita said with feeling. 'I can understand that. Telling makes it real.'

Those prophetic words hammered Sarah the following evening when Gus came for Sunday-night dinner. When she opened the door to her beautiful man-child, she didn't glimpse any criticism, only confused sadness. Guilt sliced her long and deep like the sharp, stinging sweep of a razor blade.

'Come in, darling.' She smiled so brightly her face hurt. 'I've cooked your favourite, spag bol.'

Every book and counsellor suggested both parents be together when they informed the children about a separation. But not only was she still in shock, she wasn't ready to call this a separation. Nor was she close to ready to sit calmly next to Alex while he explained to their children that she made him miserable and that Kelly understood him. She sure as hell wasn't remotely ready for any conciliation. She blamed Alex one hundred per cent—and then some—for ripping their life apart.

In her attempt to block Alex from blithely walking away and abandoning his responsibilities to their marriage, family and home, she hadn't factored in exactly how it would affect her and Gus. On a rational level she knew that, had she stayed at Riverbend, Gus would still be very much a part of the collateral damage of Alex's midlife crisis. But when was motherhood ever rational? Even though Gus was almost seventeen, it killed her that for the next little while she wasn't going to be at home with him in the mornings, making sure he ate a proper breakfast, checking he had everything he needed for his school day and kissing him goodbye. She ached that she wouldn't be around in the evenings when he did his homework just in case it was a 'maths sucks' night or better yet, a 'you've got to watch this YouTube video, Mum' night.

I hate you for this, Alex.

During dinner, she finally bit the bullet. 'Apparently, your father's been unhappy for quite a few months and disgruntled about things in his life. So, I've moved out for a while to eliminate one variable.'

'Is marriage a maths problem?'

'Sometimes.' Her mouth tried to smile at his joke but she couldn't manage it. 'I think it's too easy for someone to blame their general dissatisfaction on one person or one thing. Life's not that simple.'

Gus toyed with his pasta. 'So, does ... does that mean Dad'll have to eliminate me?'

'No!' Her heart twisted. 'Gus, darling, no. You don't need to move out. Your father loves you, Finn and Emma.'

'He's not happy with me about footy, though.'

'He's not happy with himself.'

Gus kept his head down and was silent for a bit. 'How long are you staying here?'

'I don't know.' She drank a glass of water, wishing it was wine, but a clear head was a must for this conversation. She injected false cheeriness into her voice. 'But I'm only a phone call away and I can see you after school. Really, it will be just like that time I was in New Zealand last year for work and Dad stayed home.'

'We ran out of clean clothes that time. And Dad can't cook.'

She almost apologised but she clamped down on it. Alex was the one who should be apologising to Gus. 'Tell Dad how that makes you feel. Oh, and remind him to do the washing.'

He shot her a look that said, *Yeah, right, like I'm gonna do that.* 'Have you told Finn and Emma?'

Her head throbbed at the thought of those conversations. 'Not yet. Finn's got exams coming up.' A thought struck her. 'When people in town start talking, and they will, do you think any of Finn's mates here might say something to him on Facebook?'

Gus shook his head. 'Nah. No one ever talks about the 'rents.'

'Do you message your brother much?'

'We sometimes Snapchat.'

'I'd like to tell Finn in person when he's home on holidays. Is it too much to ask you not to say anything to him before then?'

He shrugged. 'I guess. What about Emma? She's gonna notice you're not FaceTiming her from home or with Dad.'

Bloody hell. Nothing was straightforward. 'I'll talk to your father and work something out. She's a long way from home and I don't want to upset her if this is only short term. By the time she's home, hopefully I will be too.'

Gus was very quiet after that, dropping his gaze and eating garlic bread as if his life depended on it. Sarah tried to draw him out on school, the band he'd recently joined, upcoming parties and footy, but it was hard going. Eventually, she acquiesced to his suggestion they watch the AFL match on TV. In the midst of the mess that was currently their family life, at least the antenna at the flat still worked. At this point, she was scratching around for something to be thankful for. Struggling to even look—it was so much easier to be vindictive.

An increasingly familiar anxiety scuttled through Margaret as she stared at the bottle her hand had so confidently plucked from the cluster on the sideboard. Vodka. Russians drank vodka. Why was she holding it?

Her gaze slid to the far more familiar Waterford decanter circled by its matching cut-crystal glasses on the gleaming silver tray. For her, the decanter was the centre of the theatre of after-dinner drinks. She'd admired it and everything it represented since her first visit to Mill House. 'Dear George. I still miss you ...'

'Whiskey, Margaret?' George asked, lifting the heavy crystal stopper now that dinner was over.

'Lovely. Thank you.' George was very fond of smoky whiskey and, for him, it was an evening tradition that dated back generations. Right from the start, George had included her in the offer of a post-dinner snifter and she'd been appreciative and gratified. Not every man of his generation would have considered that a woman might drink whiskey, let alone enjoy it. When she, Kevin and the children had moved into Mill House, she'd joined her father-in-law in the nightly ritual.

'Good.' He splashed the amber fluid into the bell glass with a grunt. 'No point asking Kevin.'

'No.' She sighed. 'No point at all.'

The first time she'd learned that Kevin didn't share his father's penchant for whiskey was just after their honeymoon. Determined to create a home that was the envy of their social set and to incorporate the Jamieson traditions in preparation for when Mill House became theirs, Margaret spent days unpacking. The final task was to set up the Parker sideboard and arrange their own silver tray holding a crystal decanter with matching glasses in pride of place.

When Kevin walked in after work, she rested her hand on the heavy stopper and said, 'Drink, darling?'

'Sure. But not whiskey.' Kevin ripped opened a box and unpacked a rainbow collection of decorative liqueur bottles. Two more boxes followed until the bar was full to overflowing. The selection was far more comprehensive than the three dusty bottles on offer at the Mingunyah pub.

'But these are—' She struggled to find a word to describe the many reasons why these drinks were unsuitable.

'European,' Kevin said simply.

'You're Australian.'

'And you're the one who's always looking to Paris and Rome for fashion.'

Margaret had no comeback to that. It was the first of a limited number of occasions when Kevin dug his heels in and staked a claim in the house. The colourful bottles stayed, taunting Margaret for years. Although he didn't drink liqueurs when they had guests, his routine was to enjoy a different one each night. Whether it was sipping Frangelico or savouring Baileys splashed over ice, he'd always sit, sip, close his eyes, sigh, and silently disappear somewhere.

It drove Margaret nuts.

Prior to her marriage, if anyone had asked her about Kevin's drinking habits, she'd have told them that if he felt it necessary to seal a business deal, he'd drink wine, but otherwise he preferred beer; she'd certainly seen him drink enough of it at the footy club. Football. Margaret shivered. The club was the bane of her life. She hated the game. She hated the camaraderie. She hated how much football excluded her and influenced Kevin. Most of all she hated how much Kevin loved it. From the moment they'd returned from their honeymoon, Margaret worked towards separating Kevin from football —and from Gary Longmuir. As disappointing as Sarah's gender was, her daughter's arrival had become the unexpected solution to this sticky problem. Cameron's wonderful and timely arrival ten months later set it in stone.

The day Margaret came home from hospital with baby Sarah, she delegated the evening and early-morning feeds to Kevin. It was the reason she'd chosen not to breastfeed—that, and her breasts belonged to her, thank you very much. The idea of having to curtail her wardrobe and only wear clothes that allowed for breastfeeding, not to mention leaking milk and having a child paw at her, made her both indignant and squeamish. Fortunately, Kevin took to fatherhood like a duck to water and happily did the late and early feeds while Margaret slept. Sarah was a relatively content baby and the first month of motherhood was tolerable.

Kevin, who was sitting on the chesterfield sipping Amaretto, opened his eyes. 'Gary and Pete are going shooting this weekend.'

Margaret felt herself stiffen and forced herself to appear unaffected by the news. 'Really? Kaye told me that she and Pete have a family reunion in Euroa.'

Kevin frowned. 'Perhaps you misunderstood which weekend she was talking about. Anyway, I thought I'd tag along. If I leave Saturday morning, I'll be back by mid-morning Sunday. You'll hardly notice I'm gone.'

Margaret knew she hadn't misunderstood Kaye, which meant, in typical Pete style, he'd got the dates wrong. Pete would pull out at the last minute but as Gary didn't have a wife or girlfriend, the trip would still go ahead. The perennial bachelor was a thorn in her side. Not content with seeing Kevin at the footy club, Gary called around to the house uninvited and stayed for hours. Not even a crying baby put him off; in fact, he seemed to enjoy holding Sarah and bouncing her up and down during her periods of colic.

Before the wedding, Margaret sensed she was in competition with Gary for Kevin's attention and now, ten months later, she still hadn't managed to boot Gary out of their lives. There'd been occasional moments of success but then Gary would turn up like a bad penny. This time, she was determined not only to win but to force change.

'I'd rather you didn't go.'

Kevin gave her his bone-melting smile. 'I've been home every night for a month. Don't I get some time off for good behaviour?'

No. 'Of course you do.'

'So what's the problem?'

She bit back the word 'Gary' and thought fast. Kneeling between Kevin's legs, she pressed her manicured hands on his thighs and pouted. 'I just wish you'd asked me earlier.'

'I checked the calendar as instructed and it's blank. We don't have anything on.'

Damn. 'Actually, we do. It was supposed to be a surprise.' Her hand brushed his crotch as she trailed it up to rest on his chest. 'A lovely, romantic surprise.'

Understanding slowly dawned in his hazel eyes. 'I thought the doctor said we had to wait six weeks.'

Sarah was a honeymoon baby and Margaret had experienced a difficult pregnancy, starting with extreme nausea followed by worrying bleeding. Her doctor had banned sex, saying it was far too risky. Her new husband took the news stoically, not complaining once. She'd offered to pleasure him but he'd said it wasn't fair that he got to enjoy himself if she couldn't, so kissing and cuddling was as intimate as they'd been in months. But now, four weeks after Sarah's birth, Margaret's libido was at fever pitch and every time she watched Kevin dress or undress, her body throbbed and ached for him.

She unbuckled his belt. 'Six weeks is only a recommendation.

Other women might use it as an excuse but not me. After all your patience over these long months, you deserve a treat.'

His hands moved, resting over hers and stalling her progress. 'The thing is, Margaret, I promised Gary I'd go.'

Anger blew through her so hard she almost lost control and screamed. But a short fuse didn't win a long game. 'Darling ...' She breathed out the endearment, giving herself time to regain composure. 'I know for a fact that Pete won't be going. Meanwhile, I've gone to a lot of trouble arranging for someone to mind Sarah so we can have a day and a night alone. I know you didn't mean to spoil my special surprise and it's not like Gary will lose a deposit like I will if we don't go. Surely the best and easiest thing to do is to reschedule the shooting trip for a time that suits the three of you?'

First thing in the morning, she'd be on the telephone finding a babysitter, booking a night in Melbourne and then systematically filling every weekend for the next few months until the idea of a shooting trip was forgotten. By the time the next footy season was upon them, Kevin would be so deeply involved with fatherhood and outings with other young families, there'd be no time for football or Gary. Better yet, she'd talk to George about promoting Gary to a position at the Swift's Creek saw mill, four hours and a very difficult drive away.

She pulled her hand out from under Kevin's and slid it down his fly. 'Gary will understand. After all, he's a good friend and he knows what we've been through these last ten months. He wouldn't want you to miss out on a weekend of this.' She lowered her mouth.

Sarah's cries rent the air.

Kevin tensed, his hands delving into her hair. 'Sarah's telling us we should wait for the special weekend you've planned.'

Margaret ignored him and, taking him deep into her mouth in the way she'd learned made him hard, she smiled. The baby could wait. She had her husband by the balls, just the way she liked it.

A thudding sound brought Margaret back to the present and she was surprised to see a bottle of vodka lying on the carpet. As she picked it up, she got a craving for a Bloody Mary. She opened the bar fridge but the familiar box of tomato juice wasn't in the door so she carried the bottle out of the living room. As she entered the east-facing kitchen, sunshine streamed in, hitting something and dazzling her with refracted light. She stopped short and squinted. The bright light was bouncing off gleaming copper pots, which hung from a rack over the Aga. Willow-pattern platters decorated the walls, which were suddenly cream in colour instead of the pale green they'd been for years.

Agitation sank its tenacious claws into her. What was going on? This didn't look like her kitchen. She'd never liked Kevin's mother's Willow pattern and she'd certainly never used it, leaving it instead to languish at the back of the cupboards. Not once had she used the copper pots; they took far too long to clean. She spun around and was instantly reassured by the familiar sight of her blue woollen coat hanging on the hall stand, the portrait of George painted when he was in his prime, and a family photo with Ellie sitting on Kevin's knee, her blonde curls vivid and golden against his darker hair.

The portrait was the last photo taken of them all together as a family. It froze the five of them in a time she'd come to refer to as 'before the accident'. A time before everything changed. Although, if Margaret were honest with herself, and she'd avoided that sort of scrutiny most of her adult life, change was already hiding in plain sight well before the accident, visible to anyone who cared to look. Neither she nor Kevin chose to look and thankfully the children had no inkling there was anything amiss.

Margaret's initial reaction on seeing the photo was to burn it, but grieving widows didn't destroy a family portrait taken two weeks prior to their husband's tragic death. There'd been no way on God's green earth she was doing anything that might draw attention to her and tarnish the image of a perfect marriage and family she'd spent years refining. Twenty-six years later, people still commented in awestruck tones on her enduring love for Kevin. She had no intention of disabusing them of their opinion.

Margaret, we've been lying to each other for years. It's time we told the truth.

The faded voice was a passing breeze on banked coals and her anger flared. 'Bastard!' Her hand shot out and slammed the photo face down, and then she swung back to the kitchen. Again, she was caught off-guard by the pots and platters. Bloody Rita Bosco. She'd been telling Sarah for weeks that instead of doing the hard cleaning, Rita was spending her time doing easy things like polishing furniture. More than once she'd caught her fiddling with her things and rearranging them so Margaret couldn't find anything. Hiding some things to taunt her. But this! Redecorating was too much. Rita Bosco was toast.

As soon as she'd made herself a Bloody Mary, she'd ring Sarah and get her to come straight over and see for herself what the meddling woman was doing now. Walking into the floor-to-ceiling pantry, she stared up at clearly marked containers stacked on every shelf. No wonder her bathroom had mould; Rita was busy in here instead of scrubbing the shower. She better not have touched her supply of tomato juice. Margaret bent down to retrieve a Tetra Pak from the box of twelve but her hand only touched cardboard and air.

Hell's bells. There was nothing for it but to drive to the IGA.

CHAPTER EIGHT

'WHAT DO you mean I can't fire her?' Sarah paced around Dan Horton's office on Tuesday morning, her anger a living, breathing beast growing bigger every day. 'I sure as hell can't work with her.'

Dan, who'd already suggested twice that Sarah take a seat, took one himself. 'Have they had sex in the office?'

'No!'

'Has Kelly ever been issued with a workplace warning?'

'No. Right up until making a play for my husband, she's been the perfect employee.'

'Going on what you've told me, you don't have any grounds to sack her. If you do, she can file a very expensive unfair dismissal claim against you and win.'

'Dan, I don't think you understand.' Sarah pressed her hands on his oak desk, a beautiful piece of furniture that bore the scars of the previous generations of Horton solicitors, and leaned in. 'This woman wants to have sex with my husband.'

Dan flinched. 'I'm sorry, Sarah. I really am, but if she's doing her job well, that's not grounds for dismissal.'

'The law sucks.'

'Perhaps she'll do the right thing and resign.'

Sarah snorted. 'If she had a moral code, she wouldn't be having an emotional affair with my husband.'

'You've got a point.'

'I've got a lot of points. Morality and ethics are on my side. It's the law that's got it wrong.' She slumped into a chair. 'You've been to our offices, Dan. How can I go to work every day with her sitting mere metres away from me?'

He pressed two fingers of his left hand into the crown of his head in the exact same way he'd done when they were lab partners in Year 11 chemistry. 'It will be uncomfortable.'

'You think?' She leaned forward and picked up her coffee cup, needing to do something. 'Are you charging me for this useless advice?'

'Mate's rates.' He pushed a plate of Mint Slice biscuits towards her. 'What about taking leave?'

'And leave her and Alex alone together?' Her chest tightened. 'Whose side are you on?'

'Yours. Alex's.'

She sat up straight and shot Dan an accusatory stare. 'How does that work?'

He looked as if he was sitting on shards of glass. 'Sarah, you know I'm not just Mingunyah Bread and Cheese's lawyer. Lacey and I consider you both close friends.'

'You've known me longer.'

He ignored her pouty tone. 'I'm not a counsellor but I do know this. You and Alex have different business strengths. It's what makes you a great team. If you stop going into work, he's going to notice your absence.'

She thought about Mother's Day. 'I'm not so sure about that. Kelly's pretty good at the admin stuff.'

'Yeah, but anyone can do admin. Not everyone has the ideas. You're the creative person in the business.'

Her battered ego accepted the balm. 'Thanks, Dan.' Would taking leave help or hinder the situation? God, she wished she had a crystal ball. She could have done with one weeks ago to detect her husband's dissatisfaction and Kelly's opportunistic sympathy.

'You're welcome.' He stood up to see her out. 'Your mum's looking well.'

Sarah, who was busy searching in the depths of her handbag for a tissue, was only half listening. 'Oh?'

'Yeah, she was in the other day. Whenever I see her name in the appointment book, I wish I had the ability to bring Dad back from the grave.'

'My mother's formidable.' It occurred to Sarah that her mother had only been a few years older than she was now when she was widowed. Margaret had lost her husband in a car accident on a wet, dark and cold July night and Sarah was fighting not to lose her husband to another woman. She wasn't sure which was worse. At least her mother hadn't suffered the indignity of her husband telling her she didn't understand him or that she made him unhappy.

'My dad always said your mother had a better head for business than Kevin.' Dan suddenly looked aghast. 'Sorry. I didn't mean to say that out loud.'

'Don't be silly, Dan. It's no secret that the finances at the saw mill weren't great when Dad died. I know Mum valued Robert's sound financial advice. We all appreciated his fatherly interest in Ellie, especially given how difficult she got after Alex and I went to France. I really don't know how Mum would have survived without his help.'

'Thanks.' Dan got a wistful look in his eyes. 'Dad was pretty special. I miss him every day. I'm convinced Margaret thinks I'm a poor replacement. She always scared the bejesus out of me when we were kids and not much has changed. By the end of the hour, I was feeling emasculated and Cam was looking like he'd regretted his offer to drive her.'

'Cameron brought her?'

'Ah, yeah.' His gaze slid to the door as if he was expecting it to open. 'Something about your mother's car being serviced and it was raining pretty hard. Not a good day to walk.'

It struck Sarah that both her husband and her brother were acting out of character. Perhaps the universe operated on a limited amount of goodness and Alex had gifted his generosity to Cameron and accepted her brother's self-centeredness in return.

'I don't suppose she asked your advice about selling Mill House and buying something smaller?'

A pained look crossed his face. 'You know I can't breach client confidentiality. I probably shouldn't have even told you she'd come in.'

She sighed and kissed his cheek. 'Sorry. Didn't mean to make you uncomfortable.'

'I'm sorry I couldn't tell you what you wanted to hear.' His hand paused on the door. 'Sarah, this thing with you and Alex, it puts me in a difficult position. If you need a family law specialist, Rebecca Chin in Valley View is scarily good.'

Every muscle in her body tensed. 'I don't want a divorce lawyer.'

A doleful look appeared into Dan's big brown eyes. 'But you might need one.'

A squall of fury at Alex propelled Sarah from Dan's office and onto the street. It wasn't until she'd pressed the ignition button on the car and thought about where she was going that she realised she was utterly displaced from her life. On a normal day after an early appointment with Dan, she'd pop into the bakery for a coffee and a chat with the staff. After she'd dealt with any issues there, she'd drive to the office. Today, the office was out; going there required monumental amounts of emotional energy that she lacked. She didn't have enough reserve to deal with the day-to-day demands from staff, let alone Alex and Kelly.

Thinking about Dan's suggestion, she turned off the ignition and dictated an email using her phone.

Good morning,

As of today, I'm taking annual leave. During my absence, Alex Hadfield will be dealing with the day-to-day running of the business, so any and all concerns should be directed to him either at alexh@mingunyahcheese.com or on 0457 754 547.

Best wishes,
Sarah Hadfield

She brought up her address book and selected all their staff, customers' and suppliers' email addresses, including Alex's. As the swishing sound of a departing email winging its way into cyberspace filled the car, a rush of righteous rebellion filled her. 'That's going to keep you well and truly occupied, Alex.'

But what would keep her occupied? Usually, when she had a free hour in her day, she shot home to Riverbend and threw on a load of washing and unloaded the dishwasher. Only Riverbend wasn't currently home and any dirty washing was now Alex's domain. Thoughts of washing led to thoughts of Gus and her heart crumpled.

The day before had been a public holiday, so today was his first morning at school since she'd moved out. She texted him: *Remember, you have a geography excursion tomorrow. Have baked you triple chocolate brownies. See you after school. Love you. Mum x*

Now what? The idea of returning to the flat didn't appeal. Holed up there over the long weekend and surrounded by happy memories had been bad enough. She only had to cross the threshold to remember their return to Australia when she was pregnant with Finn, learning to be parents of a baby and owners of a fledging business. During those frenetic days, she and Alex had unwittingly combined three of life's top six stressors. According to the experts, it should have been an incredibly fraught time that stretched their relationship to breaking point. She laughed and the bitter sound reverberated back to her. How ironic that she and Alex had thrived on the challenges that sank other couples, but now, when life was less stressful and far more stable, their relationship was floundering.

She caught sight of Stella across the street. As she sank low in the seat, praying the woman didn't see her, a jet of wrathful indignation flared. *What the hell are you doing? Why are you hiding? You're not the one who upended your life. You haven't had an emotional affair with another man. You have the moral high ground here, so sit up straight!*

Decision made, she did exactly that. Instead of hiding from Stella, she'd meet her for coffee and give the notorious gossip the correct information. At least that way she was exerting some control over her story.

She was texting Stella when a knock on the car window made her jump. With her heart thumping wildly, she pressed the button on the door and the window slid down with a gentle whirr.

'Edmund.'

'Sarah, I am sorry,' he said in his precise and Afrikaans-accented English. 'I did not mean to startle you. I was waiting a couple of minutes for you to look up but—'

'I was sending a text.' She forced a smile, trying to ease the consternation that was furrowing his forehead. 'So, how are you?'

'I am well.' He slid his hands in his pockets and rocked back on the heels of his boots. 'But are you?'

'I'm fine,' she said too quickly. 'Touch wood I've dodged the bug that's going around.'

'And everyone is well?'

'Uh huh.'

The creases on his forehead became crevasses. 'Really? You look very tired.'

She waved away his comment. 'Just busy, but we're all good. Alex is still mad on cycling, Emma's loving France, Finn's gearing up for exams and Gus has joined a band, of all things! He's playing the guitar.'

Edmund usually listened to her with close attention—his head tilted slightly and his eyes fixed on her face—then asked follow-up questions. But today his head was straight and the tendons in his neck taut.

'If everyone is well and everything is fine, why did you miss Hibiscus's opening on Saturday night?'

Sarah's stomach dropped and her head spun, making silver spots dance in front of her eyes. With everything that had happened over the last few days, the invitation to the opening had totally slipped her mind. Even if it hadn't, she'd been in no fit state to drive up the mountain and be social, but the fact she'd let Edmund down made her feel ill. 'Oh God, Edmund. I'm so sorry. I feel awful. I mean what sort of friend am I—' *We!* 'What sort of friends are we to forget such an important event. Did it go well? I'm sure it was amazing—' *Stop! You're babbling.*

'Sarah,' he said quietly. 'You never forget anything.'

It was true. She'd inherited her mother's mind for detail and even during the busiest times she never forgot anything. Apparently, all it took to vanquish memory was a husband accusing her of a lack of understanding, blaming her for his unhappiness and desiring another woman. 'I'm so sorry your event was the first time it happened.'

'I am too. Also, it surprises me that the reminders I know you set on your phone did not work.' Edmund's sea-green gaze bored into her like a drill.

She swallowed, feeling totally exposed. 'How can I make it up to you?'

'Tell me what is really going on.'

The problem with good friends is that they know you too well, making it almost impossible to hide anything when your emotional fortitude is already on the skids. Over the years, she and Edmund had shared a lot and he knew her almost as well as Alex did.

A sigh rumbled out of her. 'On Friday, Alex more or less told me he doesn't know if he still wants to be married to me.'

Edmund blinked, shock clear on his face. 'No.'

Her laugh was brittle. 'Sadly, yes.'

'But, I do not understand ...'

She looked beyond him and saw the Lindsays power walking towards them. Janine and Alan would have been guests at Hibiscus on Saturday night and she wasn't up to fabricating a story about why she and Alex had missed one of the social events of the season. An urgent desire to flee filled her.

'Edmund, get in the car.'

'What?'

She pressed the ignition button and the engine roared into life. 'Quickly. Get in the car.'

He jogged around the back of the vehicle and swung in next to her. 'Where are we going?'

'Somewhere that isn't Mingunyah.' She threw the car into reverse, pulled out of the parking space and crunched into first gear. As she approached the roundabout, she read the brown tourist sign and flicked on her indicator. 'Hell's Falls sounds absolutely perfect.'

Standing at the base of the falls with Edmund, Sarah let the negative ions float around her and groaned inwardly at the irony of something negative being good for her. The roar of the water filled her ears and she gave in to it, preferring the sound to the circular conversations in her head that never ceased. She'd been using a similar technique with music, radio and television over the long weekend. None of it worked for long.

On the drive up the narrow and winding road to the falls, she'd filled the car with music for the same effect. Edmund had been silent. She couldn't tell if it was because he'd been too busy gripping the Jesus bar, worried that if she talked about Alex she'd take one of the hairpin bends too fast and slide over the edge of the road, plummeting them both to their deaths, or if he was politely waiting for her to start talking. Edmund was always excruciatingly polite.

She stamped her numb feet, trying to get some warmth back into them. The insidious cold easily permeated her fashionable leather boots and laughed at her one-hundred-denier tights. 'God, why did I come up here without gloves, hat and a down jacket? Clearly, I've lost my mind.'

'Here.' Edmund started to slip off his coat.

'No. Don't freeze on my account.'

'We can share it.' He stepped in close and threw the heavy, silk lined woollen coat over both their shoulders. The coat, combined with his body heat, went some way to combatting the below-zero wind chill.

'We could just get back in the car.'

'Sure.'

But there was something about the primal roar of the water and the sunshine-laden mist that kept her rooted to the spot. Standing here on the mossy lookout with Edmund, it was the first time since Friday she'd come close to a semblance of calm. Was that why relaxation soundtracks played burbling brooks and breaking waves? Or was it Edmund's presence? Perhaps it was a bit of both. This wasn't the first time Edmund had been there for her in the middle of an emotional maelstrom. Mind you, this wasn't quite the same as the time she'd gone into labour with Gus. Yes, that had been terrifying and excruciatingly fast but mostly exhilarating and exciting. This situation with Alex was devoid of exhilaration and excitement, leaving only terrifying uncertainty and rage. A malignant and all-consuming rage unlike anything she'd ever experienced. It took her mind to evil places, made her entertain base thoughts and at the same time it mocked her for sinking so low. She'd always considered that her education and wealth elevated her above such primal urges as revenge. She'd been utterly wrong.

Alex, why are you doing this to us?

Every time she thought about her husband, she wanted to yell and scream and scratch him until he bled. She wanted to hurt him like he'd hurt her. She wanted raw pain to pull at his handsome face and see tears well in his eyes. But at the same time, the idea of inflicting pain on the man she'd loved for as long as she could remember made her recoil—until she remembered what he'd done and then the cycle started all over again. The intensity of her feelings frightened her.

'Alex says I don't understand him but Kelly Bamfield does.'

'Fuck,' said Edmund softly. The vowels sounded ridiculously round and defined.

Sarah shivered. 'That's what I said.'

'But he cannot be serious?' Mist clung in tiny bubbles to Edmund's blond hair and thick eyelashes. 'Kelly Bamfield is a perfectly nice woman in a nondescript kind of a way, but she is not you.'

Tears prickled the backs of her eyes. 'Unfortunately, not being like me is the attraction.'

Edmund's arm tightened around her. It felt as natural as breathing to lean against him and give in to the relief of allowing someone other than herself to hold her upright. He muttered something in Afrikaans, which Sarah didn't understand, but she appreciated the harsh sound of the words and the guttural delivery. She imagined them crashing down on Alex like the basalt boulders that lined the creek.

'Whenever I think about it, I'm so furious with him I find it hard to breathe but at the same time I feel like half of me is missing. I've moved out. I've taken leave so I don't have to go to the office every day and see Kelly, but part of me wants to storm back in and drag her out by the hair.' She gave him a rueful smile. 'Dan has advised me against this.'

'Dan is a wise man.' He brushed some damp strands of hair off her cheek. The warmth in his fingers fired a line of heat along her skin, breaking apart the chill that gripped her. 'You need to keep busy or your mind will drive you crazy.'

The heartfelt words carried his own pain and she gave herself a shake. Here she was leaning on Edmund when he'd suffered a far greater loss than she had. 'You're right. Thank you.'

'What will you do?'

'I don't know.' Her voice sounded shaky. 'For twenty-two years, my life has been Alex, the kids and the business, and now there's this huge hole.' She sucked in a steadying breath. 'Mum's been dropping hints lately that she doesn't see enough of me so I'll do more things with her.'

'And?'

'Take up yoga. Eat chocolate. Bake for Gus. Watch a decade of movies that I've missed.' She sighed. 'The evenings are long and I can't sleep so I've already made a solid start on the movies.'

'Sleeping is the tough one,' he agreed, his eyes filled with understanding. 'Have dinner with me tonight at Protea. Chef has a new menu and the staff and I are tasting. I would appreciate your thoughts before we go public.'

A wave of emotion hit her and she didn't know if she wanted to burst into tears or hug him. He was only the second adult she'd told and unlike Anita, who'd been hungry for details, Edmund wasn't judging or warning her. Instead he radiated kindness and consideration. She needed every gram of it. However, he'd spent the last eighteen months fighting his way out of his own black hole of grief and he didn't deserve an evening of her struggling to be bright and chirpy.

'Are you sure? I'm not fabulous company right now and I don't want to drag you down.'

'Very sure.' The mist on his hair combined to form droplets and two fractured their surface tension, splashing down his forehead into his eyes. 'Can we discuss this further in the car?'

'For sure.' Sarah's ringtone screeched, making them both jump. 'Wow, I didn't think there was reception up here.'

'Running Hibiscus, I have learned the altitude affects everything from boiling point to phone signals.'

She pulled her mobile out of her pocket and frowned. 'It's my brother. He never calls me.'

'Take it.' Edmund adjusted the coat over her shoulders and stepped away.

Despite the warmth of the heavy wool, she shivered, instantly missing his heat. 'Thanks. Don't get wet. Go back to the car.'

He shot her a grateful smile before turning and jogging down the path. She watched his long legs eating up the distance and by the time she'd accepted the call, he'd vanished from view.

'Hi, Cam.'

'Where are you?' he asked, his tone oozing *I'm a very busy and important man*. 'I've rung four times and left messages.'

She suddenly remembered the chant Cameron had frequently hurled at her when they were kids: *You're not the boss of me*. The temptation to say it to him now was so strong she was surprised to hear herself say, 'Halfway up the mountain. You know the reception's dodgy. What's up?'

'Mum's had a minor car accident.'

'Oh God. Is she all right?'

'She's fine but Sergeant Plod says the front of the car isn't. Look, she's been trying to call you and so have I.' His criticism that she wasn't available when he needed her to be blasted down the phone. 'The hospital wants to discharge her so you need to pick her up.'

The hairs on her arm rose in a rush. 'Where are you?'

'Benalla. And before you ask, it's one of Annie's client mornings.'

Sarah's hand gripped her phone tightly as treachery trickled through her. Today was Tuesday. She was Anita's Tuesday morning client! Surely her sister-in-law wasn't at Riverbend filling the freezer with home-cooked food for Alex? Not when she knew what he'd done to her. 'Why didn't you ring Ellie?'

A long, put-upon sigh rumbled down the line. 'I know Alex is being a prick and you're all emotional and not thinking straight, but Ellie? Seriously?'

Sarah didn't know if it was because half of her was already consumed by bitter rage at Alex's perfidy or if years spent carefully controlling her reactions to Cameron had finally broken containment lines, but flames of frustration and fury ignited in an almighty whoosh, almost blowing her head off her neck.

'Oh, I'm deadly serious. I'm over an hour's drive away and Ellie can be in Mingunyah in less than thirty minutes. It's time she stepped up.'

'You can ring her if you want,' he said in a sing-song voice that clearly implied she was stark raving mad, 'but I've told you about Mum so my job is done.' The line went dead.

'You're such a prick, Cameron!' Her yell barely penetrated the noise of the waterfall so she added a scream for good measure. It felt amazing. Then she brought up Ellie's number and as the phone rang, she prayed that the one bar of reception would hold.

'Hi, Sarah.'

'Ellie, hi. Sorry to bother you.' God! Why did she sound so tentative? But she knew why; it was just the way things were between her and her sister.

'Oh.' A quick intake of breath echoed down the line. 'Is there a problem at the dairy with the guys? Do you need me to come out?'

Bloody hell. She'd totally forgotten today was the Burmese men's first day. Right now, she was supposed to be running their orientation. Her rush of regret was suddenly replaced by cool and clear-headed spite. It was good she wasn't at work; the orientation was another thing Alex would have to deal with on top of all the other general business that followed a Monday public holiday.

'I'm not calling about work. It's about Mum. She's fine but apparently she's had a slight bingle and they took her to hospital to get checked out. The thing is, Cam and I are both over an hour away from Mingunyah. Can you please pick her up?'

There was a long silence and Sarah automatically checked the reception.

'Ellie? Are you still there? Did you hear what I said?'

'Yes.' Ellie's tone was flat. 'I heard. You want me to pick Mum up from hospital.'

Sarah bit off the urge to ask, 'Is that okay?' as irritation prickled her from top to toe. She rolled her shoulders like a boxer facing up to an opponent. 'That's exactly right. Thanks. I'll meet you at Mill House.'

The moment she finished the call, four texts pinged in. Three were the messages Cameron had told her he'd left and the last one was from Alex. This was the first piece of communication between the two of them since she'd left Riverbend on Friday afternoon. Feeling like a bomb disposal expert, she tentatively swiped it open and braced herself for an explosion.

Margaret keeps ringing me. Are you late picking her up? Can we meet at 7 tonight? We need to discuss telling Finn and Emma. Alex

Sarah's stomach cramped and she doubled over for a moment before her fire-breathing rage ignited again. *Oh, no. You don't suddenly get to be the responsible parent and call the shots. Not when you've lobbed a grenade into the middle of our lives.* With thick and ungainly fingers, half numb with cold, she typed a reply.

Tonight not suitable. I have— Her finger paused. An appointment? Prior engagement? A word pinged into her sluggish mind and she automatically moved to discard it and stopped. *Stuff it.* She knew what she was about to type wasn't remotely accurate but why let the truth get in the way of one-upmanship?

I have a date.

CHAPTER NINE

When Ellie arrived at the hospital, the first person she met was Graeme Atkins. The police sergeant was an old classmate of Cameron's, although the two men had never been friends. As he crossed the foyer towards her, she realised with a flash of insight why Cameron always referred to him as Sergeant Plod—her brother was jealous. Even though Ellie didn't spend time scoping out men, a person would have to be blind not to notice that the policeman was not only fit but his muscles were likely ripped under his dark navy shirt tucked neat and flat behind his utility belt. Not only that, he wore his uniform with a 'don't mess with me' air of command that even she conceded was sexy in a pin-up-calendar kind of way.

In contrast, Cameron enjoyed Anita's excellent cooking just a little too much and was developing a paunch. She couldn't imagine him doing anything more physical than a round of golf but she had no trouble picturing Graeme easily scaling fences like the cops on TV shows. Mind you, that probably didn't happen much around here as most of the fences in the district were barbed wire.

'Ellie, can I have a quick word?' Graeme managed to combine professionalism with the right tone of familiarity as he flipped open his black notebook, fact checking before he spoke. 'Your mother's fine, by the way. I only brought her in as a precaution because of her age.'

'Thanks. What happened exactly?'

'She was approaching the IGA car park from the north east and the vehicle she was driving mounted the raised garden bed that creates a border between the carpark and the footpath. She collided with the light pole that's located in the centre of the bed and came to a halt.'

Ellie tried not to smile at the police talk. 'Was she avoiding another car?'

'She says she was.' He sighed. 'I'd like to think that if a local was involved, they'd have stopped to help.'

'Maybe it was a South Yarra skier. They tear through here as if the snow will melt before they get up the mountain. Did anyone see it happen?'

'No one's come forward yet but I'm asking around.' He rubbed the back of his head as if he was trying to find the best way to tell her something. 'I'm sorry, Ellie but because of the accident and the fact Margaret's seventy-six, she needs to have a "fitness to drive" medical assessment.'

Ellie wasn't expecting that, especially as her mother's driving record was impeccable and she held gold-class status with her insurance company—facts Margaret was forever reminding Sarah and Cameron of when they got pinged for speeding at least once a year. 'Are you saying you don't think she's competent to drive any more?'

'I didn't say that. It's up to the doc to determine her fitness. Mind you,' he said dryly, 'if her reflexes and eyesight are as good as the tongue lashing she's just given me, she'll pass with flying colours.'

Ellie grimaced in sympathy. 'You're a very patient man, Graeme.'

He gave a rueful shrug. 'It gets tricky when you're dealing with elderly people who've known you since you were a shitty kid throwing rocks on their roof. By the way, the car's gone to Sorenson's.'

Despite herself, Ellie got a flash of a dimpled smile and the memory of a teasing laugh. Her heart rate sped up, but for the first time in years she couldn't tell if it was protective anxiety or something less sinister. Not that it mattered when the reaction was identical. Surely that was a warning worth heeding? She swallowed and tried to sound not just normal but slightly uninterested. 'Oh? Does Luke have a sideline in cars?'

Graeme looked disconcerted. 'Have you forgotten that Otto Sorenson owned the garage? He retired a few years ago and the boys took over. Luke's the only brother who didn't go into the business. Max and Henry still service cars but they've expanded to include a panel-beating workshop that's always busy.' He snapped his notebook closed. 'They're raking it in. I sometimes wonder if Luke regrets not joining them.'

She thought of Sarah and Cameron. 'I doubt working with family is easy.'

'Oh, I dunno. The Sorensons are a pretty tight family, much like yours. And working together hasn't hurt Alex and Sarah. I read in the paper they just won some big cheese award.'

Ellie didn't disabuse Graeme of his presumption that she was 'tight' with her family and went instead to find her mother.

Robyn, the nurse in charge of Urgent Care, met her at the nurses' station. 'Margaret's fine. She's adamant she didn't black out and she passed the conscious state test except for naming the prime minister. But really, given the shenanigans in Canberra, that's a bit of an unfair question, isn't it? I'm hard-pressed to keep up myself.' Robyn handed her a card. 'We've made an appointment for her to see her GP tomorrow, but if she shows any signs of disorientation or complains of a headache, bring her straight back here.'

'Will do.'

'You can go in.' Robyn waved her towards the cubicles.

Ellie walked into the small Urgent Care department and stopped just outside the curtains. Right up to this point, she'd cheerfully avoided spending any one-on-one time with her mother since returning to the valley. Sucking in a deep breath, she parted the curtains and stepped inside.

'Hi, Mum.'

Her mother glanced up from a magazine, her expression perfectly schooled in what Ellie had long ago dubbed 'Margaret's polite face'. The small smile vanished and a combination of annoyance and disappointment rushed in to replace it.

'Oh, it's you.'

Ellie was simpatico with her mother's reaction; she'd felt similarly when Sarah rang and delegated the collection task to her. She'd have preferred the jab of a rusty nail deep into the ball of her foot instead of taking her mother to Mill House. It seemed to Ellie that the only point of difference in their reactions was that Margaret didn't appear to experience one iota of guilt about her dismay. Ellie didn't want to feel guilt—after all, she'd spent years telling herself she had no reason to feel any guilt whatsoever. But despite her best efforts, the devious and manipulative emotion slithered in, flashed brightly and burned her like the sear of a brand.

'I was expecting Sarah,' Margaret said grumpily and dropped the magazine with dramatic flair.

Ellie passed her mother her shoes. 'She's on the mountain so you've got me.'

'Hmph.' Margaret slipped on her shoes. 'What's she doing up there?'

'No idea.' She swung the wheelchair into position. 'Do you need a hand?'

Margaret did a very good impersonation of the Queen. 'I'm perfectly capable of walking to the car, thank you very much.'

'Hospital rules, Mrs J.' Robyn breezed in, swishing back the curtains. 'We have to escort you off the property.'

Margaret cooperatively sat in the chair, giving a regal wave to everyone she met along the corridor between Urgent Care and the car.

Fifteen minutes later, safely back at Mill House, Ellie placed a steaming cup of tea in front of her mother. 'Here you go, Mum.'

While she poured herself a cup, she took another look around the kitchen, trying to wrap her head around the unexpected changes. Granted, Ellie hadn't been inside Mill House in a very long time, but some things stay the same no matter how many years pass. Her mother's decorating passion had always been focused on the public rooms of the house and her bedroom. She kept these in immaculate condition and took great care to decorate them in the traditional plain features that suited the Georgian house. However, Margaret had little interest in cooking and the kitchen had never received much consideration other than the occasional lick of paint. Today it looked like something straight out of a photo shoot from *Australian Country* magazine.

'Aren't you going to drink your tea?' she asked, noticing that Margaret was gazing at the cup and saucer as if they were a sad disappointment to her.

'I'd prefer a Bloody Mary.'

'It's not quite noon.'

Her mother frowned momentarily before quirking a well-maintained eyebrow. 'For an organic vegetarian, free trade coffee–drinking lesbian, you're such a stick-in-the-mud.'

Ellie gaped slightly, not knowing whether to laugh or be offended. Although Margaret grumbled about her mostly vegetarian food preferences and her clothing choices—'Goodness me, I've seen sacks with more style'—she'd never said the L word to her before; that was Cameron's party piece. Then again, the last time she and her mother had discussed sex was nineteen years ago, and to be accurate, it hadn't come close to a discussion.

Ellie had been the one to raise the topic and she'd done all the talking. Margaret looked as if she was listening to the words but her interpretation of them had been so very different from Ellie's that she may as well have been speaking a foreign language. Margaret's eventual response of 'You always have to make everything about you, don't you?' had effectively slammed the door shut on any future conversations. They had studiously avoided the topic ever since.

Her mother, who always wore her social filter like armour, appeared to have let it slip and was suddenly dropping truth bombs.

'Are you sure you didn't bump your head when you hit the pole?'

'What?' Margaret sounded distracted.

The clink of a teaspoon against china sounded loudly in the room and Ellie realised with a jolt of surprise that her mother was stirring sugar into her tea. Margaret never took sugar. Growing up, Ellie was told sugar was the devil's work, the root of all evil, and if she wanted to maintain the beautiful figure she'd inherited from her mother, she should forsake the sweet temptation. Sitting in the utterly unfamiliar kitchen with Margaret sipping sweetened tea without flinching, was utterly surreal. Had the minor prang rattled her mother more than she was letting on?

'Are you sure you're feeling yourself, Mum?'

'I'm fine. I'd be better if Sarah was here.'

Don't react. Do. Not. React. Ellie forced a smile. 'What about having a bit of a lie down?'

'Good heavens, Eleanor. I don't have time for that. I need to freshen up before your father gets home and so do you. You know he likes it when we both dress up for him.'

Despite the intervening decades since she'd last heard the old and dust-encrusted words, they were very familiar even if they were utterly out of place.

'Mum,' she said carefully, 'Dad died when I was eight. Remember?'

Margaret pursed her lips into the thin and disapproving line Ellie was all too familiar with, having been on the receiving end of that look for many years. 'I could hardly forget that, now could I? And for his sins, the man left me virtually bankrupt.'

Ellie blinked. *This isn't good.* As a teenager, Ellie was often the recipient of Margaret's contempt but not once had she ever heard it directed at her father. Usually when her mother talked about Kevin, her voice dropped in reverent tones imbued with sadness. He was the man she'd loved and death had snatched him from her far too early. If Margaret was taking a swipe at Kevin then something was seriously wrong. Perhaps she should take her mother back to hospital.

'Thank God for good friends. Tonight's party is all about

celebrating that.' Margaret rose to her feet and jabbed a finger at Ellie. 'Go and get out of those disgusting clothes and put on the dress I bought you. When everyone arrives, you're to be welcoming and polite. I won't have you ruining the evening with any of your silly nonsense. Do I make myself clear?'

The last time Ellie had heard those words was in 1997. This time they froze her to the chair and turned her boots into lead weights. Her heart rate escalated wildly and blood boomed in her ears, throbbing like the bass in a heavy metal band. Chaos spun her mind, thoughts leaping wildly, but amid the confusion, she was vaguely aware of her chest rising and falling far too quickly—like she'd just run up a hill and couldn't catch her breath. She tried to speak. Tried to tell her mother today's date and day, but her mouth wouldn't work. Her skin burned unbearably hot and the temptation to rip at it, peel it off her body, sent her nails digging into her arms. Like an earthquake shaking the foundations of the house, the kitchen walls pressed in on her, threatening to bury and suffocate her. *Get out. Get out, now!*

'Oh, there you both are.' Sarah appeared in the kitchen along with the delicious doughy scent of freshly baked bread. She held up a green enviro bag. 'I brought us some lunch.'

'Can't. Stay,' Ellie managed to croak before standing on rubbery legs, grabbing her bag and flinging it over her shoulder.

'Surely you can spare me five of your precious minutes to fill me in on what the hospital told you?' Sarah's tone was the same one Ellie heard her use when the kids or Alex stretched her patience to breaking point.

Nothing would induce Ellie to stay in the house a second longer. Without a word, she half walked, half ran down the hall to the front door.

'Ellie! Wait!'

As she slammed the door shut behind her, she heard Sarah yelling, 'Bitch!'

Stumbling across the portico and down the worn bluestone steps, she fell into the garden bed and vomited all over the hellebores.

Ten minutes later, just after Ellie drove across the bridge and officially left Mingunyah, she pulled onto the small patch of gravel where anglers fishing for trout parked their cars. She reached for her phone and was surprised her hand was steady when every other part of her was still soaked in tremble-inducing adrenaline. Bringing up Sarah's number, she stared at the flashing cursor on the text box and pondered the best words to use when none would help.

Mum acting very weird. Seems confused. Needs to go back to hospital. She wants you, not me. Ellie

She re-read it and worried her bottom lip as the word 'bitch' replayed in her head. Sarah had never exposed her opinion of Ellie with such bluntness before. Did it matter that rushing out of the house had only reinforced Sarah's opinion of her? Wasn't that a good thing? Ever since Ellie's return to the valley, Sarah had been hell bent on trying to play happy families and Ellie constantly dodged and weaved to avoid the bulk of her invitations. Today's meltdown might have done her a favour. Sarah and Anita now had every reason to kick back, drink wine and enjoy bitching about 'the bitch', free of any familial guilt. They could bask in their own superior commitment to the extended family. Ellie was finally off the hook.

It was that easy.

The tumble of conflicting emotions churning her gut mocked her. *Crap.* It was an unwelcome surprise to discover there was a big difference between her assumption that Sarah thought she was thoughtless and self-indulgent, and hearing herself actually being called a bitch.

Come on. This is a get-out-of-jail-free card. A total gift. Accept it and move on.

Only some things were much easier to say than to do. A motivation greater than her resistance moved her finger on the screen. She adjusted the cursor, placing it neatly between the words 'me' and

'Ellie', and tapped out 'Sorry'. She immediately hit send. Regret was instant. She set the phone to silent.

With her mouth acrid and disgusting after vomiting, she lifted her water bottle to her lips and sucked again. It was empty. She checked for a spare bottle in the door holder and inside the glove box. Nothing. Perhaps it had rolled under a seat. Hopping out of the car, she opened both rear doors and peered under the seats. God, she really should clean the car. She pulled out a library book, Noah's plastic pterodactyl toy that he'd sworn he'd lost at school, a muesli-bar wrapper and bevy of parking receipts, but no water bottle.

She heard the rumble of a diesel engine and backed out of the car before straightening up. This time she recognised the vehicle immediately and raised her hand in greeting. It occurred to her this was the third time she'd met Luke, and each time he'd driven up to her in his white ute. *Knight on a white charger?* Ellie scoffed at the thought. She was hardly a damsel in distress and if life had taught her anything it was that the only person she could depend upon to rescue her was herself.

Luke hopped out of the ute and slammed the door shut. 'We've got to stop meeting like this. You got car problems?'

'Not today. I pulled over to send a text before I hit the dead zone.'

A wistful look crossed his face. 'I quite like that twenty-K stretch between Mingunyah and Valley View. The phone's silent and it's just me, the road and my thoughts.'

She laughed. 'That sounds very deep.'

He speared her with his teasing smile. 'That sounds like you think blokes can't have deep thoughts.'

Her head suddenly moved of its own accord, sending her hair swinging in an arc as she glanced playfully up at him. 'Can they?'

Panic hit. *What the hell are you doing? You don't flirt, remember?*

'I can only speak for myself.' Luke's vivid blue eyes were doing that disconcerting intense gaze again, only this time instead of studying her face or quickly grazing her chest, they were fixed on her knees. 'Took a tumble, did you?'

Her hands automatically and ineffectually brushed at her muddy jeans. She could spin him some line about tripping over but off-the-cuff lies had a way of coming back to bite her. 'I threw up in a garden bed.'

His light-hearted expression morphed into a frown. 'You okay? Should you be driving?'

She nodded, trying not to let his kindness slide under her skin and warm her. 'It was a case of better out than in. I'm fine now, although I'd kill for some water.'

'What about a cup of tea?'

'For that I'd—' She bit off the flirty and dangerous 'be eternally grateful'. She went out of her way to avoid any sort of obligation to anyone. 'A cup of tea would be lovely, thank you.'

Luke opened one of the big silver toolboxes on the back of the ute and grabbed a thermos, some enamel mugs and a cool pack like the one Noah took to school, except Luke's wasn't black and red with a superhero on the front. His had a broad blue and pink border.

'Your daughter's?' she asked, taking the opportunity to find out some information about him as she followed him to the picnic table.

He looked at her blankly. 'I'm not married.'

She almost laughed at his naiveté. 'That doesn't mean you can't be a father.'

'I s'pose not.' His large hands gripped the top of the thermos and, with a flick of his wrist, he uncapped it and splashed hot water over the tea bags. 'I guess it's just not a scenario I've ever entertained.'

She pointed at the bag. 'In that case, I'm guessing you're a *Frozen* fan.'

Understanding dawned in his eyes, immediately followed by two pink spots that circled the dimples on his cheeks. 'It belongs to my niece. Izzy's six and we had a picnic lunch together yesterday. She was very worried I didn't have a lunch bag to keep my food cold and she made me pinkie-promise her I'd use this one. I'll be in serious trouble if I don't.' He handed her a mug of tea. 'And for the record, I'm a total *Frozen* fan. I mean, what's not to love about strong women?'

She desperately wanted to quip something smart and dismissive but her body was melting in a way it hadn't done in years and her mind was flashing the word 'danger' in bright red letters. Her hand jiggled the tea bag and she studied the action as if her life depended on it. 'You're up to speed with your Disney films then?'

'Put it this way. It got me over the line at the footy trivia night.'

She looked up quickly, not sure if he was teasing her or not, and he laughed at her expression.

'Yeah, the boys won't let me live that down for a while, but hell, there was a weekend for two up for grabs at a boutique B&B in Rutherglen. I wasn't about to let that go even if I did have to admit to knowing the lyrics of "Let It Go".'

This plumber—this country bloke—wasn't fitting into any of the boxes she usually slotted men into. 'I hope your partner appreciates the hit you took for a minibreak.'

This time he was the one to drop his gaze and jiggle his tea bag. 'Actually, I'm single.'

Unforeseen delight collided with very predictable dread, causing her hand to shake. She steadied it by gripping the mug with both hands. 'If you're single, why did you risk all the heckling?'

The tips of his ears glowed red and he took a moment to reply. 'You know that movie where a guy builds a baseball diamond in his corn field?'

'Build it and they will come?'

'Yeah.' He grinned. 'I'm a born optimist.'

She envied that life hadn't stolen that from him. 'But don't those deals normally come with an expiry date?'

He shrugged. 'I've got a few months left and, worst case scenario, I can always mind Izzy for the weekend and give the voucher to Max and Claire.'

This time she choked on her tea. 'Are you sure you're actually real? Next you'll be telling me you like cooking, snuggling on the couch and watching BBC period dramas.'

'I love to cook but I hate cleaning up. I've been told more than once that makes my cooking less of an endearing skill.' His eyes twinkled. 'As for BBC dramas, can you keep a secret?'

You have no idea. 'That depends,' she said coolly, trying to douse the definite skitters of attraction spinning through her. It had been a very long time since they'd woven their magic and not only did she distrust them and their delicious feelings, she feared the chaos they brought.

He pulled some rye bread sandwiches from his lunch box and offered them to her. 'Cheese or corned beef?' She accepted the cheese. 'Once, I tried watching *Pride and Prejudice* to impress Brianna Thornton.'

'Crikey? All five hours? I'm surprised you're not still together.'

'I lasted twenty-five minutes and got kicked off the couch for taking a crack at Mr Darcy.'

She didn't want to smile but she lacked the ability to keep her mouth in a firm line, especially when his baby-blue eyes twinkled with impish glee. 'A wise man never trashes a woman's book boyfriend.'

'So I learned. I've avoided BBC dramas ever since.' He bit into his sandwich and chewed thoughtfully. 'What about you?'

'Do I like a BBC drama?'

'Are you single?'

After all the banter, the direct question took her by surprise. 'Ah. Yes.'

'You don't sound very certain. Are you and Noah's father ...?'

'God, no. We were never together.'

Luke's brows shot to his hairline.

'Okay, obviously, we came together once. It was—' *TMI! TMI! What are you doing?*

'You don't have to tell me.' Except the words were at odds with the curiosity on his handsome face.

'I'm quite aware of that.' She heard the cutting tone she'd perfected over the years waft into the air and join the tumbling yellow poplar leaves.

'Right. Good to know.' He pressed the lid back on the sandwich container with a brisk snap.

The sound carried his pique and disappointment, and regret slapped her hard. Normally, she didn't care if she was brusque and rude to a guy—it was her modus operandi to keep men at bay and it worked like a charm—but Luke had only ever been casually considerate. His solicitousness unnerved the hell out of her. Besides, the story of how Noah came to be was hardly a state secret. Lots of people knew it; just no one in her family. They'd never asked and she'd never offered.

'I'm happy to tell you,' she amended, a tad too late. The set of his mouth said, *Don't do me any favours*, and she hurried on. 'I'm sorry I sounded prickly, especially as you've shared this amazing sandwich—'

'It's the quince paste.'

'What?'

'The secret ingredient that lifts it out of the ordinary and puts it squarely into the realm of spectacular.'

'Okay.' Her heart picked up at his random chit-chat, flustering her. 'Are you deliberately changing the topic?'

'No.' He shot her a wry smile. 'Maybe. You know you can be a little bit scary sometimes, Ellie Jamieson.'

Squads of butterflies swooped and tumbled in her stomach and she was back to being twelve again and watching Luke running backwards. *You know I'm faster than you, Ellie Jamieson.* 'Are you sure you're not just a little bit of a wimp, Luke Sorenson?'

He sat up straight, his shoulders rolling back fast. 'Hey, I'm the one who risked a bit of biffo confessing to knowing Disney lyrics in a town where sport rules, men are men and the arts are for city wankers.'

'I take it back. You're very brave.'

'Damn straight.' He refilled her mug. 'So, Noah's father?'

'Is Dev Vichitrananda. He's Thai.' She settled into the story. 'We worked in the same team for an NGO and we did a lot of work in the refugee camps close to the Thai/Myanmar border. Dev's a friendly guy and was slightly bemused by my decision to work so far from home. He and his wife, Mali, adopted me, insisting I join them for any and all of their family celebrations. They've got three gorgeous daughters and I become an honorary aunt. We were nothing more than colleagues and friends but there was one occasion …' She shivered as she always did when she talked about it. 'We were on our way to visit a camp when floodwaters swept our four-wheel drive off a bridge.'

'Shit.' A deep V carved itself between Luke's brows and his hand rose and hovered as if he was going to reach out and touch her. It fell back to his workwear-clad thigh.

'Oh yeah.' She sipped her tea, welcoming the warmth and staving off the thoughts of muddy, swirling water sucking at her and filling her mouth. 'I still don't know how we survived it. I guess the universe must have decided our time wasn't up that day.'

'I'm glad about that,' Luke said softly.

There was something more than just automatic sincerity in his words and with deadly stealth, they tried to wrap around her heart. She blocked them like she always did and focused on her story.

'Somehow, we managed to get out of the car and out of the rapids. We grabbed overhanging tree branches, vines and each other. We slipped and slid our way to safety and hauled each other up the muddy bank. We were stranded, shocked and traumatised. We'd lost the vehicle and everything in it. Our shoes and hats were gone, Dev lost his shirt and my pants were shredded. By sheer luck we found a village and the headman put us up. It sounds clichéd but that night, the sex just happened. Some survival instinct, I s'pose. Neither of us was thinking straight and we didn't have contraception but to be honest, it didn't even cross my mind. That alone tells me how traumatised I was. We clung to each other to prove we'd fought death and won. Some sort of primal drive. I dunno, really.'

An agonised look crossed his face. 'I get it. It must have been terrifying.'

She nodded slowly, appreciating his lack of judgement. 'Of course, once we were safe and sound and back in Chiang Mai, I regretted it. Dev didn't. He was keen to have an affair but I didn't love him and I adored Mali. She'd only ever been kind to me and I didn't want to do anything that would hurt her. Working with Dev got tricky but I could handle things in the office. When he started visiting my apartment with the expectation of sex, I knew what I had to do. The day after I resigned, I discovered I was pregnant with Noah.'

'But you don't regret him.'

'God, no. He was an unexpected gift.'

'So does Dev know about him?'

'Yes. I send a yearly photo and letter via the office, which is all the contact he wants. It suits me.'

'What about Noah?'

She heard the jangle of judgement in his voice. 'Noah knows he's a special gift to me and that his father lives in Thailand with his family.'

'Won't that come back to bite you in the bum? The kid with the dad who doesn't want him?'

She crossed her arms defensively, glad to finally find a chink in Luke Sorenson's apparently perfect armour and get her wayward body back under control. 'It's not ideal, but even if I'd stayed in Thailand there was no guarantee of Dev being involved. If Noah gets to the point of asking to meet him, then we'll cross that bridge. Meanwhile, Noah is growing up with plenty of love from me, thank you very much. Not everyone grows up with two parents. My father died when I was young and I—' Her throat unexpectedly thickened, blocking the words, *turned out all right.* Not for the first time, she wondered if things would have been different had her father lived. She knew the statistics proved there were no guarantees.

'Sorry, Ellie. That was out of line.' He linked his fingers and stared down at them. 'It's just I'm a big brother and—'

'Are you?' She thought about what Graeme said to her. 'I thought you were the youngest.'

'I'm the middle kid. What I meant was, for the last few years I've volunteered in the Big Brother program.'

'Of course you have,' she muttered, concentrating on reining in the traitorous bubbling attraction that fizzed seductively inside her.

Reminding herself sternly of the times she'd given in to lust and how it never ended well. Fighting the voice in her head that was gleefully singing, *It's okay to like him. This guy's different.*

Only they were never different.

'Anyway,' Luke continued, 'it's made me overly sensitive for kids who have parents who don't want to know them.'

'Yes, well, you don't need to worry about Noah. He and I are just fine.'

'Having extended family helps. I loved growing up with my cousins, and my bachelor uncle used to let me get away with stuff Mum and Dad never allowed.'

'Hmm,' she responded neutrally, not wanting the conversation to head down the path of the joys of family. She jumped to her feet. 'Thanks for the tea and lunch, but I better get going. Work waits for no woman and all that.'

Have you lost your mind? What are you saying?

But Luke wasn't looking at her as if she was crazy—he was just giving her his usual friendly smile. 'Do you need a hand moving?'

'I haven't found a place yet.' She read surprise and concern on his face and pre-empted him. 'Please don't tell me I'm cutting things fine.'

He held up his hands in a gesture of surrender. 'I wouldn't dare but when you find somewhere, give me a shout. I can borrow Max's van and save you some bucks.'

It will put you in his debt. Ellie didn't want to take him up on the offer but she thought about her meagre savings; money she'd earmarked for a promised theme-park holiday for Noah. Professional removalists would decimate the tiny nest egg and those plans, and she didn't want to disappoint her little boy. Perhaps she could counter the debt with one of her own. But what? She wracked her brains. *Build it and they will come.* The voucher for the B&B in Rutherglen represented the relationship Luke was seeking.

There was a new English language teacher at the neighbourhood house who was single, actively looking for the man of her dreams and getting RSI from swiping left on her phone. Luke ticked most boxes on

Cassie's wish list; they'd be a perfect match. When moving time came, she'd invite Cassie to help. There was nothing like bonding over lugging boxes and wrangling a fridge.

And when Luke's no longer single, you won't have to worry about those zips of attraction that terrify you so much.

She didn't realise she was grinning widely until Luke said, 'Is that a yes to helping you move?'

'It is.'

'Good.' He gathered the picnic gear, walked to his ute and stowed it away. 'See ya around, Ellie Jamieson.'

'See ya.' As she watched him drive away, she couldn't help wondering what deeply hidden character flaw kept him single in a district where women lamented the lack of eligible men without ex-wives or children.

CHAPTER TEN

'Sarah's a bloody drama queen,' Cameron grumbled as he stomped through the back door.

'Hello, darling.' Anita jumped up and kissed him. She'd been surfing through photos of decadent and indulgent high teas, gathering ideas for her bookings. The big girls would be home soon on winter school holidays and they were keen to dress up in period black and white maids' uniforms.

Just like on Downton Abbey, *Mum*, Ruby texted.

'I can play my cello,' Phoebe offered over the phone.

Anita had accepted, knowing the cello would make the high tea even more appealing. She'd already filled two dates and was hoping to run four during the school holidays when Mingunyah overflowed with tourists.

'According to Sarah,' Anita said, 'it's Ellie's who's the drama queen. Apparently, she's taken self-obsessed to new heights. She bolted from Mill House the moment Sarah arrived, refusing to stay five minutes, let alone lunch.'

'I told Sarah there was no point asking her and I was right. As always, Ellie's put the wind up Mum and upset her enough to plonk her back in hospital. Talk about the daughter from hell.' He sat down. 'Man, I'm starving.'

Anita pulled Cameron's dinner from the warming drawer. 'How's Margaret?'

'Sitting up like Lady Muck and tucking in to dinner. The hospital's keeping her in for observation overnight. The doc wants her to have a scan tomorrow and see a specialist. You know doctors. I bet he's just covering his arse.'

'She'll have to go to Melbourne for a scan.' Anita slid the plate onto the cork-backed placemat and poured each of them a glass of wine. 'I guess Sarah will drive her.'

'I'm going to take her.'

'Are you sure you can spare the time?'

'It will kill two birds with one stone. I need to see Rupert about that tax issue anyway, and Mum's not happy with Dan Horton. I've made her an appointment to talk to Rupert before the scan so she can get an unbiased opinion on her finances.'

'Have you seen her will yet?'

'No.' He grimaced. 'The other day she got so cross with bland Dan, she left before I could broach the topic.'

'But you've got power of attorney. Can't you just demand Dan show it to you?'

'Maybe. But I know Dan and he's just as likely to tell Sarah.'

'Why would that be a problem?'

Cameron gave her an indulgent look. 'Because Sarah's got a bee in her bonnet about wills and personal finances being private. I know she's my sister and your friend but I can live without the inevitable rant that will come my way if she finds out I want to look at it.'

'Sarah's forgotten what it's like to live on a budget.' Anita took a sip of her wine. 'We've got the girls' education to think about. We deserve to make some plans for our future. I know it's totally Margaret's right to leave Mill House to whoever she wishes, but I don't want to build the business around it only to discover it's not going to be ours. That would be soul destroying.' She sighed. 'I'd really like to know her plans for the house.'

'Exactly. I'm pretty certain it's all going to work in our favour, because she's letting you use the house for the business.'

'I hope so.' But Anita had learned the hard way that nothing in life was guaranteed. 'I'd still like to know either way. Are you certain your mother doesn't have a copy of her will in one of those filing cabinets in the office? I could look through them tomorrow when you and Margaret are in Melbourne.'

He kissed her. 'I like the way you think.'

After Alex's bombshell, Sarah should have known that life can change direction without notice and been prepared. Perhaps, she reflected, it was the human condition not to dwell on possible disasters but to face the day with the belief that all would be well, otherwise no one would get up in the morning. Today had put paid to that ideology. First there was her mother's accident and then Ellie's bizarre behaviour at Mill House. Despite her aggravated disappointment in her sister, she had reluctantly heeded Ellie's text and returned their mother to hospital. The staff didn't seem unduly concerned and Margaret was lapping up all the attention, but given Sarah's recent experiences, she was struggling to feel positive about much at all. She'd rung Edmund from the hospital to cancel dinner.

'Your mother's in good hands, yes?'

'Yes, the staff are great and her doctor's running every test under the sun.'

'Surely, then, you are allowed a couple of hours off? I think you need to forget about everyone. Come to dinner and just be yourself.'

She'd caved to the care in his voice and driven to Protea. Strung out and anxious, she'd stepped into the beautifully appointed restaurant, accepted a glass of Mt Morag Chardonnay and a Freycinet oyster with finger lime roe and lemon foam, and immediately relaxed.

'You have the best staff, Edmund,' she told him as they ate, seated at the end of the long table with a view out onto the street. 'They're fun, entertaining and passionate about food.'

'Being passionate about food is my one non-negotiable when hiring. They can learn the finer art of waiting on the job.'

'It's paid off. It's obvious they adore you.'

'I learned from the best.'

'Stefan?' Before opening Protea, Edmund spent a summer working with the famous chef.

Edmund shot her a rueful smile. 'Stefan is brilliant with food but not so brilliant with staff. I was talking about you.'

'Me?' Pleasure fluttered in her chest.

'Why so surprised? I had no cheese-making skills and you took me on when I needed a job.'

She laughed lightly, remembering those heady days when sheer exhilaration mixed with gut-churning dread. 'When you turned up looking for work, we were so tired and desperate I probably would have hired you even if you'd said you hated cheese.'

'I doubt that. You have great people skills. You find their passion and match it to the job.'

'It's a shame I didn't know Kelly's passion was Alex.'

Edmund's fingertips brushed the back of her hand. 'Tonight is about taking a break from all of that.'

She wanted to yell, 'How can I?' but then she remembered his own loss. 'Is that how you cope?'

'In the early days.' He rubbed his jaw. 'Taking breaks where I refused to think about any of it was the only way I survived.'

She locked her fingers with his and squeezed gently. Whenever she thought about what life had inflicted upon Edmund, she always gave thanks it hadn't happened to her. Everyone did. 'In that case, I bow to your experience.'

And she did. She spent the evening enthusiastically sampling everything the chef had prepared for the degustation menu. She savoured the perfectly matched wines and joined in the discussion on which food and wines made her palate sing. It was years since she'd eaten or drunk so much.

With her body buzzing and her arm linked easily through Edmund's in the relaxed way of old friends, she appreciated the bracing winter-chilled air on the walk home. When they reached the front door of the old cheese factory, the thought of being alone in the flat surrounded by all the happy memories Alex had now tarnished hit her like a brick.

'Nightcap?' she asked and immediately wondered if there was anything still in the small cupboard she and Alex used as a bar all those years ago.

'Why not?' Edmund followed her up the stairs before helping her off with her coat. He hung his and hers on the wobbly coat stand she'd found in the op shop nineteen years earlier. Back in a time when her wallet held more dust particles than dollars.

'Sorry about the mess.' She picked up a half-full coffee cup, suddenly acutely embarrassed by her depression-induced slothfulness. 'I've been a bit distracted since I moved in.'

'No need to apologise for anything, Sarah.' Edmund was squatting down in front of the drinks cupboard. Despite everything life had thrown at him, she was struck by how square his shoulders were. How straight his back. Why hadn't she ever noticed that about him before? Glass clinked against glass and her fuzzy mind finally decoded that Edmund was talking again.

'Sorry?'

He held aloft a dark green bottle. 'Port?'

'Lovely.' She rummaged through another cupboard and found some dusty liqueur glasses. After a quick rinse and dry, Edmund filled the crystal glasses before carrying them to the couch. They sat, sipping the rich tawny liqueur, and she welcomed the mellow warmth stealing through her, stripping the tension from her muscles.

'Thank you for a lovely evening. For being such a good friend.'

'Always.' He leaned in, kissing her gently on the forehead. 'You know I'm always here for you.'

She wasn't so drunk she didn't notice he'd dropped his usual 'and Alex'.

Surrounded by memories and too tired to hold her head up any longer, she let it fall onto his shoulder. 'Remember the night we stayed up until 4 am filling our first big order for the Lygon Street Deli?'

'I remember you filling me with coffee and berating me for crooked labels.'

'Presentation makes people buy the cheese,' she said automatically, the mantra as much a part of her as her limbs.

'And then we hook them with the taste,' he said, attempting to mimic her voice and smiling. 'You taught me that too. I say it to my staff.'

'That order was our first big turning point. It put us on Melbourne's foodie radar.'

'And then you moved to Riverbend.' Something in his voice made her look up. 'For a long time, I missed this place. Missed working so closely with you.'

The quietly spoken words combined with the soft touch of his fingers in her hair and it lit along her veins. Suddenly, she was very awake. 'But you and Catriona were ...'

He shook his head. 'Not then. That came later. Months after the new cheese factory. For a long time, it was you. In a way, it's always been you.'

She stared at her dear friend, her mind spinning. 'I ... I didn't know.'

He shrugged. 'I didn't let you know. There was no point. You were in love with your husband. But now Alex has hurt you. He has no idea what he has in you. If he did, he wouldn't be doing this. You don't deserve it.'

Now his hand was on the back of her neck, gently cupping her skin. His warmth and tenderness infused her and her blood pumped it quickly around her body in a heady rush. For the first time in days—hell, weeks—she felt cared for and cherished instead of judged and discarded.

'You're a beautiful woman, Sarah. Inside and out.'

Gratitude almost made her weep.

The kiss was natural; the coming together of two close friends who were used to greeting each other with warmth and affection. Her response to it, however, was far from familiar. Her body leaped, surging on the heady elixir of being wanted and utterly deaf to the tiny voice of reason saying, *Unwise*.

Whether it was the culmination of the days of shock from Alex's betrayal, anxiety about her mother's health, concern for her kids, her large intake of alcohol or a mixture of everything, she let go of her pain and heartache. Giving herself over to the blissful and delicious sensations that strummed her body, she tumbled into bed with Edmund.

With the pearly rays of dawn peeking in around the blinds and sneaking under her eyelids, Sarah opened her eyes. The peach light swooped in across the bedclothes and a sharp pain dug into her head. She quickly squeezed her eyelids shut and without the distraction of sunshine, slowly tuned into the body heat warming her back. She stiffened from head to toe. Edmund's arm lay across her chest and his leg was hooked high and snug between her thighs. Her very naked thighs.

Oh God. She'd had drunken sex with Edmund.

Her vagina fluttered involuntarily and hopefully at the thought and she stifled a groan. It had been good sex, which, considering the circumstances, was totally unexpected. Wasn't sex with a stranger supposed to be fraught with fumbling and missteps? Not that she had any real idea, given she'd slept with the same man for twenty-four years. She and Alex knew each other's bodies intimately and knew exactly what turned each other on. Before Alex, her experience had been limited and very fumbling.

But she and Edmund hadn't fumbled at all. Despite her

intoxication—or perhaps because of it—they'd had surprising rhythm. On the back of misery and fuelled by far too much booze, she'd given in completely to the heady addiction of being adored. A delicious shiver ran across her skin. Edmund had held nothing back and offered her everything. She'd taken it all and then some.

Shame flared hard and fast, spreading an itching discomfort that came close to guilt. Oh God. She'd committed adultery. What would her mother say if she ever found out? Margaret talked *a lot* about the sanctity of marriage. Hell, she still invoked it twenty-six years after her husband's death, especially if someone asked her why she'd never remarried.

What on earth are you on about? This is Alex's fault. Alex broke our marriage vows first.

He didn't have sex with Kelly!

Shut up! He will have by now. I'm just evening the score.

The idea should have soothed her but instead it made her heart race. She'd just had sex with her dearest friend. *It's okay, you love him.* Of course she loved him; he'd delivered Gus. Still, she had a gnawing feeling that perhaps she didn't love Edmund with quite the same intensity that he loved her.

'Good morning.'

She jumped as Edmund's mellow voice stroked her ear. With anxiety pressing painfully on her chest, she rolled over to face him. 'Good morning.'

The smile that greeted her—filled with love, admiration and contentment—flipped her stomach with a jolt of longing. Perhaps she should listen closely to her body. It was clearly telling her that her mind was an idiot and she loved and wanted Edmund plenty.

He kissed her gently on the forehead. 'I should go before the joggers hit the streets.'

'Okay.'

'I'll call you later.'

'Okay.' *Okay?* She should be using big, grown-up words in cohesive sentences but her heart and mind were too busy competing for supremacy.

He laughed fondly. 'You need coffee. I'll brew you some before I leave.'

Appreciation and trepidation flooded her. 'Thank you, but as amazing as last night was, I don't think you have the time to make coffee and miss the joggers. I'm not ready to share what happened with the town and have it driving the gossip mill.'

'I understand.'

It crossed her mind that Alex would have said something like, 'I *was* pretty amazing last night, wasn't I?' before kissing her and demonstrating once again exactly how amazing he could be. Did he say things like that to Kelly? Her heart twisted and she made an involuntary sound.

'Is everything all right?'

'Everything is perfect.' The lie was far less fraught than the truth. Besides, it was too early in the day to contemplate the mess that was currently her life, especially when her body was still delighting in the lingering effects of good sex.

Edmund swung out of bed and shoved his long legs into his trousers. She didn't know whether to lie there and admire the body she'd explored in the dark with her mouth and her hands or look the other way. Excitement duelled with decorum. This situation was a perfect example of why she'd loved being married: there were well-established protocols. She could gaze at Alex dressed or naked as little or as much as she wanted and she'd gazed plenty, having lost all skerrick of embarrassment years ago. But this was different—she was clueless on the rules of morning-after behaviour. Some people might find it exciting and exhilarating; she found it both those things as well as daunting and exhausting.

The mattress moved again and then Edmund was squatting by her side of the bed. 'I hope your mother's test results are good.'

She touched Edmund's cheek. 'Thank you.'

He turned his head and pressed a kiss into her palm before

standing and striding across the room. She heard the front door close and then she rolled onto her back and stared up at the ceiling, thinking about the night before. She was grinning widely when reality hit her. *Shit.* Having sex with Edmund meant she'd just gone and squandered the moral high ground with Alex.

You're overcomplicating this. Alex doesn't know. He doesn't need to know. No one needs to know. You're a grown woman. Take responsibility for your actions.

But they were actions she would never have contemplated, let alone taken, if Alex hadn't pulverised her heart into a thousand tiny pieces.

'Argh!' She threw off the covers and got up, welcoming the chill of the floorboards against the soles of her feet. As she padded to the shower, the irony of her current situation hit her. For a month, she'd wanted some time to herself and now that she had it, she craved the back-to-back busyness of work to still the machinations of her mind.

After a slice of breakfast seed loaf slathered in homemade strawberry jam and far too much coffee, Sarah telephoned Cameron. He was driving to Melbourne with their mother and he answered on speakerphone. Margaret kept asking, 'Where are you, Sarah?' and Sarah finished the call wearing a heavy coat of remorse. She should be the one driving her mother to her appointment. She should have insisted on it, but she'd been so taken aback by Cameron's unexpected offer that she'd agreed without thinking past, *It's about time you did something to help.* Now her selfishness was causing her mother anguish and grief. As much as Margaret adored Cameron, Sarah knew her mother appreciated her for her sensitivity and caring; two things Cameron wasn't known for.

There was more than one way to help her mother and she picked up her keys, gripped by the need to compensate for this lapse. She'd spend the day tackling Margaret's filing cabinet—a task that would not only assist Margaret but keep her mind away from the tangled mess that was Alex and Edmund and the tingling sensations of pleasure that whipped her whenever she thought about the night before. Lust and guilt were a hell of a cocktail.

Just like when she was a kid, she amused herself on the short walk to Mill House by blowing into the fresh alpine air and watching her breath vaporise. Mrs Makin gave her a wave as she passed and Sarah got the same grip in her stomach she always did when she remembered the magnificent elms, oaks and bunya pines that had been felled to make way for the new estate. Her childhood garden was now covered in cookie cutter–style housing lacking any architectural character. Sarah and Cameron had both strongly argued with Margaret over the decision to subdivide the large property Mill House once sat on. In fact, it was one of the few times they'd joined forces either for or against their mother, but it was an alliance of convenience. Cameron, who had still been angry over the sale of the saw mill, considered the subdivision another betrayal.

Sarah had grieved for the garden; for the chance to show yet-to-be-conceived children the joys and wonders of playing hide and seek in the grove of silver birches. She also grieved for the gauzy memories of time spent there with her father, both of them escaping from the house and Margaret's critical comments. In the end, despite aligning herself with Cameron, neither of their arguments prevailed. It was Robert Horton who won the day—again. He'd invested the profits from the sale of the land and gone on to double them for Margaret, giving her more financial security than she'd ever known.

The familiar and worn bluestone steps of the red-brick Georgian house welcomed her, as did the faded gold lettering above the door. *Mill House 1845*. As she slid the key into the lock, the door swung open before she'd turned it. The hairs on her arm stood up. The door should be locked. Had the thieves who'd stolen her mother's car returned?

You're being ridiculous. It's probably Anita.

But it's Wednesday. There's no reason for Anita to be here.

'Hello! Anita?'

'Sarah?' Her sister-in-law's voice floated from the depths of the house. 'Yes. It's me.' Anita met her just as she reached the kitchen door and gave her a kiss. 'Hello. I wasn't expecting you.'

A prickly feeling ran up her spine, a righteous sense of ownership for her childhood home. 'I wasn't aware I needed to call.'

'No, of course not,' Anita said, her words breathy and her cheeks flushed pink. 'I'm just surprised to see you. I've been ordering things for my first high tea.'

Sarah, who was still on the fence about the entire project of using Mill House for Cooked By a Friend, wondered why Anita needed to be here to place an order. Surely she could have done that from home? As she was thinking it through, Anita's words suddenly registered.

'High tea?'

'Yes!' Anita clapped her hands like an excited six-year-old. 'I'm having so much fun planning it.'

'I thought you were only doing the occasional cooking class here?'

'I am, but high teas are all the rage. This house is the perfect setting and Margaret has the Spode to make it really special for the guests.'

Sarah felt her jaw clench. Guests? They were paying customers. 'And Mum's okay with all of this?'

'Of course.' Anita touched Sarah's arm. 'You know I wouldn't be doing it if she wasn't.'

Sarah took in Anita's worried expression and sighed. 'Of course you've run it past her. I'm sorry. It's just with everything that's going on with Mum and Alex and ...' *Don't mention Edmund.* The warning surprised her because Anita was the first person she'd wanted to tell about Alex's perfidy. 'The kids.'

'You're stressed. I get it.' Anita glanced at her watch. 'I have to be at the Farrells' out on Tannery Road by ten thirty, but I can squeeze in a quick cup of tea.'

Chatting over a cup of tea put Sarah at risk of blurting out something about Edmund. 'Thanks, but you'd be cutting it fine to make it on time. I'm good. Really. I've got a list of things to do for Mum that will keep me occupied for most of the day.'

'Well, if you're sure ...' Anita was already fishing for her keys from a designer handbag Sarah hadn't seen before and heading to the door.

Sarah walked with her, waved goodbye and then threw the lock on the front door before going directly to the study. Although the room had been painted and the chesterfield reupholstered, it still looked much the same as it had when her grandfather was in residence. As a child, the painting 'Hounds on the Hunt' fascinated her not only because of its content but also because, to her knowledge, her grandfather and her parents had never hunted. Her mother's decorating choices were always a mystery to her; some things Margaret modernised with ruthless efficiency and others she refused to change. The painting was a perfect example.

Sarah switched on her mother's computer. Although Margaret was 'on the line', as she insisted on referring to the internet, her computer was five years old and slow. For over a year, Sarah had been suggesting that Margaret invest in a new computer and that Finn or Gus would set it up for her and teach her how to use it. Her mother, however, was resisting in her obstinate way that could never be predicted. Each time Sarah was secure in her anticipation of her mother's reaction to something, Margaret would do the complete opposite. The computer was a case in point. Her mother prided herself on being the first of her social set to acquire a computer and later a smartphone. Email and texting were now part of Margaret's way of life and she was often heard to say, 'I love the internet.' But then she asked Sarah to book theatre tickets and accommodation for her because 'I don't trust the internet'. Sarah was happy to help but occasionally wondered at Margaret's logic that it was fine for her daughter to risk her credit card to hackers when she wasn't prepared to risk her own.

Plugging her phone into the computer, Sarah turned on the speakers and selected her '80s music playlist, starting with Duran Duran. She turned to face the walnut filing cabinet. As well as being functional, it was a beautiful piece of furniture. Should she start with the top or the bottom drawer? Starting at the bottom meant she could sit so she sat, tugged on the brass handle and then pulled out the green expansion files. The first four contained instruction manuals for long-gone items such as her father's pride and joy, the 1983 Bose sound system. She pictured Kevin standing in the centre of the lounge room, head tilted, listening intently to the crisp sound and smoking his pipe. When he noticed her watching him, he'd smile and open his arms. Even if she didn't like the music, she always snuggled in next to him just to be near him.

Oh, Dad. You would have loved the kids. She shook off the melancholy, wondering why her father had been popping in and out of her thoughts recently. Was it because he'd only been forty-nine when he'd died and Alex was now forty-seven?

Kevin had died before Sarah met Alex but she felt sure her father would have liked him. They certainly shared a lot of traits. Well, they had, right up until last week. Over the years, she'd sometimes pondered the similarities between the two men she loved. Had part of her attraction to Alex been that he reminded her of her father? They certainly shared the ability to fix just about anything.

She tossed the manual for the Victa lawn mower into the discard pile. It had been a lemon from the moment her mother bought it, and she'd given it to Sarah and Alex when they'd first returned to Australia. Alex immediately took it apart and rebuilt it, only to discover one piece left over. Despite the machine running better than it ever had, he dismantled it again, just like Kevin would have done, and started over. Alex always lavished love and care on engines; apparently he was only cavalier with relationships.

Sarah ditched more aged and expired warranties and manuals for a variety of household items, including the colour television her parents bought in 1975—they were one of the first families in Mingunyah to own one; a 1980 state-of-the-art Molineux food processor that came with every possible attachment and Sarah barely remembered her mother ever using; two fridges; one freezer and three washing machines. Then she started on the ten— *ten!*—manila folders of receipts. Had her mother kept a receipt for everything she'd ever purchased? Sarah could understand the meticulous care of jewellery receipts—they were important for insurance purposes—but the rest of the receipts were yellowed with age and could have been chucked out years ago.

The playlist moved into '90s music and she needed the soaring beats of Coldplay as she started on the middle drawer. The first few expander files held old tax returns and bank statements, which she was hesitant to throw away so she invoked a 'decade' rule and put the rest in an archive box just in case Margaret freaked out. Dust clung to her nostrils, making everything smell musty and old, and her stomach rumbled. She pushed the drawer closed and pondered her options for lunch. She could duck out to the bakery but when she'd done that the day before, the staff had presented her with a raft of issues and expected her to solve them. Best to stay in and rustle up something from the fridge.

As she left the study her phone beeped with a message from Edmund. It was short and sweet: *Thank you.*

A fizz of delight spun through her. He wanted her. He appreciated her. Unlike her husband, he didn't want space from her. But as Alex's words came at her with the accuracy of a long-range missile, they cast doubt and uncertainty over Edmund's message. What did 'thank you' really mean? *Thank you and let's do it again? Thank you, but the real you didn't live up to my long-held fantasy, so goodbye?*

Stop it! She hated how wayward and runaway thoughts invaded her mind and totally took over. Five days ago, she'd rarely second guessed anything about herself or her life; she'd never needed to. She'd known exactly who she was—a loving and loved wife, a loving and loved mother and daughter, and an award-winning businesswoman running an internationally successful business. Her life was full albeit slightly out of balance, but she'd been planning on rectifying that. All it had taken to upend her equanimity and make her question everything was Alex saying, *I need space from you.*

'I need food,' she said out loud to shut up the voices. She opened the fridge with a jerk.

Her jaw dropped. Instead of the usual bottle of milk, the two main shelves in the door were filled with one-litre Tetra Paks of tomato juice. At first she thought they must belong to Anita, but then she remembered Anita was using the fridge in the butler's pantry; the health department had approved that one because the food for her classes had to be kept separate from Margaret's.

Why did her mother have eight boxes of tomato juice in her fridge? Seeking answers, Sarah's gaze shifted to the interior shelves. There was an opened container of yoghurt, a black banana, a Tupperware container labelled 'Chicken Casserole' in Anita's distinctive Victorian modern cursive script, some cheese slices—*seriously, Mum? Plastic cheese?*—a box of her mother's favourite chocolates and a packet of batteries.

Batteries? She was reminded of the time when the kids were little and she'd been so distracted that she'd once put a Lego toy in the fridge and the jam in the toy box. Picking up the batteries, she turned them over. The day before, Ellie had insisted their mother was confused. Sarah hadn't seen any evidence of disorientation and was convinced that if Ellie spent more time with Margaret, she wouldn't be making such outrageous claims. But batteries in the fridge and a surfeit of tomato juice did give her pause. She reminded herself that Margaret had been on the way to the supermarket when the accident occurred, which would account for the lack of food in the fridge.

She was relieved to find half-a-dozen frozen meals, a loaf of bread and a tub of salted caramel ice cream in the freezer. Given the limited lunch options, Sarah overrode her foodie soul and made herself a toastie with the mass-produced cheese. She chased it with an apple and some tomato juice.

She was just rinsing the plate when her phone rang, displaying her brother's name. 'Cameron, how's Mum?'

'That's why I'm calling.'

A pain twisted in her chest. 'What's happened?'

'Apparently, she's had a mild stroke.'

Sarah sat down hard as memories of her grandfather with a tightly clawed hand and a drooping, drooling mouth assailed her. 'Oh God, how bad?'

'Jeez, Sarah. I said mild. Why are you always such a panic merchant?'

And just like that she was fifteen again and visualising slamming her fist into his handsome, sneering face. 'Define "mild"? Can she talk? Walk?'

'To be honest, I can't notice too much difference. She's got some problems swallowing and her speech is a bit slurred. They're admitting her to monitor her overnight. If there's no change by noon tomorrow they'll transfer her to Mingunyah for rehab. They're talking about physio and stuff so she'll probably be in hospital for a few weeks but it's easier at home than down here.'

'I'll drive down.'

'It's not worth it. Even if you leave now, you'd get stuck in peak hour traffic and by the time you arrive, visiting hours will almost be over. I'm staying at the apartment tonight and we can discuss it all in the morning when we know more. If she needs to stay longer in Melbourne, you can drive down and bring her some nighties.'

'Well, if you're sure.' Sarah hated conceding that his plan made sense.

'It's what you'd tell me if the situation was reversed.'

And she couldn't argue with that. 'Can I talk to her?'

'She's having tests.'

'Oh, right. Well, please send her my love.' A loud rumbling noise that sounded a lot like a tram filled her ear. 'Where are you?'

'Outside the hospital.'

Granted, it had been a long since she'd been to Heidelberg, but she was fairly confident that no trams ran past the hospital. 'I thought her appointment was at the Austin?'

'It got changed. I have to go. I'll text you the details.'

The line went dead just as she asked, 'But where's Mum?'

Fuming, she stared at her phone. Why was it that even when Cameron was being helpful, he still managed to annoy her? Without thinking, she opened a new text message and was halfway through typing it when she stopped. Were you supposed to tell your estranged husband about your mother's mild stroke?

You're not estranged. It's time apart.

I slept with Edmund.

Had that one act pushed her over an invisible line into separation territory?

It doesn't have to. You didn't promise Alex you wouldn't sleep with someone.

That's because I was never going to do it!

According to the *Cosmopolitan* magazine she'd found in Emma's room a couple of months earlier, young women now owned their sexual needs and monogamy wasn't guaranteed. She remembered saying, 'Rubbish!' before tossing it into the recycling. As much as she wanted to think that she'd owned her sexual needs the night before, she knew it was alcohol and a floundering self-esteem that had taken total control. She felt lost and at sea in a life devoid of all the usual anchors and now her mother was sick, adding to her discombobulation. Needing the routine job of filing more than ever, she returned to the study and pulled open the top and final drawer.

Unlike the previous drawers, this one contained more recent paperwork, although it lacked the rigid labelling system of the older files. The first suspension folder contained a mishmash of photos: Emma, Phoebe and Ruby on horseback; Noah standing proudly next to a sandcastle; her parents' wedding; Cameron in his christening frock; and one of her and Alex looking young and happy, bouncing Finn and Gus on their knees. A lump rose in her throat, fast followed by a wave of anger.

Why, Alex? Why?

Tossing the folder aside, she picked up the next one. It appeared to be bills: phone, power, property rates, home and contents insurance and car insurance. She set the car insurance aside; her mother's car would need some panel work. When she returned to the untidy pile she glimpsed the words 'Tack and Co'. Wondering what her mother could have possibly bought from Mingunyah's horse-riding equipment store, she pulled out the paper. She blinked at the $5125 invoice for an equestrian saddle.

She immediately recalled Anita telling her that Ruby was thrilled with her new saddle. Sarah had assumed Cameron had bought it, but it appeared it was their mother who had paid the big bucks. Given Margaret wasn't known for her generosity outside of birthdays and Christmas, and even then her giving was fiscally prudent, the saddle was an incredibly munificent gift. A twinge of jealousy scurried uncomfortably through Sarah. Margaret had never given a gift to Finn, Gus or Emma that came anywhere close to the price of the saddle, and they were the grandchildren who'd received most of Margaret's attention.

Ruby is Cameron's child. The needy and traitorous voice from her childhood—one she hadn't heard in years—rose shrilly in her mind. *Cameron's the golden child, the favourite. She loves him more.*

Sarah shook herself. Her mother had the right to spend her money any way she chose and if she wished to give a saddle to Ruby, who was a very talented rider, then Sarah had no right to comment.

She returned her attention to the job at hand, tossing the utility bills that were older than a year along with the expired insurance certificates. The recycling pile grew larger by the minute.

It was inside the last suspension folder, stuck between a brochure for a cruise and an invoice for travel insurance, that she found a plastic sleeve containing an invoice and a certificate of authenticity for a cello.

Her mind boggled at the five-figure sum. This must be the documentation for Phoebe's cello. The cello both Anita and Cameron constantly bemoaned the cost of while at the same time bragging about how much talent blessed Phoebe, and how the purchase of a lesser instrument would disadvantage her. Cameron had stood in Sarah's kitchen a year earlier saying, 'We had no choice but to fork out the big bucks. But dear God, if the little girls want to learn an instrument, it has to be the recorder.'

'Jesus!' Were Cameron and Anita lying because they wanted to spare her feelings that their daughters were receiving incredibly generous gifts when they knew the other grandchildren were not? Did they assume that her kids had already received gifts like this in the past and, as nothing had ever been said, there was a tacit agreement to obfuscate? Or were they lying because they'd asked Margaret to pay?

With the deft skill of a clerk with an ink-blackened rubber thimble on her finger, she determinedly raced through the paperwork. Finally, she sat back, sweat pooling on her eyelids and she tried to slow her racing heart. She'd found six partial payments to her older nieces' exclusive and expensive Melbourne girls' school. Cameron and Anita had not only lied to her; they'd done it on multiple occasions. That Cameron had lied didn't shock or surprise Sarah as much as it should, but Anita—her lies cut like a knife, the pain sharp and eviscerating. Anita was her sister and confidante. They told each other everything.

You haven't told her about Edmund.

That's totally different.

From the day Cameron had introduced a young, wide-eyed and overwhelmed Anita to the family, Sarah had loved her and had been determined to be the sister Anita never had. In turn, Anita became the sister Sarah had wished for in Ellie but had never known. Anita joked she and Sarah were so close that if she turned up with a dead body, Sarah would just grab the gloves and shovel and later provide the wine, no questions asked. So why had she lied about the cello, the saddle and the school fees?

Was it Cameron's idea to lie? Anita's unquestioning spousal allegiance always puzzled Sarah, but then again, what did she know? Cameron wasn't the husband who'd told his wife he wasn't happy and hadn't been for a long time. Even so, Sarah couldn't fathom Anita's behaviour unless she was an unwilling participant. That idea made more sense and she was momentarily reassured until a voice inside her head said, *What else don't they want you to know about?*

As if on cue, Anita's name lit up her phone.

'Hi, Anita,' Sarah said tightly, then forced herself to add in friendlier tones, 'What's up?'

'Oh my God, Sarah. What a shock about Margaret. Just as well she was in Melbourne when it happened.'

'Just as well it was mild.'

'Yes, of course, that too. But Cameron says she's going to need rehabilitation.'

'And we might need to seriously talk about her moving.'

'I hope that won't be necessary.'

Something about the way Anita said the words ran up a warning flag. Was her sister-in-law's concern for Margaret or was it for her cooking classes and high teas?

'The most important thing is we do what's best for Mum.'

'Absolutely. But really, it's too early to be making any big decisions, especially when we don't know all the details.'

Details was right! Sarah knew nothing about the details of a saddle, a $15,000 cello or $20,000 worth of school fees. 'How's Ruby enjoying her new saddle?' The question was petty and she instantly regretted it. This situation needed to be finessed and tackling Anita about it over the phone was not the way to go.

'Oh, she loves it. Did I tell you that the first time she competed using it, she got a blue ribbon in the schools' equestrian event?'

Sarah knew she should just say, 'How exciting,' and change the subject. But she glanced at the invoice for the saddle and, with the bit between her teeth, threw caution to the wind. 'I bet Cameron had fun beating Rob Bartlett down on the price.'

'You know how he loves to haggle. He got a good price but it still cost us a small fortune.' Anita gave a tinkling laugh. 'But I'm not telling you anything. You bought a new saddle for Emma last year.'

She had, but it had cost a fifth of what Ruby's had. Hang on! Anita just said, 'it still cost us a small fortune'. Not 'it cost Margaret a small fortune' or even 'it cost a small fortune'. Fury blew through Sarah like a hot north wind, leaving treachery and mistrust swirling in her gut. If Anita was lying about the gifts, then it was only a small leap to assume she was lying about other things. Suddenly the idea of Anita having free run of Mill House without Margaret there to monitor things seriously bothered her.

CHAPTER ELEVEN

Ellie listened to Noah reading to her, his mouth slowly forming the challenging words, and tried not to let her concentration wander. She wanted to be present, wanted to enjoy his childhood, but her responsibilities pressed in on her. She inhaled her son's sweet, clean scent and absorbed the heat from his soft, warm body. Unlike the summer, when it was hard to get him inside and sitting still, the early fall of winter darkness lent itself to early bath time, dinner and snuggling up.

'Pen-ell-lope.' Noah sounded out the name on the page.

'Pen-ell-o-pee,' she corrected him.

He was on the second last page of the book when he suddenly stopped reading and scrambled to the edge of the bed. 'Someone's here.'

She grabbed the back of his pyjama top. 'Everyone's here and you know the deal. You can't go and play with Bree until you've finished your reader.'

'No, silly,' he said with an exaggerated eye roll. 'I mean a visitor.'

'It's not polite to call people silly.'

Up until the eviction notice, drop-in visitors had been rare at the old farm but that didn't mean the household wasn't social. To be accurate, Wendy, Grace and Rachel were very social and Ellie enjoyed being included in their slipstream. Her housemates' friends were an eclectic group and in the past two years, they'd thrown them a winter solstice dinner, a spring blossom frolic and an autumn harvest picnic in the orchard. Without a dam, a pool or access to the river, summer was just too hot for entertaining at home.

Home. The word dragged across her mind like a blunt blade. It wasn't going to be home for very much longer. Already it had an air of ennui, with packing boxes stacked in the hall. What had been the happiest household she'd ever lived in was breaking up and whenever she thought about it, she fought back tears. For the previous couple of weeks, friends had been dropping in unannounced— often with wine—to grieve with them and say a last farewell to the quaint old house and orchard.

Noah strained forward. 'But I want to see who it is.'

Her son was far more sociable and interested in people than Ellie, which she conceded was a good thing. From the moment he was born, she'd been determined to do everything in her power to protect his innocent trust and enthusiasm.

'It's probably Grace's friend, Liz. She said she might call in.'

Noah's face fell. 'She's no fun.'

Ellie tousled his hair. 'In that case you're not missing out on a thing. Come on, you were up to here.'

In a begrudging tone, Noah read, 'Penelope watched the bees—'

'Ellie,' Wendy called. 'You've got a visitor.'

'Wow.' Noah gave her a wide-eyed look that initially made her smile before it backhanded her with a stinging and rebuking slap. 'No one ever visits us.'

Because she never invited anyone.

'I wonder who it is?' *Luke?* His name came uninvited and a fizz of either dread or anticipation—it was hard to tell—made her feel giddy and shivery.

'I'll go.' Noah was already at the door.

'Wait.' But he was gone before Ellie could shove her feet into her uggies.

She hated that she paused on the way to the door to check her face in the mirror. *You don't do that, remember? You don't care.* But the mocking laugh she heard in the back of her mind said otherwise.

'Mummy!' Noah met her in the hall, grabbing her hand and tugging her towards the lounge room. 'It's Sarah.'

A wave of disappointment hit her with the nerve-tingling shock of icy water. She didn't have the time or the desire to analyse the intensity of her feelings: they said far too much about her to be comfortable. What did strike her was that if it had been Luke standing in her lounge room, his presence would seem more normal than Sarah's. Even before yesterday's uncomfortable incident at Mill House, Sarah had never visited Guthrie Farm.

Ellie was used to seeing Sarah in her work wardrobe of black pants, white blouse and a smart, fitted fleece-lined shell with Mingunyah Bread and Cheese stitched over her left breast. Today, she wore faded jeans and a pretty Liberty print blouse that was buttoned up crookedly. Sarah's cheeks bore two red hot spots and her hair was hat flat, making her look both angry and sad all at the same time. Although Sarah was never as put together as Anita, it was unusual to see her without foundation and lipstick.

Ellie girded herself for a lecture on familial responsibilities. 'Hi, Sarah. This is unexpected.'

'I suppose it is.'

'Sarah!' Noah slipped his hand inside his aunt's. 'Do you want to listen to me finish my reader?'

Ellie formed a sentence, ready to temper his disappointment when Sarah inevitably told him she'd come to speak to his mum, but her sister was giving her son a fond smile and tousling his hair.

'I'd love to, Noah, and after that I need to talk to Mummy.'

'I'll put the kettle on,' Ellie said, surprised by Sarah's acquiescence. *That's not fair. Sarah's always been good with Noah.*

'I brought wine.' Sarah thrust a brown paper bag at her. 'Pour this instead.'

As Sarah followed Noah down the hall, Ellie slid the bottle out of its covering and surprise gave way to appreciation. Unlike some members of her family, her sister could never be faulted on her generosity. Even if Sarah planned to give her a serve for running away from Mill House, at least she'd do it over good wine.

When she returned, Sarah said, 'I hope it's okay, but he's watching TV with Bree. He said you'd promised but my kids used to play Alex and me off each other to get what they wanted. They probably still do.'

Ellie pushed a glass towards her sister, already filled with the expensive and full-bodied cab sav. 'He's telling the truth. It's his post-reader reward.'

Sarah took a seat on the couch that was disappearing into a removal van in forty-eight hours. She glanced around. 'This room's warm.'

Ellie bristled. 'We do have heating.'

Sarah sighed. 'That's not what I meant. I think it's warm and welcoming. I like the decor.'

'Thank you.' Ellie failed at not sounding stiff. 'Sadly, it's all about to be broken up. The only thing that's mine is the bookcase.'

'Have you found somewhere to live yet?'

A week after the eviction notice, the four women had conceded that the household would have to split up because rambling old houses with six bedrooms were rarer than hen's teeth. Rachel and Grace had signed a lease on a new townhouse in Mingunyah and Wendy and Bree were moving into a granny flat behind Wendy's mother's house. Each morning and afternoon, Ellie checked in with the two Valley View real estate agents, ever hopeful that a miracle had happened in the intervening hours and that the perfect rental property had magically appeared on the books.

'Something will turn up.'

Sarah sipped her wine. 'About yesterday—'

Ellie tensed. 'How's Mum?' she asked even though she didn't want to know.

'She's had a mild stroke.'

Guilt, fear, anger and sadness tangled with the disconnection Ellie always experienced when she thought about her mother. 'What does "mild" mean?'

'I've only got third-hand information. It happened in Melbourne when they were running some tests. Cameron's with her and the doctors are talking about rehab in Mingunyah Hospital before she comes home.'

'I thought you'd have rushed down to Melbourne.'

'Me too.' Sarah grimaced slightly. 'But for once, Cameron's taken charge and, given everything else that's going on in my life, I'm happy to let him do it.'

Something in her sister's voice made Ellie glance up from the wine she'd been studying. 'What's everything else? It's not a work problem, is it? Alex told me that my Burmese guys are settling in well.'

'I'm glad to hear it.'

'Hear it? Didn't you do their orientation?'

'Didn't you get the email saying I was on leave?'

'No.'

Sarah took a long sip of her drink before setting her glass on the coffee table. 'After you left the dairy on Friday, I found Alex giving Kelly Bamfield a rather personal shoulder rub. He then told me that he hasn't been happy for some time and,' she made quotation marks with her fingers, 'he "needs space".'

'Oh, Sarah. I'm sorry.' Ellie might not wish to be in a relationship but it didn't stop her from appreciating that others felt differently. Sarah and Alex always appeared to be a tight unit and it was obvious in all that Sarah said and did that she loved her husband. If the news was a shock for her, she could only imagine how Sarah must be feeling. 'When did he move out?'

'He didn't—I did. I'm back at the old cheese factory.'

'But ...' Ellie's mind grappled with the scenario. 'I don't

understand. If he wants space, why are you the one moving out of Riverbend?'

'So I have some control over his midlife crisis.' Sarah sat a little bit straighter, her mouth a grim line 'Why should Alex get to call all the shots and be free to screw Kelly whenever he wants?'

Ellie flinched at the aggression in her sister's usual sanguine tone. 'How long have they been ...'

'He told me they hadn't had sex.'

'Oh! That's a good sign, isn't it?'

Sarah snorted. 'Not doing it just makes the longing, the excitement and the anticipation even more delicious. And a lot more dangerous. Personally, I'm hoping they've had sex now and that it was a massive disappointment for both of them.'

Ellie squirmed on the couch, excruciatingly uncomfortable. She and Sarah never talked about anything this intimate or personal and despite—or perhaps because of—her own experiences, she was the last person to have anything useful to offer on sex or relationships.

'But I didn't come here to talk about Alex.' Sarah suddenly reached down and pulled a plastic folder out of her handbag. 'I came because I've been doing some clearing out for Mum. I found this.'

Ellie accepted the document holder. 'What is it?'

'Read it and see.'

She withdrew the pages and quickly scanned them. 'Mum's bought Phoebe and Ruby some very expensive presents.'

'And?'

Ellie hated playing games at the best of times let alone when she had no idea of the goal. 'They're a saddle and a cello?'

Sarah refilled her glass and leaned forward. 'Not to mention the contributions to the school fees.'

'Okay.' Ellie slid the papers back into the folder and dropped it onto the coffee table.

'Aren't you outraged?'

'No.' She'd held onto outrage for a long time but had let it go in a muddy, raging river in northern Thailand.

'Well, you should be.' A suspicious look crossed Sarah's face. 'Unless ...'

'Unless what?'

'Has Mum been helping you out? Buying things for Noah?'

Ellie sat up straight. 'No!'

Sarah startled and her wine sloshed up the deep bowl of her glass. 'There's no need to shout.'

'Sorry.' It was easier to apologise than to explain to Sarah why she didn't want any help, financial or otherwise, from their mother, or why Margaret was unlikely to give it. 'Surely Mum has the right to spend her money any way she chooses?'

'Of course she does,' Sarah snapped. 'Although outside of gifts to herself, she isn't usually this generous.'

'Perhaps she's mellowed.' Ellie's attempt at a joke fell flat. She couldn't imagine her mother ever being mellow. 'I don't understand. If we both agree she can spend her money her way, then why are you showing me all of this?'

'Because, instead of telling me that Mum bought the cello and saddle, both Cameron and Anita have made it sound like they paid for them. Why would they do that?'

Ellie didn't care and she really couldn't be bothered discussing it, but as Sarah had brought great wine, hadn't lambasted her about her behaviour at Mill House and was in the middle of major marriage problems, she felt she should at least try to contribute some suggestions. 'Embarrassment?'

'Ha! Very funny. You know as well as I do that our brother doesn't have that gene. Thirty years ago, he'd have taunted me with the fact that he got an expensive gift and I didn't. He's always competing with me even when I'm not aware it's a competition.'

'Perhaps Anita asked him not to say anything?'

Ellie didn't know her sister-in-law very well. By the time she'd met her, Anita and Sarah were a closed group of two. This had suited Ellie and she hadn't made any effort to infiltrate and join their group. Although she and Anita had children of a similar age, they shared little in common. Anita loved clothes, accessories and makeup and spent a large part of her life pursuing the perfect combination; Ellie avoided anything to do with fashion. Clothes were something to keep her cool or warm depending on the season.

'I thought you and Anita were BFFs. Why not ask her?'

Sarah bristled. 'I asked her about the saddle today in a roundabout way. She gave me the same line she's been spinning since Ruby got it. Phoebe's cello was bought a year ago and not once have they mentioned it was Mum who paid for it, let alone saying anything about her contributions to the girls' boarding fees. Now Anita's using Mill House for Cooked By a Friend—'

'Is she?' Suddenly the unrecognisable kitchen made sense.

'Yes!' Exasperation clung to the word. 'Honestly, Ellie, would it kill you to take a bit more interest in the family?'

Yes. 'In my defence, there was no mention on Mother's Day about Anita starting a business or using Mill House. Apart from Gus's play, that's the last time I saw them.'

'Hmm.' Sarah seemed to give herself a little shake. 'Well, anyway, from the moment Anita told me about her plans for Mill House, I've had concerns. It's Mum's home and she's using it as a commercial enterprise. I've tried to be supportive but on the back of this huge omission of thirty-five thousand in gifts, I'm starting to wonder what else she's hiding.'

This was the first time Ellie had glimpsed this side of Sarah. 'Don't you think you're being just a teensy bit paranoid?'

'When your husband betrays you after twenty-two years of marriage, you can't help but question all the other relationships in your life.'

Ellie drank her wine, letting the uncomfortable silence tinged with Sarah's pain sit in the room. She wasn't touching the topic lest it put their already prickly relationship under the microscope. She had a horrible feeling that, if they examined it, a bubbling and toxic bacteria filled with all her failings would rise out of Sarah and choke her.

'I want you to move into Mill House.'

Wine bubbled in Ellie's nose. '*What?*'

'I want you to move into Mum's house. It's the perfect solution.'

'For what or for whom?'

Sarah rolled her eyes. 'For you and Noah of course.'

Not in my world. 'It's Mum's house, not yours to loan out. Plus you've just been banging on about Anita invading it—'

'Yes, but this is different.'

'No, it's not.'

'Yes, it is. You're Mum's daughter.'

She tried not to wince at the statement that the relationship gave her preferential treatment. 'And with that logic, Anita is her daughter-in-law, so still family.'

'Okay, fine.' Sarah thumped down her glass on the stained coffee table. 'I'll get straight to the point. While Mum's in hospital, I want someone living in the house.'

'Why?'

'To keep an eye on what's going on.'

Ellie crossed her arms. 'So, you move in.'

A triumphant smirk broke over Sarah's tense face. 'Unlike you, I already have somewhere to live.'

The hairs on the back of her neck rose. 'I am *not* moving back to that house.'

'For God's sake, Ellie! Why on earth not? You just told me you haven't found anywhere to live. This is the perfect solution.'

'For you maybe.'

'It's win-win for both of us.'

It was so far removed from a win that Ellie's heart was flinging itself against her ribs. 'Sarah, I'm thirty-four and a grown woman. I'm not taking a retrograde step and moving back in with my mother.'

'You're thirty-four, a mother and you're about to be homeless.' Sarah's lips pursed. 'You can choose to be homeless and live out of your car if you wish, but you're not the only person involved. Noah's an innocent child and he shouldn't have to suffer for your selfish choices.'

Anger propelled Ellie to her feet. 'Jesus, Sarah, don't hold back. I guess I should be grateful after all these years that your opinion of me's finally out in the open and untainted by any ambiguity. But while you're up there in the heady atmosphere of "I know best" land, know this. You can call me selfish, irresponsible and the rest, but *not* when it comes to Noah. When I left Mingunyah, it was for good. No way in hell was I coming back here, but then the perfect job presented itself. It was a job that matched my skills and was single-parent friendly. The *only* down side, and believe me it was a sinking, squelching trough of a big one, was its proximity to Mingunyah. I sacrificed what I wanted and I compromised for Noah. He's the *only* reason I'm in the valley.' Ellie didn't care that Sarah's face tightened as if she'd struck her.

'That's called motherhood, little sister. And now you have to do it again.'

'No!' Her head shook so hard her brain hurt. 'I *will* find somewhere to live.'

'Yes, but will you find somewhere in time?' Sarah said quietly. 'I think you already know the answer to that.'

The idea of moving into her mother's house made her gag. She already knew being there made her vomit. How could she spend one night in Mill House let alone many? She couldn't. She wouldn't. A wave of foaming hatred for Sarah surged through her. As she was about to unleash a barrage of hurtful words, her anger did a one-eighty and the wave dumped back over her.

Mummy, where are we going to live?

For the last week, the first thing Noah said when he woke up and the last thing he said before he fell sleep was, 'Where's our new house?' or 'Why can't we live with Wendy and Bree?' That afternoon his teacher had telephoned her, concerned that Noah had been both uncharacteristically naughty and quiet over the last few days: 'Can you think of anything that might be bothering him?'

Noah's fear of the unknown was causing him a level of anxiety Ellie needed to banish. No mother wanted their child to suffer, let alone suffer because of their actions or inaction. A memory of Margaret sitting on the end of her childhood bed, pantyhose-clad legs elegantly crossed and Bloody Mary in hand, slugged Ellie hard. Okay, *most* mothers didn't want their child to suffer. Ellie was determined not to be her mother and equally determined that Noah shouldn't suffer because of her. As his mother, it was her responsibility to take that hit. As hard as it was, she had to move into Mill House for the foreseeable future. But there would be rules. Very strict rules—it was the only way she was going to survive.

Ellie sat down, refilled her glass and took a large mouthful of Dutch courage. '*If* I move in, it will be short term. I'll keep looking for a place. And Sarah, know this. I won't become Mum's carer.'

'I don't think she needs a carer, but yes, okay.' Sarah rubbed her temples. 'Really, I just want you as a presence in the house while Mum's in hospital. You know, doing the things Mum would do.'

Ellie doubted she'd ever do the things her mother did. 'What things?'

'Make sure Anita doesn't take over any more rooms of the house.'

'What's she allowed to use?'

'The agreement was the kitchen on Saturday afternoons but today she told me she's starting high teas in the dining room. And she's using all of Grandma's china. The next thing we know, she'll be planning to host weddings in the stables.'

Ellie tried not to sigh. 'Last time I checked, Anita wasn't an events planner.'

'And yesterday I would have agreed with you.'

Ellie understood her sister's world had been rocked to its core but despite not wanting to get involved, it bothered her that Sarah was questioning everyone's actions. It was one thing for her to do it, but not her loving, trusting sister.

'Have you talked to a counsellor about Alex?'

Sarah shifted on the couch. 'Do you still have your key for Mill House?'

'God, no.' She tried to block a rising memory that she'd stashed down deep and out of harm's way—an image of the last time she'd held the key to her childhood home. Her gut lurched. If Sarah's reasons for avoiding answering her question about counselling were as strong as hers were about the key, then she understood the silence.

Sarah made a soft grunt that said, *Why did I even ask?* She selected a key from a large and congested bunch.

'I'll get Rita to clean your old room,' she said, handing her the key.

'I'll sleep in the guest room.' The words rushed out faster than Ellie had intended. 'After all, I'm a guest and I'm not sleeping in a single bed. Perhaps Noah can sleep in your room?'

'Mum turned my room into a clothing depository and dressing room years ago. Yours and Cam's are still intact,' Sarah said snippily.

It was on the tip of Ellie's tongue to say, 'I wish mine was something else,' but she stopped herself. No point inviting comment on something she had no plans to discuss. 'In that case, Noah can sleep in Cam's room.'

'Hallelujah. You're finally being practical. I'll sleep well tonight knowing you're not homeless.'

Ellie raised her glass to her sister in an ironic toast. At least one of them would sleep.

Margaret opened her eyes, frowned and shut them. Giving herself a shake, she tried again but the visuals didn't change. Where were her dove-grey drapes? Her carved mantelpiece and antique gilt mirror? And who had taken her beautiful armchair and replaced it with this horrible vinyl monstrosity that burped whenever she moved? She'd sat on a dreadful chair like this once before. A straight-backed chair in a cold hospital corridor on the night Kevin died …

Two nurses helped her up from the chair before flanking her as she half walked, half stumbled into the morgue to identify her husband's stiff body. Thankfully, the nurses thought her so grief stricken they didn't twig to the fact she was more drunk than bereft.

Gripping the edge of the trolley for support, Margaret stared down at Kevin's handsome but now alabaster face and tried to focus. She pressed her lips together hard to stop from crying out.

'Yes. That's Kevin. You know it's Kevin, Phillip.'

The police sergeant spun his cap in his fingers. 'I'm very sorry to put you through this, Margaret.'

'Please accept our sincere condolences,' the doctor added. 'Kevin's done so much for Mingunyah Base—'

'May I have a few minutes alone with him?' She was in no fit shape to listen to platitudes.

'Of course, Mrs Jamieson.' The obsequious medico was probably thinking about his fundraising target. 'Press the buzzer when you're ready.'

When the door clicked shut behind the two men and their footsteps faded, Margaret raised her hand and slapped Kevin's cold face hard. 'You stupid, idiotic, useless excuse of a man. You even screwed up dying. I suppose I should be grateful for small mercies.'

'Yoo-hoo, Mrs Jamieson? Did the physiotherapist wear you out?'

Margaret startled and the past scuttled away like a cockroach slipping under a skirting board. A woman with greying curls and wearing navy pants and a colourful blouse was setting down a small tray containing a teapot and a slice of cake.

'A cup of tea's the perfect pick-me-up after a chair nap.'

'I don't nap,' Margaret said indignantly. 'I'm far too busy for that.'

'Don't get your knickers in a twist, Mrs J. You're not the first person here to have a quick kip. I'll leave a second cup for Sarah, shall I? She usually visits about this time.'

Before Margaret could reply, the woman left the room and Sarah walked in clutching a big bunch of white eyeliner lilies.

'Hello, Mum.' She kissed her on the cheek. 'I thought you might enjoy these.'

'Why? The perfume makes me sneeze and the pollen stains everything it touches. You know I never have them in the house.'

Sarah's mouth formed a familiar yet quiet smile tinged with

restraint. Kevin's smile. 'In that case, I'll take the flowers home and enjoy them there ...'

'Margaret,' Kevin said, holding something in his hand and waving it at her. 'I've got tickets to the Melbourne Symphony Orchestra at the new concert hall. I thought you might like to come?'

'Seriously, Kevin? If it was the opening, I'd have tolerated the classical music, but it's not so I won't.'

'In that case, I'll go and enjoy it on my own.'

Margaret looked at her daughter and tried not to sigh. 'That's exactly the sort of thing your father would have said.'

'I'll take it as a compliment.'

'I wouldn't,' Margaret muttered, making a grab for the cake.

Sarah's eyes widened and the teapot clattered onto the tray. 'Mum, is everything okay?'

'No! Why am I here? I want to go home.'

'I know you do but you've had a stroke, remember? If you want to keep living at Mill House, you need to be steadier on your feet.'

No one told Margaret Jamieson what to do, especially not her daughters. 'You can't keep me here against my will.'

'No one is keeping you against your will,' Sarah said quietly as she put her hand gently over Margaret's. 'The sight in your left eye isn't great and neither is your balance, which is why you're here in rehab. All I want is for you to get better.'

Margaret pulled her hand away and straightened in her chair. Her eldest daughter lacked Cameron's and Ellie's model good looks and she had too much of Kevin's personality in her for Margaret's taste, but Sarah was her most biddable child; the one who always tried to please her.

'I'm your mother. If you love me, you'll take me home.'

'Of course I love you, Mum.'

Familiar anguish tinged the words and Margaret relaxed. As soon as she got home she'd—

'Which is why you need to stay here until you're capable of doing things without assistance.' Sarah poured the tea. 'The OT's assessing your cooking tomorrow and then she'll do a home visit in preparation for your discharge.'

A white rage exploded inside Margaret and she trembled all over. 'I am going home and you can't stop me. No one can stop me. I demand to talk to that nice young man who told me not to let anyone take advantage of me.'

Consternation pulled Sarah's brows together and she leaned back in her chair—shoulders straight, chin lifted—in the same exact and measured way Kevin always had when Margaret yelled. 'What nice young man, Mum? One of the nurses? The physiotherapist? A doctor? What does he look like?'

The questions came at Margaret like the ack-ack fire of a machine gun. She lifted her hands to her ears, trying to block the sound. *Think.* But her mind was encased in lead and filled with cotton wool as it often was now and she struggled to conjure an image. 'Black hair.'

'He had black hair?'

Margaret's head ached so badly all she wanted to do was sleep. 'Who?'

Sarah leaned over and pressed the buzzer that rested on the neatly made bed. 'The nice young man with black hair who told you not to let anyone take advantage of you.'

Ray ... Rodge ... Rex ... No! 'Rupert.' The name brought exquisite relief. 'Yes, I want to see Rupert. I was very impressed by him.'

A nurse appeared in the doorway. 'You rang the bell Mrs Jamieson?'

'Go away!' Honestly, no one here had a clue about anything. She could teach this lot a thing or two. After all, she'd made a vast amount of money out of not very much.

Sarah turned in her chair. 'I rang it, Jenny. Is there a Rupert on duty?'

'Rupert?' The nurse looked thoughtful. 'I don't know any Ruperts. I can check the agency staff list to see if anyone with that name worked the night shift but it's a pretty distinguished name. I think I'd have remembered it.'

'Rupert isn't here, Sarah,' Margaret said irritably, pressing her fingers onto the cake crumbs before sucking the granules into her mouth.

Sarah's eyes took on the wild and crazy look she got whenever someone exasperated her. 'If he doesn't work here, where does he work?'

Margaret couldn't remember. 'His office has a magnificent view. You really should see it for yourself.' The *Women's Weekly* magazine next to the tea tray caught her attention. She picked it up, flipping straight to the fashion section.

'Jenny,' Sarah said, rising to her feet. 'Is Doctor Kafi available?'

CHAPTER TWELVE

'Have fun with Daddy.' Anita kissed the little girls goodbye before leaning in to kiss Cameron.

His hand squeezed her behind as he said quietly, 'And when you get home tonight, we can have some fun.'

An electric shot of desire thrummed between her legs and she squirmed deliciously against him. 'There's a divine gown that's split to the thigh.'

His grey eyes shone like polished ore. 'I like the sound of that.'

The sales of Margaret's dresses were exceeding expectations. Even in their wildest dreams they could never have imagined the strength of the demand and they were working hard at cataloguing outfits. The moment they uploaded the detailed description and the accompanying photos that showcased all aspects of the dress, someone bid. There was something utterly addictive about watching the last few moments of an auction. Her heart pounded, her stomach churned and she squeezed Cameron's hand hard, withholding squeals of delight as the price ratcheted up. But most of all, Anita loved that Vintage Glamour was a family project that not only helped her mother-in-law, but gave her precious time and fun with her husband. After the sale of the tenth dress, Cameron suggested that, as a reward for all their hard work, they use their commission to buy themselves something.

The idea of a commission thrilled her but it was offset with a general unease. The roles and responsibilities inside a family were vague and untested concepts for Anita as she had no similar experiences to draw on. Just before her ninth birthday, her father had vanished. Abandoned and ill-used, she couldn't forgive him for sticking her with a mother who was incapable of functioning without him. As Anita had watched her mother drink herself to death, she'd lurched between guilt, hating her father and fantasising that one day he'd walk through the door and restore her life to the way it had been before he left. The closest he ever got to walking back through the door was via a police officer, who'd confirmed that her father's abandonment of her was complete.

The only man who had ever entered her life with good intentions was Cameron. She'd told him the basics of her childhood—'Dad left, Mum drank and I started planning my exit from home at thirteen'—but she'd avoided the details. She'd certainly never revealed the sordidness of their poverty; Cameron just assumed that money in her household was tighter than in his. She'd never told him how she'd hidden money from her mother so they could eat. How her part-time job waitressing at the local pub meant enduring having her bum pinched, her boobs stared at and a barrage of misogynistic comments. How she had no choice but to put up with the sexism, because it was the only job on offer and she couldn't afford to quit.

As far as she was concerned, the past belonged firmly where it was and all that was important now was that she had a real family— one who loved and supported her.

'A commission? But I thought this was a love job for Margaret. You know, something family just did?'

'Absolutely it is, but think about it: we've both spent hours working on Vintage Glamour on top of our own jobs. You're getting Cooked By a Friend off the ground, running after the girls and me, and hell, my work's flat out at the moment. When was the last time we sat on the couch together after dinner and watched TV? Vintage Glamour is a job in itself and it would cost Mum a hell of lot if she was paying a professional to do it.'

'That's true, but we're having fun doing it. It doesn't really feel like work.'

He'd given her an indulgent smile. 'Perhaps "commission" is the wrong word. Really, it's just a gift of appreciation from Mum for all our hard work.' He'd kissed her. 'And you know it's considered bad manners to refuse a gift.'

He'd chosen new golf clubs and she'd selected a small but brand new Valentino handbag instead of a preloved one. Sometimes, the thrill she got holding it was better than sex. Although recently, courtesy of Margaret's clothes, the sex was the best it had been since before they had children.

She carefully placed her handbag on the front seat of the car before swinging into the driver's seat. 'See you tonight, darling, and please don't let the girls run riot today.'

Cameron closed the door for her. 'I'm a better babysitter than that.'

'Exactly. You're their father.' She kissed him again and reversed onto the street.

Apart from the tourist traffic in the main street, Mingunyah was quiet this Saturday as the Tigers had a bye, so it was a surprise when she turned into Sawmill Lane and had to brake. The narrow, but usually tranquil, road was crowded with cars and the Sorenson's Motors van was parked outside Mill House. Surely Hamish Makin wasn't buying another souped-up vehicle? She pulled in behind an old Subaru wagon with a black Sea Shepherd Conservation Society sticker and a distinctive 'Coexist' bumper sticker. *Ellie's car.*

A new sticker had been added: Valley View Alpine Ranges Football Club. Anita rolled her eyes. Even she, a relative newcomer to the valley, knew the rivalry between the two footy teams was fierce and a sticker like that in Mingunyah was a red rag to a bull. As Noah idolised Gus, she couldn't imagine he'd been the one to insist on it. Honestly, why did Ellie do stuff like this?

A familiar streak of chagrin charged with jealousy made her grind her teeth. Once again, Ellie was giving Mingunyah and her family the finger. Anita had little time for Ellie, who'd both thrown away and turned her back on all the golden opportunities she'd been offered growing up—opportunities Anita would have killed for. Why was Ellie even here? She never visited Margaret, and now that her mother was in hospital there was absolutely no reason for her to be at Mill House unless ...

No. Anita scotched the idea. Ellie wasn't thoughtful enough to come and collect something Margaret might want or need from the house. Besides, the day Margaret had arrived by ambulance from Melbourne, Anita had come to the house and packed a bag for her mother-in-law. She had also bought chocolates, flowers and a stack of magazines. While she was packing everything into the car to take to the hospital, Sarah had turned up, but instead of thanking her for her thoughtfulness and help, she'd quizzed her on exactly what she had packed.

Anita had indignantly recounted the episode to Cameron saying, 'Sarah might be going through a marriage break-up but that doesn't give her carte blanche to be rude.'

'Oh, baby girl.' He'd shaken his head fondly. 'I'm surprised it's taken this long for the scales to finally fall from your eyes. Sarah needs to control everything. When she can't, she's a right bitch.'

'I want to be on her side but part of me is wondering if Alex might have a point. If she keeps on like this, I'll be wanting some space from her too.'

Exiting the car carefully, Anita opened the hatch, lifted out the esky and walked past Ellie's car, critically noting the encrusted mud clinging to the duco. Her cooking class started in an hour but she liked to be early so she could double-check everything and light the wax-melt burners, giving time for the scent of lemongrass and ginger to waft through the house.

As Anita approached the front door, Ellie and a tall, good-looking man stepped out. Her sister-in-law stopped abruptly in the portico, surprise written clear on her face, but the blond-headed bloke kept walking, meeting Anita halfway down the path.

'Can I take that for you?'

Before Anita could reply, he lifted the bulky esky out of her hands.

'Where do you want it?'

'I—the kitchen. Thank you.'

He flashed her a smile, his vivid blue eyes crinkling around the edges. 'Too easy.'

Anita watched him bound up the steps, appreciating the view, and gave a momentary thought to suggesting to Cameron that he dress up in navy blue cotton work pants and strap on a tool belt. Who was this man? Cam was convinced that Ellie was gay and in a secret relationship with one of the women she lived with. Given Ellie's clothing and food choices, Anita agreed wholeheartedly, and yet Ellie was in the company of a male every heterosexual woman would sneak a second look—or just plain stare—at with open admiration. Her mind boggled.

Ellie, who'd jumped sideways to give the man room to enter the house, finally spoke.

'Hi, Anita.'

'Who's that gorgeous specimen of manhood?'

Ellie frowned. 'You do realise you've just objectified him.'

And *this* was another reason Anita had little time for Ellie. She was a politically correct killjoy. Although Ellie was much closer to her in age than Sarah, her elder sister-in-law was a lot more fun— or at least she had been. The old Sarah would have responded to her comment about a sexy man by fanning herself and saying, 'Well, my day's just been made.'

'If I objectified him, we're even. He just inflicted gender bias by not letting me carry my own esky.' Not that Anita believed that for a second; she loved it when men showed good old-fashioned manners. It was one of the traits that had attracted her to Cameron.

Ellie's mouth twitched in wry amusement. 'Touché. Who knew

you were such a radical feminist? His name is Luke Sorenson. He's a plumber.'

Anxiety raced along Anita's veins. 'Oh God, has the guest toilet blocked? Is that why you're here? I told Cameron the other day it was playing up and he said I was worrying over nothing but I've got six women arriving for a cooking class and—'

'Settle, petal.' Ellie held up her hand. 'He's not here as a plumber. He's helping me move some stuff.'

'Really?' Anita mounted the concave steps. 'After all this time, you've still got stuff here?'

'Oh, yeah,' Ellie said flatly. 'In fact, as of today, I've got more stuff here than I've had in seventeen years.'

Anita, who was only half listening, stepped inside and stopped short. Cardboard boxes lined the hall and a clothes airer leaned against them. A woman she'd never met before was talking as she jogged down the front stairs.

'Ellie, I put the—Oh! Sorry I didn't see you there. Hi, I'm Cassie.'

'Anita Jamieson,' she said automatically despite her rising panic. 'I'm Ellie's sister-in-law. Would you excuse us for a moment please, Cassie? I need to speak to Ellie privately.'

Without waiting for the woman's acquiescence, Anita grabbed Ellie's arm and tugged her into the formal lounge room. 'I know you're moving out of your place but you can't store your stuff here. I've got a cooking class in an hour and the hall looks like a warehouse.'

This time Ellie didn't frown, although her baby-blue eyes filled with resignation. 'Ah. Sorry. I thought Sarah told you.'

'Told me what?'

Ellie sighed. 'Until I can find a suitable place to live, Noah and I are moving in. Believe me, it won't be for long.'

Panic morphed into disbelief. 'You can't do that! I'm running a business here. I won't have Noah running wildly through the house ruining the ambiance while I'm hosting elegant high teas.'

Ellie stiffened and her expression changed from embarrassed

regret to iron-clad determination. 'I promise you, Noah will be as well behaved as Ava was on Mother's Day.'

It was a shot across the bows. Ava had thrown a spectacular tantrum that included screaming at the top of her lungs and lying on the floor, pummelling the boards with her arms and legs.

Anita, feeling battle lines being clearly drawn, decided to amass some supportive troops. Pulling out her phone she said, 'I'm calling a family meeting.'

Ellie's low laugh mocked her. 'I never took you for a sadist, Anita.'

Ten minutes later, an irritated Sarah arrived, followed by a fuming Cameron, with the little girls in tow. Noah, who'd apparently been upstairs the whole time, whooped in delight on seeing his cousins. Now all three of them were charging around in circles on the front lawn like excited puppies.

'Was it absolutely necessary to pull me away from—from visiting Mum?' Sarah's gaze shot to the children. 'And who's looking after them while we talk?'

In her rattled state, Anita hadn't thought as far as that. 'I don't know. I—'

'I think we've found our solution.' Sarah pointed to Luke, who was holding a ball aloft and ducking and weaving between the kids. Three little people dived at his legs trying to stop his progress, with scant effect. 'Apparently, he's not just a good plumber and boundary umpire.'

'I'll ask Cassie to help,' Ellie said tightly.

'Luke doesn't look like he needs any help at all. Who knew my sexy plumber had hidden depths? He's got those kids eating out of his hand.'

'Can we focus?' Anita snapped. 'Ellie, ask your friends if they'll keep an eye on the kids. It won't be for long.' As Ellie turned away,

Anita shooed everyone with her hands. 'Come on, inside. I've got a cooking class in forty minutes!'

'You don't have a monopoly on busy, Anita,' Sarah muttered as she trooped inside.

Cameron closed the door behind him, which Ellie opened a moment later. 'I hope you weren't planning on starting without me.'

'Why?' Cameron crossed his arms over his chest. 'We do most family things without you.'

Anita had attended enough family gatherings to know that if left unchecked, things between Ellie and Cameron disintegrated quickly, each giving as good as they got. 'Let's stick to the issue at hand. Before Margaret went into hospital she gave me permission to use Mill House for Cooked By a Friend.'

Cameron picked up the baton. 'That's right, and Anita needs free use of the house.'

Anita glanced at Sarah, who'd seated herself on the club chair Margaret always referred to as 'Kevin's chair'. Although her father-in-law had died years before she'd met Cameron, she'd heard all the loving stories numerous times from Margaret. Anita took pride in the fact her marriage to Cameron was as strong as his parents' marriage had been. 'Sarah, you agree, right?'

'Actually, I don't.'

Surprise slapped Anita hard and it took her a moment to catch up. 'What do you mean? You've been on my side from the start.'

'There are no *sides*, Anita. My understanding is that Mum gave you permission to use the kitchen for some cooking classes on the occasional weekend when she was busy and out of the house. That's a far cry from free use of the house twenty-four-seven. It's a big house and I can't see any reason why Ellie can't live here.'

'Jesus, Sarah.' Cameron thumped the mantelpiece. 'You know as well as I do Ellie shouldn't be living here.'

'Excuse me,' Ellie said sharply. 'I'm standing right here. Exactly why shouldn't I be living here?'

'You don't deserve it,' Cameron said bluntly. 'Why should Mum bail you out by giving you a roof over your head when all you've ever done is cause her grief? You ran away from this house, so why the hell are you moving back?'

'For God's sake, I was fourteen.'

Cameron shrugged. 'Has much changed? You were a spoiled brat then—'

'I didn't—'

Sarah shot to her feet. 'That's enough, Cam. This is simple maths. Mum's in hospital and Ellie needs a place to live.'

'Temporary place to live,' Ellie clarified. 'Very, very temporary.'

'This is my workplace,' Anita ground out in frustration as betrayal beat at her like the flames of a grass fire. 'You run a business, Sarah. You know what's important, what's at stake. I can't believe you're supporting Ellie over me when we all know how flaky she is.'

'I love you too, Anita,' Ellie said sweetly.

'Ellie has as much right to take advantage of what this house offers her as you do,' Sarah said sharply. 'I'm trying to support everyone.'

'It doesn't look that way to me. God, you didn't even tell us she was moving in! I've got a cooking class in thirty minutes and the hall is full of boxes!'

'This doesn't need to be complicated.' Sarah's tone was the firm one she used when she spoke to staff. 'Ellie, move the boxes out of the hall and put a hold on moving in the rest of your gear until after Anita's class has finished.'

'I can move the boxes but if Luke needs to return the van before five—'

'Go and ask him. Anita, take a few deep breaths and go and do your preparation.'

Anita wanted to object to Sarah's high-handed approach and tell her she wouldn't need to be taking deep breaths if her sister and best friend hadn't screwed her over. But damn it, the clock was ticking and she couldn't risk any more hiccoughs. She needed to project a calm, professional demeanour, which was going to be a challenge given her roiling anger and the stabs of treachery inflicted by both sisters-in-law.

She kissed Cameron on the cheek and whispered, 'Do something. Please. Don't let her move in.'

While Sarah waited for Ellie and Anita to leave the room, she glanced out the front window of Mill House. The view was slightly distorted by the 160-year-old glass but she could see the little girls showing off to Luke by doing cartwheels. Noah was valiantly trying to match his cousins but the poor kid didn't have their rigorous calisthenics practice under his belt and his arms kept collapsing. She read his disappointment and her heart went out to him. She could relate—Cameron had absorbed all the limelight of her childhood.

Anita's unexpected phone call had pulled Sarah away from an equally unexpected lunch and matinee with Edmund. He'd arrived with a bottle of her favourite sauv blanc and when she'd opened the door, his gaunt face relaxed into a caring smile.

'I thought you might need a break.'

His kindness had made her fight tears and she'd instinctively leaned in and kissed him, giving in to the relief of being able to rest her weight and worries against another person. Edmund had always been her rock. From the first day he'd started working for them, he'd always been there ready to listen. Unlike Alex, he'd let her rant and rave until she ran out of steam before giving his counsel, advice that was usually spot on. During the second expansion of the business, when she and Alex were burning the candles at both ends and she had the added responsibility of a toddler and a baby, Edmund had offered not just a listening ear but practical help as well. Now he was doing both those things again.

Are you serious? You're calling sex practical help?

Totally! It was about the only thing giving her any joy. Good sex and listening. Edmund gave her his undivided attention as if she were the centre of everything and nothing else mattered. They'd been in bed when Anita's hysterical telephone call had interrupted them. The coincidence wasn't lost on Sarah—she'd been in the middle of telling Edmund about her suspicions about Anita and Cameron, her mother's odd behaviour and her plan to move Ellie into Mill House. Reluctantly, she'd thrown on her clothes and left him. Now, after the brouhaha that had just gone down, she knew whose company she'd rather be in.

The door closed behind Anita, and Sarah turned away from the window. 'Cam, the girls look happy. Do you have a minute?'

Her brother gave a brusque nod. 'To talk about Princess Ellie moving in here? Hell yes.'

'Actually, I want to talk about Mum.'

His forehead creased. 'What about her?'

'She's having periods of confusion.'

'Are you sure?' He sat on the couch, swinging his feet onto the ottoman. 'I haven't noticed.'

She returned to her father's chair and experienced a moment of melancholy. Sitting here took her back to when she was little, cuddled up on Kevin's lap and breathing in his scent of freshly shaved wood and peppermint. He'd always kept a pack of Steamrollers in his pocket and he'd pop one in his mouth to quell his urge to smoke. He was a snuggler and, with one arm holding her close against him and the other holding the book, he'd read to her until her mother appeared in the doorway saying, 'Enough. Bed.'

'We better do as we're told,' her father would say, giving her a wink before sliding her off his lap. As a wife and mother herself now, Sarah appreciated that her mother had likely borne the bulk of the childrearing and that her father had done the fun stuff. It probably wasn't fair to Margaret that Sarah remembered her father as the more affectionate parent.

'When I visited Mum at the hospital, there was an incident where she insisted on seeing someone I've never heard of. It wasn't anyone at the hospital. She also said something about Dad.'

Cameron rolled his eyes. 'She's always talking about Dad.'

'I know, but this was sarcastic.'

'Sarcasm's Mum's party trick. We've all enjoyed a laugh from her caustic commentary on people.'

'Sure, but when have you ever heard her be sarcastic about Dad? The night he died, she put him high on a pedestal and no one's been allowed to say a word against him since. That's why yesterday was so odd and unsettling. I've spoken to Doctor Kafi. Apparently, the part of Mum's brain that was affected by the stroke means she's likely to have ongoing memory loss and confusion.'

Cameron frowned. 'Are you sure? I mean, she was fine when I saw her.'

'Did you ask her any questions or did you do most of the talking?'

'I told her about the girls. Oh! I see what you mean. Still, she was making sense, so surely with a bit of support, she'll be able to come home.' He clapped his hands as if the discussion was over. 'If it makes you feel any better, you don't have to worry about her finances. I've got that all covered.'

'How?' Her mother was always very cagey about her money.

'Oh, I've got power of attorney.'

Sarah sat forward so fast her head spun. 'How long have you had that?'

'Mum and I discussed it when I moved back last year. I thought it was prudent given she's not getting any younger. This health scare is a case in point.' He tilted his head as if he was a disapproving headmaster. 'To be honest, Sar, I was surprised you hadn't already organised it.'

Cameron's patronising tone generated a rage inside her that was reminiscent of the time she'd been sixteen and Cameron had told her crush, Russell Dallimore, that she didn't want to go out with him. Every muscle in her body tightened, ready to spring her out of the chair and body slam him to the ground, but she curled her fingers into the leather arm rests to keep herself seated. On and off over the last five years, she'd tried discussing both power of attorney and medical power of attorney with Margaret, but each time she raised the topics, her mother always shut her down.

My finances are private, thank you very much. I'm not prepared to discuss this with you, Sarah. My doctor and lawyer know my wishes and they're the only people who need to know.

Jealousy and hurt stormed in over her fury. All she'd ever done was try to be a caring and loving daughter while her other siblings were off for years doing their own thing. In the line of duty, she'd put up with comments like 'Honestly, Sarah, I'm starting to think you're only interested in me because you want to know exactly how much I'm worth.' Discovering that Cameron had been given a responsibility she'd been offering for years almost choked her.

Cameron must have taken her paralytic silence as agreement. 'Anyway, you don't have to worry. I'll make sure all her bills are paid.'

The roar of blood in her ears increased. 'I bet you will. Will you also make sure some of yours are paid too?'

Affronted, his features darkened. 'That's a low blow even for you.'

'Is it?' She stood quickly, fuelled by a raw dislike sparked by the remnants of childhood grudges never fully resolved. 'Don't bullshit me, Cam. I know Mum paid for Phoebe's cello and Ruby's saddle.'

He had the audacity to scoff. 'I thought you prided yourself on not keeping score of gifts. Mum loves the girls and she wants the best for them.'

'I agree, but why the secrecy? Why act as if you'd paid for them?'

His arm sliced through the air. 'For this exact reason. I knew you'd be jealous.'

The arrow hit but she took the pain and rode it. The purchase date of the cello was ambiguous territory but not the saddle. 'Did you use your power of attorney to access her money and buy the saddle?'

'Now you're accusing me of stealing? Oh, that's nice. Very nice. Listen, Sarah.' His voice was a low growl. 'You're not the only Jamieson child to love their mother and want the best for her. I'm sorry your feelings are hurt and that Mum trusts me with her money more than you, but tough. Deal with it. And as I've got power of attorney, Ellie's not moving in.'

'That's not your decision to make.'

'Oh, but it is. You just told me Mum's confused. If that's the case, then she's not competent to make these sorts of decisions.'

The triumphant sneer on his face turned her gut, and the thought that Cameron had total control over her mother's estate sucked the air from her lungs. *Stay calm, stay calm, stay calm.* 'Dan Horton might disagree with you.'

'That's immaterial.'

'I don't think so! He's her lawyer. He knows her wishes and he's mandated to act in her best interests.'

'Not any more.'

'What do you mean? Mum's always been with Horton's.'

'She asked me to take her to see a solicitor in Melbourne so I did. She engaged him as her lawyer. Dan's been notified.'

Sarah flashed hot and cold as memories boomed. Cameron unexpectedly offering to drive Margaret to her medical appointment in Melbourne. The screeching noise of a slowing tram interrupting their phone call. Her mother being admitted to the Alfred Hospital instead of the Austin where she was supposed to have the scan.

'You took her to a lawyer instead of her medical appointment?'

'No! Of course not and I resent the implication. Her scan was in the afternoon but she never got there because she had the stroke at lunch, *after* the solicitor's appointment.'

I want to talk to that nice young man who told me not to let anyone take advantage of me. His office has a magnificent view.

'Rupert?' Sarah's delicious lunch curdled in her stomach. 'As in Rupert Grimes, your mate from uni? *Your* lawyer?'

'That's the one.' Cameron threw her a triumphant smirk. 'Mum liked him a lot and he's a damn sight better lawyer than bland Dan.'

She tried reassuring herself that for years she and her mother had used the same solicitor without fear or favour. That Dan was her friend as well as her lawyer, just like Rupert was Cameron's friend and lawyer, but it didn't help. Dan swam in a different pool from slimy Rupert, whose ethics she'd always considered questionable.

'Did Mum see him alone?'

'No, why would she? I'm her power of attorney, so I need to know what's going on and what her wishes are. But you know Mum, she knows her own mind.'

Oh, Sarah knew that very well. But she was still reeling over the fact Margaret gave Cameron power of attorney when she'd always told Sarah, 'that sort of thing's best handled by a solicitor'.

It was out of character.

No, it's not. Cam's always been the favourite.

'And what are those wishes?' She hated asking, because it gave him power, but she had a horrible, suspicious feeling that he already held the power.

'Oh, Sarah, Sarah, Sarah,' he said slowly, shaking his head. 'How ironic is this? You've always been the one telling us we need to respect Mum's privacy yet now you're asking me to break her financial confidentiality?'

I hate you so much. She didn't trust him as far as she could throw him and since his descent into the flabby forties, that wasn't very far. The only way to get the information she wanted was to play the humility card straight into Cameron's need to feel superior, and try not to gag.

'You're right. I'm sorry. I shouldn't be putting you in a compromising position. Forget I asked.'

His expression was the smug one he always used when he thought he'd won. 'We're family, Sarah, and I trust you. Instead of Mum giving bland Dan instructions on her share portfolio and other investments, she's giving them to Rupert.'

'So, Dan's still the executor of her will?'

'The last will she made is years old and with the grandchildren growing up, Rupert suggested she make a new one.'

Sarah had never been privy to the contents of any of Margaret's wills. 'Is it different from the old one?'

'I have no idea. I never saw it. But given the precise way Mum reeled off her instructions, I reckon it's the same. It was obvious she'd committed them to memory a long time ago. In the long-held Jamieson tradition, she's leaving Mill House to Anita and me.'

This was no real surprise. Given the house's heritage, Sarah always knew it was a possibility, even if the feminist in her wasn't happy about it. But from the hints her mother had dropped on her more mellow days, Sarah was confident that Margaret's investment portfolio held approximately double the value of the house, meaning all three siblings would get an equal third.

'So Ellie and I get the shares. That's fair.'

Cameron stretched and linked his fingers behind his head. 'Mum's very happy that you're already independently wealthy.'

A zip of unease narrowed her gaze, bringing him more sharply into focus. 'What the hell does that mean?'

'It means that unlike Ellie and me, an inheritance isn't going to change your lifestyle. You can already afford whatever you want.'

This was true, but if she and Alex divorced, her net worth would halve. 'What does that have to do with my inheritance?'

'I believe you recently stated that inheritance is a gift not a right.'

Her mind spun. 'Are you saying I'm not being left anything?'

'No. Mum wouldn't do that to you.'

The relief was extraordinary but it had barely settled over her when Cameron sent it scattering to all four points of the globe.

'I think she's left you a bracelet.'

'You mean a brooch.' Grandma Jamieson's diamonds were not only worth a lot of money, they held sentimental value.

'No. I think it's that coral bracelet she got for the 1986 Melbourne Cup. She said you'd always liked it.'

Costume jewellery? Sarah breathed in so sharply she was gripped by a paroxysm of coughing. *Mum loves you less. You've always wondered and this is the proof.* The barbed words hooked into her, flooding her body with pain. She tried fighting them, tried to understand her mother's thought processes and to see things from her point of view, but logic struggled under the onslaught of rejection. Sarah couldn't argue the fact she enjoyed a large disposable income, but she wasn't alone. Cameron always intimated he earned good money too, granted not quite at the same level as her and Alex, but if his spending habits were anything to go by, he was earning plenty. If any of the Jamieson siblings needed an inheritance to substantially change their lifestyle, it was Ellie.

Without a doubt, her sister had been a spoiled and difficult teenager, a university dropout and pretty much absent from their lives during her twenties. Yes, she continued to baffle Sarah with the way she kept them all at arm's length, but Sarah couldn't fault Ellie for not working hard. For all her sins, she'd always held down a job and not once had she asked for a handout. Ellie's share of the inheritance would buy her a house in Mingunyah or Valley View and give her and Noah stability and security. There'd be money to replace her ageing car and there'd be money left over to invest for treats like holidays.

Margaret wasn't overlooking Sarah; she was taking care of Ellie and Noah. Sarah tried using that thought to assuage the insidious rejection that was amplified by each beat of her heart.

'I think Mum's made the right decision leaving Ellie the share portfolio.'

It was Cameron's turn to look baffled. 'Why on earth would Mum leave Ellie anything?'

'No.' She shook her head violently. 'No. Mum wouldn't do that to her.'

'And that's where you're wrong. That's exactly what she's done.'

The unforgiving nature of the will tangoed with the woman she thought she knew. Yes, her mother was opinionated and could be uncompromising but she hadn't rejected Ellie's return to the valley. At family functions, the two of them were civil and Margaret took as much or as little interest in Noah as she took in Cameron's younger daughters. So why cut Ellie out of the will?

'We both know Princess Ellie's been a bitch to Mum. Why should she reward her for years of heartache and pain?'

When Cameron talked about Ellie, Sarah had always heard derision, exasperation, frustration and annoyance but this was the first time she'd ever heard dislike. He was always cocky but today there was an added something. It took her a moment and then it hit her—triumph. He was *gleeful* that Margaret was disinheriting Ellie.

Dazed, she stared at him as if he was a stranger. They'd never been close but he was her brother and wasn't blood thicker than water? Except right now, that shared blood was congealing in horror.

Perhaps her mother had bypassed Ellie but left the money in trust for Noah's education.

'And the grandchildren?'

'She wasn't going to include them but I suggested she make a small bequest to each of them and give the girls some of her jewellery.'

'You suggested ...' That's when his treachery hit her.

This is your doing. You're the architect of this will and Rupert's the draughtsman.

No! You're being paranoid.

Her mother gave the instructions for the new will before her stroke, when she was of sound mind and—Oh God. The vice-like pain in Sarah's temples brought her hands to her head. Was this the key to the will? In the past, despite loving Cameron more than Sarah, Margaret had been deaf to his pleas regarding the sale of the saw mill and the subdivision. She'd certainly resisted giving power of attorney to anyone in the family and yet, in the last twelve months, Cameron had wrested it from her.

And he'd kept that secret too. If Margaret had been of sound mind, surely she'd have resisted Cameron's suggestions to cut both daughters out of the will? It distressed Sarah that she couldn't answer that question with any degree of certainty. The reality was, she saw her mother almost every day, so if there were any changes in Margaret's cognitive abilities before the stroke, she would have noticed them. Of course she'd have noticed them.

But doubt lingered like rogue malignant cells and a series of inconsequential events trickled through her mind. On their own they meant nothing much, but as more and more tumbled in, they came together, forming a collage that told a very different story. Her meticulous mother opening the front door in her underwear. The overly generous gifts from a woman who'd always carefully meted out her money to others. The supposedly stolen car on Mother's Day being found undamaged in the IGA carpark. The increasing paranoia that Rita Bosco was hiding things from her and a growing distrust of people she'd always placed a great deal of faith in, like Dan Horton.

Sarah bit her lip so hard she tasted blood. Individually, none of those things had flagged to her there was anything wrong. Only the eight boxes of tomato juice and the batteries in the fridge had hinted that something might be slightly off and even then, she'd laughed them away. Shame burned hot on her skin. She'd got angry with Ellie for insisting their mother was confused, but Ellie was right. Her sister, the sibling who spent the least amount of time with their mother, had the perspective of distance.

'Dad will be turning in his grave about this will. I'm going to talk to Mum and convince her to change her mind.'

'Mum was very clear about what she wanted. I doubt you talking to her will make any difference.'

Sarah's mind raced, looking for loopholes and a way to slow things down. 'She only saw Rupert last week, so she hasn't signed the new will yet, right?'

'She signed the notes.'

'Yes, but that's not the will. I doubt any doctor will say she's competent to sign it now, so that means the old will stands.' Not that she knew if the old will was any fairer, but she sure as hell planned to find out.

'Not necessarily. She also wrote a statement saying the notes are intended as an informal will. If she's not able to sign, I have power of attorney.'

She hated the superiority in his voice and struggled to sound dispassionate. 'I don't think it works that way.'

'I think you're wrong but either way, we have very clear instructions. Rupert can apply to the court to have the notes accepted as her will.'

And seal a deal that was one hundred per cent in Cameron's favour and exceedingly unfair to Ellie and her. 'I'll fight you on this every step of the way.'

He shrugged as if her threat was of no consequence. He may as well have said, *I'm gonna beat you, I'm gonna beat you*, in a sing-song tone, the same one he'd taunted her with each time he threw the dice, served a tennis ball, run a race and opened Christmas presents when they were kids. His confidence made her want to spit.

'You won't win, Sarah.'

She tugged at her jacket. 'Will too.'

CHAPTER THIRTEEN

'ARE you sure my life's not in danger?' Luke was screwing a faceplate to the back door at Mill House. 'When I offered to help you move, I didn't realise it was going to be under cover of darkness.'

'You and me both,' Ellie said tightly.

The move was supposed to have been quick and easy and a chance for Cassie and Luke to spend time together, but all hell had broken loose, sending Ellie's plans pear-shaped. Instead of being tucked up in his new bedroom, Noah was staying the night with Sarah and Sarah was paying Luke to change all the locks at Mill House. This left Ellie alone with him, and moving in at eleven thirty at night.

'Again, I'm really sorry about this.'

'Stop apologising. This is the most excitement I've had in ages.'

He flashed her his smile, the one that always sent her into turmoil. First excitement surged, making her hope that he might be a person she could trust. That cautionary optimism was instantly boiled in red-hot anger at herself for being foolish enough to contemplate such a scenario. A blanket of sadness followed, settling over her like the heavy, scratchy and itchy touch of wool. Sarcasm always came next.

'You really don't get out much do you?'

'I get out plenty,' he said equably, not rising to her bait. 'It just hasn't involved sneaking around in the dark since I was seventeen and missed curfew. You do this sort of thing often?'

'Not at all. I shouldn't be doing it now.'

One minute that afternoon she'd been outside checking with Luke about delaying the move to five o'clock and the next, Sarah had come storming across the lawn with a face like thunder. Catching her by the elbow, her sister had said, 'Luke, I'm borrowing Ellie for half an hour. Noah, you stay here and play with Luke.'

Instead of looking confused or pissed off at being summarily instructed without any consultation, Luke had waved cheerfully before picking up a whooping Noah and throwing him over his shoulder. Ellie had been the one to object.

'I can't leave Noah with someone I barely know.'

'Oh, for heaven's sake, Ellie. I know Luke. He's great with kids and he runs Auskick and the junior cricket—'

'That doesn't mean any—'

'Listen,' Sarah said tersely as Noah squealed, 'Again, Luke, do it again!'

'Noah's having fun. Just. Get. In. The. Car.'

'This better be life or death.'

'It's worse.' Sarah crunched through the gears and drove around the corner to the nature reserve. 'Walk with me.'

As Ellie jogged to keep up with Sarah's power walking, she listened to her sister explain their mother's confusion, the new will, the suspected role Cameron played in its creation and his refusal to let Ellie move into Mill House. Of all the information Sarah shared, it was her apology that shocked her the most.

'I should have believed you when you said Mum was confused. I'm sorry about that.'

'I thought you did believe me. I mean, you took her back to hospital.'

Sarah grimaced. 'I thought you were being dramatic. But let's not revisit that. More than ever, you have to move into Mill House.'

'I don't think it's a good idea. I was only moving in so Noah felt safe and secure. If Cameron's going to be difficult that nukes the whole point. I don't need the hassle.'

'It's not his house yet. Mum's still alive and you have just as much right to live there as Anita has to use it. We're not letting him throw his weight around and walk all over us.'

'Have you actually asked Mum what she thinks about me moving in?'

'There's no point. I'm not even sure Mum's been thinking straight for months. But that's another issue for another time. First things first. We're changing the locks.'

Ellie stopped walking. 'That's aggressive.'

Sarah's hands hit her hips. 'And Cameron calling that shots isn't? We're pre-empting him. Occupancy is nine-tenths of the law.'

'I think you mean possession is nine-tenths of the law.'

'Exactly! If you're living there it's going to be hard for him to shift you out. Plus, it's leverage.'

Every part of Ellie recoiled from getting involved in this drama. Sarah and Cameron's childhood antipathy for each other had softened over the years, and Ellie thought they'd even been amicable since he'd married Anita. But now the hostility was back with a vengeance, bubbling fiercely on the surface like sulphur, complete with an acrid stench.

'This isn't my fight, Sarah.'

'No, it's *our* fight. It's about being women. Sisters. It's about equality and fairness—'

'They're not the same thing.'

'Bloody hell, Ellie! Do you want Cameron to get away with stealing from us?'

She wanted to say she didn't care about the money—she truly didn't—because living at Mill House was going to be difficult enough for her even before it had become the battleground in a family feud. But Sarah's 'our fight' burrowed in, finding memories she'd forgotten: Sarah teaching her to ride a bike after Cameron, who'd promised, kept reneging; Sarah coming home from uni three months after their father died expressly to organise Ellie's ninth birthday party, because her mother was too distraught with grief; Cameron pinching her on the couch and Sarah telling her to pinch him right back; Sarah meeting her bus at Spencer Street in Melbourne and taking her to a musical, *The Secret Garden*, when she was twelve. The following day, when Sarah put her on the bus home, she'd bought her a copy of *Dolly*—a magazine Margaret not only disapproved of but said she was too young to read. *It can be a sister secret, Ellie. They're the best kind.*

All of it belonged to a foreign place and a hazy time when she and Sarah were sisters instead of strangers.

Now, standing in the dark at Mill House holding the torch so Luke could see to work and with the chill of the night air stinging her back, she pondered the fickle emotions surrounding her memories. Memories that couldn't be separated from the unwanted tug of family ties. Her time living in Asia, and even in Sydney, made it easy to keep the ties loose but it was harder now she was living in the valley. Despite her resolve to keep her distance, those ties snuck in under her resistance with ninja-like stealth, binding her tighter and tighter to her family.

Not the family—to Sarah. Why else would she plonk herself in the middle of this pitched battle between her elder siblings?

'There you go.' Luke pushed to his feet and opened and closed the door, checking the fit of the pins. 'You now have the ultimate protection and convenience in locks,' he quoted from the blurb on the packaging.

'Thanks.'

'No worries.'

For the first time since she'd met him out at Riverbend, he looked awkward, as if he didn't know what to do or say next. It surprised her, because he'd always seemed to be laid back and relatively unflappable. What was more astonishing was her need to put him at ease.

'I should probably—'

'Cup of tea or twenty-one-year-old whiskey?'

He grinned. 'You realise you're not actually offering me a choice, right?'

She laughed, enjoying the feeling. 'Dedicated tea drinker, are you?'

'Absolutely.'

'Whiskey it is then. It's about the only Jamieson family tradition I'd like to be able to afford.'

Luke followed her into the dining room and she hoped he didn't notice her shiver as she crossed the threshold.

'I guess we can turn the lights on now.'

'What will you do if your brother turns off the power?'

'As much as he might want to, I doubt he'll do it. Without power, Anita can't run her cooking classes or high teas.'

'And it's your mother's house.'

'Oh, yeah. It's definitely my mother's house.' She grabbed the whiskey decanter and two glasses. 'Come on. The den's a lot less stuffy.' She turned off the light and closed the door behind her, planning on keeping it permanently shut.

The den was originally part of the old servants' quarters and located at the top of a narrow wooden staircase at the back of the house. It had been Sarah and Cameron's teenage hangout long before it became Ellie's escape room. Her mother had generally left her alone when she was up there. Going by the cobwebs, Margaret didn't use the room for anything and Ellie was surprised to see her teenage posters still gracing the walls.

Luke shook his head, mirth rolling across his cheeks. 'You were a Hanson fan?'

'Weren't all fourteen-year-old girls?'

'I just never took you for a teeny-bopper.'

'I think I bopped with the best of them.'

His expression disagreed. 'On my fourteenth birthday, Mum and Dad took me and my brothers to Tony's. Back then, pizza was my favourite food.'

'And now?'

'Medium rare, truffle-salt-infused Angus steak.'

'Not to be specific or anything.' She wanted to laugh but stopped herself. He constantly surprised her and that made him far more dangerous to her equilibrium and her long-held commitment to herself.

'Hey, you won't scoff when you taste it.'

'I'm vegetarian.'

He pressed his fist to his chest. 'You're breaking my heart. Anyway, back to my story. You walked into Tony's dressed head to toe in black and wearing a T-shirt with some sort of "up yours" slogan. I figured you'd got into grunge music. I planned to ask you but I never got the chance—you left for boarding school soon after that.'

She knew exactly which night he was talking about but it stunned her that twenty years later he was mentioning it. 'Why would you even remember that?'

Just like the time he told her he knew the lyrics to 'Let It Go', the tips of Luke's ears burned red. 'Jeez, I really shouldn't drink whiskey. It's like truth serum.'

'Too late now,' she said with a grin and refilled his glass.

'Well, the thing is, Ellie Jamieson,' he said, clearing his throat, 'I ... I had a bit of a crush on you back then.'

'Really? You used to tease me that I ran like a girl.'

He shot her a sidelong glance from under his messy hair, his eyes bright with mischief. 'And you chased me. It worked pretty well until we went to high school and you realised the older boys had far more sophisticated pickup lines.'

She laughed. 'You mean things like, "You're hot. I'm hotter. Meet me behind the shelter sheds?"'

'See? Up against poetry like that, I had no hope. I was benched with the mortals and you were this vivacious whirlwind of colour that made everyone else look pale and insipid. My brothers teased me mercilessly. Eventually even Mum and Dad gently suggested you were way out of my league and that your mother wouldn't let me anywhere near you. After that photo of you in the paper at Sarah's wedding, there were rumours that you'd got a modelling contract in Melbourne.

I think that's why, when you arrived at Tony's in head-to-toe black instead of the bright colours you always wore, it stuck with me.'

She glanced down at her black boots, baggy pants and bulky polar fleece and an old ache burned. *No.* 'Looks like the only thing that's changed is I lost the "up yours" T-shirt.' The quip fell flat.

'You still into grunge music?'

'I'm into comfortable clothing.'

He sipped his whiskey, deep in thought. 'What happened to colourful Ellie?'

Her heart twisted. 'She grew up.'

'Did she come out?'

Deflect. Deflect. Deflect. The direct question shot her protective barriers into place with the speed of a falling guillotine. 'You should have warned me that whiskey totally destroys your filter.'

He shifted his weight and set down his glass. 'Actually, it's got nothing to do with the whiskey. I've been wanting to ask you that question for weeks.'

It wasn't the first time someone had asked her if she was gay, but it was the first time the question came from someone she didn't want to lie to. If she told Luke the truth, she had a very strong suspicion he'd take the answer as an opportunity to ask her out. She didn't want to hurt his feelings by saying no.

'I told you how I got pregnant with Noah.'

He shrugged. 'Traumatic situations make us do crazy things. You said so yourself.'

'Gay, straight or bi, it doesn't change who I am.'

'I get that. But I need to know.'

'Why?'

'Because you've been living with three out and proud lesbians. Because ...' He ran his hand through his hair, tugging at it. 'Sometimes I get this amazing flirty vibe from you that makes me walk on air. Other times, it's like there's this enormous patch of bindii stretching between us and if I stand on it, it's gonna hurt like buggery. It's confusing the hell out of me.'

'Sorry.'

'Sorry?'

'I don't know what else to say.'

'Okay then, how about this. Do you feel a vibe?'

Don't touch it. Leave it alone. It will only end badly. Say no.

But the quiet voice of her counsellor rose in her mind. *There are good men in the world, Ellie. Only you can decide if you believe that.*

She drained the glass as hope and fear split her in two. 'I ... I've felt it.'

'Thank God.'

He was suddenly close, his body solid in front of her. Alarm leaped, skittling along her veins and sending her pulse soaring. *No escape. No way out.* The edge of the bookcase pressed hard against her back, reinforcing her stupidity.

'Ellie?'

The hesitancy in his voice made her look up. The smile on his face dazzled her like the diamond sparkle of snow on a sunny day and she glimpsed the young boy she'd once raced along the perimeter of the school grounds.

This is Luke. He brought you coffee. He made you tea. He's only ever been kind.

You know kind is just an illusion. That nice always gift-wraps the ugly truth.

Panic ramped up, detonating bombs of agitation in every cell, and sweat drenched her. For the first time in years she'd let down her guard and now she was trapped. The outcome was inevitable: he was going to kiss her. He would wrap his arms around her, pull her in close and whisper in her ear. A silent scream shrieked in her head. Amid the swirling fear, the survivor in her struck out, separating herself from the situation with chilling calm. Seizing control, she pressed her hands against Luke's shoulders to keep his body from touching hers, and then she leaned in and kissed him.

Nine years had passed since she'd last kissed a man but somethings didn't change. She knew exactly what she was doing. Tilt the head.

Close the eyes. Press lips against lips. Flick tongue along lips. Slip tongue in mouth. Roll tongue on tongue. Flick—

Luke pulled away.

Her eyes flew open and focused.

He was frowning at her.

'What?'

'I can't work out if you want to do this or not.'

This is your out. Take it and run. 'I guess the vibe is off. We're obviously not kissing compatible.' She ducked sideways and crossed the room, positioning herself closer to the door and a clear exit, should she need it. 'Win some, lose some.'

'Don't go pulling any punches.' He rubbed his face. '*This* is exactly what I've been talking about. Why tell me you feel a vibe and then kiss me like you're painting by numbers?'

She'd expected aggression and was ready to match it but he sounded utterly poleaxed. The hurt in his voice slayed her.

'I'm sorry.'

'No!'

The word hung in the room, but he didn't move towards her or try to get close to her again. Instead, he lowered his considerable frame onto the old couch and crossed his arms. He was an immoveable, bewildered and decidedly pissed-off force.

'Sorry's way too easy.'

His ability to cut straight to the essence of an issue scared the hell out of her. 'You do realise I can just walk out and leave you sitting there.'

'I know.'

'So ...?'

He shrugged. 'Talk to me.'

She opened the door. 'Or you could just leave.'

He dropped his head for a moment, looking like the weight of the world rested on his broad shoulders. As he sat back, a sigh rumbled out of him. 'Ellie, I like to think I'm evolved. My dad taught me no means no and my mother would hang, draw and quarter me if I ever disrespected a woman. God knows, I'd love to kiss you senseless, but I'm not going to do it if that's not what you want. And that kiss you just gave me pretty much screamed, "Give him what *he* wants and get it over and done with fast."'

She couldn't deny it; it was a modus operandi she'd used from her teens to her early twenties until the day it put her in physical danger.

'I like you, Ellie. Sometimes I'm convinced you like me just as much. I'd love nothing more than to have the opportunity to get to know you and explore the possibilities of something deeper. If there's any chance a part of you wants to try, I've got the time. There's no need to rush into anything.'

Dread drowned the last few strands of possibility and a sob she didn't know she'd been holding back rose in her throat. 'You're too nice, Luke. And I'm too difficult.'

'I doubt either of those are absolutes.'

'Oh, they are.' She wrung her hands against the tug of his sincerity. 'I'm too much like hard work. No, scratch that. I *am* hard work. You deserve someone easier and a lot less screwed up than me.'

'This isn't my first rodeo, Ellie. I can decide that for myself.'

She pressed her lips together to stop the sob from escaping. 'You say that now, but you'll change your mind. I don't want to hurt you.' *I don't want you to hurt me.* 'And there's Noah. I won't let anyone hurt him. He's at a vulnerable age. Plus, all this shit with my family ...'

'I think you're busy lobbing roadblocks at me so you don't even have to try.' He caught her gaze, his own intense and searching. 'What's really going on? Has some bastard done a number on you, Ellie? If he told you that you don't deserve to be happy, he's wrong.'

His words crashed into her like storm waves pounding onto the shore and she fought back. 'Oh, right and this is when you tell me that unlike every man who's preceded you, you're the one who'll make me happy.'

'Nope. I'm optimistic but I'm not stupid. You're responsible for your own happiness. But I reckon I could contribute to it if you opened the door just a bit. Let me try.'

'You scare me, Luke.'

His shoulders dropped. 'That devastates me.'

A rogue tear rolled down her cheek and she blinked rapidly. 'You know I'm prickly and sarcastic. You said yourself I blow hot and cold. I might make your life miserable.' *You might make mine miserable.* 'Why do you even want to try?'

He held out his hand. 'Because you're you. You're worth the risk.'

His honesty sent all her protective instincts into freefall. She scrambled to pull them back, brick them into place and stay safe. It had been such a long time since she'd dared to trust anyone and she didn't know if she had it in her to do it again. But suddenly it was harder not to try than to take his hand.

She pressed her palm to his and their fingers entwined. 'For your sake, I hope I am.'

CHAPTER FOURTEEN

Sarah checked the leg of lamb and turned the vegetables. Gus was coming for Sunday lunch. It had been a leap of faith to use the old oven in the flat, but it appeared to be maintaining its temperature perfectly and the potatoes looked crisp and golden brown. The idea for a roast hit her late the night before after she'd made a to-do list and written 'Mum's old will' and underlined it. She planned to be on the doorstep of Dan's office at eight thirty Monday morning.

Ideally, she'd wanted to phone him that morning, but Mary Horton still cooked a traditional Sunday roast lunch just as she had all her married life, despite the fact Robert was no longer alive to carve and hold court at the end of the long mahogany table. Regardless of the busy life Dan led, and the fact he now had a family of his own, he attended his mother's Sunday lunches. This both bemused and humbled Sarah. Politicians should reference the Hortons when they banged on about 'traditional family values'; unlike her family, the Hortons had it in spades. Sarah's roast lunch was an attempt to give Gus something that resembled normal.

She was preparing the beans when his knock sounded on the door.

'Come in, Gus,' she called as she walked to the door. 'It's open. You don't have to kno—'

'Hello, Sarah.'

'Alex.' She stumbled over his name and the shock of seeing him standing in the doorway stilled her feet. She hadn't seen him since she'd left Riverbend. The first thing she noticed about him was the fatigue lines dragging at his eyes. Concern flickered, but anger squashed it hard and fast, almost knocking her sideways. She rose on her toes and glanced over his shoulder. 'Where's Gus?'

'I don't know.'

'You don't *know*?'

Alex's jaw clenched at the screech in her voice. 'He told me he's getting here under his own steam. Something about Ebony and Jack.'

'Then why are you here?'

'Because we need to talk.'

'Oh, really? And that went so well last time.'

'Christ, Sarah. I never took you for a bitch but you're doing a bloody good job proving me wrong.' He stepped past her into the flat, aggression rolling off him. 'By the way, great stunt taking leave without notice, but that's not why I'm here. I don't appreciate being made a fool of.'

She had no idea what he was talking about but it didn't stop her taking the cheap shot. 'I think you're doing a good enough job of that on your own with a woman fifteen years younger than you.'

'Leave Kelly out of this.'

'I don't see how that's possible when she's the reason we're in this situation.'

'She's not the reason,' he muttered before swinging around to face her. 'I've deliberately kept things quiet so less people get hurt. No one knows—'

'I know!' His betrayal burned all over again. 'I fucking know, but apparently my feelings don't matter.'

'Your feelings?' His voice rose. 'What about mine? I'm doing my best to protect the kids and half the town sees you staggering home drunk with *Edmund*.'

A stinging swoop of shock hit her. *He knew? How?* She couldn't recall seeing anyone that night but then again, she'd been more than tipsy. And the only reason she'd drunk so much was because Alex had upended their lives for no good reason.

'Half the town? Wow. I didn't see that many people when I *walked* home with Edmund after dinner at the restaurant. I'm surprised that anyone even noticed two old friends walking together.'

'Oh yeah, the two of you have always been good friends.'

The hardness on his face made her start and guilt slithered in. 'The *three* of us are close friends,' she reminded him. 'For eighteen years, Alex.'

'No, Sarah.' The edge in his voice was as sharp as a Stanley knife. 'You and Edmund are close friends. I was only ever his employer.'

Did a midlife crisis alter reality? 'Don't be ridiculous. You've played golf with him. He delivered Gus—'

'And I can hardly forget that when you remind me of it almost every damn time we see him.'

She rolled her eyes. 'Oh, you mean once a year on Gus's birthday? Gus loves hearing that story. And what about the ski trips and the houseboat holidays we took together before Catriona and the girls died? Friends do things like that together. When the bank refused his loan to start the restaurant, it was your idea to lend him the money. Only a close friend or family would risk that sort of cash.'

'I gave him the loan so he'd quit.'

What? They'd never employed anyone she trusted as much as Edmund. Back in the early days, she'd called them all the three musketeers and when Edmund left, it had placed a lot of pressure on her and Alex for months as they recruited and trained his replacements.

'We had to employ *two* people to do his job.'

Alex crossed his arms and his mouth thinned. 'And I'd have

employed three if it meant he wasn't in our office and our home every damn day with you like a slobbering puppy.'

She stared at him, gobsmacked. Surely Alex wasn't jealous of Edmund?

Why not? The moment things went pear-shaped with Alex, you slept with Edmund.

Her stomach rolled and she sat down hard on a dining chair. 'I had no idea you felt that way. Why didn't you say something?'

Uncharacteristically, he ducked his head for a moment before bringing it back up. 'Would there have been a point? You'd have defended Edmund.'

She opened her mouth to give an outraged, 'No!' and closed it again. It bothered her that her feelings were ambiguous. 'At least I'd have known how you felt. I hope I would have understood.'

'Maybe I didn't want to take the risk that you wouldn't.' He ran his hand across the back of his neck. 'But it's a moot point now, isn't it? Poor Edmund's been back in our lives full time since the accident, seeking comfort from you.'

His callousness shocked her. 'His wife and daughters died!'

'I know!' he yelled back. 'Do you think I want to hate him for losing his family? That his tragedy brought him back into our marriage and for eighteen months I've had to share you with him all over again? It makes me sick to my stomach that I feel this way but at least I can stop beating myself up about it, because the inevitable's finally happened. For someone who was so outraged about Kelly, you turned to Edmund pretty bloody fast.'

Pangs of conscience made Sarah's grip on her resentment slippery. 'It's totally different. This isn't some lust fest with a gold-digging bimbo. I've known Edmund for years. He's a friend!'

'And I bet he comforted you just the way he's wanted to for years.' Alex's eyes narrowed, pinning her with vitriol. 'Now the boot's on the other foot, Sarah. You're slumming it on the lowlands with the rest of us. If I find out he's sleeping here, I'll make things very difficult.'

'Oh, take a number,' she said, her anger deflating as exhaustion rushed in.

'What?'

His furious expression had changed to perplexed and two familiar concentration lines carved deeply across the bridge of his nose. They always appeared when he was trying to nut out a tricky problem and her heart ached. *I miss you.* The need to talk to him was so strong she kicked out a chair and poured two glasses of water from the jug she'd set on the table for lunch.

'Cameron and Anita have joined you in making things difficult.'

He hesitated a moment and then sat. 'How?'

'I think they've been committing elder abuse.'

He laughed and she shot him a stony look.

'Oh, come on, Sarah. Fair go. Surely you can see the irony in that statement? Margaret's as tough as old boots. If there was any abuse involved, it's more likely she'd be the perpetrator. Remember when she toppled Mary Horton as CWA president? Even you agreed it was a vicious campaign, especially so soon after Robert's death. It was one of the few times you stood up to her and told her what you really thought.'

'That's why this situation with Cameron and Anita's such a shock. But hindsight is a bugger and, given recent events, I think Mum's been slowly losing her memory for some time. I hate that I didn't see it. Worse than that, it kills me that they've been taking advantage of her right under my nose.' She told him about the gifts, the will, the power of attorney, Cameron refusing to allow Ellie to live at Mill House and how she'd moved her in the night before.

'You changed the locks? Go you. Cam won't be expecting that.' He grinned at her, his eyes as warm as melted chocolate.

There's my Alex. Delight filled her as she saw his pride in her. If he could look at her like that, surely he must still love her? If he still loved her, then they could come back from this nightmare they were currently living. She grinned back at him and the angst of the last nine days dimmed a little. Hope dared to glow.

He sobered. 'Did you talk to Dan about it first? It's probably not legal.'

'Probably, but the police aren't going to get involved in what they consider a civil matter. If Cam wants, he can file an application at VCAT and force a hearing or he can be reasonable and let Ellie live there. I'm talking to Dan in the morning. It's all one big mess and I'm struggling to wrap my head around it. I mean, up until Friday, I assumed Mum would be well enough to return home in a couple of weeks.'

'Gus told me Margaret's in hospital. It must be a worrying time for you.'

His sympathy was an unexpected balm and she floated in it. 'It is. Oh, and thank you for sending her flowers.' On her most recent visit to Margaret, she'd been surprised to see the pretty bouquet of pink roses and white gerberas in a pink box wrapped with organza ribbon, and his *Sorry to hear you're in hospital. Get Well Soon* message. Alex wasn't known for sending flowers. 'It was very thoughtful.'

He swallowed and at the same time tugged at the crew neck of his jumper. The action itself was unremarkable except that she'd been married to Alex for twenty-two years and knew him too well. It was like a knife to the heart and her rage rushed back, furnace hot.

'Oh my God! Kelly sent them.'

His face flushed but his body stiffened in hostility. 'I paid for them. It doesn't matter who placed the order.'

She shot to her feet, screaming, 'Of course it bloody matters! You asked your fuck buddy to send flowers to my mother!'

'God, Sarah, you can be fucking unreasonable.'

'Mum? Dad?' Gus stood just inside the door. The look on his face destroyed her.

'Gus. Darling. We didn't hear you come in.'

'Yeah.' His knuckles shone white against the strap of his backpack. 'That'd be because you're too busy swearing at each other. Nice. Really nice. Lucky you don't have neighbours.'

'That's enough, Gus,' Alex said wearily. 'This is between your mother and me.'

'Sometimes adults—' Sarah started and faulted. *What? Behave like children? Brawl like cats and dogs?* 'Lunch is almost ready. I've cooked a roast.'

Her son was looking at her as if she'd lost her mind. Perhaps she had.

'I'm not hungry. You two keep screaming at each other. I'm going to Jack's.'

'Gus, please.'

But he'd closed the door on her.

She grabbed her keys. 'I'll go and talk to him.'

'He won't listen to you right now. Best thing is to leave him to cool down.'

She hated that Alex had a point. Hated that her darling son had heard them tearing each other apart. Before this awful impasse, they'd rarely argued and when they had, they'd made sure it took place away from the children. Back then, their arguments had respect woven through them, preventing them from deteriorating into a vicious slanging match. But now they were savage with the intent of inflicting flesh wounds and drawing blood. Alex had reduced their marriage to this crippled and bleeding vessel.

'This is *your* fault, Alex. You're one hundred per cent to blame.'

'You keep telling yourself that, Sarah. I hope it helps you sleep at night.'

He slammed the door and she grabbed the nearest thing to hand and threw it. As the heavy glass jar of marinated goat's cheese dented the wooden door and cracked, the symbolism wasn't lost on her.

Anita listened to Cameron ranting about Sarah and Ellie. Given the speed he was shovelling her apple and rhubarb crumble into his mouth, she worried he'd give himself indigestion.

'And on top of all the sister bullshit, today at the hospital the doctor pulled me aside. He said Mum's blood pressure is all over the shop and she's got something called rapid vascular dementia.'

'Oh God. What's that?'

'Not enough blood's getting to her brain.'

'What can they do?'

'Not very much.' His voice broke and he gulped another mouthful of crumble. 'Old age is such bastard. One minute everything's normal and the next it's shot to hell!'

'Breathe, darling.' She squeezed his hand. 'I'm really sorry about your mum, but if you keep on like this, you're going to make yourself sick too.'

He looked at her wild-eyed and bewildered; childlike. 'You asked me to do one thing for you. You said don't let Ellie move into the house. Now she's bloody living there.'

'It's not your fault, Cam,' she said stoutly. 'I blame Sarah completely. I can't forgive her for not telling us or backing us up. Ellie virtually said to me that she didn't want to live in Mill House so I thought once you laid down the law, she'd back down. I mean, who moves in the middle of the night to a house she doesn't like and changes the locks?'

'That's Sarah's work. Ellie can barely pay her rent let alone drop three hundred and fifty bucks on an out-of-hours locksmith.'

'Can we kick her out?'

'We can, but Sarah's no fool. I talked to Rupert today and it's going to take weeks.'

'Weeks?' A flutter of despair lodged in her chest. 'What if you find Ellie a place to live?'

'In her price range? Unlikely.'

'I can't be locked out of Mill House for weeks. I'm just getting traction with Cooked By a Friend. Do you think if we compromised, Ellie would meet us halfway?'

'Hah! When have you ever known Ellie to be compliant?'

She considered his statement. 'I know you said she was an out-of-control teenager and we both know she was pretty wild in her twenties and Noah was the result. But since she moved back to the valley she's participated in some family things. For the sake of the business, we need to try to negotiate with her.'

'The idea sticks in my craw.' He pushed the empty bowl away, the spoon clattering against the china. 'This is my fault. I made a tactical error telling Sarah about the will, thinking she'd respect Mum's wishes. Turns out, Mum's been the sensible one all this time. She knew exactly what she was doing, keeping the contents of her will a secret. I should have too.'

Cameron's hangdog expression drew Anita out of her chair and into his lap. With all the weekend drama and the day being consumed by talking to doctors and lawyers, they'd been too busy to debrief on the particulars of the two wills. The details of the new will both delighted and shocked her.

'I suppose I can sort of understand Margaret leaving Ellie out of the will, but Sarah? I think it's crushed her.'

'Yeah, it's tough. At first I was furious with bland Dan for letting Mum write her will like that but now I see it wasn't his fault. Both Rupert and I tried to convince her it was a bad idea but she was adamant she was sticking to her guns.'

'You've finally seen the old will?'

'Yeah.' He laughed. 'No wonder you couldn't find a copy in the study. When we popped in to get it on our way to Melbourne, she went straight to the bookshelves in the lounge room and pulled it out of a copy of *Bleak House*.'

'*Bleak House?*'

'It's a classic. Charles Dickens.'

That didn't enlighten Anita at all. 'Why would she keep it there?'

'It's a joke.' He patted her arm. 'There's a legal case in the book all about an inheritance.'

'Oh.' Anita's ignorance wrapped her up in humiliation. Every now and then her lack of a tertiary education filled her with a keen sense of shame. 'I suppose I should read it.'

'Why bother?' Cameron kissed her. 'I love that you know more about the latest blockbuster than the dusty old classics.'

Reassured, she brought the conversation back to the will. 'Sarah's always been Margaret's go-to person.'

'Yeah, but Mum's got a point. Sarah and Alex are completely loaded. And I know you said she hasn't told Mum about her and Alex yet, but if they get divorced, she'll still have plenty.'

'But an inheritance is more than just the money. It's love. Unlike Margaret, my mother was a totally crap mother and she didn't have much, but at least she left it all to me.'

His brows rose. 'You sent everything to the Brotherhood— except for that cheap necklace you won't wear because it turns your skin green.'

'I know, but that's totally different from her not leaving me anything. Nothing at all would be a permanent message from the grave that I wasn't even worth her cheap furniture.' Anita swallowed past an unwanted lump in her throat. 'I like to think it was Mum's way of apologising.'

He gave her waist a squeeze. 'That's way behind you, baby girl.'

She snuggled into his chest, grateful and thankful all of it was very firmly in the past. 'I can't believe Margaret's left Mill House to me. I mean, I never thought she really liked me.'

He stroked her hair. 'She loves you. You've got more in common with her than either of her daughters. She's leaving it to both of us, it's just right now we're better off financially if it's in your name. It's all to do with asset loading.'

She didn't quite understand but it clarified what had seemed to her to be an odd decision. 'And that's why she's breaking tradition?'

'Not breaking, exactly. More like tweaking tradition to help us out. She said as long as Dad's wishes were honoured and I got the house, it was all good, otherwise Dad might haunt her.'

'Your mum's remarkable the way she always honours your dad. God, she must have loved him.'

'Why sound so surprised?' Cameron slid her off his knee with a gentle slap to her behind before standing up and walking to the couch. 'I'd like to think you'd be just as loving if I died.'

She sat next to him. 'I'll always love you but would you really want me to be alone for twenty-six years? I don't get why she didn't remarry. It's not like she didn't have a choice. Even now, the old blokes at the bowls club fall over themselves to buy her a drink.'

'I'm glad she didn't remarry. Imagine if we'd had to share her wealth with another family.' He shuddered. 'Lucky for us she didn't. Even better, she's looking after us. The one change she did make in the new will was a suggestion from Rupert.'

'What?'

'An education trust for the girls.'

She stared at him, too thrilled to speak until she reached bursting point and a squeal of delight slipped out. 'Oh my God! I can't believe it. First Mill House and now a trust. Oh, Cam. We can finally relax.'

Kissing him, she gave over to the joy sweeping through her, letting it drive out the constant niggling fear their current debt level triggered. She wanted her daughters to have the best education possible, and what parent didn't want that? Even with Margaret's current assistance, the school fees hovered over their heads like an ominous cloud. Now the little girls were assured of the same high-quality education as their older sisters.

Thinking about Ava and Chloe brought Noah to mind. Despite his boisterous enthusiasm, which was so different from the girls and often overwhelmed her, he was a happy and loving little boy. Ellie, for all her flaws and general thoughtlessness, had at least got that right. But Anita had learned from an early age that society doesn't always honour the dictum that the sins of the mother should not be foisted onto an innocent child.

'The trust includes Noah too, right?'

'Mum was very specific. There's just enough for our girls.'

'But—'

'Sorry,' he said softly, pressing his finger to her lips. 'I did my best.'

'I'm sure you did.' Anita blinked, disconcerted by the sudden sting of tears.

'Someone's taken my cigarettes.' Margaret shook out her handbag before opening the drawer of a horrible mass-produced bedside table. 'You've abandoned me to live with thieves. Your father would be furious.'

'No one's taken them.'

Margaret shook off Sarah's hand. 'I want a drink and I want a cigarette!'

'Let's go for walk. You can have one in the garden.'

Sarah held out her navy woollen coat and Margaret slipped her arms into the sleeves, craving the familiarity of it. It was a classic Perri Cutten and one of her favourite pieces. Anticipation tingled in her fingertips as she dropped her hand into the hidden pocket seeking the solid, reassuring touch of sterling silver. Her fingers splayed. She rolled her wrist. All she felt was the coolness of silk. Frantic, she whirled around.

'You stole my hip flask.'

You little bitch. It's not yours. He gave it to me. Give. It. Back. Right now, Ellie, or you're grounded.

Why would I want that stinking hip flask? If you weren't half drunk all the time, you'd know you left it in the bar. It's sitting next to the empty space where your vodka used to be. I stole that.

'I'm not drunk!'

'Mum, it's okay. I know you're not drunk. Here, hold onto your handbag and we'll go outside.'

'Sarah?' Her eldest daughter's voice startled her. 'What are you doing here? When did you get back from France?'

'I've been back a while. Let's talk outside.' Sarah ushered her through the sliding door out into the garden.

'You and Alex should have come home earlier. It was bad enough you left me, but I've had to cope with your sister on my own. She's totally out of control. I'm beside myself with worry. Do you know she's sneaking out at night and drinking and doing God knows what down at the river with those Malevich boys?' Margaret tugged her coat tightly around her. 'If she's going to be a slut at least I've got her on the pill. The last thing I need is her pregnant to that uncouth family.'

'She'll grow out if it, Mum. Ellie *will* be okay.'

'Hmph! That's what people say but I'm the only one who really knows what she's like. I'm the one dealing with the lies and the stealing. I've made up my mind. I'm sending her to boarding school.'

Sarah indicated a wooden seat and as they sat, she produced a packet of cigarettes and a lighter.

'Oh!' Margaret clapped her hands. 'You really are my favourite daughter.' She accepted the lit cigarette and inhaled greedily. The warm smoke drifted into her lungs and then a divine coolness swept her body, bringing a tingling and relaxing bliss. 'God, this is almost as good as sex.'

Sarah made a choking sound.

'Oh, for heaven's sake, Sarah. I might be a widow but I'm not dead.'

'I know, it's just that since Dad died, I thought ...'

Margaret laughed, delighted to have shocked her prudish daughter. She had no idea how Sarah had managed to land the extremely good-looking Alex Hadfield when she was utterly clueless about using her body to hook a man and keep him interested. Ellie, on the other hand, had far too much of that particular talent. 'I'm having more sex now your father's dead than I ever had when he was alive.'

Sarah's brown eyes widened. 'I—that's—I didn't know ...'

'Oh, yes.' Margaret drew in another long draught of smoke. 'I've always been a big fan of sex ...'

'You use sex like a weapon, Margaret.' Kevin pushed her away from his lap. 'I won't be used any more.'

'Used? Oh, that's rich coming from a man who needs more help getting it up than a eunuch.'

'Has it ever occurred to you that perhaps it's you I can't get it up for?'

Her hand shot out, palm open, but he caught her wrist.

'I've had enough, Margaret. Neither of us deserves this. I want out.'

A cold sweat broke across her skin, emanating the stench of fear. It had been years since it filled her nostrils, clogged her throat and seared her tastebuds with poverty, powerlessness and social ignominy. She'd worked far too hard for this comfortable and privileged life to lose it. Staying married to Kevin was essential to maintaining it.

'I'm pregnant.'

He stared at her, his face ashen. 'How?'

'Oh, for God's sake! Have you conveniently blocked out the Lovetts' party?'

'Christ.' He shoved his hands through his grey-streaked hair. 'But we decided no more kids. Hell, you made that decree years ago when Cameron was born.'

'You should have thought of that before you raped me in the pool house.'

'I did not rape you. You're my wife.'

'That doesn't give you the right to force yourself on me.'

'Don't bullshit me, Margaret. You've always liked it rough.'

'There's a big difference between consensual sex and rape. I said no.' She hadn't. She'd taken advantage of his drunken state and lured him there. The next morning when he was sober, she'd showed him the dress she'd ripped and told him he was the one to ruin it. As she'd expected, Kevin was mortified and she'd filed his reaction away for future ammunition. Now she fired it.

'Who knew all it took was anger to maintain your erection long enough to do the job? Well done! After all these years of subpar work, you've knocked me up.'

He winced and looked as if he was about to throw up. 'What about an abortion?'

Margaret had considered it. Three months earlier, the thought consumed every waking moment and most of her dreams. Terminating an inconvenient pregnancy was the practical thing to do and she'd got as far as booking an appointment in Melbourne. When the day arrived, she'd cancelled. Not because she couldn't go through with the procedure but because, for months, she'd had a growing suspicion that her mostly compliant husband was bubbling with dissatisfaction. A baby was leverage. Kevin was toast.

'Of course I considered an abortion. It was the first thing I thought of the moment Andrew gave me the horrifying news. But it's too late. I'm already four months.'

'Four months? Surely you had suspicions you were pregnant long before now?'

She thought fast. 'I'm forty, Kevin. I thought it was early menopause.'

He stared at her, clearly perplexed. 'But every time you're pregnant, you're sick for weeks. Surely that was a clue?'

'I haven't been sick this time.' This was the truth. 'It has to be the only upside of being pregnant at forty.'

'When were you planning on telling me?'

She wrung her hands and forced herself to sound penitent. 'I've wanted to tell you for days but since your last trip to Melbourne, you've been virtually silent. When you're not at the mill, you're out in the shed. That's why I made an effort with dinner tonight, I was trying to smooth things over between us. Not that you appreciated it but one of us had to do something. You know things between us have been ... difficult ... since the pool house.' She sniffed and brushed away a tear. 'Our blameless baby doesn't deserve to grow up in a broken family just because we didn't try hard enough.'

Haggard lines tugged at Kevin's features and she saw the struggle playing out clearly on his face; it was exactly as she'd hoped. Kevin loved being a father and he was a good one. Loving and far more patient than she was, he went to every boring sports match and every interminable music concert with cheerful good grace. Although he always came on the family holidays she arranged— somewhere warm and luxurious where she didn't have to cook—he also took the kids camping, bringing them home filthy and happy. He might want to leave her but he'd hate leaving the children. This was her first weapon. Her second was George. Although her father-in-law was in his late seventies, his opinion still ruled. Margaret was secure in the knowledge that George would side with her. Kevin knew it too.

Kevin poured himself a whiskey; a sure sign he was at breaking point. 'Exactly how do you propose we make this work?'

'Mum?'

Margaret opened her eyes. 'What?'

'Did you and Dad ... have problems?'

'Of course not,' Margaret said indignantly, stubbing out the cigarette with a vicious twist. 'Honestly, Sarah, sometimes you say the most ridiculous things.'

CHAPTER FIFTEEN

Ellie slid into her office chair, pleased to be back in the warmth of the neighbourhood house. The morning had been consumed by home visits and the afternoon was earmarked for follow-up phone calls. Consulting her volunteer list, she wondered who would be the best person to give a couple of Burmese women some driving lessons.

'Knock knock.'

Delight swooped in before she even looked up. All it took was Luke's rumbling voice for a delicious tingle to skate across her skin. As part of her need to protect Noah and their decision to 'go slowly', Luke dropped into the neighbourhood house if he happened to be in Valley View. It seemed he was in town at some point every day.

Skating her chair back from the desk, she stood. 'Hello.'

'G'day. Just passing by, thought I'd drop in,' he said in an exaggerated accent. 'Got time for a picnic lunch?'

She pointed to the window. 'It's six degrees out there and sleeting.'

'I didn't say it was going to be outside.' He leaned in and she tried hard not to tense as he dropped his head and planted a kiss on her cheek as if they were a normal couple.

She craved normality but she feared it too. Since the night at Mill

House, when she'd accepted his outstretched hand and he'd gently cuddled her against him, she'd been working on relaxing into his touch. Not that they'd done much more than cuddle and kiss, but he did both particularly well. Each night after Noah was in bed, Luke Face Timed her and they talked; sometimes for two hours. He always started by asking about her day. He sounded genuinely interested in the goings on at the neighbourhood house. They talked politics, books and films, Mingunyah gossip, his family—never hers—and the night before, at his suggestion, they'd streamed the same TV show simultaneously, talking on the phone as they'd watched it. It had been like sitting together on the couch and she was both surprised and relieved that she missed having his arm around her and snuggling in. Missed putting her head on his chest and hearing his heartbeat. Missed his body heat and musky male scent.

True to his promise, Luke hadn't mentioned sex. She was grateful for that but at the same time she couldn't stop feeling that sex was the baby elephant in the room that was only going to grow bigger. But for now, instead of passion, excitement and high-octane sex, she was mostly embracing and appreciating old-world courting. She'd never experienced anything like it and she wanted to believe it was a sign of intrinsic good. However, that was a part of the problem. Her instincts with men were never good and in the past they had done nothing to protect her.

There are good men in the world. Only you can decide if you believe that.

'I thought we could have a carpet picnic.' Luke pushed back some chairs to create a space and spread out a rug before producing two baguettes and two piping hot lattes from Le Fournil, Valley View's very own French bakery. It was a recent and blessed addition to the town courtesy of Phillippe, a baker from Bordeaux who had fallen madly in love with a local winemaker. Phillippe had the lightest touch with pastry and even the most homophobic folk in the district could be seen enjoying one of his eclairs or profiteroles.

'One vegetarian baguette for you and the charcuterie for me.'

Luke bit into the fully loaded sandwich and bliss broke over his face. She watched him with a freedom that was both foreign and enjoyable, trying not to let her mind catastrophise that this liberty might come back to bite her.

'Food isn't just fuel for you, is it?'

'Just fuel?' He gave an exaggerated shudder. 'My taste buds are offended. Mum's a fantastic cook and I was raised on the mantra that good food is one of life's joys.'

She tasted the memory of burned chops and gluggy tuna casserole. 'Not when my mother cooked.'

'Is that why you're vego?'

'Not really—I kind of fell into it. It started in Thailand as meat was scarce and continued in Sydney where meat was expensive. Then, when I moved to Guthrie Farm, the household was vegetarian. As we shared the cooking, it was just easier if I was vegetarian too.'

He cocked his head and his hair fell into his eyes. He brushed it back. 'So it's not an ethical issue? If I cooked you a roast, would you eat it?'

She considered the question. 'If it was a free-range chook, I might be tempted.'

'You're on. When?'

He looked ridiculously happy at the idea of cooking for her and she worked on relaxing into his delight. 'I have to work tonight and it can't be tomorrow, because I'm not leaving Noah two nights in a row.'

'Noah can come. The more the merrier.'

'Not yet, Luke.' She steeled herself for a snide or manipulative comment but he merely shrugged.

'Fair call. It's early days.'

'Thank you.' Relief made her lean over to kiss him. 'Really.'

'Wow. If that's all it takes for you to kiss me, I'll have to agree with you more often.' He put down his baguette and pulled her into his lap. Sliding his large hands into her hair, he kissed her long and deep but without demand; giving far more than he took.

Her limbs liquefied and she looped her arms around his neck, returning his kiss. This time her mind was thankfully out of the game and her body took advantage of its silence, revelling in responding uninhibitedly to his touch and taste.

When they both drew back for breath, he rested his forehead against hers.

'I've fantasised about this for longer than I'm prepared to admit.'

'Kissing me at work?'

'Kissing you full stop.' He tucked an errant curl behind her ear. 'But I have to admit there's a definite thrill sneaking a kiss from you at work.'

She caught sight of the clock and scrambled out of his lap. 'I don't want to shock the good women of Valley View who offer their time free of charge to tutor English on a Thursday afternoon.'

'I dunno. A bit of voyeurism can be healthy.'

She laughed and stood up. 'Time to get back to work, plumber boy.'

'Yep. The Parrys' state-of-the-art AC system awaits.'

'They're organised. The first hot day's months away.'

'And sadly, they'll never use it.' He scrunched the white bakery bags before tossing them into her bin with the accuracy of a basketball player. 'Warrnbatt's down on the river flat with a clear view of Mount Defiance. Between the sound of rushing water and the cacophony of bird song, it's idyllic, but I reckon they fell in love with the dream. That and probably watching too many re-runs of *Grand Designs*.'

'What do you mean?'

'They overcapitalised on the reno. Then they got hit by last year's flood. Chris took a job in Albury and they figured—wrongly—that Warrnbatt would sell fast, so they bought a place there. The bridging finance has gotta be killing them. Anyway, your brother's the agent and he called me the other day to set up the job. He reckons the lack of a decent heating and cooling system is putting off his city-slicker buyers.'

'I would have thought being close to the river was more of a problem?'

'Could be. It's flooded twice in the last five years and given how weather events are changing ...' He lifted the picnic rug she'd folded out of her hands and kissed her. 'Catch ya later.'

She almost asked, 'When?' but she wasn't doing needy ever again so she said, 'Totally,' and immediately felt foolish.

Operation Get the Key to Mill House was keeping Anita fully occupied.

With Margaret's favourite coconut and jam slice tucked in her basket, Anita hummed as she walked down the hospital corridor to visit her mother-in-law. She had the visit all planned. After tea and as much jam slice as Margaret could eat, Anita would mention the new locks in passing. Margaret would be appropriately shocked and horrified by the situation and immediately instruct Sarah to give Anita a key. Sarah, who, unlike Ellie, found it almost impossible to refuse Margaret anything, now had an added incentive to comply: the thorny issue of the will and the inheritance. Sarah would oblige her mother. The Mill House key was in the bag.

Margaret was resting on the bed and Anita opened the conversation chattily, mentioning how well Vintage Glamour was doing. 'That gorgeous early Jenny Kee jumper of yours almost melted eBay.'

But the mention of it seemed to catapult Margaret back into 1975 and she became increasingly agitated about her diamond brooch.

'You've stolen it, you little tramp.'

Anita jumped at the vitriol in the words but reminded herself Margaret was unwell. 'I'm your daughter-in-law, Anita. I love you and I haven't stolen your brooch.'

Margaret's laugh was vicious. 'You can't sweet talk me, Anita. I know all about your wide-eyed innocent pixie act. You covet those diamonds as much as I did the moment I first saw them. We're a lot alike, you and I, except I'm not a doormat. I know how to handle my husband.'

The words slashed Anita like the slice of a knife and her heart thumped faster. In fifteen years, Margaret had never said anything like this and the accusations rattled her. How should she handle it? What should she say? Where did she even start? She rang the bell.

The personal care attendant came quickly, took one look at Anita and said, 'Being difficult is she? Take her for a walk and a ciggie, love. That always calms her down.'

Tucked away in a pretty garden nook by the pond, Anita lit two cigarettes with a shaking hand and passed one to Margaret. Despite all her years of not smoking, it was alarming how desperately Anita craved to slip under the heady nicotine spell and escape for a few precious minutes.

Be a love, Anita. Go and buy me some smokes.

There's no money in your purse, Mum.

You hate me drinking and I'm trying hard not to but I'm stressing out here. You know I wouldn't normally ask, hon, but you've got some money. Just one packet. For your mum. You know they relax me.

They're not good for you, Mum. I'm not getting you any.

You little shit. You'll bloody well buy them if you know what's good for you.

When Anita got home, she didn't mention the brooch, the cigarette or his mother's accusations to Cameron. All she said was, 'I didn't realise how much damage the stroke did. I'm not even sure Margaret knows what year it is. There's no way she's going to be able to help us with Mill House. Our only choice now is—' She braced herself for an explosion. '—for you to make peace with Ellie.'

'Fine,' Cameron snapped. 'Leave it with me.'

Sarah walked into the house at Riverbend and tried to staunch the flow of heartache. How could the artwork still hang on the walls? Why was the winter sunshine defying the gloom that should be shrouding the house? How could their resident kookaburra sit patiently on the deck railing waiting for his afternoon strips of beef as if everything was normal and her world had not suffered a violent schism?

'Gus?'

Silence met her.

After the disastrous non-lunch on Sunday, she'd telephoned Gus that night and they'd talked. Who was she kidding? She'd talked and he'd made unintelligible grunts, but she'd wrung a promise out of him to visit her after school. Now it was Thursday and Gus had still not visited, so if the mountain wouldn't come to her ...

Dropping her handbag onto the island bench, she glanced around at the upsettingly neat and tidy house, seeking evidence of Kelly. She hated herself for doing it. Hated that the whole situation was turning her into a paranoid and angry woman always looking for ways to hurt Alex, but at the same time she felt powerless to stop it. Where were the piles of clean washing waiting to be folded and put away? Where were the dirty dishes in the sink? Was Kelly responsible for the unexpectedly organised house? Did she think keeping house would weld Alex to her? Hah! If that were the case, Sarah would still be here.

The whiteboard on the fridge sported Rita Bosco's distinctive writing: *Buy more Domestos*. Of course. This was the answer to the clean house—Alex had upped the cleaning woman's hours. After all, it wasn't like he couldn't afford to have someone come in daily and pick up after him. An empty Cooked By a Friend container sat by the sink, taunting her. *Bloody hell, Anita!* Whipping open the freezer, she saw neatly labelled meals stacked high. She slammed the door so hard, it bounced open on the insulating rubber.

Sarah had assumed Anita would be supporting her by not continuing to cook at Riverbend now she was no longer living here, but she'd got that wrong. Boy, had she got so much about Anita wrong. How had she fallen for her sister-in-law's shining eyes and heartfelt declarations over the years, telling her that marrying Cameron and gaining her as a sister were the best things that had ever happened to her? What a load of crap. Anita was as money-grubbing and as unprincipled as Cameron. Sarah had never laboured under any illusions about her brother, but she'd always assumed he had familial feelings for her and Ellie. Not once had she thought him cruel but his betrayal hurt almost as much as Alex's. As much as her mother's. Had she gone through life totally blind to the faults of the people she loved?

Crossing the light and airy family room, she walked down the hall and found Gus sitting on his bed, headphones on and playing his guitar. Her heart rolled at the sight of her beautiful and talented son. God, she missed him.

'That's sounding good,' she said loudly to penetrate his noise-cancelling headphones.

He looked up, a momentary flash of surprise in his eyes before the shutters slammed shut. He pushed one earphone aside. 'What are you doing here?'

Hurt and despair hit with the spasm of a cramp and she gripped the architrave to prevent herself from doubling over. *Smile. Act normal.*

'I came to see you. I miss you.'

His mouth turned down as if he didn't believe her and her heart rate picked up. *Be honest.*

'And I came to apologise. To say how very sorry I am that you overheard Dad and me arguing. It's not something I wanted you to hear.'

Gus fiddled with the guitar pegs.

Mother annoyance bubbled. 'Gus, did you hear what I said?'

'Yeah.'

The antipathy in the word was new and it sucked the air from her lungs. Anger at Alex leaped with new energy. 'Have you talked to Dad about what happened? He's part of this too and—'

The chords from 'Smoke on the Water' drowned out her words, the message clear: *I don't want to listen to you.*

'Darling, I love you. I'm sorry you're hurting. I'd do anything to make it better but I can't. Dad's the one who—'

The off-key strum of D flat twanged. 'Did you have sex with Uncle Edmund?'

'Wh-what?' Two hundred and forty volts couldn't have shocked her more. 'Why would you ask me that?'

'I overheard Mrs Riakos on the phone telling someone it was inevitable.'

'Your maths teacher?' Sarah's face flamed with shame but the rest of her burned with fury. How dare gossips devoid of any professional etiquette or regard for Gus's feelings make her a topic for their amusement. Her legs twitched, instructing her to march straight to the school this minute and accost the woman, tell her that the Hadfields' private life was none of her goddamn business.

'She had no right to say that.'

Gus raised his head from the guitar and his long hair fell back to reveal the anguish on his face. 'So it's not true?'

Like a caged animal, scared and cornered, her heart slammed against her ribs. The first time she'd fallen into bed with Edmund she'd been propelled by anger, hurt and betrayal. The next two times it happened had more to do with a craving to be loved and cherished and Edmund did that so well. Each time she saw him, sex hovered between them, a living and breathing entity, tempting her with the promise of escape and losing herself in its mindless bliss—a euphoria that drove out everything wrong in her life. In her more reflective moments, she glimpsed the attraction mind-altering substances offered people who wanted to forget, but she was learning that relief was short lived—an hour after orgasm, the endorphins dropped and the awfulness and anger flooded back, bringing guilt with them. Despite her self-righteous belief that Alex had pushed her into this, she couldn't always ignore the guilt. She was adrift in her life without an anchor or buoy in sight.

Surely this was the one occasion where lying to your child was the safest course of action? After all, she had no idea what the future held.

'Uncle Edmund and I are friends, Gus. That's all. You know your dad and I have been friends with him for years. He's your godfather.'

Gus's head dropped, his hair falling forward like a curtain, and the chords played out again. 'I think you like him more than Dad does,' he muttered.

Denial rose to her lips and stalled as Alex's accusation played in her head: *He's your friend.* 'Nonsense.'

Gus shrugged. 'Whatever. I have to practise.'

And just like that the conversation was over.

During the drive back to town, Sarah couldn't shift Gus's words. If her son detected antipathy towards Edmund from Alex, why hadn't she? Had she always known on some level that Edmund desired her as more than a friend? Worse still, had she subconsciously chosen to ignore Alex's feelings to keep Edmund close because he was the yin to Alex's yang?

I haven't been happy for a long time, Sarah.

With a spray of gravel, she accelerated onto the main road. Back in range, her mobile rang and Finn's name lit up on the dashboard screen. She was yet to speak to her other two children about the separation. Emma's host family had taken her to Italy for a holiday and she'd been letting Finn concentrate on his exams.

Pressing the accept call button on the steering wheel, she forced herself to sound upbeat and cheery. 'Hello, darling.'

'Hey, Mum. Just wanted to tell you I'm going to Queensland.'

'You are? When? Where?'

'End of next week. We're going to Surfer's.'

No. The timing was awful; she wanted Finn home not only so she could tell him about the situation between her and Alex in person but so he could be at Riverbend with Gus during the school holidays.

'I thought you were broke?' she said.

'Dad gave me the money and I bought my ticket yesterday.'

He did what? She took a bend too fast and fright and fury whipped her. Heart racing, she pulled over before she killed herself. Alex had been complaining for weeks that their eldest son was dragging his heels getting a part-time job. 'I'm paying twenty-five thousand in college fees so Finn's housed, fed and watered. If he expects me to pay for his beer and shots, he's got another thing coming.' Sarah had wholeheartedly agreed with him, but now, without discussing it with her, Alex was paying for Finn to drink beer and shots on the Gold Coast.

Speechless, livid and despairing, she pressed her forehead against the steering wheel. This was blatant power play. It was bad enough she and Alex were wounding each other at every opportunity, but she'd never anticipated that he'd fail to consult her on a parenting decision, especially when she was one who usually came up with the plan.

'Mum? You still there?'

'Sorry, darling, lost you for a minute.' *Sound calm and collected.* 'So, Queensland. Aren't you lucky? You must have got Dad in a good mood. When will we see you?'

'I've invited some college mates to come up to ski, but before you go all details on me, I'll text you exact dates and numbers when I get back. But it won't be before the fourteenth. Gotta go. Love you, Mum.'

He hung up before she could say, 'But that's after school's gone back.' University holidays were a month long and Finn understandably wanted to ski on a quiet mountain but it left Gus alone for the entire school holidays. Any other year she'd have been thrilled Finn was bringing friends home, but not this time. Then again, perhaps having friends at Riverbend might take his mind off the fact his parents' relationship was imploding more and more every day.

She bit her lip. Should she and Alex FaceTime Finn and tell him that way? No. She wanted to tell him and hug him, reassure him—although how she'd do that when she had no idea what the future held, she had no idea. Her tattered and bleeding marriage now consisted of curt texts, because face-to-face meetings devolved into vicious contests. Alex's request for space was morphing into a vast void. For more than twenty years, her husband, her kids and the business had defined her. Without all three, she was floundering. She missed work and the kids desperately. Missing Alex was a double-edged sword; right now, she was so furious with him it vaporised any desire to see him. It was better if she avoided seeing and thinking of him, because every time she did, she lurched between tears and intent to maim.

She pulled back onto the road and had only travelled two

kilometres when the phone rang again. *Ellie?* Ellie communicated by text. She almost never rang.

'Hi, Ellie. What's up?'

'Hi, Sarah. Um, it's the neighbourhood house community dinner tonight and I've just realised I don't live in a shared house anymore. I was wondering ...' The hesitancy in Ellie's voice held a combination of reluctance and hope. 'Do you have plans tonight?'

Did she have plans? Sarah wanted to say, 'Oh, yes, I'm very popular. I've got a thousand invitations to choose from.' The reality was that Edmund was tied up with the restaurant from five, and Alex and Gus were barely talking to her, and neither was Anita. Not that Sarah would welcome her sister-in-law popping over. Book group was tonight but as the book was about a marriage breakdown and the members would be ripe for the details of her own split, she was skipping the meeting. Her evening was indeed wide open.

'I can babysit. It will be nice to have some kid company. If you ring after-school care, I can pick up Noah now.'

'Thanks, Sarah.' Ellie's relief flowed down the line. 'I appreciate it.'

Ellie rang off and Sarah wondered at the turn her life had taken. Two weeks ago, she'd counted Alex and Anita in her top three go-to people for fun, support and unconditional love. She'd been confident she was in their top three too but Ellie had never been in her top three, thirty or three hundred. How could she be when she was standoffish, unreliable and totally uninterested in Sarah's life? Ellie didn't come close to being a go-to person and Sarah would have bet money that she was not in Ellie's top anything ... and yet her sister had just created history and asked for her help.

Sarah smiled, humming a tune about miracles as she turned into School Road.

'I'm only hungry for rainbow cake, Sarah,' Noah said hopefully as he clambered onto a chair in the Mill House kitchen.

She smiled, thinking about the lines her children had tried out over the years. 'Are you now? How about you drink the smoothie and eat the cheese and biscuits and then I might be able to find you something sweet.'

He shot her a gap-toothed smile. 'Okay.'

Sitting opposite him, she tried capitalising on his easy acquiescence. 'Mummy says you've got spelling and reading homework.'

His bottom lip fell. 'Can I watch TV first?'

It was Finn and Gus all over again. Emma always raced home, bolted a snack, completed all her homework and then played. The boys, on the other hand, delayed for as long as possible. She'd learned if they took a break, they eventually settled better and completed the homework. Besides, if Noah watched cartoons for half an hour, it would give her time to continue her search of Mill House. She was looking for hard evidence that her mother's mental acuity was failing well before her stroke. She needed it to persuade Dan that Cameron had coerced Margaret into making the new will. She'd failed to convince him on Monday.

'Sarah, the last time I saw your mother, she was her usual acerbic self,' Dan had said, offering her a Mint Slice. 'And unless her GP says she was compromised before the stroke, well ...' He'd given his 'my hands are tied' shrug. 'I know it's hard, Sarah, and hurtful, but she has the right to change her solicitor and her will.'

'She hasn't signed it, so is it even a will?'

'Not until she signs it.'

'I'll fight tooth and nail if they try to get her to sign it now. Come on, Dan. Show me her old will?'

'You know I can't do that. And until the new will is signed, it is *the* will.'

'Look, I don't even know if her new instructions are different but I'd bet my bottom dollar they are and Cameron's responsible.'

'Proving undue influence is really tough.' He'd sighed then and given her a reluctant smile. 'See if you can find me some evidence that she's been failing and we can go from there.'

Sarah had kissed him and, ever since, she'd been on a mission. Her current routine was to arrive at Mill House after Ellie left for work and spend the morning searching for evidence. Then she'd visit her mother at the hospital over lunch and enjoy a couple of hours with Edmund before he started work at the restaurant. The busyness kept her mind from sinking into the dark morass that pulled at her whenever she thought about Alex, their marriage and the kids.

She smiled at Noah, who now sported a white smoothie moustache, and she tried hard not to tumble into the tugging sadness that it wasn't Gus sitting in his place.

'I tell you what. You can watch TV for a bit while I look for something I've lost.'

Noah's eyes sparkled. 'Is it treasure?'

'I think you could probably call it that.'

He shot off his chair. 'I can help! I'm good at helping. Where do you think it is?'

She'd already turned the study upside down and was now widening her search in a methodical, room-by-room approach. 'I'm not sure. I'm going to start in the dining room.'

Noah shook his head slowly and solemnly. 'You can't go in there.' His seriousness surprised her. 'Why not?'

'Mummy said so.'

Sarah smiled. 'There are a lot of precious things in there that a little boy might accidently break, but I'm a grown up and I promise to be careful.'

'No,' he said firmly. 'Mummy said no one's allowed to go in.'

'I think she'll let me.'

He looked unconvinced, almost worried. 'You have to ask her first cos she said there's bad air in there that makes people sick.'

'Bad air?' What? Why would Ellie say that? Was she trying to reduce the amount of housework by closing off some of the rooms? No; Sarah was paying Rita to clean, so that didn't make any sense. Besides, Noah was old enough to obey the 'look don't touch' rule. As a kid, she'd spent hours gazing into the locked vitrine, fascinated by the delicate Dresden lace skirts on the porcelain figurines and the detailed carving of the netsuke. Cameron had been equally intrigued by the antique compasses. Even if Ellie wanted to keep Noah out of the dining room, why invent such a story? If anything, Ellie usually over-explained situations to Noah instead of just saying 'No.'

'Sarah?'

'Hmm?'

'Is Gran sick because of the bad air?'

'No, sweetie.'

'Are you sure?'

'Yes.'

'But her room's next to one with bad air.'

Sarah blinked. 'There's more than one room with bad air?' He looked at his feet and mumbled, 'Yes.'

The poor kid was scared stiff. She wrapped her arms around him, hugging him close, and wondered what the hell was going on. 'I tell you what. I've got some special masks that will protect us. We can put them on and then we're going into every room and opening all the windows. We'll push the bad air out and welcome the fresh air in.'

The monthly Valley View Neighbourhood House women's dinner was growing in popularity every month. Ellie got a great deal of personal satisfaction from watching women from two very different cultures discover that, when it came to their men and their children, they had a lot in common. The fantastic food was also an added bonus. That night, Susie Faraday from the dairy had come along specifically to meet the wives of the Burmese men working at Riverbend. Watching these sorts of connections build was gold and not only validated Ellie's decision to take this job, but gave her a zip of happiness.

Like every activity at the neighbourhood house, the monthly

dinner depended on the generosity and enthusiasm of a marvellous band of volunteers. These good women cheerfully set up trestle tables, organised the food and then cleared everything away after the dinner, leaving Ellie free to chat and make certain everyone felt included. One of the great things about the dinner was that it not only forged links between other women, but it was considered a safe place. It surprised Ellie what women would share around a table when they were relaxed, issues they otherwise might not air, but it also heartened her. The day after a dinner was always busy with referral phone calls to local agencies and the female GP.

Tonight was no different and she'd been flat out all evening, but now it was eight thirty, everyone had left and the neighbourhood house was blessedly quiet. Weary from a twelve-hour day, Ellie realised that by time she got back to Mill House, Noah would be asleep. Asking Sarah to mind him felt both right and wrong. No doubt Noah had loved every minute spent with his aunt; Sarah had the ability to make a fuss of children while at the same time ensuring they did their homework, ate their vegetables and cleaned their teeth. It was her special power—love and kindness within the parameters of routine.

Ellie admired it but also resented it, especially when it spilled over to her. Sarah tried to mother everyone whether they wanted to be mothered or not. It made it hard to be grateful and tonight Ellie knew she should be filled with gratitude. God, she missed Guthrie Farm and the easy rapport. It was hard enough returning to Mill House each evening but tonight she'd have to make polite conversation with Sarah. At least there would be wine. She knew she wasn't being fair, but being fair was hard work when estrangement was so much easier. The threat of homelessness had bulldozed the long-established buffer between them, bringing Sarah back into her life. It was like the curate's egg—good in parts. Ellie just had to work out how to handle it.

The dishwasher beeped its electronic tune and, in perfect procrastination mode, she turned up the music and unloaded the dishes, getting an inordinate amount of satisfaction from stacking crockery in neat piles.

She was swinging her hips and belting out a very off-key version of 'Absolutely Everybody' when strong arms curved firmly around her waist. They pulled her against a solid body and then hot breath grazed her ear.

Fear froze her and a silent scream exploded in her mind. Adrenaline surged and years of self-defence classes kicked in. She shoved her booted foot into his kneecap, scraped it down his shin and stomped on his foot. His grip loosened. She dropped down then pushed up, bashing her head against his face and managing to throw off one arm. Grabbing his other hand, she turned fast and struck his elbow with her forearm before using everything she had to pull him forward. He fell face first to the ground. Panting hard, she pushed her foot onto the base of his skull and leaned her weight into it. It had probably taken less than twenty seconds but it felt like a decade.

Sweat drenched her, blurring her vision, and the roar of her blood in her ears deafened her. Meanwhile, her mind raced, trying to solve the logistics of how to get to her phone to call triple-o while preventing the intruder from moving and trying to hurt her again.

'Jesus, Ellie. It's me.'

The muffled voice became clearer.

'Luke. I'm Luke.'

Luke? Her legs buckled and she crumpled to the floor, grabbing her knees and rocking. 'Oh God, oh God, oh God.'

He sat up gingerly. 'Are you okay?'

'No!' Her body shook so violently she could barely speak. *There are good men in the world.* 'I—You—Why?'

Culpability wove into every plane of his face. 'I'm really sorry. I wanted to see you one more time today and when I saw the lights on and the door open ... I called out but I guess you didn't hear me over the music. And you're so sexy. You were doing that thing with your hips and it seemed like the best idea in the world to go up and hug you and dance along with you.'

Her shocked brain struggled to decode the words. 'Dance?'

'Yeah. Obviously, I shouldn't let my dick think for me. Shit, I'm sorry I terrified you.' His hand touched her shoulder and she flinched. He pulled it back fast and she heard him stand and walk away. Then he was back.

'Ellie. Drink this.'

She raised her head and accepted the glass of cordial with a shaking hand. Somehow, she managed to drink it without spilling any down her front. It washed away the caustic taste of terror from her mouth so she could concentrate on slowing her breathing.

'Mum says hot sweet tea's good for shock.' Luke was back again, this time holding a mug.

'Whiskey's better.'

'Sorry, I'm all out.' He glanced at the white cabinet on the wall. 'Do they have brandy in the first aid kit?'

Her wobbly mouth managed a smile. 'Tea is fine.'

She sipped it under his watchful gaze, feeling the glucose streaking into her cells, firming up her concentration and strengthening her limbs. She noticed he was wearing an icepack on his shoulder, there was blood on his lip and a lurid bruise was rising on his cheek.

'I'm sorry. I have a hard head. You look like you've been bashed.'

'Please don't apologise. I deserve it for being such a bloody idiot. I can't believe I did something a stupid teenager would do.' He gave her a rueful smile. 'The problem is, when I'm around you, I feel like that teenager. I promise I'll never sneak up on you again.'

'Thank you.'

'You did warn me you were hard work but you never mentioned you were lethal.' His smile took any sting from the words. 'In the future, whenever I'm behind you, we need a safe word.'

She laughed but tears fell too. She'd wrenched his shoulder, cut his lip and likely given him a black eye, but instead of blaming her, he was cracking jokes. 'I understand if you want out.'

'No chance. I very much want in.' He hesitated, clearly weighing his next words. 'Is there a particular reason you learned how to do the move that felled me?'

She didn't want to tell him. Didn't want to relive it. She'd worked hard to leave all the ugly behind a long time ago, so she gave him a partial and sanitised version.

'Safety. I met a guy who, over the course of a year, changed from charming and exciting to controlling and terrifying. I never wanted to feel that vulnerable again so I took up martial arts and learned a few skills.'

His nostrils flared. 'He hit you?'

'Once.'

'Bastard! I hate that he did that to you.'

She blocked the rising memory of how she'd been in too deep and isolated from her friends before she realised Ryan was Jekyll and Hyde. 'As horrifying as this sounds, that hit was the best thing that happened. I'd been constantly doubting myself for months, lost in a mire of emotional abuse. The punch freed me.'

Luke's breathing was hard and heavy.

She put her hand out and touched him. 'Don't. It's over.'

He covered her hand with his. 'But not forgotten, right?'

'Actually, I got some professional help and I don't think about Ryan at all any more.' Even if it wasn't her entire story, that part was true. She convinced herself it was enough.

He shot her a questioning look. 'Are you sure? It's just sometimes when I touch you, you flinch. When that happens, it kills me.'

Guilt and shame twirled their damaging dance and she fought the pull. 'Surprise touches make me jump.'

'But I'm not that bastard.'

'No.'

'Jeez, Ellie. Can you sound a little more confident? I want you to trust me.'

She reached out and brushed his hair out of his eyes. 'You need a haircut.'

'You're changing the subject.'

Why did Luke have to be the only guy on the planet who wanted to talk about feelings? 'Luke, please believe me. I already trust you more than I've trusted any man since—' *No!* 'In a long time. I'm sorry you're the guinea pig for my first real attempt at a relationship in over a decade. I'm not sure you deserve it. Or that I deserve you.'

'Don't say that.' He stared at his hands. 'How can I fix this?'

The past battered her and she held onto everything she'd learned, trying to believe. 'I don't need fixing.'

Bewilderment emanated from him and he raised his hands in surrender. 'I didn't say *you*. I said *this*. I need some help here. I come from a physically demonstrative family. I'm a hugger. It's automatic for me to reach out and brush your shoulder or stroke your face. I want to be able to touch you without you flinching. I want you to touch me. It's what people do when they're attracted to each other.'

'I want that too,' she said softly.

'Awesome. Okay, well, um ... Obviously, I'll never ever touch you again from behind as much as for my safety as for your peace of mind.'

'Thank you.'

'But do I need to give you a warning for other stuff like, I dunno? "Incoming hug"?'

Her heart wobbled. '"Incoming hug" sounds great.'

He opened his arms wide. 'Incoming hug.' He held her tightly and she lay her head against his shoulder, breathing him in.

'Incoming kiss,' he announced loudly.

Laughing, she tilted her head, opened her mouth and welcomed him in.

CHAPTER SIXTEEN

The winter school holidays found Sarah and Noah spending two hours of each day playing a game called 'What's this?' It featured taking Mill House apart room by room, opening every cupboard and drawer, and seeking behind every book, nook and cranny. Noah's favourite job was pulling the entire contents of cupboards onto the floor. He wasn't as keen about putting it all back. When he lost interest, he played with his Lego, chattering away to Sarah as she pushed on with the search for evidence that her mother's state of mind had been failing for months.

Sarah had contacted Alzheimer's Australia and spoken with a very helpful woman before downloading and reading all their information brochures. Apparently, people with dementia lived in survival mode and often hoarded or hid things of value. So far, Sarah had photographed money hidden in a tin in the bathroom and jewellery hidden in the pantry, although she wasn't convinced that was enough to prove pre-stroke dementia. She'd been known to hide things of value in her own pantry when they went on holidays but the fifteen bottles of vodka her mother had stashed all over the house were another matter. Margaret enjoyed a drink and she'd never hidden that from them, which is why so many secreted bottles raised a flag. Some bottles were open but most still had intact seals, as if she considered them something precious she must protect.

The state of her mother's dressing room was a shock. Margaret treated her clothes with meticulous care and normally this room could be photographed at a moment's notice and featured in a storage system commercial. Now clothes spilled wildly from drawers, hung precariously from hangers and were even thrown in piles on the floor. If Sarah hadn't known better, she'd have been on the phone to the police telling them a burglar had ransacked the place.

'Boo!'

Noah's game of hide and seek came with prompts, reminding Sarah to seek, otherwise she got distracted and forgot to look for him. She was pleased he'd suggested the game, because it meant he was happy to go into all the rooms of the house. The week before, after they'd opened the windows and doors and shooed out all the 'bad air', he'd finally relaxed.

She was still trying to find a good time to discuss this crazy room ban thing with Ellie. She'd intended to tackle the topic the night she'd learned about it but when her sister had arrived home uncharacteristically happy and glowing, Sarah had hesitated, not wanting to burst her balloon. At least, that's what she told herself. In more honest moments, she knew she was stalling in case Ellie got snippy, told her she was interfering and no longer wanted Sarah to mind Noah during the holidays. Either way, Sarah was enjoying this new and slightly less strained relationship with her younger sister. She'd hardly call her and Ellie close, but there was a definite shift between them. It was an improvement she didn't want to lose.

'Boo!'

Sarah realised she'd been too slow to react the first time so she jumped and pressed her hand to her chest, feigning fright. 'Noah! You tricker.' She spun around but she couldn't see him. 'Where are you?'

There was no reply so she pretended to look for him in the drawers while she searched for—what exactly? She didn't really know.

'Perhaps you're on the shelf.'

She heard a giggle but ignored it and got up on the step stool anyway. She looked under cashmere jumpers, hats and handbags. She found a couple of wrapped Christmas presents but again, she'd been guilty of hiding gifts and forgetting all about them.

'Nope, you didn't magic yourself up here.' Hopping down, she kneeled and peered into the dark. 'Are you hiding in a forest of shoe boxes?'

Noah giggled again. She pulled out box upon box until she felt a bony knee.

'Gotcha!'

He scrambled out from the back of the wardrobe and into her lap, giving her a hug. Missing Gus, she squeezed him back. God, she loved how affectionate little boys could be before hormones hit, complicating everything.

'Why does Gran keep books with her shoes?'

'Does she?'

'Uh huh.' He shot back under the clothes before returning with an ageing book.

Sarah wiped away the grey film of dust, exposing her mother's name embossed in gold on a green leather cover. Opening the book, she recognised Margaret's distinctive script crawling over the first page. Was it a journal? The title read *My Year in Mingunyah* and it was dated to 1969, the year her mother arrived from Melbourne to work at the high school. The early pages contained witty descriptions of Margaret's first impressions of the town and the people, and her father's name was underlined twice. Her mother had always told her that when Kevin walked into a room, every woman stopped talking and turned to admire him. Obviously, her mother was smitten at first glance. Sarah paged through a bit further but the writing stopped and the rest of the book was blank. Life must have got too busy for journaling.

A newspaper article, yellow with age, slipped out from between the leaves. It thrilled Sarah to see a photograph of the grandmother she never knew looking exceedingly stylish in a fur-trimmed hat and coat and with the famous diamond brooch glinting on the lapel.

'Are there more books in there, Noah?'

'I dunno.'

'Let's use a torch and look.' She touched the torch app on her phone and crawled in after him. Dust bunnies and dead insects dominated. The light caught the edge of something bulky—an old and battered leather hat box in the far corner. 'Can you pull that out for me, please, Noah?'

Her little helper dragged the hat box into the centre of the room. Fearing a rush of silverfish and spiders, Sarah hesitantly lifted the lid. Thankfully, nothing live leaped out. Inside were piles of crystals—the remains of decomposed mothballs—along with neat bundles of letters tied in a variety of coloured ribbons. She picked up the top bundle. The stationery was heavy-weight cream paper and the envelopes had neither a stamp nor an address written on them, only the word 'Margaret' in black ink. The penmanship was beautiful. Despite not having seen the familiar writing in decades, a lump rose in her throat. Her parents had shared nineteen years of marriage and, twenty-six years after her father's death, her mother still kept his love letters. Letters he must have written to her when, exactly? Trips to Sydney and Canberra for work?

That seemed unlikely but then again, she was holding her own jaded relationship up against one that had maintained a spark. Sarah remembered receiving funny postcards from her father from time to time. Perhaps he'd saved postage and put the letter to Margaret and the postcard inside the same envelope. Had she and Alex ever written to each other? No. They'd met at university, got married young and been together ever since—or had been. With each passing day, the idea of being together again felt increasingly unlikely. Their 'letter writing' consisted of prosaic instructions on Post-it notes: *Pick up kids from tennis. Out of coffee.* In recent years, the Post-its were increasingly replaced by texts: *Gone riding. Back by 3.* Sarah added emojis to her texts and Alex signed off with *Ax* but, now that she thought about it, the x had gone AWOL a few months earlier.

The envelope felt heavy in her palm and she wondered at its age, guessing it could be anywhere from thirty to forty years old. During her Alzheimer's research, one article talked about 'sundowning'; a phenomenon that affected some sufferers in the late afternoon. Margaret was most definitely experiencing it, with increased confusion, anxiety and restlessness. Seeking refuge in her past must be more familiar and secure to her than her present. Sarah was experimenting with different ways to settle her mother and was trying to surround her with familiar things, but she was yet to hit the mark.

She fingered the blood-red silk ribbon binding the bundle. Would these letters soothe her mother's late-afternoon anxiety? Would touching them or having them close remind her of Kevin and happier, more secure times?

'Zoom, zoom.'

Noah drove the ATV Lego toy he'd made up the 'wall' of one of three 'shoebox-skyscrapers'. With him happy and occupied, Sarah undid the bow, turned over the first envelope and pulled out the beautiful, thick paper.

Darling Mags,

Thank you for last night. Enjoy the diamonds. Wear them, and them alone, next time we meet.

Sarah stared at the note, utterly immobilised by the contents and the lack of a signature. Her mother hated being called Maggie or Mags. The only person she'd ever allowed to call her those names was Grandpa, and Sarah had always assumed the reason was because he'd given her Grandma's diamond brooch. Was the handwriting familiar because it was her grandfather's, not her father's?

Blood drained from her fingers and she dropped the letter. Her breakfast surged to the back of her throat. Surely Margaret hadn't slept with Grandpa?

You're being ridiculous.

With a shaking hand, she opened another envelope. And another, and another. It took eight letters before she found a signature and even then, it was only an initial: R. It had a bold swirl at the top and a flourish on the tail. She'd seen it before, but where? Her grandfather's name was George Joseph Jamieson and her father was Kevin Henry Jamieson, so the R couldn't have belonged to either of them. Unless it was a nickname, but to her knowledge her mother only ever called them George and Kevin, refusing point blank to use Kev, which the townsfolk always used. Sarah spun the paper in her hand, studying the R from different angles and, as she righted it, she gasped, knowing exactly where she'd seen it before. The initial didn't belong to her father or her grandfather. It belonged to Robert Horton, Dan's deceased father. Their family's solicitor, dear family friend, and now it appeared, her mother's very married lover.

I'm having more sex now your father's dead than I ever had when he was alive.

Her mother had stunned her with that little titbit. At the time, she'd assumed Margaret must have meant a widowed friend she'd kept hidden. Now Sarah knew exactly who she'd kept hidden and why. She could barely wrap her head around it and yet so many things fell into place. Robert's solicitude for Margaret when Kevin died. Why her mother became so hideously rude to Mary Horton after Robert's death.

Like a knife plunging into her flesh all the way to the hilt, an awful thought stabbed her. She rifled through more letters, urgently seeking a reference she could use to date them. Robert had been a very good friend of her father's. They'd played golf each week. They'd served on the hospital board together. Surely the affair started after her father's death? She pulled out letter after letter with frantic fingers, paper fluttering around her as she scanned the mostly short, but occasionally longer, correspondence.

I was stunned speechless when Kevin asked me to be Ellie's godfather. Oh, the irony. You could have warned me!

The words swam and her mouth dried. Her mother, Mingunyah's paragon of virtue, professional widow and social commentator on the sanctity of marriage, was screwing her father's best friend—a married man—when she was still very much a married woman. Sarah eyes raced across the page so quickly she was reading forward before she'd absorbed every word.

I discussed it with Mary and she wholeheartedly approves. Said she thought it was a fitting connection between the two families. Hah! I almost had apoplexy trying not to laugh. Was it your idea, you clever thing? Can't wait to see you; it's been far too long. I've booked the Windsor under the name of Lewis and ordered room service for lunch at noon.

Bastard! Bitch! Sarah didn't know if she wanted to throw up, lie down, or both. Her legs quivered and her head spun. Her mother and Robert had betrayed her father in the worst way and going by this correspondence, they got their rocks off over their duplicity. Anguish twisted her gut and she ached for her darling father. *Oh, Dad. I hope you didn't know about their treachery.* But she couldn't help wondering if his world had fallen apart just like her own. If the affair had started soon after Ellie was born, surely he would have twigged something was going on? Hell, she'd caught Alex and Kelly out after only after a few weeks. If her father knew, why hadn't he left his traitorous wife? Especially as divorce was increasingly common in the early eighties. Or had he known and stayed, sacrificing his own happiness for her, Cameron and Ellie?

Either way, Sarah's heart broke for her wonderful father. She reread the letter, slowly this time, and when she got to *you clever thing* she realised her eyes had completely missed a line.

Me being her godfather is the perfect way to hide our beautiful little mistake in plain sight.

Sarah gagged. Her fist rose, pressing hard into her mouth, and her heart jittered like it did after a caffeine hit. Did this mean what she thought it meant? *No! No way!* Surely the affair was the mistake? And yet 'our beautiful little mistake' made a certain calamitous sense. Ellie was as blonde as the rest of the family was dark. It certainly threw a light on the huge age gap between Cameron and Ellie, especially when Sarah considered Margaret's oft-quoted, 'Thank God I stopped at two'—words hurled at her and Cameron for years whenever they got into trouble.

It also answered the question that had dogged and diminished Sarah growing up: Why, when Ellie was a daughter too, had her mother loved and doted on her in ways she never had with Sarah? Well, doted on her right up until Ellie hit her teenage years. But the clincher that Robert Horton was very possibly Ellie's biological father was how very different in personality Ellie was from her and Cameron. As a teenager, Ellie had rejected everything Sarah and Cameron valued.

Sarah thought about the other Horton children. The sons, Dan and Michael, were stable and settled, both living in Mingunyah. Megan had left the district years ago but from all accounts she was happily living somewhere in Queensland. Kathryn, however, had been as wild and as out-of-control as Ellie, and she'd died from a drug overdose at twenty-three. DNA was such a powerful force.

The urge to tell Ellie about her suspicions was so strong Sarah sat on her hands to prevent herself from picking up her mobile. This wasn't fact, just a hunch generated by shock, and therefore unreliable. She didn't want to upset Ellie unnecessarily, especially when she could be way off course and totally wrong. *Please let me be wrong*. She sure as hell didn't want Cameron getting a whiff of her suspicions. He didn't need any more ammunition to keep Ellie out of the will.

Talk to Alex. She rubbed the jab of pain between her breasts. No, that door was not only closed but sealed shut. Her only choice was to keep her own counsel until she found a way to get her confused and demented mother to tell her the truth.

Piece of cake! She sighed. Why did life sometimes suck so much?

'Sarah,' Noah said sternly, looking at the confetti of letters scattered around her. 'That's a big mess.'

'You're not wrong, mate.'

'Are you going to clean it up?'

'I'll do my best.'

Anita placed the wicker basket at her feet inside the Mill House portico and tugged at her cropped jacket. It had been almost two weeks since she'd been inside and with a fully booked high tea looming, she was fast running out of options to gain access. Earlier that morning, the idea to visit Ellie had seemed like a fool proof plan. Now collywobbles spun in her stomach, reminding her of her other failed 'fool proof' plans.

A week had passed since Cameron agreed to talk to his younger sister and he was yet to even set up an appointment. Yes, he was busy with two new and prestigious listings on the books. Yes, schmoozing his contacts with lunches and dinners was important and it all took time. Yes, she understood clients needed to be wooed not rushed, but Cooked By a Friend was important too. She'd tried gently reminding him. She'd asked if there was anything she could do for him to free up some time so he could visit Ellie. She'd even offered to go with him if that would get the ball rolling, but the night before he'd got cross and said curtly, 'Stop nagging.'

The unfairness of the accusation still stung. Making a success of Cooked By a Friend benefitted him as much as it did her.

She didn't want to go over Cameron's head, but the time had come to take the situation into her own hands. Twelve women were excited about coming to an elegant high tea and she refused to cancel. She had a bunch of fragrant jonquils, freshly baked scones, homemade raspberry jam, high-country cream and a packet of Ellie's favourite coffee beans in her basket.

'When we go inside, girls, I want you to—'

'Take Noah for a walk,' Phoebe started.

'And buy him ice cream,' Ruby finished.

'We know, Mum!' they chorused. 'You've told us ten times already.'

The older girls were home for the school holidays and it always took Anita a few days to adjust to the way they seemed to start and finish each other's sentences.

'Us too,' the little girls reminded their big sisters. 'We want ice cream too!'

'Shh.' Anita needed quiet to concentrate—to have one last run-through in her head before Ellie answered the door. With the big girls looking after Noah, she and Ellie would sit down at the beautiful dining-room table surrounded by all the accoutrements of a civilised life and calmly discuss the situation.

Anita knew she could be calm with Ellie but she couldn't be calm with Sarah. For the first time since she'd joined the family, she was angry with her eldest sister-in-law. Sarah's high-handed approach of changing the locks clearly left them on opposing sides. No matter which way Anita came at the situation, she couldn't imagine Ellie caring enough to take sides. In general, her younger sister-in-law went out of her way to avoid any real connections with the family.

And that's what Anita was counting on: Ellie's lack of interest in the family. She had her spiel all planned and practised. She would cite her shock and stress as reasons for her rudeness and say that if Sarah had told her Ellie was moving in, she'd have had time to process the news and wouldn't have reacted in quite the same way. Finally, she would express her heartfelt regret and apologise. Ellie was a community worker and used to mediating, so doubtless she'd accept the apology. Then they could negotiate the high tea. Anita's bargaining tool was offering the twins as babysitters to give Ellie time to house hunt or do something just for herself. Not that she had any idea what Ellie might do. Going by the clothes and shoes Ellie wore, shopping wasn't a hobby.

'Right,' she said to the girls, picking up the basket with both hands. 'Ring the bell, Phoebe.'

'I want to do it,' said Ava.

'No, me. It's my turn,' insisted Chloe.

'Oh, for goodness sake.' Anita jutted her elbow into the brass button and heard the long ring echoing faintly back to her.

The thump of running feet followed, then Noah's voice called out, 'I can do it,' and the door opened.

'Surprise!' Anita said in her cheery childcare worker's voice that always seemed to rise unbidden when she was talking to children other than her own. She walked inside and the girls followed.

'We're getting ice cream,' Ava said, tossing her hair.

'Ice cream!' Noah cheered, his eyes filling with delight. 'Can I have chocolate?'

'Let's check with Mummy first,' Anita said, not wanting to do anything to upset Ellie.

'Who's getting ice cream?' a voice asked from the dim of the hall.

Anita's mouth dried and her hands tightened on the basket. 'Sarah?' Her presence had not featured in Anita's scenario. 'Oh, hi.

I didn't see you there.'

'Hello, Anita. I see you let yourself in.' Sarah strode up the hall. 'Hello, girls. Welcome back.'

'Hi, Sarah,' they chorused.

'Is Gus here?' Phoebe asked hopefully.

'He can come for ice cream too,' Ruby added.

'I'm sure he would've loved to, but he's at Riverbend.'

'Can I go, Sarah?' Noah pleaded. 'Pleeeaaase?'

'I really think we should check with Ellie,' Anita tried again.

'Of course you can go, mate, but you have to listen to the girls and do exactly as they say. Hold hands when you cross the road.' Sarah glanced over Noah's head at Anita. 'Ellie's at work and I'm babysitting.'

'Right.' Nausea spun her stomach. *New plan! New plan!* 'I brought morning tea,' she said brightly, holding up the basket. 'Let's eat the scones while they're hot.'

'If you've come to sweet talk me, it won't work.' Sarah threw the words over her shoulder as she marched to the kitchen.

'Funny. Your mother said the same thing to me the other day.' Anita tried to joke to keep things light.

'Oh? What were you trying to con her out of at the time?'

'Nothing!' Unbridled resentment made her drop the basket onto the table harder than she'd intended. China clinked. 'That's unfair, Sarah. I've never asked Margaret for anything.'

Sarah leaned against the bench, arms crossed. 'Perhaps not. You let Cam do the asking and then lie about it.'

'I don't lie!'

Sarah's mouth knotted at the corners and animosity rolled off her in waves. 'Are you sure you don't want to rethink your answer? Tell me something you should have told me a long time before now?'

An unwanted zip of guilt tingled Anita from top to toe and she swallowed. 'I'm sorry I didn't tell you about Vintage Glamour. Margaret asked me not to and that's the only reason I kept it a secret. She was worried you were going to give away her clothes.'

Sarah's expression of certainty slipped. 'What's Vintage Glamour?'

Anita took the chance to prove to Sarah she only had Margaret's best interests at heart. 'We've set up an eBay store to sell Margaret's designer clothes. It's insane how much money it's making, but she's always had sensational taste. The money's going into a special Vintage Glamour account so everything's itemised and we can easily track the payments and the postage. Cameron's set it all up.'

'I bet he did.'

Anita's cheeks burned hot as if Sarah had slapped her. 'I can assure you that everything's completely above board.'

'That's very reassuring, Anita. Is it as above board as Phoebe's cello and Ruby's saddle?' Sarah raised her brows. 'That's right. I know Mum paid for them. What I don't know is why you lied about it.'

Anita wrung her hands. 'I didn't have a choice in that either. It was part of the agreement.'

'What agreement?'

Anita felt like she was in the witness box being cross-examined by a particularly vitriolic barrister. 'How about we put the kettle on and talk about this?' She lifted the cloth-wrapped scones and the dishes of jam and cream out of her basket. 'I've missed our chats.'

For a few uneasy moments she thought Sarah wouldn't cooperate but then her sister-in-law moved jerkily, flicking on the tap, filling the kettle and slamming it onto the electric base. 'Fine. I'll make tea. You tell me about the agreement.'

'It's not a state secret, Sarah. Surely you've benefitted from the grandchildren's slush fund? Margaret asked us not to mention that she paid for the cello and saddle, because she didn't want people getting upset or feeling left out. She said it all evens out over time as everyone benefits.'

The kettle boiled and Sarah poured the steaming water over the leaves. 'And you heard Mum say that?'

'She told Cam and he told me.'

'Hah! And you believed him?'

Anita's patience snapped. 'Yes, I believe him. I have no reason not to. He's my husband. He's your brother.'

'Frankly, neither of those titles raise him out of the dross.' Sarah carried the pot over to the table and put it down so hard tea slopped out of the spout and snaked along the table's grooves. 'I assume you know about the will?'

Anita's body clenched, riddled with anxiety. All she wanted was the key to the door but apparently to get it she had to navigate her way through the rocky shoals of Sarah's hurt and disappointment. 'I—Yes. God. This must be so hard for you. First Alex and now this. I was shocked. Well, not so much about Ellie not getting anything, but definitely shocked for you.'

Slow down. You're gabbling. 'I know you're well off, but as I told Cam, inheritance isn't just about the money, is it?' She pushed a scone laden with jam and cream towards Sarah as if the food might soothe but at the same time knowing it was ridiculous. 'Cam's furious with Dan for allowing it to happen in the first place. He and Rupert tried really hard to get her to reconsider but—'

'Wait. What?' Sarah's gaze was suddenly glued to her face. 'What's "the first place"?'

'Five years ago. You know, when Margaret made the will before this one. It was just after you and Alex broke into China. I know you think Dan's marvellous but I think he really dropped the ball on this one and let you down. Yes, Margaret can be tricky, but he must have known it would cause upset and angst in the family. He should have given her better advice.'

Sarah silently poured two cups of tea and then stirred hers around and around, watching the milk slowly mix into the black liquid. Anita noticed strands of grey in her sister-in-law's hair, flecks that hadn't been there a month ago. Then again, with Alex virtually leaving her and her mother basically telling her she didn't love her, Sarah was having an extremely tough time of things.

'Is this the will Mum was determined none of us would ever see until after she died?'

'Yes. And sadly, now we know why.'

'I thought she'd written her will much earlier than five years ago.' Sarah stopped stirring and clinked the spoon against the rim of the mug. 'Have you read it?'

'No, of course not. I'm just the daughter-in-law. I haven't even seen it. I'm only going on what Cameron's told me.'

Sarah's head shot up. 'He told me he's never seen the will.'

'I doubt he said that. In fact, he told me a funny story about how Margaret hid her copy of the will inside *Bleak House*.' Sarah stared at her blankly and she added, 'Because, you know, how much she loves Dickens.'

'Mum hates Dickens.'

'Perhaps it was ironic?' A bead of sweat broke out on her hairline. 'I've probably got it mixed up because I've never read Dickens. The point is, Cam's seen the old will and I think you've misunderstood what he said.'

'It's a bit hard to misinterpret "I never saw it".'

'So, what are you saying? That Cam's lying?'

'That's exactly what I'm saying.'

Every part of Anita leaped to defend him. 'How dare you! My husband doesn't lie.'

Sarah's top lip curled. 'You keep telling yourself that.'

It was rare for Anita to stand up for herself in this family and she'd never questioned Sarah on anything before, but the bitchy remark lit a fuse. 'It's not his fault Margaret left you out of her will. Just because you're hurting doesn't give you the right to make false accusations about us or lock us out of this house. Mill House is ours. It's *never* going to be yours. Or Ellie's. It's not our fault your life is spiralling out of control. Perhaps it's time you asked yourself why your husband and your mother have abandoned you.'

Sarah stood up so fast the legs of the chair scraped against the stone floor. 'Get out.'

'No.'

'Leave. Now.'

Anita stayed seated but her heart thundered as if she'd run five kilometres. She was giddy and light-headed and the room swam. 'I'm not leaving without a key.'

'Make yourself comfortable then, because you're going to be here for quite some time.'

'I'd planned to starve her out.'

Ellie watched Sarah glumly eat another scone. 'Really? With all this food she brought? You didn't think it through, did you?'

'No.'

'What if Cameron had turned up? It would have got ugly.'

'Uglier.' Sarah sighed. 'Sorry.'

Ellie had arrived home to find Noah and his cousins watching a movie in the den, Anita camped in the kitchen, Sarah sitting like a sentry on a chair outside the door and tension oozing through the house like poison.

'I should charge you for my mediation skills.'

'I'd pay. You're very good.'

Ellie searched Sarah's face for sarcasm but found none. 'Thank you.'

After talking with Sarah and hearing her version of events, Ellie had sequestered herself in the kitchen with Anita, listening first and negotiating second. She saw no point in banning Anita from Mill House and agreed to provide access at specified times so her sister-in-law could run her high teas and cooking classes. They'd tussled over free access to the house, but as much as Ellie wanted to believe Anita when she said she understood Ellie was only living here temporarily and she was fine with that plan, the problem, from Ellie's point of view, was Cameron.

Sarah pushed her plate away. 'Thank you for not giving Anita a key.'

'Don't think I was doing it for you.' She laughed, surprised to find herself teasing Sarah. 'It's pure pragmatism. I can't afford to lose my babysitter.'

'Noah's good company. Believe me, you're helping me out more than I'm helping you.'

Ellie was slightly discombobulated about how the sister tables had suddenly turned since she'd moved into the old family home. Sarah, who'd always been purposeful and optimistic, was struggling and increasingly sought out Ellie's company. Ellie knew Sarah missed her kids and fretted about them even more, especially Gus. She understood the worry; it seemed to be an integral part of being a mother. Although she'd stake her life that her own mother had never been affected by such misgivings.

'Have you spoken to Gus?'

'He still isn't taking my calls. He either ignores my texts or replies "later", and later never comes. I drove out to Riverbend again yesterday hoping to ambush him, but he wasn't home.' Sarah slumped in her chair. 'I was always the parent he talked to. Now I'm worried he's not talking to anyone.'

'Maybe he's talking to Alex?'

'Hah! If Gus was talking to Alex, I could find a way to accept it, but Alex isn't talking to any of us. I called him to find out where Gus is and he told me he's been staying at Jack's house for the last few nights.

When I said surely that should have been a joint parenting decision, he told me to chill.'

'"Chill"?'

'It's hardly Alex's vernacular, is it?' Her face hardened. 'He's probably trying to hide the fact he's forty-seven from hipster Kelly.'

Ellie didn't correct Sarah on the incorrect use of the term 'hipster' and there was no way on earth was she going anywhere near the spiky topic of Kelly. One inadvertent mention of the woman set Sarah off on a rant that lasted longer than Ellie considered healthy, but then again, betrayal was a vulture that feasted luxuriously and long.

She was desperately seeking an inconspicuous segue away from the topic when the doorbell rang. She rushed to her feet, her Noah-like eagerness not lost on her. 'I'll get it.'

'Use the peek hole,' Sarah called out as she approached the door. 'If it's Cameron, don't let him in.'

'You think?' Ellie muttered but she doubted it would be her brother. She'd been very surprised Anita had come to Mill House on her own to negotiate; so surprised, in fact, it had made her question if Cameron even knew his wife had visited. Ellie couldn't imagine him backing down enough to be open to compromise, but then again, it had never occurred to her that Anita had the guts to go against his wishes.

So far, Anita and Sarah were her only visitors at Mill House and she felt a momentary panic ringed by delight that this visitor might be Luke. She'd worked a half-day today and even though she'd lingered half an hour longer than necessary, he hadn't managed to drop into the neighbourhood house before she left.

As her hand reached for the door handle, she knew it couldn't possibly be Luke. He respected her wishes too much to come to the house when Noah was home. As much as she valued and wanted that respect—needed it—the ache of disappointment that he wouldn't be on the other side of the door surprised her. She was still thinking about what it all meant when she peeked through the door viewer.

Astonishment sent her thoughts skittling off in another direction. She swung open the door. 'Edmund?'

'Oh.' His smile was tinged with uncertainty, as though he hadn't expected her. 'Ellie. Hello. How are you?'

'Good thanks. What can I do for you?'

'Is—'

'Edmund?' Sarah reached the door and edged past Ellie to stand in the portico.

In a fluid movement, Edmund slid his arm around Sarah's waist, closed the distance between them, bent down and kissed her with a familiarity that startled Ellie. Sarah flushed and splayed her hand against Edmund's chest, but Ellie wasn't sure if the action was from embarrassment or enjoyment. With her mind fully occupied trying to decode her sister's body language, it took a moment for the full significance of the blush and Edmund's proprietary touch to hit her. *Oh. My. God!* Sarah and Edmund were having sex.

Sarah, who was so vocal about Alex's betrayal, and searingly scathing about Kelly, was having sex with her and her husband's closest friend. The hypocrisy of it rocked her. She spun around and stomped to the kitchen, furiously turning on taps and filling the sink with sudsy water as she battled uninvited emotions. She told herself she didn't care what Sarah did with her life; that it was none of her business. After all, she'd deliberately distanced her own life from that of the family's for years so they couldn't comment on her actions, therefore she shouldn't comment on theirs.

Except her gut churned and agitation quivered in her limbs. Right up to this moment, if anyone had ever asked, Ellie would have said she was not a judgemental person. But as she plunged dirty dishes into the sink, the stinging heat of her own criticism burned. Why did she care that Sarah was having sex with Edmund?

'Sorry about that.' Sarah breezed back into the kitchen. 'Edmund misunderstood where I was meeting him.'

'Good to know.' Ellie thumped a soapy plate into the dish drainer. 'I've sacked babysitters for less.'

Sarah laughed and grabbed a tea towel before picking up the plate.

The tinkling sound dug in under Ellie's anger, hitting a soft and tender spot that exploded in pain. 'Tell me you weren't planning on having sex here this afternoon with Noah in the house?'

The plate hit the slate floor; the crash echoing around the room as shards of china scattered widely. 'What? No! Of course not.' Sarah's voice trembled as she bent to pick up the pieces. 'What possessed you to say something like that? God! You know Edmund and I have been friends forever.'

Ellie rigorously scrubbed at the saucepan and water splashed up from the sink, dampening her T-shirt. 'I'm not blind, Sarah. Edmund's touch was the one of a man who either believes he has the right to intimacy or has been given permission to do it. Going on your expression, he's got permission.'

Sarah, now on her knees, was silent for a moment. 'Not that it's any of your business,' she finally bit out, 'but yes, Edmund and I are having sex. To be perfectly honest, it's the only thing in my life right now that's giving me any happiness. And you know what? *He* doesn't judge me. All he does is tell me I'm wonderful.

'And before you dare criticise me—although God knows, as a single mother with a child who has no apparent father, you don't have the right—this thing with Edmund didn't start until after Alex left me. I doubt you've got any idea what it's like to be told you're surplus to requirements. How that reduces everything you've ever held dear to nothing much at all and leaves you questioning if your entire marriage has been a meaningless sham.'

Sarah's pain filled the room and for the first time in years, Ellie was tempted to let the angry words go, allow the cheap shot about being a single mother to flow over her and instead kneel next to her big sister and hug her. But before she could move, Sarah rocked to her feet.

'But you know what bothers me the most about your accusation? That you think I'd bring a man into this house and have sex with him when I was responsible for Noah. How dare you!'

'How dare I?' Sympathy vanished, sucked dry by an old fury far more powerful than good intentions. Suddenly, Ellie was yelling. 'Oh,

I more than dare! It wouldn't be the first time a supposedly responsible adult betrayed a child.'

Her words hit the air and hung there, dark, ominous and far too revealing. More than anything, Ellie wanted to snatch them back. She desperately hoped Sarah was too angry at their shrewish volume to have really heard them.

But Sarah wasn't yelling back; instead she was silent, her red-rimmed eyes staring straight at Ellie.

'What are you talking about? I've *never* had sex in this house.' Sarah shuddered. 'I'm not about to start.'

'Well, good for you,' she said aggressively, trying to lure Sarah back to a personal attack and keep them both far away from the edge of the hole she'd just dug for herself. *Tell me I'm irrational. Tell me I'm a spoiled brat. Call me Princess Ellie. Please!* But she could see the cogs of her sister's mind at work.

'Has someone had sex when they were supposed to be minding Noah? Did he see it? Perhaps he didn't even know what was—Oh God.' Sarah's hand rose to her mouth as her eyes dilated. 'Oh, Ellie. Is it worse? Poor, darling Noah. How awful for both of you.'

Sarah's stricken expression combined with her unsolicited empathy undid Ellie. No matter how much she wanted to protect herself, she couldn't let her sister think that Noah had been witness to, or forced into, sex. 'Noah's fine. Nothing's happened.'

'Oh, thank God.' Sarah visibly relaxed and then immediately stiffened. 'Hang on. I don't understand. If Noah's fine and nothing's happened then why did you say it wasn't the first time an adult betrayed a child?'

'Slip of the tongue. Forget I said anything.' Ellie stripped off the rubber gloves. 'It doesn't matter.'

'I think it does.'

'No. It doesn't.'

Sarah's brows drew down. 'Bad air ...'

Oh God. Ellie tried to feign nonchalance. 'It's the fog. We need some wind to clear the valley.'

'This is nothing to do with the fog. A couple of weeks ago, Noah was upset. He said you'd told him some of the rooms in the house had bad air and he wasn't to go into them. I thought it was an odd thing for you to say, but I didn't mention that to him. He was convinced he was going to die of a toxic gas so I made up a game. We threw open every window in the house and let the fresh air in. He's been happier since and I've been meaning to talk to you about it.

'Ellie, I'm sorry about the unfair crack I made before about you being a single mother. You're a great mum. That's why I can't think of a reason why you'd risk upsetting Noah with such nonsense except now I can't help but think ...' A pensive look crossed her face. 'Something horrible happened to you here, didn't it?'

Despite the cold day and the cool house, sweat doused Ellie. 'Shit, Sarah.' She forced a laugh and it came out strangled and tight. 'And you tell me not to be dramatic.'

'I'm not being dramatic,' Sarah said quietly. 'I'm trying to understand what's going on.'

'Nothing's going on.' Ellie pulled the plug from the sink and the noisy gurgle of water blissfully blocked further conversation. 'I have to check on Noah.'

'Noah's fine. He's got another half an hour left of the movie. But I don't think you're fine.' Her voice softened. 'I want to help, Ellie. Let me help.'

Many years before, abandoned and utterly alone, Ellie had sobbed her heart out because Sarah was in France and not there to listen or help her when she desperately needed it. She opened her mouth to hurl, 'You're too late,' even though she knew that was unfair. She glimpsed the closed dining room door across the hall.

Noah was upset.

For seven years, she'd done everything in her power to shelter and protect her little boy so he only knew love. Yet, since moving into this bloody house, he'd started wetting the bed. She wanted to blame the house, blame Sarah for making her move in. Blame Cameron, blame her mother, hell, blame her entire dysfunctional family, but that was too easy. For years, she'd prided herself on having moved past blame. Noah's anxiety lay squarely at her feet; it was feeding off her reaction to this house. As much as she craved to hide from the uncomfortable truth, she had enough years of counselling to know where denial led. She was the one with the demons that filled this house, scaring her little boy.

Perhaps she should ask Sarah if she could live at the old cheese factory and Sarah could move in here instead? The solid advice of her counsellor came back to her: *The future can only happen when you let go of self-blame and shame, and leave the past where it belongs.*

Bone-jarring fatigue hit with the force of a ten-tonne truck. The thought of moving her pinkie, let alone lugging boxes, was more than she could handle. It was time to deal with the ghosts and banish them from this house so that while she and Noah lived here, her son felt safe and happy. It was time to stop running from Mingunyah. No matter how hard it was going to be for her, no matter how difficult the unpredictability of Sarah's response might be to bear, it was time to air this secret to her sister.

'You're right, Sarah. Something did happen.'

CHAPTER SEVENTEEN

With a sickening feeling crawling along her veins, Sarah followed Ellie from the kitchen into the dining room and straight to the bar.

'Don't judge me,' Ellie said. 'I can only do this with a drink.'

'Pour me one too.'

'God, Mum has so much vodka she could be Russian.' Ellie sorted through the bottles until she found the rum. 'Are you absolutely certain Noah has half an hour left of the movie?'

'Yes.'

'He can't hear this.'

I'm not sure I want to hear it. 'I'll close the door.'

'No!' Ellie sloshed rum and Coke into glasses. 'Leave it open. If we sit here we'll see him if he comes downstairs. If he does, we stop talking. Sarah, are you clear on that?'

'Yes, very clear.' *And anxious, very anxious.* Sarah accepted the drink before sitting next to her sister on the wide window sill. More than anything, she wanted to say, 'Just tell me,' but instead she stared down at her drink and waited, fearing if she forced Ellie to speak, her sister would change her mind.

Ellie sipped her drink and then rested it on her knee, her knuckles white around the glass. 'Remember how excited I was, being one of your bridesmaids?'

'I remember how gorgeous you looked in your dress. Not that you were ever an ugly duckling but it seemed like, overnight, you went from being my baby sister to a beautiful young woman.' A memory she'd forgotten flew to the surface. 'Mum was so proud of you that day. She told me it was lucky I'd already snagged Alex, because you were much prettier than I was and all eyes would be on you.'

'Jesus. What a thing to say to a bride on her wedding day.' Ellie took another slug of her drink. 'Why did you put up with the crap?'

Sarah shrugged, not exactly sure. 'I guess by then I'd accepted that you and Cam got the looks so it wasn't like it was news to me. Besides, I was about to marry a man I adored and nothing could possibly dent my joy.' She was suddenly blinking back tears. God, she'd been so happy that day and now look at her and Alex. How had it gone so wrong? Giving herself a shake, she reminded herself that this conversation wasn't about her but about Ellie. 'You were talking about being my bridesmaid?'

'Yeah. I got so many compliments that night, I floated on air. I suddenly saw myself completely differently and I was determined I was never going back to being that little kid. I took advantage of Mum's passion for dressing me like a doll and we both got new wardrobes. Looking back, she dressed me a bit too old and herself a bit too young. My psych got a heap of mileage out of that.'

'Your psychologist?'

Elle shot her a self-deprecating look. 'Sometimes people need professional help. You and Alex might benefit from it.'

'You're changing the subject.'

'Yeah.' Ellie sighed. 'Okay. The thing about being the popular girl is the addictive sense of power. I loved it. I had boys fighting over me at school and I flirted outrageously.'

'That all sounds pretty normal teenage stuff.'

'It was normal. Right up until the moment it wasn't.'

'What do you mean?'

Ellie drained her drink. 'I mean that flirting with boys my own age was one thing but flirting with an adult was stupid.'

'We all did that when we were kids, Ellie. It's like we're wired to practise. Any normal adult knows it's just part of growing up and ignores it.'

'That's the thing. He wasn't normal. He showered me with compliments and gave me gifts. He singled me out from other girls, paid me a lot of attention and I felt so special and superior. He had the easy knack of treating me like an adult and yet he still managed to be fatherly and give me advice. He'd ask me about the boys I liked and I'd share my silly, girly, thirteen-year-old secrets with him.

'He'd pat me fondly and tell me conspiratorially that, unlike Mum, he totally understood me. He encouraged me to tell him everything and anything and reassured me that all my secrets would be safe with him. I missed Dad so much and I missed you, and Mum was well, you know, self-obsessed, so I fell for his shtick hook, line and sinker. Once I was confident, safe and secure in his affections, thinking of him as my substitute father, he started to slowly and surely change the rules.'

'Oh God.' Sarah's mouth dried and she grabbed her sister's hand. 'He groomed you? Who? Who did this to you?'

'Who isn't important right now. I need you to hear what happened first.'

As far as Sarah was concerned, *who* was vitally important. If she knew the scumbag, she was going to murder him. 'Sorry. I'm listening.'

'He'd always kissed me on the top of the head and stoked my hair but Dad did that, so ... The sexual touching started innocuously. The first time it happened, he reached across me for something and brushed my breasts. He instantly apologised. Called himself clumsy. The next time, I was at his house visiting his daughter. He came out and rubbed sunscreen on her back and offered to do the same for me. With his daughter lying next to me with her eyes closed, he let his fingers slide under my bikini bottom and then my top and fondled my nipples.' Ellie sucked in a breath. 'When something like that happens, your brain goes into meltdown as you struggle to understand if you'd imagined it—was it an accident or did he mean to do it? Within a few short weeks, he'd twisted everything I trusted and believed until I didn't know what was real, what was right or what was wrong.

'Things changed fast and suddenly everything that had been good was evil and he blamed me. He told me it was all my fault. I taunted him. I flirted with him. He said my beauty was both a sin and a gift from God. One night, when Mum was hosting a summer cocktail party and there were seventy people out on the terrace, including his wife and family, he cornered me over there.' She pointed across the room. 'As he digitally raped me, and his hot, beery breath panted in my ear, he told me in lurid detail what he wanted to do to me and how lucky I was he was giving me what I'd begged him to do for weeks. Later that night, holding me tightly against his aroused body, he hugged me goodbye in front of his family and whispered that he'd kill me if I ever told anyone what happened.'

Sarah gulped air, finding it hard to breathe as the horrific images battered her. 'Oh God. Did he—did he ever ...' She couldn't form the words.

'Rape me with his cock?' Ellie's voice was harsh and raw and Sarah flinched. 'No. Not that it would have been any less traumatic, Sarah. Being violated is just that, no matter the method. I'm sure the only reason he didn't do it was because he lacked the opportunity. I'd been raising hell at home for weeks. At first it made matters worse, putting me straight in his path. He'd ingratiated himself so well into our lives that Mum trusted him implicitly. She invited him over to "talk some sense into me". He'd come into my room and berate me for causing Mum problems. He'd call me a dirty slut and spank me, telling me he was only doing it because he loved me and wanted me to be happy. Then he'd pull me into his lap, fondle and hug me, all the time whispering that everything would be fine. All I had to do was trust him.'

Silent tears ran down Sarah's cheeks. All her unasked questions about Ellie's behaviour over the years suddenly had an answer; a horrendous and devastating answer. 'I didn't know. God, Ellie, why didn't you tell me? I would have flown home.'

'Would you?' Ellie didn't sound angry, just resigned. 'From the outside looking in, I was an over-indulged fourteen-year-old who was running wild. It was my word against the word of a man everyone in this town held up as a pillar of the community. He'd convinced me no one would believe me and I was petrified by what he might do to me if I spoke out.'

'But you're my baby sister. I'd have moved heaven and earth to protect you if I'd known you were in danger.' Sarah frantically looked for options. 'What about Mum? You were so close back then. You could have told her?'

Ellie pulled her hand out of Sarah's and stood before crossing the room and refilling her glass. Sarah watched her beautiful sister's face framed by the blonde curls she'd envied more than once growing up. Ellie's head was the only part of her body that was visible; the rest of her was hidden behind her signature baggy, grunge-coloured clothes. Clothes Sarah suddenly understood hid her body from the world. From the prying eyes of men. A strangled sob escaped as the realisation of exactly how much had been stolen from her younger sister engulfed her.

'The night he raped me in this room changed everything. Up to that point, he'd befuddled me with his clever mix of fatherly affection, discipline and shame. But after that night, I knew without a doubt that he wouldn't stop there. What would follow was inevitable and ongoing, and it would kill me as much as he would if I betrayed him.' Ice clinked in Ellie's glass. 'I told Mum.'

Sarah's heart hammered but instead of pumping hope, sickening dread trickled through her. 'And?'

'Before I tell you, I think it helps if you know that my counsellor believes our mother is a narcissist.'

'You mean someone who loves themselves?'

'Sort of. It's more complicated than that. It's a mental health issue.

Narcissists need to be admired. They need to be the centre of attention and they've got little or no empathy for others. Sadly, my metamorphosis from gangly kid to young woman made me, in our mother's eyes, the competition. I received far too much attention for her peace of mind. Jealousy and envy are not normal maternal emotions but unbeknown to me, they'd become the bedrock of our relationship.' Ellie laughed tightly. 'Of course, it's taken years of counselling to recognise what was going on. At fourteen, I was clueless. All I wanted was to be rescued and protected.'

'Of course you did. You deserved to be,' Sarah said hotly as the word *competition* burrowed in, bringing with it a sinister premonition. She'd read every one of the letters in the ribbon-tied bundles she'd found in her mother's wardrobe but even as the thought dangled itself in front of her, it was too horrible to contemplate. She rejected it out of hand. 'What did Mum say?'

'When I told her what her esteemed family friend and financial advisor had done, she slapped me for making up such scandalous lies. She promptly sent me to boarding school, which saved me, but not quite in the way I imagined.'

No. No. No. No. No. Sarah's hands flew to her face, cupping her mouth as she dry retched. 'I—it—was Robert?'

Ellie's head tilted almost imperceptively. The savagery of Margaret and Robert's brutal betrayal of her sister rained down on Sarah, spinning her head and bringing the façade of a mostly functioning family crashing down around her feet. As she struggled to think, she didn't know which was worse: that her mother had abandoned her daughter for the love of a man or that the same man had abused her sister. Her hands pulled hard at her hair, the stinging pain a welcome distraction from the hideous possibility that the despicable man might also be Ellie's biological father.

'It's hard to get a handle on, isn't it?' For the first time, Ellie's face contorted, pain and suffering twisting it into ugliness. 'While you're struggling to come to grips with the fact that my abuser was Mingunyah's finest, a dedicated family man, an upstanding member of the church and my godfather, you can understand why it was so hard for me to say anything at the time.'

Guilt, shame and rage filled Sarah. 'He's lucky he's dead or I'd be banging his door down. I fucking thanked him for looking after you. I told that bastard more than once how grateful I was for his support of Mum. When I confided in him, telling him how worried we all were about you, he colluded, saying, "Sometimes, no matter how much we love someone, we can't help them until they want to help themselves." That lying prick told me I had to have faith that you'd eventually find your way. And all the time he was the lowlife pushing you off your path into the dark and stealing your childhood.'

A sharp pain jagged through her and she doubled over, her throat burning with acid. 'Oh God. Mum colluded too. I've been so critical of you and your life choices and the two of them let me believe their lies. No wonder you never came back here.' Sobbing, she jumped to her feet and ran to Ellie, hugging her close. 'I'm ... s-ss-sorry,' she sobbed. 'I am so, so sorry.'

Ellie wrapped her arms around her and patted her back. 'It's okay, Sarah. Please don't hyperventilate on me. Just breathe.'

Getting air into her objecting lungs took effort but slowly, her jerky breaths steadied. She dug for a tissue in the pocket of her pants and thankfully found one to swipe at her eyes and blow her nose on. When her vision finally focused, she studied her sister. With her smooth skin, blue eyes and Shirley Temple curls, she looked like a porcelain doll—perfect and untouched by anything sordid. Dear God, how looks could deceive.

'How can you stand here so calmly and dispassionately and comfort me when—' Words failed her.

Ellie sighed. 'I'm not calm or dispassionate but I'm no longer letting anger control me. I was lost for a long time. All that stuff you worried I was doing, I did all of it and then some, including a few things I'm not proud of. For a long time, I struggled to stick with anything. I chopped and changed courses and jobs and made more than my fair share of bad choices in men. When you hate yourself, you don't expect anyone to treat you well. But the night I found myself dodging a fist shocked me into getting help.

'The Latrobe student health service was fantastic and after a lot of hard work, I've found my own version of peace. That man stole my adolescence and early twenties, but he's not part of my adult life any more.' She grimaced. 'Well, mostly he isn't. There are times when he sneaks back and creates havoc. Living here has been a challenge.'

Sarah was suddenly frantic. 'You can't stay here. You have to move. You and Noah can live with me.'

Ellie's mouth curved into a wry smile. 'Yesterday I would have jumped at that. Even an hour ago, I would have accepted the offer, but now I've told you and you believe me, I don't have that same frantic need to flee. Don't get me wrong, I don't want to live here forever, but right now, it's important for Noah that we don't rush off anywhere.

'You were right, Sarah—I've stressed him out so much that when we move again, it's going to be to somewhere with a lease for at least a year. Meanwhile, although I don't plan to ever eat in this room, I'll open it up and encourage Noah to play with the netsuke. Besides, if Noah and I did move in with you, we'd cramp your style with Edmund.'

Sarah's cheeks burned. 'Edmund and I are—' She faltered. *Are what?* The weight of her failing marriage bore down on her. Alex, Kelly, Edmund; everything was complicated. She couldn't talk about it, because she wasn't sure she could articulate how she felt about her and Edmund. Besides, right now, she needed to know more about Ellie.

'Why didn't you tell me about the abuse after your counselling? You know, when you were feeling better?' She heard the hurt in her voice—did she even have the right to be hurt? She glanced at Ellie, anxious about her reaction.

'That's easy. He was still alive and to be honest, after everything I'd done, I just assumed you and Cameron would side with Mum.'

Sarah rubbed her face, overwhelmed with sadness and shame. 'I can see why you'd think that way. God, since you've come home, we haven't made it easy for you, have we? I've judged everything you do against all those lost years. No wonder you stayed away.'

'I stayed away because it was the only way for me to have a chance at staying healthy.'

Sarah considered that and found herself calculating time. 'And Robert died three years ago. Is that why you came back?'

'I came back because of the job. If he'd still been alive, I wouldn't have applied for it.'

'God, I hate him!' Vitriol surged so hot and fast, Sarah rubbed her sternum. 'He not only stole from you, he stole from me too. I lost my sister. I know you were only thirteen when I went to France but before we left we'd had some fun together. When we got back, I was looking forward to getting to know the young adult Ellie. I wanted to be your sister and your mentor, but by then you rarely came home to Mingunyah. And I swallowed the spoiled princess story Mum and Robert fed me.' She picked up her sister's hand. 'I should have tried harder. I'm sorry.'

'Even if you'd tried harder, it wouldn't have made any difference. When I was at MLC, I moved heaven and earth to avoid coming home as much as possible. Fortunately, I had friends whose families were happy for me to tag along on holidays and, despite what Mum told you, she was far happier when I was out of town.' Ellie's expression turned contemplative. 'This must be hard for you too, learning our mother is such a two-faced bitch. Did you know about the affair she had with him after Dad died?'

Sarah almost said yes, but then she'd have to explain the letters and she was loath to do that. Despite feeling confident that Ellie would not want to read them, it wasn't worth the risk. If she'd learned anything in the last few weeks, it was that nothing in life was predictable or dependable. Ellie had already suffered so much and bravely come out the other side. Sarah didn't want to jeopardise her recovery, so for now it was safer to lie. 'Mum hinted the other day there'd been a man in her life after Dad but I didn't know who it was. When did you find out?'

'They hid it really well, but the first suggestion was six months after your wedding. I discovered he was giving both of us gifts. When Mum found a necklace that he'd given me, she went ballistic. But I didn't know for sure until the night I told her what he'd done to me in here. During that screaming match, she said she'd had enough of me always needing to be the centre of attention. That outrageous lies were never going to make him mine when he was already hers.'

Sarah flinched at the bald words. 'I can't believe she betrayed you so viciously. God, she punished you for telling the truth. And the awful thing is that if you'd told me all this two months ago, I probably would have struggled to believe that she hadn't supported you. I'd have thought you'd misinterpreted her sending you to boarding school as banishment. But with the issues around the will and all those years of canonising Dad when she was getting it off with—' She sucked in a breath to keep her disgust at bay. 'She abandoned you. I have no idea who this woman I've called Mum really is.'

Indignation surged in over grief. 'And you know what? Even before all this awfulness, I thought you deserved your share of her money but now ... You should sue her! We'll fight this together.'

Ellie's face hardened. 'I don't want *anything* from her.'

Sarah opened her mouth to tell her sister not to be ridiculous but closed it quickly. This wasn't a battle for today, but it was a conversation she was determined they would have in the future.

Returning to the window seat, they sat shoulder to shoulder. Sarah was struck by the fact they were sitting physically closer than they had in decades and she now had a far better understanding of who her sister was—a remarkably brave and resilient woman.

'Ellie?'

'Sarah.'

'You're not gay, are you.'

'No.' She sighed. 'I'm not. But letting you think I might be was easier than dealing with your questions about why I didn't have a bloke. And before you ask, Noah is a blessing I never expected to have but that's a story for another day. His father and I came together for one night after we almost drowned.'

Another shock detonated inside Sarah. There was so much she didn't know about Ellie. 'I definitely want to hear that story when you're ready. I want to hear all your stories when you're ready so I can get to know you. Have you—do you—can you ...?' There was no easy way to frame her question so Sarah just went for it. 'Have you ever known the joy of a loving relationship?'

'Funny you should ask ...'

'What?'

'Poor Luke. He wants to try.'

Sarah squealed and bumped her sister's shoulder. 'Luke Sorenson is divine. And you know what they say about plumbers: they're good with their hands.' Busy laughing, it took her a moment to realise Ellie hadn't bumped her back. 'Hang on. Why did you say "poor Luke"?'

Ellie bit her lip. 'As much as I want to be normal, Sarah, sex is something I struggle with.'

Sarah's gut burned with anger at what one disgusting man's carnal needs had cost her sister. 'Have you told Luke what happened?'

'Sort of.'

'What do you mean?'

Ellie flicked lint off her pants. 'I told him about Ryan. The guy who hit me.'

Misery pulled tight and hard and Sarah's tears returned. Her sister had endured and lost so much. Ellie had never known the things Sarah considered her basic right—to be loved and respected for who she was and for what she believed. The right to enjoy a healthy sex life. So many things she'd taken completely for granted. More than anything, she wanted Ellie to have and to know the joy of unconditional love.

'I know I'm not your counsellor, Ellie, but if you want a chance with Luke, you have to tell him what you just told me. He needs to know or it will get in the way. Don't let that miscreant or Margaret's warped reaction drive away what could possibly be the best thing that's ever happened to you. You deserve a fine man and Luke embodies all that is good.'

Ellie's blue eyes suddenly flashed. 'How do you know he's a good man? How can we ever really tell?'

'Surely he's told you about—' She stopped, uncertain as to whether she should be saying anything, yet wanting to banish Ellie's scepticism. The information wasn't a secret; anyone who'd been in town five years ago knew. Then again, she doubted Ellie would have told anyone about her and Luke so no one would have mentioned the story.

'What?' Ellie sat a bit straighter, eyes narrowing. 'I knew he was too good to be true.'

'He's not too good to be true,' Sarah said resolutely, 'but it sounds like you're not the only person keeping secrets.'

'So tell me.'

She shook her head. 'Would you want me to tell him what you just told me?'

'No!' Ellie looked stricken. 'God, you wouldn't.'

'Of course not, but it works the other way too. It's Luke's story. He's the one who needs to tell it. If the two of you are serious about trying to make this work, you both need to sit down and have an honest-to-goodness heart to heart.'

Ellie's brows rose. 'Like you and Alex need to?'

The truth hurt and Sarah winced. 'Alex and I can barely be civil with one another, let alone talk. I imagine it won't be long before our lawyers will be doing the talking for us.'

'So why are you so keen I talk to Luke?'

'Because you deserve what I had for so long.' Sarah shoved her phone at her sister. 'Call him. Go see him. I'll mind Noah.'

Anxiety flitted across Ellie's face. 'He'll be at work.'

'Luke's his own boss and you told me he wanted to try with you. I guarantee you, if he truly means what he says, he'll take your call unless he's out of range.'

Emotions warred in Ellie's eyes. 'Even so. I'll call him after five. That's probably better.'

Sarah was having none of that. She took back her phone and brought up her contacts list, found Luke's name and hit the call button.

'Stop it.' Ellie grabbed for the phone. 'What are you doing?'

'Being the sister I should have been years ago.'

Ellie lunged for the phone just as her sister said, 'Hi, Luke. Sarah Hadfield.' She returned what Ellie assumed was his greeting and query with, 'No, my plumbing's perfect. I hear you're dating Ellie. You do realise my little sister's special?'

'Sarah!' Ellie hissed, frantically making another attempt to wrest the phone away while Sarah listened to whatever Luke was saying. But her sister dodged and weaved with similar skills to Gus when he had possession of the ball.

'I'm glad to hear you say that, Luke,' Sarah said, holding her left arm out in front of her, blocking Ellie. 'So, you'll agree with me then when I say she deserves to know—'

Thirty seconds later, Ellie's phone rang and Luke's name lit up the screen.

'Ellie, your sister can be scarier than you.'

'I heard that!' Sarah called out.

Luke sighed. 'Come for dinner tonight but do me a favour? Leave Sarah behind.'

CHAPTER EIGHTEEN

Ellie wound her way along the heavily wooded Macs Road, marvelling at how densely dark a moonless night sky was without light pollution. Shadows ducked and weaved as her headlights bounced off the massive tree ferns and towering gums until finally the beam picked up a row of roadside mail boxes. Until Luke had given her his address, she'd assumed he lived in town, not ten kilometres out. A wombat stood in the road, staring at her headlights, either blinded or unimpressed by her need to turn left. She edged forward and eventually it lumbered away. If Noah had been with her, he'd be in seventh heaven.

She drove down a tree-lined drive, wondering if the bare trees were ornamental pears. She hoped so; they were one of her favourite trees. In summer their full foliage was lush and green, defying the heat, and in autumn the leaves ignited to a vivid fire red; a defiant last hurrah before they conceded to winter's chill and fell soundlessly to the ground. But it was the trees' spring extravaganza that she loved best. They dripped with thick clusters of white blossoms, looking almost bridal, casting a magical spell over the valley and filling her battle-scarred self with energy and hope. Going on the length of this driveway, the spring display would be positively regal.

Aren't you getting ahead of yourself? Spring's two months away. Life can change irreparably in two months.

And her life could change tonight. Sarah was right—Ellie needed to tell Luke all of her story, but right now that took a back seat to the secret Luke was keeping from her. She rounded a bend and the headlights illuminated the house. Surprise made her brake sharply. The small weatherboard cottage she'd been expecting was a sprawling, modern, homestead-style brick house with wide verandas to protect against the summer heat.

It screamed family home, kids and pets. Did Luke live with one of his married brothers? Even as Ellie searched her memories of their nightly phone conversations, she knew that if he'd told her that, she'd have remembered. Unlike her, he chatted easily about his parents and siblings, freely sharing stories with her. It was as though he wanted her to get to know his family so she was familiar with them before she met them. If she met them.

Switching off the ignition, she grabbed the bottle of wine Sarah had forced on her and hopped out of the car. As she approached the front door, an old kelpie struggled to its feet to vet her. She bent down and scratched him behind the ears. 'It's okay. He invited me.'

'I did.' Light spilled onto the veranda and she looked up to see a smiling Luke leaning casually against the doorway with a tea towel slung over his shoulder. 'Hec, this is Ellie.' The dog sniffed her crotch and Luke laughed. 'Stop it, Hec. Sorry, he's out of practice greeting women. A bit like his owner.'

'Oh, I don't know. I think any tarnish you might have had from lack of use has been well and truly polished away.'

'You think so, eh?' He pushed off the doorframe, loose limbed and with eyes twinkling. 'You do realise you're engaging in blatant flirting, Ellie Jamieson?'

A rush of delight hit her. 'I've been practising too.'

'I'm honoured.' He opened his arms. 'Incoming kiss?'

'Yes, please.' She stepped into him, giving thanks for the wondrous absence of alarm bells. She rose on tiptoe, wrapped her arms around his neck and let the bottle of wine hang against his back. Pressing her lips against his, she tasted the tang and heat of chilli. It was as natural as breathing to deepen the kiss. Luke pulled her tightly against him, groaning softly into her mouth and her body leaped, hot and ready, craving him. For the first time in years, she didn't second guess her sexual instincts. More than anything, she wanted to tumble into them.

Hec barked. When they ignored him, he determinedly shoved his muzzle between them.

Luke broke the kiss with a frustrated grunt.

'Mate, you're seriously cramping my style. Back to your bed.' He pointed to it. 'Now.'

Hec threw them both a doleful look before retreating arthritically to the dog bed.

'This is for you.' Ellie handed Luke the wine and as he read the label, he gave a low whistle. Ellie hastily added, 'Sarah chose it, paid for it and sent it. My budget leans more towards cask wine.'

'Mine falls somewhere in between but I'm not saying no to this.'

'I'm really sorry Sarah gave you the third degree. If I'd known she was going to do that, I wouldn't have told her about this ...' Her hands fluttered. 'I mean ... us.'

'Us?' He grinned at her. 'I like the sound of that.'

He ushered her inside and led her through the open-plan house, past a closed door she assumed was the master bedroom, through a wide formal lounge and dining area with a large but rather dated floor vase silk flower arrangement before entering the kitchen. A long island bench separated the space from a family room complete with a flat-screen television. Unlike the other rooms, this one felt lived in—there was a worn couch, stained coffee table and what looked like hastily stacked *Australian Geographic* magazines. Numerous doors opened off the space and she assumed they were bedrooms, the bathroom and the laundry. It was an enormous house for a bachelor.

Luke set the wine on the bench then stirred a pot on the stove before turning back to her. 'Can you do the honours? Glasses are on the table. I just have to check our free-range organic chook.'

'Are you sure you don't want to keep the wine for another occasion?'

'Once I would have saved it but now I'm all about the here and now.'

Six chairs surrounded a rectangular wooden table set for two, the placemats adjacent to each other at one end. She cracked the seal on the cabernet shiraz that was worth more than the clothes she was wearing and poured two glasses.

'Can I do anything to help?'

'It's all good. I've just got to—' His mobile rang and he checked the display. 'Shit. Sorry. I have to take this.'

'No problem.' She felt uncomfortable eavesdropping on his phone call so, sipping the Baby Grange, she wandered into the lounge room to check out the bookshelves she'd been rushed past. Unlike her tatty collection of favourite novels—paperbacks she'd picked up at garage sales and fetes over the years—Luke's collection looked to be antique leather. Once again, this man didn't fit the image of the average plumber.

Wondering which of the classics he enjoyed, she peered at the closely packed titles. Not recognising any of them, she hooked her fingernail into the top of one and tugged. It didn't budge. She added another finger and pulled harder. The entire collection suddenly jerked forward, coming away in her hand. After her initial horror that she'd broken something, she laughed. The 'books' were a series of spines glued onto masonite. She hastily restored the magnificent fake collection to the shelf.

Glancing around the room, she couldn't shift the feeling that the decor wasn't really Luke. There was an upright piano on the opposite wall with its lid down and she wickedly wondered if it was real. Before she lifted the dusty lid, she paused to look at a collection of photographs. Housed in a variety of frames, the four photos positioned at the front featured the same two men. Both had muddy blond hair and a look of Luke, so much so that she didn't think it a stretch to assume they were his brothers. One photo showed them proudly holding an enormous fish aloft. Photos two and three showed each man standing next to a woman of similar age, plus a handful of children. The fourth photo included Luke, his brothers, sisters-in-law, nieces and nephews and an older couple Ellie guessed were his parents. Everyone was smiling at the camera.

There were photos of Luke water skiing and snow skiing and individual pictures of his nieces and nephews, including one of a little girl posing coquettishly in a blue full-length dress decorated with shimmering snowflakes. This must be Izzy. By now Ellie was at the back row of the photos and the frames were dustier. A young Luke proudly standing next to a brand-new ute, another of him with a kelpie puppy nestled in his arms and a photo of a woman dancing on a concrete slab. Was it the foundation of this house? Ellie picked it up and studied it but it was a distance shot and impossible to tell. When she set it back down she noticed the wedding photo.

Luke, heart-stoppingly sexy in a tuxedo and his face wreathed in a wide smile, wasn't staring straight at the camera. His gaze was riveted on the smiling bride by his side. Her heart shuddered. Perhaps he was the best man? But the unequivocal love on his face and the shining gold band on his left hand betrayed that idea. Ellie didn't suffer from envy very often but now its toxic tendrils wrapped around her heart before reaching out with strangling intent to the unknown woman wearing a strapless beaded gown. If anyone deserved to be strangled, it was Luke. Was this what Sarah had intimated? If it was, then how the hell did it make Luke a good man?

Clutching the photo and filled with questions that demanded answers, Ellie marched back to the kitchen.

Luke was just ending the call and he threw her an apologetic smile. 'Sorry about that. I've got a tender in for the new building program at the primary school and—'

'You've spent hours telling me everything about your brothers and their wives and yet you've failed to mention this.' She belligerently propped the dusty photo on the bench, not caring that she'd interrupted him.

'I see you've been having a look around.'

His mild censure briefly made her feel wrong-footed but then it fuelled her sense of betrayal. 'When were you going to tell me?'

'Over dinner.' He held her gaze. 'It's the reason I invited you.'

'Oh.' Her indignation deflated, leaving her feeling like she'd completely overreacted.

'But it's probably best I tell you now, right?'

Understanding played in the creases around his eyes, both annoying and soothing her. 'Are you always so bloody reasonable?'

His mouth twitched. 'Only when I know I'm probably in the wrong. Sarah's right. I should have told you before now.' He picked up the photo and dusted it with the tea towel. 'This is my wife, Miranda.'

'But you told me you were single. You told me you'd had a crush on me since you were eleven.' She hated how needy she sounded.

'And both those things are true. But you left town when I was fourteen, Ellie. I pined for you right up until Carly Benson got boobs. She was very good at helping me move on.'

She wanted to smile at his easy humour and the way he was gently showing her how ridiculous she was being, but the question of why he hadn't told her about his marriage ate at her. If he hadn't told her that, what else wasn't he telling her?

He flicked off the gas under the gravy and pulled the chook out of the oven before covering it with foil. 'Come on, let's do this sitting down.' He picked up his glass and walked to the couch.

She didn't want a cosy sit, she just wanted the facts. But remaining standing made her look silly so she sat on the opposite end of the four-seater couch. A couch he'd likely sat on with his wife.

'You and Miranda built this house, didn't you?'

'Yeah.' He smiled. 'We bought it off the plan to suit our idea of having a couple of kids and a guest room for when her parents visited. That was the easy bit. We didn't always see eye to eye on decorating, so in the spirit of compromise, we agreed she'd decorate the interior and I'd landscape the garden.'

That explained the feeling she'd got in the lounge room. 'It's a huge house for one person. Why didn't you sell it after the divorce?'

His mouth tightened. 'I'm not divorced, Ellie. Miranda died.'

Fuck! Fuck! Fuck! She steepled her hands in front of her mouth. 'I —Oh—It's just you both look so young in the photo, I thought ... Shit. Sorry.' She drank more wine. 'Are you okay talking about this?'

He was silent for a moment. 'The thing is, everyone around here knows my story so I don't have to talk about it. And then I met you. And not that I've dated a lot of women, but you're the first one who didn't know Miranda. Hell, you didn't even know she'd existed. I wanted to tell you. I've been going to tell you but then ...' He suddenly dropped his gaze and stared down into his wine.

Goose bumps skated across her skin. 'But what?'

He raised his head, a look of anguish bright on his face. 'You and me ... *Us* ... You're already dealing with a lot. I didn't want to add to it.'

'Oh, Luke.' The weight of his concern threatened to bury her. 'It's not your job to protect me. We won't work if you tiptoe around me, treating me with kid gloves. You've got equal rights in this relationship too. I mean ... God.' She moved in closer. 'She was your wife. You loved her. She's part of who you are. You should feel you can talk about her to me if you want to. Do you want to?'

He shrugged. 'I don't feel the need to talk about her a lot any more. It's five years since she died. The first two were fucking hard, but it's got easier.'

'How did she die?'

'Leukaemia. Bloody awful disease. Miranda was always a whirlwind of energy and suddenly she was tired all the time but as we'd just found out she was pregnant, everyone said it was the baby. When she miscarried, we stupidly thought that was the worst thing to happen to us, but we had no idea. They ran some routine blood tests at the hospital and our world fell apart.' He rubbed his jaw. 'The only thing cancer gives you is advance warning. The chemo made her so bloody sick I gave up work to look after her. At first, the treatment seemed to work and she got well enough for us to take a couple of trips. Then she stopped responding. In the end, we got ten months.'

Heartache for him and relief for herself did an odd dance in Ellie's chest. This was what Sarah wanted her to know—whoever Luke loved, he did it with his whole heart, and put them first. 'She was blessed to be loved by you.'

If he heard her, he didn't show it. 'Before Miranda died, she told me she wanted me to be happy.' He linked his fingers through hers. 'And you make me happy.'

Tell him. But she couldn't. He'd just told her she made him happy and she wasn't going to tempt fate. Tears welled in her eyes and her throat thickened. 'Do I? I don't understand how, but I love that I do. You make me happy too.'

He dropped his head close to hers, the fresh scent of soap and aftershave crisp and clean. Breathing him in, she slid her palm along his cheek and he kissed her long and deep. Her entire body sighed. As his lips pressed kisses along her jaw, her head fell back, inviting him to extend his touch to her neck … and that's when she glimpsed the silhouette of the large brown vase.

'Um, Luke.'

'Hmm.' He didn't stop the wondrous thing the tip of his tongue was doing to her, making her body sing. Her hands tightened on his shoulders and he stilled. 'Do you want me to stop?'

'No …'

He lifted his head, his blue eyes full of questions. 'I'm sensing a but.'

She sighed. 'Don't get me wrong. I love it when you kiss me. I want you to kiss me. I want to kiss you and touch you and you're the first guy I've wanted to have sex with in forever.'

He grinned at her like a puppy, his face alight with hope. 'I'm liking the sound of this.'

'But …'

'Yeah?'

'I know you said Miranda wanted you to be happy, but I'm not sure she'd be totally thrilled that I'm pashing you in her house.' She pointed down the hall to the vase. 'And it's still very much her house, isn't it? I can feel her here.'

He looked around as if he was seeing the decor for the first time. Understanding dawned. 'I see what you mean. Is it making you uncomfortable?'

'Little bit. Not so much in here. This area says "Luke", but back there, it's very much "Miranda".'

'I really only live in this part of the house.'

'But I'm guessing the bedroom still has her decorating style?'

He looked sheepish. 'Ah, yeah. It's not going to work for us in there, is it?'

'No.'

'Your place?'

'Shit, no.'

He face-palmed. 'Noah. Right. Sorry. I get it.'

'I think we need neutral territory. You still got that voucher for the B&B?'

When Ellie told Sarah their plans, her sister whisked Noah off on a boy's own adventure—indoor trampolining, junk food and a sleepover—freeing Ellie for a day and a night away with Luke.

He'd been jumpy from the moment he picked her up. Seeing him nervous was oddly soothing; it eased her niggles of disquiet.

'I've got it all planned,' he said, shoving a sheaf of tourism guides at her instead of a hello kiss. 'And a playlist, unless you prefer something else?'

'Let's start with your music and if I hate it, I'll let you know.'

They drove along the back roads, past winter-brown paddocks and sheep heavy with wool, avoiding the Hume Freeway for as long as possible until they reached a winery on the banks of Tuesday Creek, a tributary of the Murray River. Luke had arranged an incredible degustation lunch cooked by the vintner's Italian wife and served with matching wines. Luke's knowledge and passion about food and wine outclassed hers by a country mile. As much as she appreciated all his efforts, their conversation ebbed more than once and Ellie wondered if they should have gone straight to the B&B and had sex so she could get easy-going Luke back.

After a quiet walk along the river to help shift their lunch along and avoid a food coma, Luke asked if she wanted to call in to one of the bookstores in Rutherglen.

Ellie took control. 'It's after three. Why don't we check in first?'

As their host retreated, closing the bedroom gently behind her, they stood stunned, staring at the teddy bear–laden room. The bear brigade wasn't restricted to the queen-sized bed: they graced shelves, the dressing table and the window sill. The brown glass eyes of the faux-antique toys seemed to follow their every move.

'Bloody hell.' Luke breathed out. 'I wasn't counting on an audience.'

'Worried they'll rate you?' she spluttered.

'I've already got performance anxiety.'

It was the most ludicrous room Ellie had ever seen and laughter took over, holding her captive until her ribs ached and she was fighting for breath. Collapsing onto the bed, she spread her arms wide and said, 'Take a photo for our memory book.'

'No frigging way.' He grabbed at the bears, tossing the passion-killers across the room. 'I should have just ravished you under that tree by the river while my masculinity was still intact.'

Suddenly sober, she caught his hand and pulled him onto the bed next to her. 'Bears or no bears, I'm just happy I'm here with you.'

Dejection played in the brackets of his mouth. 'I wanted the weekend to be special.'

'It is special. I feel like the Queen. No mothering duties, being chauffeur driven, a six-course lunch and a gorgeous walk in the winter sunshine.' She rolled on her side and stroked his face, her love for him growing by the minute. 'If we were any other couple, we would have tumbled into bed a couple of hours after you smiled at me and gave me coffee when I was standing in a flooded house. You made me feel like I was the only woman on the planet. No planning would have been involved, just spontaneous sex. But we're not and we didn't and now sex has become this huge event and—'

'*Don't* say you're sorry.'

'Actually, I wasn't going to.'

'Good.'

'And I never thought I'd be the one saying this, but Luke, you gotta relax.'

Anxiety hovered in his eyes. 'I don't want to hurt you.'

'You won't. I trust you more than I've trusted any man since my father.'

You need to tell him. And she would, but not right now. This moment belonged to them. It was about hope and a step towards the future and she didn't want it tainted by her past or his reaction to it.

Pushing away the unwanted thoughts, she said, 'And if sex today isn't quite right and uncoordinated, it's not like it's our only shot at it.' She started undoing the buttons on his shirt and pressed her palms against the solid musculature of his chest.

His hands tangled in her curls, massaging her scalp. 'So, you're an advocate of practice makes perfect.'

'Totally.' She slid her leg between his. 'And your kisses alone get me close to coming so I'm already yours.'

He gazed at her, eyes shining, and his face filled with delicious intent. 'I am a pretty good kisser.'

'I've been told that plumbers are good with their hands. I want to test that theory too.'

'So, for you it's all about the science,' he said, slipping his hands on the hem of her jumper and tugging it over her head. A moment later, his fingers flicked open her bra and his mouth and hands were doing incredible things to her breasts.

Delicious and tingling excitement engulfed her. Desire twitched her muscles, craving to tighten around him, and she ached to feel him deep inside her. She moved quickly, rolling him under her until she was straddling him. Gazing down at his dilated pupils and flushed face, she gave thanks that he'd appeared in her life.

'To be honest, Luke, for me, it's all about you.'

And she bent down and kissed him. After that, they stopped talking, because they were far too busy using their hands and mouths to explore each other's bodies. Finding their rhythm. And if the bears thought they were a bit too noisy, they didn't comment and kept their eyes sternly averted.

CHAPTER NINETEEN

'This is nice.' Margaret smoothed her skirt as she sat down in the leather club chair beside the gleaming beaten copper fireplace.

'I thought you might enjoy a change of scene,' Sarah said, taking a seat next to her. 'You used to come here a lot.'

'Did I?' The room was familiar, but at the same time agitation fizzed through Margaret like electricity. Why was Sarah here? She couldn't shift the feeling that her daughter didn't belong here. Touching her hair to check its set and straightening her royal blue woollen jacket, she glanced around with a ready smile and was disappointed to find there was no one else in the room to admire her.

A young man appeared—anyone under fifty was young—with a tray supporting two tall glasses both containing a distinctive stick of celery and a plate of her favourite nibble: smoked oysters on Savoy biscuits.

'You darling boy.' But he was smiling at Sarah and Margaret bristled. She ran her fingers along his arm. 'How did you know this is exactly what I wanted?'

'I know your secrets.' He grinned and tapped his nose. 'Always the best for you, Margaret. You know that.'

And she did know that; she'd spent her adult life making sure of it. Not that she would ever admit that to anyone, so she laughed coyly and blew him a kiss the way she always did with men, enjoying the buzz of lightness and the zip of power that accompanied flirting. She had no idea who he was but that was irrelevant. He'd just brought her a Bloody Mary and nothing else mattered.

'Cheers.' Sarah leaned forward, picked up her drink and gingerly stirred the red contents with the celery stick as if drinking it would be torture.

Kevin set his drink aside untouched.

The uncomfortable and jittery sensation that had been with Margaret since she arrived arced up, white with warning. Why was Kevin here? He didn't belong here; this was the special place she came to only with Robert. She glanced around furtively and when she looked back, Kevin was gone.

'Can you reach your drink?' Sarah asked, sitting where Kevin had been.

Flustered, Margaret picked up her glass and took the first blessed mouthful. As the vodka hit her stomach and raced into her veins, she blinked, trying to focus. In front of her, the sombre wood-panelled walls of the private member's bar shimmered with secrets. Her secrets. Robert's secrets. Kevin's secrets. All written in silver cursive script across the dark wood for everyone to see ...

'Where have you been?' Kevin demanded, his expression stony and his skin the colour of granite. 'Ellie's been beside herself about tomorrow's costume for Read Day. You promised her you'd make it. I've stapled red circles onto her white dress but she needs a hat. She went to bed crying.'

Usually, Kevin wasn't around enough to notice Margaret's comings and goings but the last few months had been difficult. For a man who'd been fit and healthy all his life, he'd had two bouts of pneumonia already this winter and it wasn't even August. The illness sapped his usually boundless energy, keeping him away from the mill and out of his workshop but firmly inside the house. He was spending far too much time at home for her peace of mind. She'd been forced to cut back her regular assignations with Robert and cancel trips to Melbourne. That week, Robert had reached breaking point and today she'd caved to his demands and her own needs. She'd driven to Albury to meet him at the club. A very inconvenient flat tyre and a long wait for the RACV delayed her trip home by over two hours.

Margaret pushed past her husband, slipped off her coat and walked straight to the bar. If Kevin was going to be difficult, she needed a drink. 'The CWA meeting ran long.'

'Three hours longer than usual? And they serve alcohol now, do they?'

'Not enough.' She splashed whiskey into a glass and didn't bother to add water.

'Are you going to tell me where you've been?'

'Oh, you mean like you always tell me where you vanish to?' She smiled sweetly and tried not to grind her teeth. 'I don't think so.'

'At least when I vanish, I don't break promises to our daughter!' A coughing fit consumed him and as he leaned against the doorframe trying to catch his breath, she noticed his trousers. Kevin, like herself, was very particular about his clothing, having items altered to achieve the perfect fit. Now his shirt and pants hung off him and his belt was buckled two notches further in than usual.

She squirted soda into a glass and shoved it at him. 'Good God, Kevin. This has gone on long enough. I'm sick to death of being kept awake at night by that cough. I'm sick of you being sick. Go back and see Andrew.'

'I have.'

Something in his voice made her snap to attention. 'And?'

Kevin closed the door. 'Sit down, Margaret,' he said wearily. 'We've been lying to each other for years and it's time we stopped.'

Every hair on her body rose in a whoosh and adrenaline instantly evaporated her delicious post-sex, post-alcohol buzz. 'I don't know what you're talking about, Kevin. I'm very happy with my life.'

'And that's where we differ.' He sat down hard, his chest heaving. 'I haven't ever been happy.'

'Well, thank you very much! Nineteen years and three children, and this is the thanks I get for time served.'

'Spare me the self-righteous shtick, Margaret. You have my grateful thanks times three for making me a father, but you know as well as I do that the use-by date on our marriage expired a long time ago. Hell, not even you can deny we've been living separate lives for years.'

'It works.'

He shook his head. 'Not for me. Not any more. I've been in love with someone else for a long time.'

The flash of jealousy hit her so hard she glowed green, stunned by its intensity. Years had passed since she'd loved Kevin, but no other woman was going to replace her. 'And what? You think I don't have someone else? Don't tell me you're fool enough to believe I've existed on your pitiful performance of sex twice a year for fifteen years? I haven't. In fact, this afternoon I was very much refilling the well. It doesn't mean we have to upend our lives and the children's.'

'I'm afraid that's already happened. It's why I want to make my relationship official.' He rubbed his palms against his stubbled cheeks and when he raised his head, he looked much older than his forty-nine years. 'Yesterday, Andrew gave me some test results. I'm dying, Margaret, and I refuse to waste what little time I've got left with you. I'm going to die my way, surrounded by people who actually love me.'

Stunned, she stared at him. He was dying? He'd given up smoking years ago and harangued her to do the same and yet with all that coughing ... 'You've got lung ...' Her voice dropped as if saying the word loudly might give her the debilitating disease. 'Cancer?'

'No.' He closed his eyes for a moment as if seeking strength. 'This pneumonia that won't go away ... It's a complication of AIDS.'

'AIDS? I don't understand ...' Her mind veered violently away from the images of the Grim Reaper campaign. If Kevin used drugs, she would have noticed track marks, odd behaviour. It wasn't like they did everything separately; they kept up appearances for the sake of the children and their position in town. 'You've never even had a blood transfusion. How on earth can you have AIDS?'

'I'm gay, Margaret. Homosexual.'

Horror stiffened her from top to toe. 'No!'

'Yes. I've known since I was twenty.'

The whiskey glass slipped from her numb fingers and bounced on the carpet. 'But you played football. You're good at sports. You can build anything. You love being outdoors, for God's sake.'

Sadness circled him along with resignation. 'I'm sorry, Margaret, but none of those things prevent me from liking men more than women.'

'But you married me! We have three children!' She knew she was gabbling but her mind was screaming, *Did I know?*

He shrugged. 'It was 1972. I didn't have much choice. Men in their late twenties were expected to marry, especially Jamieson men.'

'But if you knew, why didn't you leave town? Go and live in Sydney or Melbourne?'

'I wanted my Mingunyah life and the man I loved.' His mouth flattened. 'Turns out he and I were both naive and stupid. We thought if I got Dad off my back by getting married, our lives wouldn't change much. When Dad suggested I marry you, I thought it was the perfect solution, because in two years of our sort-of dating, you never made a single demand on me.' He shook his head. 'Christ, Margaret! The restraint you showed must have almost killed you. Gary and I didn't bargain on the fact that the moment I slid that ring on your finger, you'd show your true colours.'

Gary! Her world tilted. She'd hated Gary, not because she thought he was gay but because he was always around and Kevin took his advice over hers. She trawled her memory. Had she known deep down they were lovers? No! She didn't know any gay men. It had never occurred to her that—she shuddered at the thought of two men having sex—*that* was part of their friendship.

'You loved Gary Longmuir? In that case, I'm even happier that I got rid of him. I hope it hurt.'

'Of course it bloody hurt. I've loved him more than I ever loved you.'

'That's not true!' Memories of their early marriage played across her mind. Certainly, their sex life had never been great. Usually, she'd been the one to initiate it, but Kevin had done it often enough that she'd never once entertained the thought he was homosexual. Even after she and Robert had started their affair, sex between her and Keven still happened occasionally.

She'd always thought his absolute insistence on using condoms after Ellie was born was because of her surprise pregnancy but suddenly the full implication of his diagnosis hit her. That was the year the HIV/AIDS pandemic swept the world. Had he known he had the disease then? Flashes of blood-stained tissues and blood-stained sheets —items she'd recently handled during his illness—bombarded her. Poisonous blood from a perverted disease.

Her insides collapsed, her gut turned to water and she leaped away from him. 'You filthy, stinking faggot! Get out! If you've infected me or Ellie, I'll kill you.'

'You're safe, Margaret. So are the children. And I anticipated this reaction,' he said levelly, rising slowly to his feet. 'I've already packed and my cases are in the car. I'm having lunch with Cameron and Sarah in Melbourne tomorrow and I'll tell them. All I've said to Ellie is that I'm leaving for Melbourne before she wakes in the morning and that I'll see her next week.'

A deadly calm stiffened her spine. 'Over my dead body you'll see her.'

'If that's what it takes.' His nostrils flared. 'She's my daughter and I will see her.'

Hysterical laughter tore out of her. 'You stupid fag. She's not your daughter. She's Robert's.'

Kevin swayed and his hand wrapped tightly around the arm of the chair to steady himself. 'That's just biology. I'm her father in every way it counts. Ellie's my baby girl.' He lifted his chin, straightened his shoulders and his frail body suddenly looked like reinforced steel. 'If you try to stop me from seeing her, I will fight you with everything I've got.'

She crossed her arms, confident of being on solid ground. 'I doubt it will matter what you do. You're a dirty homo. I'm her mother and the wronged party. The court will side with me.'

An uncharacteristic glint lit up his eyes. 'I've lived with you for nineteen years, Margaret, and you've inadvertently taught me how to be a lying and scheming bitch. Do you really think councillor Robert Horton will welcome a very public outing of his bastard child? Do you think he'll want anything to do with you after the news breaks? I don't think so.'

Fear and anger collided, staining her vision red. 'Don't threaten me, Kevin, or I'll tell everyone about your perverted little secret. No one in this town is going to believe the crazy rantings of a poofter with AIDS.'

He laughed. 'Oh, Margaret, go right ahead. I'm going to be dead within the year so the news will hurt you a lot more than it will hurt me. But it will hurt the children the most. An optimistic part of me hopes you want to protect them from salacious gossip and the hurtful judgement of the town who will ignorantly and erroneously call my life sordid. The problem is, I know you too well. It's not the children you want to protect but yourself. If you out me, you'll be tainted by all the misinformation about this horrendous disease. Robert will distance himself from you faster than a rat up a drainpipe.'

He suddenly doubled over, wracked by another coughing fit. When it passed, he straightened and this time his face was set harder than concrete. 'By the way, I've seen a solicitor. Because we haven't had sex in over a year and we've been living separate lives under the same roof, I've got a strong case for immediate divorce. I'm setting up a trust fund for the kids but you're not getting a cent. You've got the diamonds and all the other jewellery. If you liquidate those assets and get a job, you'll be fine.' His hand closed around the doorhandle. 'And I've got a buyer for the house. You might want to start looking for somewhere else to live.'

Blind fury rendered her almost speechless. 'You prick!'

'Goodbye, Margaret.' The door closed.

'But I won!' she yelled. 'You pathetic buggering bastard! I won.'

Something wet and cold startled her and she glanced down at her hand, surprised to see she wasn't in Mill House but sitting in a club chair by the fire and holding a Bloody Mary.

'Oh, dear. You've spilt your drink.' Sarah mopped at the damp patch on Margaret's skirt before offering her own drink as a replacement. 'Who upset you?'

The hairs on the back of Margaret's neck rose. 'None of your business.' She drank greedily, relaxing into the vodka and letting it sweep her up in its glorious and giddy slipstream.

'Was it Robert who upset you?'

She laughed at the absurdity of the question. 'Robert would never do that.'

'Why not?'

'Because unlike that dried-up prune Mary, I give him what he needs. He worships me.' She leaned forward, thrilling in the power she wielded over him. 'He'll do anything for me.'

'Will he risk everything and divorce Mary for you? Will he acknowledge to the town that Ellie's his daughter?'

She stiffened, instantly alert despite the confusion circling her. How did Sarah know about Ellie? Margaret had held on to that secret tighter than a drum and Robert would never tell. *Kevin knew.* She whipped her head left and right, looking for him, and gasped. Kevin was back, only this time he was standing behind the bar, pouring one of his ridiculous bright green cocktails into a martini glass. He waved at Sarah and then he grinned at Margaret—a taunting victorious smile. He tapped his nose. *I know all your secrets.*

'You bastard, Kevin!' She stood up screaming. 'Poofters like you aren't welcome here. Take your stinking, putrid, faggot body and get out before I kill you.'

'Mum!' Sarah's hands tugged at her arms. 'That's not Dad. That's Gary—'

'Longmuir!' All her secrets spun around him in a silver swirl, the words clear and bold. 'No. I sent you away, you cock-sucking pervert!'

'Gary! Call an ambulance.'

Margaret's head throbbed with a pulsing ache in her temple. Fury blurred her sight but she had to protect herself. Protect Robert. She had to get to her secrets, grab them and hide them before anyone saw them. Panting for breath, she used every ounce of strength she had to pull against arms that held her tight. Nothing moved. Flinging out an elbow, she heard an *oomph* and then the vice-like hands fell away. She toppled forward, threw out her arms and steadied herself on a chair before taking a step.

Excruciating pain seared her mind. Silver lit up behind her eyes and then her legs collapsed under her. As she fell into a tunnel, the bright lights faded and everything turned black.

Anita squeezed Cameron's hand as they walked out of the hospital, their mood sombre. 'I've read that hearing is the last thing to go. Your mum might still be able to hear you, so hold onto that.'

'I doubt it. You saw her. She can't move and her eyes ... God, they're vacant. Why couldn't it have just killed her?'

When Sarah had summoned them to the hospital, they'd been shocked by Margaret's condition. Unlike the previous stroke, this one had left her totally incapacitated, dribbling and unable to speak. The doctor told them there was no chance of recovery. Sadly, her heart was strong, so they were keeping her comfortable as death might be a long time coming. This was the first time the stylish and indomitable matriarch had been felled by her body, a vessel that had always been exceptionally good to her. Now her attractive face sagged as the damaged muscles pulled her mouth down, giving her the wizened look of a miserable and disagreeable crone. Anita shivered just thinking about it.

It wasn't until later that evening, after they'd told the girls about their grandmother, answered their questions and settled them into bed, that they had another chance to talk.

'Poor Sarah.' Anita accepted a glass of Baileys from Cameron. 'She looked absolutely devastated.'

'Poor Sarah? You've got to be kidding. She caused this.'

'Oh, Cam. I know you're upset. I know she's being a bitch about Mill House, but as much as you want to blame her, she's not responsible for Margaret's stroke.'

'She bloody well is. What the hell was she doing taking Mum to Albury for the day? Jesus!'

'We took her to the Tarrawonga races last week,' she said gently. 'The doctor said the stroke could have happened anywhere and at any time. Isn't it better to know she was out enjoying herself when it happened?'

'But she'd been getting better and now ...'

'Oh, Cam.' She stood up and hugged him tightly. Her husband was blinkered when it came to his mother. No one except him believed Margaret had been improving. Since her first stroke, her confusion had increased exponentially. The few times Anita had forced herself to visit and endured being harangued, Margaret had been heavily rooted in the past with no grasp on reality.

The day at Tarrawonga had been interesting. Cameron hosted a marquee for prospective clients, inviting them to experience a local event. The aim was that, under the influence of fine wine and hopefully a win on the horses, they'd fall in love with the idea of buying a property in the valley. Knowing how much Margaret loved fashion and the races, Anita had, against Cameron's wishes, bought her a new dress and hat for the occasion. Her mother-in-law had been giddy with excitement and positively sparkled at the event. What struck Anita the most about the day was her mother-in-law's behaviour. Whenever Margaret was on Cameron's arm meeting his clients, she appeared to make sense. But when he was occupied talking business and Margaret spent time with Anita and the girls, she was convinced she was at the 1980 Melbourne Cup and celebrating with the Sangsters. The laugh of the day was when she'd said, sotto voce, 'I'd have expected them to serve better champagne than this.'

'Darling, Margaret was always more alert with you than she was for anyone else. The only thing we can hope for is that this awful event might make Sarah easier to deal with. Family's important at times like this.'

He grunted. 'Unlikely. You'd have to be blind not to notice Sarah left the hospital as soon as we arrived. Ellie wasn't even there.'

She thought about how reasonable Ellie was being about Mill House. 'She probably visited before or after us.'

'Hah! Since when are you attributing empathy to my spoiled and self-obsessed sister?'

'I think she's put all that behind her. Right now, she's being a lot more rational than Sarah.'

He shot her a bemused look. 'Given she's forcing us down an expensive legal path to get access to what is rightfully ours, how did you manage to draw that conclusion?'

Anita was yet to tell Cameron about the agreement she'd struck with Ellie. As insurance, she'd sworn the girls to secrecy too, using much the same theory he'd proposed for Vintage Glamour: the surprise is better when you can prove your success. It had almost killed her not sharing with him the rave reviews she'd got on Facebook after the first two high teas and the new bookings that were coming in. But a tiny part of her worried that if he knew she was using Mill House, he might go storming up there to demand more access and break her hard-earned détente with Ellie.

She ran a finger around the rim of her liqueur glass. With Margaret barely conscious, surely the siblings would want, and be open to, reconciliation. Since the lock-out, Ellie was the only one of them to have extended anything that resembled an olive branch. Surely that had to count for something? Before the fight, Sarah and Cameron were closer to each other than to Ellie and therefore had less distance to travel before reaching unity. It was time to get the ball rolling.

'Ellie's letting me use Mill House for Cooked By a Friend.'

'What?' His cheeks flushed purple. 'How did this happen?'

'I went to see her.'

'*You* went to see *her*?'

'Shh, Cam. You'll wake the girls.'

'Bloody hell, Anita! Do you have any idea what you've done?'

'Yes.' A combination of annoyance and determination swept through her. 'I've gone out to bat for my business.'

'You should have consulted me first.'

'I did! We discussed and agreed on a strategy. When you didn't apologise to Ellie, I did what I had to do to save my business. I agree with you about Sarah being a bitch, but you're wrong about Ellie. I negotiated with her and she was pleasant, professional and sensible.'

He slammed his fist into his palm, the sound as loud as a clap. 'You stupid, stupid girl.'

She flinched, not able to believe he'd hurled those hurtful words. Since they'd met, he always called her 'his girl' and 'baby girl' as a nod to their age and height difference. She'd never objected because they were terms of endearment. Not once had he called her stupid. Completely thrown by his offensive remark, she fought for composure.

'I am *not* stupid. I'm the adult in this situation. Not only have I saved Cooked By a Friend, Ellie and I have created an avenue for reconciliation between you and your sisters.'

'No! What you've done is fuck everything up!'

His unfamiliar aggression battered her and she blinked, trying not to cry. 'I—I haven't.'

'You have.' His grey eyes narrowed to flinty slits. 'The *one* thing our case rested on was the fact they locked us out and banned us from rightful access.'

Relief raced in and she reached out, touching his arm. She needed to calm and reassure him and find her loving husband in the process. 'But I don't have full access. I don't even have a key. I can only be there at predetermined times and either Ellie or Sarah are always there.'

He threw out his arm, tossing away her hand. 'But you were the one seeking an agreement.'

'Yes, but I didn't get everything I wanted.'

'Christ, Anita.' He slumped onto the couch. 'You don't get it, do you? You've set us back weeks.'

Guilt, anger and frustration burned her. She hated that she'd upset him but this wasn't all her fault. 'Perhaps if you'd explained things to me instead of promising me something and then doing nothing, I wouldn't have gone to Ellie. But I wasn't going to stand by and watch my business languish after such a solid start. You'd fight for Prestige Country Properties if it was under threat.'

'Look,' he said, exasperation rising off him like steam. 'I know you love Cooked By a Friend but this issue with the house is bigger than a small, hobby-based business. We have to keep our eye on the big picture.'

Hobby? The dig hurt. She tried to rise above it, cutting him some slack for a very difficult day and acknowledging the havoc grief was playing with his state of mind. 'You said if Cooked By a Friend operated out of Mill House it worked in our favour. If that's not the big picture, then what is?'

His eyes held hers for a long moment. Finally, he sighed and patted the couch next to him. 'Sorry, baby girl. It's been a bloody awful day.'

'Huge.' She slid in next to him, welcoming his arm around her and his return to normal. 'I get it. You're in shock. Your mum kind of died today.'

'Yeah. But I shouldn't have taken it out on you. It's just with the new will still unsigned and—'

'Not signed?' She sat up with a start. 'But you have power of attorney. Why can't you sign it?'

He scratched his head. 'I was shocked too, but if seems the powers don't extend that far.'

'But if it's not signed, does that mean we could lose—'

'Shh. Rupert's on top of things but he might advise us to pull Cooked For a Friend out of Mill House until it's all resolved and ...' His sympathetic gaze met hers. 'Before you get all bent out of shape, sometimes in business we have to take small pains for big gains. But whatever happens, promise me you won't talk to Sarah or Ellie about any of this. Information is power, Annie. We don't want to give my sisters any more power than they've already got.'

Anita hated that Cooked By a Friend might take a hit but with Margaret possibly lingering for weeks or months, she was stuck between a rock and a hard place.

'If Margaret had died today, would the old will be current?'

'Yes. But the moment she dies, we lodge a caveat at the probate office and get a court date to argue our case for the new will.'

'But if that fails, Mill House was left to us in the old will, wasn't it? So that won't change?'

'It shouldn't but the law isn't always fair. Stop worrying. Rupert knows what he's doing.' He kissed the top of her head. 'Let's talk about happier things. Tell me about the high teas. Did Phoebe rock the cello?'

Anita dropped her head back on Cameron's shoulder, pride swelling at the thought of her eldest daughter's talent. 'She was fantastic and Ruby looked amazing in her black and white maid's uniform.' She rattled on about the petit fours, the ribbon sandwiches and French pastries, relaxing into Cameron's interest and trying not to worry about the future of her beloved business.

CHAPTER TWENTY

SARAH MIGHT HAVE LOOKED normal on the outside but inside her mind whirled like a dervish. If discombobulation could be bottled and sold, Sarah would be wealthier than ever. Roaming freely for days, it stole her concentration and created havoc, making her jittery and jumpy and giving her a short fuse. Not even in the sanctuary of Edmund's bed, at his mountain-resort apartment with its glorious views of the craggy blue-green Crosscut Saw, could she rid herself of its effects. Poor Edmund; he was so kind and considerate, working so hard for her pleasure, and all she'd been able to manage were the sounds of an orgasm, not the real deal. Thankfully, she didn't think he'd detected the lie.

When Alex had declared, 'I'm not happy,' he'd gutted her. Had she known that his betrayal was just the start of chaos, she might have run away and hidden from her life. Eight days earlier, her mother had not only detonated the foundations the Jamieson family was built on, she'd exposed them to be utterly false. Sarah was struggling to adjust her perception of who Margaret and Kevin really were and attempting to piece together the true story of their marriage.

The professionals advised that talking to someone about emotional trauma helped and Sarah needed to talk to someone, but every time she opened her mouth to tell Edmund that her mother was not only an adulteress, but that she'd been so jealous of her younger daughter she'd failed to protect Ellie from being sexually abused by her biological father and that Sarah's own father was likely gay, she closed it again. Telling Edmund felt wrong, which shocked her. She'd been convinced she could tell him anything. She was convinced she had told him everything over the years. But like so many other things she'd believed to be true, this too was smoke and mirrors. As dear and understanding as Edmund was, he didn't know Ellie. He didn't really know Margaret and he was ignorant of the mythology her mother had carefully constructed around the memory of her father.

He wasn't Alex.

The familiar and desperate ache hit her again, stealing her breath. Shame came hot on its heels. For six weeks she'd sought solace in Edmund, unquestioningly accepting his love for her and telling herself their current situation was a natural extension of their close friendship. Convincing herself that if she couldn't have Alex, then Edmund was the next best thing. But her family crisis exposed the huge chasm between her love for Alex and the paler version she felt for Edmund.

It hasn't stopped you from sleeping with him or accepting today's invitation. She didn't want to think about what sort of person that made her. Oh God, was she a user of people like her mother? Sweat broke out under her arms. She'd justified today's trip up the mountain as a deserved day off from sitting by her unresponsive mother while she wrestled with the secrets she wished she'd never learned.

Edmund, although clueless to the exact cause of her anguish, was accurate in detecting her guilt.

'Your mother's stroke is not your fault,' he'd said each time he caught her staring off into space instead of focusing her attention on him. 'Be kind to yourself, darling. It could have happened anywhere at any time.'

Except she had a horrible suspicion that by taking Margaret to the club and questioning her about Robert, she'd increased the odds. After

Margaret's first stroke, Sarah had noticed the dementia made her mother progressively unguarded. Out in the hospital's garden and with a cigarette in hand, Margaret was gregarious and happy to talk about her glory days, even dropping bombshells about sex. But whenever Sarah tried to get her to divulge information about her assets and will, she'd get a glint in her eye and clam up. Sarah had almost given up, thinking it an impossible task, but when Ellie had revealed her story to her, the zeal for the truth drove her every waking moment.

Her rage at Robert Horton was so primal, so savage, and terrified her so much, she was avoiding Dan. He looked almost identical to his father and he was much the same age as Robert was when he'd assaulted Ellie that she feared she'd lose control and say something. As much as she wanted to rip the blinkers from Dan's eyes and reveal the true deviancy of his father, it wasn't her story; the telling rested entirely with Ellie.

And then there was Margaret. Discovering the role she'd played in Ellie's ordeal had shattered Sarah's mother–daughter trust and destroyed all the small allowances she continually made for Margaret's 'little quirks'. All her life, she had craved Margaret's affection, turning herself inside out for crumbs and, on reflection, apparently rewriting Margaret's hurts and slights into more palatable memories. For forty-five years, Sarah had been a marionette and Margaret the puppeteer, pulling the strings to get her own way and using her like she used everyone. Her belief that she and her mother were close was pure fiction, as was the 'mother' Sarah had loved. Her desire to uncover the real Margaret had become an obsession.

After re-reading Robert's letters, the decision to take her mother to the Albury Club, one of their lovers' rendezvous, was both calculating and deliberate. Sarah had reasoned that, with its feel-good memories of Robert, a visit to the club might prompt Margaret to divulge information from her fast-dissolving mind. Only, she'd got way more than she'd bargained for. Although her mother hadn't stated that Ellie was Robert's, the look on her face and the bizarre reaction confirmed it. What had happened next was like watching a horror film as her mother unravelled, taking them back in time to shine a spotlight on a marriage that was morbidly fascinating and heart-achingly sad.

If Sarah was to believe Margaret's maniacal raving, her father was gay. It was almost impossible to contemplate but the base and vitriolic language her mother spat was so raw it couldn't have been fake. During her student days, Sarah had shared a house with a gay guy, but he'd been a drama student and outrageously camp— absolutely nothing like her father, despite his penchant for musicals. Kevin had been a man's man, quick witted and well respected by the men at the mill. Although he'd seemed increasingly distracted with work and had travelled a lot during her last few years of high school, he was there if she ever needed him: tall, solid, dependable, loving and ready with a hug. He was her go-to parent every time. But homosexual? Not a hint. Then again, she'd not been looking and her father obviously didn't want her to know.

Oh, Dad. You must have been miserable.

The day after her mother's catastrophic stroke, Sarah had worried Kevin might not be her father either. Did gay men have heterosexual sex? But she only had to look in the mirror and see her father's eyes and distinctive nose—it had always suited his larger face better than her smaller one—to know her darling dad was her father. She'd dismissed her concerns about her parentage as irrational and stupid but that didn't lessen the other questions that continued to plague her— questions that were unlikely to ever find answers. Had her father married her mother knowing he was gay or had that realisation come later? When in their marriage did Margaret find out Kevin had a lover? Was it before or after her long-time affair with Robert Horton?

Clouds gathered, easing out the previously blue sky and casting a shadow across the bed. She felt a reluctant pang for her mother. Was it worse when you discovered your husband was betraying you by loving another man instead of a woman? Margaret had done some shocking things but had Kevin played a part in who her mother had become? Sarah stomped on her empathy. No matter how much her father's secret hurt her mother, it didn't account for the appalling way she'd abandoned Ellie.

Sarah was still spending most mornings searching Mill House, but now she was looking for anything that belonged to her father. She'd spent hours googling 'Gary Longmuir' but hadn't found anything. Even if she had, it was hardly going to gift her with the words 'lover of Kevin Jamieson'. She'd drawn a blank on any evidence her father was gay but she'd learned her mother's homage to her happy marriage to Kevin was limited to an extremely thin veneer of carefully chosen photographs, including the beautiful portraits taken a few weeks before he died. Sarah's favourite was the one of her father sitting in a chair with Ellie on his lap and love in his eyes. Did he know Ellie wasn't his? How she wished the photo could come to life and answer questions, but all she saw was a man looking thinner than she remembered. Had the failing business taken its toll on him? Had his double life? Had he killed himself?

No! She discarded the horrifying thought, reminding herself he'd telephoned her on the afternoon of his death, insisting she lunch with him and Cameron the following day. He wanted to see her, not leave her. For months after that call, she'd replayed the very normal conversation over and over in her head, but the only difference she could pinpoint from other catch-up phone calls was his insistence Cameron join them. Sarah remembered being pissy about that. It was enough that Cameron had Margaret's undivided attention; she hated sharing her father with him too. Why had Kevin insisted on seeing them together? And why had he left Mingunyah at ten o'clock at night in the middle of a thunderstorm instead of his usual early-morning departure?

Her family was a black hole of secrets and lies. Was there anyone who could help? The historical society? The footy club archives? Perhaps she could talk to someone at the hospital or the police station about the possibility of finding and reading her father's autopsy report. Was there more to the car accident than she'd been told? She wanted details—hell, she wanted anything that might paint a picture of the truth, because she no longer believed anything her mother had told her.

Her thoughts drifted to Mary Horton, still spry and very much alert. Did she know about her husband's long affair with Margaret? Did she know about Ellie? Did Sarah have the right to ask?

'Earth to Sarah?' Edmund, now dressed, appeared by the bed holding a mug of tea.

She sat up. 'Sorry. I was thinking about ... Mum.'

'Today is supposed to be a day off from all that. Why don't you book yourself a massage, or we can ski some runs? I've got two hours before I have to be at the restaurant to check everything's ready for the investors' dinner.' His eyes lit up. 'You should come to dinner and stay the night.' He nuzzled her neck. 'We haven't spent a night together since our first time and waking up with you is wonderful.'

She made herself smile. 'As lovely as that sounds, I need to get back to Mingunyah—'

'The doctor said your mother is in a vegetative state.'

She sighed. 'It's not Mum, it's Gus. I live in hope he'll amble into the flat one day after school.'

'This situation with him has gone on too long, Sarah. Let me talk to him.'

Alex will have a pink fit. 'You're lovely, but it's not a good idea.'

Affronted, he sucked in his cheeks. 'Gus and I have a bond.'

'I know you do, but ...' She licked her lips. 'He's heard rumours about us and he asked me if we're together. It was just after the first time we'd ... I denied it but even so, I don't think it's a good idea for you to talk to him.'

'You denied it?'

He sounded hurt and bewildered and her own remorse and shame sat like a medicine ball in her chest. She slid her hand into his. 'Edmund, this isn't about you or me or even us. He's my son. I wasn't about to discuss my sex life with him.'

He gave her a rueful smile. 'I understand. When things are more settled and you and Alex are legally separated, we will tell him together. We will tell all the children.'

Shit! Finn and Emma hadn't even been told about the separation and Edmund was talking about their future? The thousand-count thread sheets suddenly seemed impossibly heavy on her skin. 'I— that's —Thank you,' she said lamely.

'Sarah.' His accent was suddenly more pronounced and tinged with disapproval. 'You must tell Finn. You have waited too long already.'

Her scalp tingled. 'I've waited until he's home and in the same room so I can answer his questions. He's bringing friends to Riverbend this week.'

'And Emma?'

'Jesus, Edmund.' She threw back the sheet, fished her discarded undies off the floor with her toes and pulled them on. 'My daughter's across the other side of the world. I'm not telling her until I can face her and hold her in my arms. If you don't agree with this decision, then tough. They're my kids.'

'I know they are.'

His quiet words slashed her. Oh God. How could she have said that to him? She fell to her knees beside him on the bed. He'd always been so loving with her kids both before and after one wet night ended his life as a husband and father and left him totally alone.

'Edmund, I'm sorry.' She wrapped her arms around him and rested her head on his shoulder. 'With everything that's happening ... I'm floundering. It's no excuse. Please. Forgive me.'

'You're forgiven.' He kissed her and as she leaned away, her naked breasts brushed his chest and he kissed them. Her body shivered involuntarily and he smiled. 'Look,' he said, pointing to the window with its view across the back country. 'It's snowing. As you're not dressed yet, I'm taking that as a sign.'

Guilt drove her to acquiesce. She owed this generous man more than lying on her back and letting him pleasure her.

She unbuttoned his shirt and was trailing kisses down his chest when Alex's ringtone blared from her phone. Her head snapped up so fast, she almost took out Edmund's jaw. Alex never called her anymore, he only sent curt texts.

'Sorry, it might be Gus,' she lied, rolling away and grabbing her phone from her bag. 'Hello.'

'Sarah, we've got a problem.'

She tried not to snort her derision. 'Just one?'

'It's Gus,' he said, ignoring her quip. 'He's been arrested.'

'What?' She frantically picked up her clothes. 'Why?'

'The school said he punched some kid. Look, I'm leaving Riverbend now. I'll be at the police station in half an hour. Don't talk to anyone before I get there.' The line went dead.

Stunned, she turned to face Edmund. 'I have to go. Gus is in custody at Mingunyah Police Station.'

Edmund bounded to his feet. 'I'll come with you.'

If she walked into the police station with Edmund it would be like throwing a lit match into a box of fireworks. Alex would go apeshit and they were still suffering the fallout from the last time Gus heard them hurling insults at each other. As much as she didn't want to upset Edmund, Gus was her priority.

'In this weather, it's over an hour down the mountain let alone how long we'll have to wait. You need to be at Hibiscus for the investors' dinner.' She kissed him. 'I'll be fine.'

'You'll need chains. Call me when you're safely off the mountain.'

'Of course.' But her mind was already moving away from Edmund to her gentle son, who'd never struck anyone in his life, not even playing footy.

'You took your sweet time,' Alex said grimly as the constable ushered Sarah into a private waiting area.

Once you would have hugged and kissed me hello. 'I wasn't in

Mingunyah when you called,' she said, stating the obvious. 'I'd have told you if you hadn't hung up on me so fast.'

His eyes raked her body, taking in her puffer jacket and her black après-ski pants. 'No, I can see that. How is life on the mountain with Edmund?'

'I could ask you how life is with Kelly, but can we please not do this right now?' She glanced around. 'Where's Gus? Surely we should be with him?'

Alex filled a plastic cup with water from the dispenser and handed it to her before pouring one for himself. 'That's what I said, but Graeme suggested he sit in a cell for a while and reflect before we rush in.'

'What? So we just wait here?'

'Yep.'

'What about the other boy? Is he here too? His parents? God, who are they? Do we know them?' All the questions that had been racing around her head on the drive down the mountain spilled out.

'Ever heard of Mason Raith?'

She shook her head.

'No, me neither. The family's new to the valley but our son has put their son in hospital with a broken nose. Christ, Sarah.' Alex paced. 'First Gus throws his chance at the firsts and now this. What the hell's going on with that kid? Thank God we didn't have a fourth child.'

His words scratched the scab on a wound that had never fully healed. 'Yes, well, you took that decision out of our hands.'

'Really?' He stared at her, flabbergasted. 'You're bringing that up again? *Now?* For Christ's sake, it's been fifteen years. Let it go.'

'That's right, blame me. Add, "I had a vasectomy without telling my wife and she won't let it go" to your list of Reasons Why Sarah Makes Me Unhappy.'

His jaw stiffened. 'It was the right thing to do.'

'Do you realise that no matter how many times you say that, it doesn't make me believe it? That it doesn't change the fact that you made a life-altering decision without discussing it with me?' The urge to hit something made her scrunch her plastic cup. The cracking sound reverberated around the small room and Alex flinched. 'And as for "let it go", I saw a counsellor for months to try to do just that.'

His head dropped. 'I didn't know.'

'No. Well, you wouldn't, would you? I was the one with the problem, wasn't I? I was the one who needed help to understand why my otherwise loving husband did something so drastic and so deceitful.' She sat on the edge of the plastic chair. 'I got as far as forgiving you, Alex, but as much as I've tried, and as much as I've wanted to, I can never fully forget. Sometimes it comes back and hurts me all over again.'

The words tumbled out, driven by his absolute breach of faith and his cavalier treatment of her heart. 'Do you want to know why I saw a counsellor? Because I loved you. You'd summarily taken a sledgehammer to our marriage and I wanted to save it. And I truly believed that we'd found our way through that dangerous and difficult time. That we'd come out intact and you were never going to hurt me that badly again. Boy, did I get that wrong. Guess the joke's on me.'

Emma had been four months old when she discovered Alex had gone in for a vasectomy. Sleep deprived and struggling to care for a baby, a toddler and a pre-schooler, as well as being sentient for Alex, his confession had blindsided her so badly she hadn't been able to talk to him about it. That he had done something so significant without consulting her and savagely destroyed their long-time plans for a fourth child had encased her in a black fog of despair for weeks. By the time she'd come out of it, he'd taken her silence on the subject as acceptance. After that, whenever she tried to raise the topic, he became defensive. Now, seeing his taut and unsmiling face, she knew nothing had changed.

Alex sat down hard and huffed out a breath. 'I didn't do it to hurt you.'

But you left me bleeding just the same. It was pointless responding to his statement. They'd been over this ground so many times before there was nothing left to pick over. If she asked him why he'd done it, he'd just trot out the same answer he'd always used: three children were enough. She'd get angry and remind him that he was the one who'd always wanted four kids. And he'd yell, 'I changed my mind, okay? People are allowed to do that.'

She was sick and tired of arguing with him. In the weeks since she'd moved out of Riverbend, all their conversations had deteriorated into a slanging match at some point. Knowing they could both hurt each other so cruelly devastated her. How did two people who'd loved each other so well and for so long find themselves here?

'Can I ask you something?'

He pulled at his ear and grimaced. 'That depends. I'm not arguing with you here. They're just as likely to throw us into the cells.'

And just like that, the version of the man she loved, the man she'd glimpsed so infrequently lately—her Alex—was in the room.

'You don't have to answer if you don't want to.' A flicker of surprise registered in his eyes but his face remained stony. She pushed on. 'Do you have any regrets at all about the vasectomy?'

He was silent, his gaze drifting to the 'Dob in a Dealer' poster on the wall.

She waited, working hard on staying silent and not jumping in early—she knew he hated it when she did that, but it was a struggle. When a good minute had passed and he still hadn't said anything, she rose and walked to the water cooler. It had nothing to do with thirst and everything to do with moving, doing something, anything, to temper her disappointment. But what had she really expected of him? Alex could talk about the goats, cheese, the global marketplace, and their machinery ad infinitum but his feelings almost never.

'I thought you were going to die.' His voice cracked on words that sounded as if they'd been wrung out of him.

'What?' Icy water cascaded over her fingers and she fumbled with the tap. 'When?'

'When Emma was born.' He rubbed his hands back and forth on his thighs and shuddered. 'There was so much blood. I can still hear the alarms screaming on those bloody machines. You were whiter than the sheets, you could barely talk and the midwife looked terrified. I watched them running. Yelling. Pushing you on the trolley into theatre and I had no idea if you were going to live or die.'

His left leg bounced and the plastic chair creaked. 'Later, they told me I was only waiting twenty minutes before the paediatrician came and found me and told me we had a daughter. But to me, those twenty minutes were eternity. It was a lifetime lived without you and raising the boys alone. I was in the nursery cuddling Emma when the obstetrician came in. Unlike the paediatrician, he looked like shit. He said it had been touch and go. You'd needed two blood transfusions and it was going to take you a while to get your energy back, but you'd be okay.

'For weeks, my breathing sped up whenever I thought about how close I came to losing you. All I could think about was that I never wanted to live through anything like that again.'

Her memories of that time were hazy. After the birth she'd been chronically anaemic, battling exhaustion and trying to breastfeed Emma while recovering from a caesarean section. No one at the hospital or at her post-natal check-up had ever mentioned she'd almost died. But they'd told Alex? Dear God, what a burden to carry alone.

'I almost died? No one ever said.'

'No. You had enough to deal with.'

Her mind slipped and slid, trying to process this new information. 'Are you telling me that you had a vasectomy so I couldn't get pregnant again and die?'

Humiliation hovered in the creases around his mouth. 'Something like that.'

'Oh, Alex.' Compassion and sadness rolled in, moderated by frustration as the same old question raised its head again. 'Why didn't you talk to me about it?'

'Because you'd have tried to stop me. You'd have told me I was being ridiculous, that I was worrying unnecessarily and that everything would be fine. But you weren't there, Sarah. You didn't have to watch everything unravel so fast you questioned if it was even happening.

I've never felt so powerless in my life as I did that day. I don't regret having the vasectomy then and I don't regret it now.'

He suddenly slumped as if all the fight had drained out of him and, for the first time in his life, he looked as old as his years. 'But I do regret what it did to us.'

She recognised the softly spoken words as the apology she hadn't known she was still waiting for after all these years. Up until the last few awful weeks, that year had been their most difficult. Devastated and grieving, she'd thrown herself into mothering, myopically focusing on the children as she struggled to come to terms with what Alex had done. The house at Riverbend became her domain and motherhood her mission. Alex retreated into the business, working harder than ever, frequently coming home late just as she'd got the boys settled. His arrival would hype them up again. She accused him of being an absent father. He accused her of side-lining him from the children's lives.

Emma's first birthday had brought the turning point. As she surveyed the jumping castle, the open bar for parents and the cake with more fondant icing than an entry in the Royal Melbourne Show, she'd compared it to the small family gatherings she'd thrown for the boys. 'Alex, I've gone completely overboard with this party, haven't I?'

'Yep.'

'I think I need to come back to work.'

'Thank goodness.'

He'd leaned over and kissed her, relief bright in his eyes, and her world—off-kilter for so many months—found its axis. They gradually rediscovered their rhythm at work and quickly became the team they'd always been—equal partners—but at home she never completely forgot the child she'd hoped to have. She mothered everyone within her orbit and was the domestic controller of all their lives.

Now, in the harsh white LED light of the police station, she studied Alex's face. The lines around his eyes, the sooty stubble that appeared every day by three in the afternoon, the small white scar under his nose from a hockey injury and his dark caramel eyes were all so very familiar to her. Yet these last weeks proved they were a façade that stood in front of hidden depths.

At home you treat me like one of the kids.

He'd hurled that accusation at her the day she'd left Riverbend and she'd hotly denied it. But now she wondered if there was some truth to it. She could confidently say she didn't treat him like a child at work, but at home ... Her gut cramped. Up until this year, before Finn left for university and Emma went on exchange, home life was frantic. Just the sheer logistics of coordinating the kids' diverse activities so one of them was in attendance was sometimes more complicated and strategic than dealing with DFAT to get a shipment of cheese to China. She'd once read that families with structure were happier, so with that in mind, and to minimise chaos, she'd organised. She'd shouted commands. She'd told Alex what they were doing, when they were doing it and the times and places he was required—then she'd plugged it all into his electronic calendar. She'd thought she was helping.

Apparently, he didn't see it that way and it had taken him fifteen years—*fifteen years!*—to tell her.

The expected anger didn't come. Instead, desolation rolled in like rain in the valley on a frosty winter's day—bone-chillingly damp and making everything seem hopeless and forlorn.

'I thought we'd recovered from that terrible time, Alex. Made our peace. Now I'm wondering if we just papered over the cracks.'

The squeak of the door made them shoot to their feet and Graeme walked in with a woman they didn't recognise.

'Alex, Sarah, this is Pamela Darcas. She's the youth justice worker in the region. She's going to have a chat with you.'

Sarah smiled tightly and said a quick hello to the woman before turning to Graeme. 'When can we see Gus?'

'Have a seat, Mr and Mrs Hadfield,' Pamela said kindly. 'Gus is safe and will be released into your care when we've finished here.'

Sarah glanced at Alex, who gave an almost imperceptible shrug. She sat down. Alex took a seat opposite her. Pamela, glancing between them, pulled up a chair and sat in no-man's land.

'Gus tells me the two of you are currently separated.'

'That's right,' Alex said gruffly.

'And how's that going?'

'Look, we're not here to talk about us,' Alex said curtly as Sarah said, 'We're here to talk about Gus.'

Pamela nodded, her face impassive. 'And what's going on at home can't be separated from what Gus did today.'

'Hang on,' Alex blustered. 'We've never condoned violence. I've never hit Sarah. Hell, neither of us have hit anyone and we've never slapped the kids.'

'That's not what I'm saying, Mr Hadfield. Gus hasn't said much at all, but he did tell me that he's the only one of your children who knows about the separation. Do you agree that's a huge responsibility for a seventeen-year-old?'

Sarah's stomach heaved. 'We thought we were doing the right thing. Our situation's complicated by the other children being away and all the books say you should tell the children in person—'

'It doesn't explain why he punched a kid!' Alex interrupted.

'Young men's brains are still developing. Sometimes they can be overwhelmed by their feelings,' Pamela said.

Alex frowned, confusion clear on his face. 'That's not an excuse for breaking a kid's nose.'

'No, but it may explain why it happened. The two of you have imposed your separation on Gus and he has no power in the situation. During the argument with Mason, he could and did take control. He seized the power.'

'Control? Power?' Alex's voice rose. 'It's more like bloody anarchy. What the hell were they arguing about anyway?'

Pamela sighed. 'He won't tell me. I'm hoping the two of you will be able to coax it out of him.'

'Alex.' Sarah looked at him, thinking about the current secrets she couldn't share with anyone and how weighted down they made her feel. 'Obviously, Gus hitting Mason is indefensible but we did ask him not to tell anyone and he ...' She swallowed. *He might know about*

Edmund and Kelly. But she wasn't prepared to say the unpalatable words in front of Pamela; words that laid bare her and Alex's less than stellar behaviour. 'He isn't blind or deaf.'

Alex's troubled gaze held hers for a moment and then he rubbed his face and sighed. 'We'll sit down together and talk to him. But what happens now? Is he going to be charged? Do we need to get a lawyer down here?'

'Given this is Gus's first offence and the fact he's a local football star who's won best and fairest most seasons, Sergeant Aitkens and I agree that mediation is the best way to deal with the case. But for it to work, Gus must open up about what actually happened.' She stood up. 'For now, take him home, feed him and make sure he gets some sleep. I think the recent holidays, parties and couch surfing haven't done him any favours. Talk to him tomorrow when he's rested.' She opened the door. 'I'll send him in.'

'She doesn't pull any punches,' Alex said, when the door shut behind her.

'No.' Sarah blinked back tears. 'I hate that we've done this to Gus.'

Alex's head jerked around as if he didn't believe what he'd just heard. He studied her closely. It took her a moment before she realised it was the first time she hadn't placed the blame squarely on him. 'We should have handled things better. Done things differently.'

'Yeah,' he said. 'We should have.'

CHAPTER TWENTY-ONE

Anita strolled up to the school gate a few minutes before the afternoon bell and hesitated, torn between an easy chat with Tam or taking the wise business decision and talking to Jess. The free lasagne all those weeks ago had paid off in spades, and she now had a regular fortnightly cooking gig for Jess and two of the other pony club mothers. Decision made, she was about to walk over to Jess when Tam looked straight at her. As Anita took a step towards her, the usually friendly woman turned away as if they hadn't just made eye contact.

Taken aback, Anita stalled, stranding herself in the centre of an expanse of grey asphalt. There was little ambiguity in Tam's action; Anita knew a slight when she saw one, having been victim of many when she was a school girl.

Oh my God, what are you wearing? You smell, you stinky povvo. Go away. You can't play with us.

'Anita!' Jess's voice roused her and she accepted her air-kiss greeting. 'God, Anita, how do you do it? You always look amazing. Are those a pair of Stuart Weitzmans?'

Anita followed Jess's gaze to the brown suede ankle boots with fur trim that she'd bought a few weeks before. She and Cameron had treated themselves, celebrating the details of the new will and the amazing windfall of the education trust.

'I was a little bit naughty,' she confessed, appreciating the woman's confidence-bolstering admiration. 'But I couldn't resist them.'

'I know what you mean. They're darling and they suit your look to a T. Were you celebrating your new acquisition?'

Anita smiled hesitantly, not certain what Jess was talking about. Margaret was still hovering in a state of limbo—more dead than alive but still breathing—which meant Mill House wasn't yet theirs. Despite all her arguments to the contrary, Rupert Grimes had banned her from visiting, let alone using, the house for Cooked By a Friend. She seethed every time she thought about his high-handed manner. He'd spoken to her as if she was one of the little girls, instead of a thirty-seven-year-old businesswoman. Although Cameron had rolled his eyes, indicating he understood the lawyer was being patronising, he hadn't said anything to rectify the situation.

'I've always loved Warrnbatt,' Jess continued. 'When do you move?'

The missing pieces of the conversation fell into place. 'Oh no, we're not moving to Warrnbatt. Cameron bought it as an investment property for the business. Being right on the river, it's ideal for holiday rentals.'

'Savvy plan. Greg says your husband's no fool.' Jess glanced at Tam, who was chatting with her fellow sustainability sisters. 'I know business is business, Anita, but just a word to the wise: Tam's good friends with Jane Parry. Rumour is, they've lost their house in Albury.'

Anita's chest cramped as the past rushed up to greet her.

'That's—how awful for them,' Anita managed to stammer, her face burning. She was far too familiar with how losing a house put a family one step away from poverty and homelessness. *Pack up your toys, Anita. Someone else is going to live here now.*

Jess tutted. 'I don't know what they were thinking with Warrnbatt. I mean, even if Jane grew every damn vegetable and piece of fruit they ever consumed, recycled everything and made the kids' clothes, there's no way they were ever going to afford those renovations on Chris's salary. Jane's earth-mother calm must be struggling to stay zen. She didn't want to move to Albury in the first place and now they're stuck.'

'I don't really know them,' Anita said. 'One of their girls was in Ava's class but they moved soon after we arrived.'

'You're not missing much. Not really our type,' Jess said conspiratorially. 'Can you do coffee tomorrow at ten?'

Anita nodded distractedly and greeted the little girls as they rushed up to her.

'Look, Mummy,' Ava said, holding up a painting of stick figures standing in front of a house. 'It's us.'

'Lovely, darling,' she said, ushering them out the gate and along the footpath towards home.

'We're doing family trees,' Chloe added excitedly. 'Ava's little so she just has to draw but Mrs Novak says we have to write down everyone's names. Noah and I already started 'cept he can't spell his dad's name but I can spell Cameron. C-A-M-E-R-O-N,' she sang, skipping along.

'I want to write down everyone's names too!' Ava stamped her foot, her face lined with determination.

'Well, you can't. You're too little,' Chloe countered.

'Let's have something to eat first,' Anita said, recognising the symptoms of post-school hunger. 'Then I'll help both of you with your trees.'

Happy with the decision, the girls ran on ahead. Anita had laid out afternoon tea before pickup so twenty minutes later, fed and watered, the girls were ready with notebooks, pens, pencils and paints. Ava was cheerfully drawing a tree and Chloe, concentrating hard with the tip of her tongue protruding from her mouth, was carefully copying out all the names of the immediate Jamieson extended family and connecting them along the tree lines.

Anita glanced over, admiring her daughter's penmanship. 'Well done, Chlo. Very neat.'

Chloe chewed her pencil. 'It's crooked.'

'No it isn't. You wrote on the lines beautifully.'

'I mean the tree. Your side is empty. Who was your mummy?'

'Her name was Lena Jankovic.'

Ava screwed up her face. 'That's a funny name.'

What sort of name is that? You're weird.

Anita gave herself a shake. 'It's Serbian. Serbia is a country in Europe and she was born there.'

'Were you born there?' Chloe asked, looking at her mother with new eyes.

'No, I was born in Melbourne.' Anita suddenly felt hot, which was ridiculous as it was so cold the heater was struggling to maintain a comfortable temperature.

'Was it a pretty house?' Ava asked, adding flowers to her painting.

The scent of rotting food assaulted Anita's nostrils and suddenly she was back picking her way around empty bottles, overflowing ashtrays and half-eaten meals.

'Very pretty.'

Ava splotched pink onto one of the stick figures. 'That's your mummy. Did you have a daddy?'

Old anger reared its head and this time she couldn't lie. 'No, I didn't have a daddy.'

'But everybody has a daddy,' Chloe said emphatically. 'Even if they don't live with you, like Noah and Casey and River.'

Anita was going to march down to the school in the morning and talk to the teacher. The older girls didn't have a project like this at their city primary school because of this very issue. It was time the country caught up.

'Write down Peter Smith and then pack everything up because we need the table for dinner.'

But as she whipped up zucchini slice for the girls and a curry for her and Cameron, she couldn't shift the image of her father standing in the front garden of their house surrounded by most of their furniture carefully labelled with the price tags he'd asked her to make while her mother lay on her bed, sobbing. Memories came thick and fast. Their neighbours walking through the house. The boy who wanted to buy her Derwent pencils and her father making her sell them. Her father threatening the men who clamped the wheel of their second car and towed their boat away. Her father telling her he was 'just nicking down the shops, love' and never returning. Moving houses, moving suburbs, moving schools.

'Mmm, that smells good.' Cameron walked into the kitchen and kissed her before pulling open the fridge and grabbing a beer. 'I see the girls are watching crap TV. Everything okay?'

She dumped basmati rice into boiling water. 'Can I have a wine please?'

'I just sat down.' He threw her a hangdog look. 'You're closer.'

'You're lucky I love you.' She poured herself a glass and sat down too. 'Something happened at school pickup today and it threw me. A woman I've become friendly with, Tam Simpson?'

Cameron showed no recognition at the name.

'I work with her in the school garden and she teaches yoga ... Anyway, she deliberately turned her back on me today for no apparent reason. Then Jess Kincaid mentioned Warrnbatt. Turns out, Tam's a close friend of Jane Parry's.'

'Hmm.' Cameron's eyes had strayed to the *Mingunyah Herald* on the table.

'You paid a fair price for the house, didn't you?'

He looked up then, his jaw jutting. 'Bloody hell, Annie, of course I did. Where is this coming from? You know how hard I worked trying to sell that property. I showed it to people desperate to get a stake in the valley but it's a weird design and it gets fog-bound in winter. People don't want to pay big bucks when there's a risk the river will fill it with mud and insurance companies won't touch it. For the record—and you can tell this bloody Tam woman—Chris Parry came to me wanting to do a deal.'

'Did he?'

'Yes. And he accepted my offer.'

'Jess told me they just lost their house in Albury.'

'Shit.' Cameron took a long pull on his beer.

'It all sounds horrible.' She fiddled with the edge of the placemat. 'I've never told you this, but when I was nine, my parents defaulted on their home loan. We lost the house. It changed my life. My father ...' She pushed back the anger and pain. 'He ran. Abandoned us. My mother completely lost it and well, you know the rest.'

She looked up imploringly. 'Chris and Jane have three kids. I need to know we haven't added to their pain in any way.'

Sympathy crossed his face and he picked up her hand. 'It was bad decisions, bridging finance and being too heavily geared that caused the Parrys' problems. I promise you, we've helped them by diminishing their debt.'

'So why is Tam treating me like I'm a social pariah?'

'Finding a scapegoat is easier than accepting Chris is financially incompetent. Ignore the gossip. It was a private deal, so they're only speculating on the price.'

Memories shifted like sand, making her heart bleed. She may not know the Parrys but she knew their heartache. She'd lived the bewilderment and fear of watching everything familiar disappear.

Draining her glass, she tried to keep her own apprehensions at bay. 'Cam? Promise me nothing like that that will ever happen to us.'

'With me at the helm? No way. I promise.' He kissed her on the top of her head. 'So how about dinner? I'm starving.'

Sarah and Alex drove a silent and black-eyed Gus home—Mason had apparently managed to land one blow. Even though it had almost killed both her and Alex, they followed Pamela's advice about not quizzing him. They fed him, apologised for asking him to keep their separation a secret from Emma and Finn, told him they loved him and tucked him into bed. After leaving Gus's room, they telephoned Emma's host family in France and explained the situation before Face Timing Emma. She cried. So did Sarah. Even Alex's voice wavered. They offered to buy her a ticket if she wanted to come home.

Half an hour after the offer, Emma sent a message. *I want to stay in France.*

More than anything, Sarah wanted to jump on a plane and rush to her daughter but with everything else that was going on, it wasn't possible. Instead, all she could do was accept the kind reassurances of Collette, Emma's host mother, that she would keep a close eye on her daughter.

While they were still reeling from the emotional fallout of the conversation with Emma, Finn surprised them by walking through the door two days early.

'Hello, parents!' He dropped his bag and hugged them both. 'Thought you'd want to spoil me before the guys arrive.'

They sat him down at the kitchen table and told him about their separation, the words no easier to say despite their increasing familiarity.

'What does this mean for the business?' Finn's dark chocolate eyes flashed at them. 'Is there even going to be a family business for me to be part of when I've finished uni?'

The veins in Alex's neck pulsed. 'Your mother and I haven't discussed what it means for the business yet.'

'You're messing with me, right?' Finn looked disgusted. 'How can you split up and not have talked about the business? I mean, it's all the two of you ever talk about! We can't have a meal without you discussing it. You *are* the business.'

'I'm taking leave because of Gran,' Sarah said, obfuscating. 'And there's a lot going on with your uncle and aunts and Gus ... I don't have the head space to deal with anything else right now.'

Alex gave her a grateful but surprised look. Had he thought she'd spill the beans on why she'd really taken leave? But she was too battle scarred to play games any more; she just wanted to protect her kids. If she'd learned anything from this debacle, it was that Alex had the right to tell the kids about Kelly when he was ready and not be forced into it because someone else told all to score points or get off on salacious gossip.

'I don't plan to sell the business,' Alex said carefully, as if he was swimming through shark-infested waters. 'And if your mother wants to stay involved then we'll find a way to work it out.'

'Oh, right, so you can't live together but you can run a business together?' Finn made a derisive sound. 'That's fucked up. I'm going to bed.'

When the echo of slammed doors faded, Alex said wryly, 'That seemed to go pretty well.'

Sarah mustered a faint smile and stood up. 'If it's okay with you, I'll come back early in the morning. I want to be here when Gus wakes up.'

'You should stay,' he said flatly.

She looked at him—this man whose body was as familiar to her as her own, and yet in so many ways he was now a stranger. Exhaustion emanated from every pore and she ached to reach out and touch him. Console him. Seek consolation from him. But there was nothing in his expression or in the planes of his body that intimated she had that right anymore. It was surreal. She was standing in her own home with her husband but she may as well be a guest at a B&B with the owner offering her the use of a room.

'I'll make up the spare bed.' She pushed her chair under the table and turned to go.

'Sarah.'

'Yes.'

'I meant what I said about the business. It's not the same without you.'

She read genuine regret on his face but emotions duelled inside her. He'd missed her but he was the one who still had his lover on their staff. 'I was telling Finn the truth when I said I can't talk about this right now. The stuff with Mum and the family, it's—' But she was in no fit state for that conversation either. 'I'm barely staying afloat as it is.'

'There's no pressure to come back,' he said quickly. 'Whenever you feel ready.' His usually confident demeanour dimmed and his body looked as if it didn't know how to sit comfortably. 'Kelly's taken a job at Gunderson's. We thought it was the best solution.'

We? Sarah swallowed hard and pressed her nails into her palms as every emotion from anger to sadness pummelled her. What was the protocol here? Did an estranged wife thank her husband for moving his mistress out of their shared business? No way was she doing that. A rational voice rose above the melee of indignation: *You're missing the point. He's cleared the way for you to return to work.*

Could she work with Alex again? Could they navigate this new way of being together as business partners and parents but not friends and lovers? She had no idea.

'I appreciate the information,' she finally managed to say. 'Goodnight, Alex.'

'Goodnight, Sarah.'

Sleep didn't come. Her mind was too full of the kids, Alex's work-related olive branch, Edmund's intimation of a shared future, her mother's bombshells, the questions about her father and her dilemma over whether to tell Ellie about Robert. All of it put Cameron's likely shifty dealings with the will in the shade. She tossed and turned on the pillow-top mattress and didn't need the alarm to wake her. As she rolled out of bed, she heard the distinctive snap of cleats and saw the red flashing taillight of Alex's road bike. In a sea of change, some things stayed the same.

It had been seven weeks since she'd last made breakfast in the Riverbend kitchen. Opening cupboards and drawers, she noticed Alex and Gus now stored some things in different places. The coffee machine was in its usual position, however, and as she brewed herself a strong black, she watched the pink of the dawn spread across a cloudless sky and waited for the boys to wake up.

She'd downloaded the paper and was drinking her second cup of coffee when Gus ambled into the kitchen. She jumped up.

'Morning, darling. Would you like pancakes? Eggs?'

'Pancakes.'

'Right,' she said brightly, re-whisking the sitting batter. 'You're up early. Dad's just back from his ride. He's in the shower so he won't be long.'

Gus poured himself some orange juice. 'I thought he'd go ballistic.'

'Last night?'

'Yeah. I mean he went mental about the footy and the play, but I punch someone and he's like, "I love you, Gus."'

'I do love you, Gus.' Alex appeared in the kitchen, dressed in his work uniform of drill pants, a blue chambray shirt and a Mingunyah Bread and Cheese polar fleece. 'I don't like it that you hit someone, but I love you.'

'Sweetheart.' Sarah heard the hesitancy in her voice. 'You understand about the mediation process, don't you?'

'Yeah. I have to apologise to that cunt, Mason.'

'Gus!' Pancake mix splattered onto the bench at the unexpected profanity.

He shot her a mulish look.

'What did the cunt do?' Alex asked conversationally.

Astonished, Sarah looked between father and son, struck by the role reversal. Usually Alex was the reactive parent and she was the proactive one.

Gus looked at his father. 'Nothin'.'

'You're my son. I know you wouldn't hit someone without a great deal of provocation.'

'Gus. We don't want you to be charged but unless you explain what was going on in your head when you found yourself whipping back your arm and flattening this boy, apologising won't be enough.'

Gus shrugged. 'I'm having a shower.' He left the room.

'Alex.' Everything she felt, all her frustrations and fears, clung to his name.

He huffed out a long sigh. 'I know.'

'Graeme said he was sober and the saliva test didn't detect any drugs but—I know he's angry with us, but is that enough for him to forget everything we've ever taught him and hit some kid?'

'I haven't been the best role model recently.'

Regret rolled off Alex, regret she shared. 'Neither have I, but we haven't hit anyone.'

'Not physically. But we've hit each other pretty hard with our words and our behaviour, and he's witnessed it.' Alex accepted the coffee she was surprised to realise she'd automatically made for him. 'I suppose we should probably search his room. See if we can find anything.'

'I hate that we should,' she said reluctantly. 'And how are we dealing with his school suspension? I don't want him to be on his own like he was during the holidays.'

'There's plenty of work on the farm.'

'He should study.' But even as she said it, she knew it was a vain thought. 'What if he goes skiing with Finn?'

Alex looked at her sharply, clearly taken aback. 'You want to reward Gus for decking a kid?'

'More like I hope he'll tell his brother what really happened.'

Alex stared out the window at the chorus of magpies. 'You always say that side-by-side thing works with boys. What if the four of us go skiing today?'

First Alex had been calmer with Gus than she had, and now he was suggesting a family outing? He never suggested family outings. She'd probably never given him the room or the opportunity. The rueful truth slugged her hard. Skiing meant another day not visiting her mother but in so many ways, Margaret was already dead to her and Gus came first.

'It's worth a shot.'

'That's what I'm thinking.'

'My legs are jelly.' Sarah pivoted on the heel of her ski boot and sank inelegantly onto the bench seat, miraculously avoiding spilling her hot chocolate. 'I held my breath coming down that last run.'

The four of them had spent the day together on the mountain; she and Alex skiing and Gus and Finn snowboarding. They'd shared the chairlift up the runs and met again at the bottom to do it all over again. They hadn't spoken much, but the alpine air between them all was calm. Although Gus hadn't said anything to either of them about what had happened the day before, he'd lost his haunted look. Sarah had even glimpsed him smiling a few times. It was a start.

The boys were keen to revisit the double black diamond area and had invited their parents along, but Sarah knew her limits. With twenty runs under her belt by three in the afternoon, if she risked Big Slide again now, she was likely to break a leg. Alex surprised her by declining the boys' offer too and joining her at the outdoor café. 'Remember when they were little and we'd be desperate to keep skiing but they'd be exhausted?' Alex pulled off his gloves. 'Now it's the other way round.'

She laughed, thinking about those early days with young children. 'We'd melt in the drying room, battling to get them dressed in their snowsuits, helmets and gloves, finally get them out on the slopes, and they'd do one run and then need to wee. I don't miss that.'

'I miss the energy I had then.'

She glanced up from stirring the marshmallows into her drink. 'This from a man riding three hundred kilometres a week?'

'Two-seventy, but yeah. I can't keep up with Finn and Gus any more.' He downed his lukewarm hot chocolate. 'Jesus, Sarah. I'm fifty soon. We've got a kid at uni. How did that happen?'

His salt and pepper hair was wild from being trapped under a hat and despite the lines around his eyes and mouth, she could still see the twenty-two-year-old she'd fallen in love with. She heeded the unspoken warning not to point out that he was still three years away from turning fifty.

'You've packed a lot into the years.'

'Yeah, but you heard Finn at lunch today. He's got so many ideas and ... I dunno ...' He shrugged. 'I remember when my life was that open and full of possibilities.'

Once, she would have laughed and told him not to be ridiculous, but this time she heard his bewilderment. 'It still is.'

'I've lived more years than I've got left.'

Alex had always been so driven and busy with life that she'd never once thought he might stop and reflect. His father certainly didn't and he was fit and vital at seventy-two, still slaying dragons with some part-time agronomy consulting.

'And if you pack as much into these upcoming years as you've done with the ones you've had, you'll have lived a remarkable life.'

His expression told her he didn't agree.

'Alex, we're the biggest employer in town. Our cheese wins awards and sells around the world. Finn wants to work in the business and who knows? Maybe Gus and Emma will too. Either way, you've created a legacy.'

'It doesn't feel enough.'

Was this a fear of death thing? Every part of her ached for this over-achieving man she loved. 'What do you want to do?'

'I don't know.' She jumped at the anguish in his voice. 'We got married young and then Finn came and life took over. I just got pulled along.'

Pulled along? Seriously? But she breathed deeply and let it go. 'And we came back to Australia earlier than you wanted to.' Her words came out of nowhere, surprising them both.

'Yeah.'

Perhaps, deep down, she'd always known she'd been the one who wanted to come home. The original plan was five years in France. Alex had just signed his second contract with the engineering company in Toulouse when she'd discovered she was pregnant. It was a huge surprise; she hadn't known it only took one missed pill for a baby to settle in and get comfy. Once the shock wore off, she'd embraced the pregnancy but at the same time, the idea of mothering in a foreign country so far away from everything familiar overwhelmed her. She'd pushed to return to Australia and Alex had reluctantly capitulated.

'Do you want to go back to France?' she asked, floundering in his misery.

'No. I don't know.' He shredded the edge of his cardboard cup. 'God, we've worked so hard to get the business to this point so we can have a bit more time. Now I feel like I'm treading water.'

She studied him carefully, looking for clues. Had Anita been right when she'd said Alex might need a new project? 'The double-edged sword of a successful business?'

'I didn't expect it to be like this.'

His unhappiness settled over them both. More than anything, she wanted to wave a wand and see him happy again, but she had no such magic.

'I had no idea you felt this way. I thought you loved your newfound freedom and the cycling, but ... Have you thrown yourself into a less satisfying challenge?'

A reluctant smile curved his mouth. 'You might have a point.'

'Last night Finn said all we ever talk about is the business. Who knew our man-child was so perceptive?' A tight laugh scratched her throat. 'But he's right. We talk about the business and the kids, but somewhere along the way we stopped talking about us. I've been struggling too, Alex. For months, I've been feeling sandwiched between the demands of the kids, you, Riverbend and Mum. And how's this for irony? I've been jealous of your cycling and free time when I couldn't seem to find any for me.' She brushed the scattered cardboard into a group. 'I wish I'd known you were so unhappy.'

'I wish I'd known you didn't want to be superwoman.' He hooked her eyes with his as the tips of his fingers brushed the tips of hers. 'We're as bad as each other.'

It was the first time he'd touched her in weeks and his cherished and familiar warmth spun into her, rushing to fill empty places. Was this a peace offering? A chance to rebuild? Or was it a stoic acknowledgement that they'd once loved and had now lost.

'Sarah?'

Her pulse leaped at the voice behind her. Edmund. *No. Not now.*

Even if he hadn't called her name, the change in Alex would have signalled Edmund's presence: his vulnerable and conciliatory mood had vanished and his mouth was a thin, grim line.

Alex stood as quickly as ski boots allowed and thrust out his hand. 'Edmund.'

'Alex.'

Sarah watched the two men eying each other like boxers in a ring. One fair, tall, straight and thin; the other dark, not quite as tall, but definitely straight, broad and solid. With animosity burning brightly in their eyes, they puffed out their chests. Holy shit. How blind had she allowed herself to be for all these years?

Edmund turned to her. 'Are you okay?'

She nodded.

'And Gus?'

'I'll tell you later,' she said hurriedly, not wanting to have this conversation with him here or now.

Edmund bent down quickly and kissed her, a clear marking of what he believed was his. 'Call me, yes?' he said softly before straightening. He gave Alex a curt nod and left.

Her cheeks burned with mortification. A few weeks earlier, she'd have been thrilled if Edmund had kissed her like that in front of Alex, but now it felt tawdry. More concerning was the fact she couldn't shake the feeling she was more than partly responsible for Edmund's action. What other conclusion could he possibly draw from their frequent afternoons of sex?

'I'm sorry,' she said to Alex, who was still standing. 'God. He shouldn't have done that. It was—'

'Petty? Competitive? He obviously feels he has the right.' Alex picked up his gloves. 'What we were talking about before ... In the spirit of full disclosure and telling each other things, I never slept with Kelly.'

He turned and walked away before her stunned mind could muster up a single word.

CHAPTER TWENTY-TWO

Ellie invited Luke to the park so he and Noah could spend some time together. After having fun kicking the footy and being silly on the play equipment, they'd returned to Mill House for the early-evening kid rush. With Noah now tucked up in bed, Ellie was watching Luke move around the kitchen.

'I can cook, you know.'

'I know. I saw the spag bol you gave Noah for his dinner.'

'But you think I can't cook for grown-ups?'

He held out his hand and she took it, allowing him to pull her in close. 'I think you have a lot of skills and talents, but you've been in the vegetarian wilderness a long time.' He kissed her. 'Besides, I like cooking for you. I like watching the look on your face when a flavour you love hits your taste buds. It's almost as good as watching you come. And talking of orgasms—'

'We were? I wasn't aware.' She watched him grin like a kid caught raiding the lolly jar. She didn't know what she appreciated more, the joy she got from teasing him or the relief that she could.

He tucked a wayward curl behind her ear. 'How do you feel about the Valley View motel one night this week? I checked and they don't have any bears.'

She laughed. 'I'd love to but it seems wrong to be spending money to have sex.'

'I thought you didn't want to have sex here because of Noah and you said my place is haunted.'

'Hello.' Sarah rushed in. 'Sorry I'm late. Has Noah gone to bed?'

'He's probably still awake hoping you'll read him a story.' Ellie accepted the bottle of wine Sarah was holding. 'How's Gus?'

'Back at school but still not saying anything.' Fatigue clung to her sister. 'I hope it's okay with you, but he's coming here at eight straight after band practice.'

'No problem,' Luke said. 'There's plenty of food. Seeing there's four of us, why don't we eat in the dining room?'

Sarah's head whipped around so fast, Ellie thought it might snap off. Her big sister was spearing her with a tight look of disappointment barely tempered by understanding. Ellie couldn't move; her feet were rooted to the floor as eddies of anxiety washed through her. She still hadn't told Luke, because the bubble of happiness they were floating in was so amazing she didn't want anything to burst it. That and she couldn't forgot how upset he'd been when she'd told him about Ryan. This news would traumatise him.

Luke must have felt something because he was glancing between them, clearly confused. 'What's going on? No, don't tell me ...' He laughed. 'The dining room's haunted too.'

The silence that followed was so loaded even the slightest movement would trigger an explosion. Ellie's mind seized and her tongue grew thick and stuck to the roof of her mouth.

Sarah spoke first. 'Ellie will tell you. I'm going to read to Noah.' She walked out of the kitchen, her fading footsteps echoing back to them.

'El? You're looking a bit green around the gills. What's the big story?'

She hugged him, letting her head rest on his chest for a moment, wondering where to start. Not wanting to start anywhere. Finally, she raised her head and gazed up into his open face, feeling his love and care cocooning her. She cupped his cheek.

'I love you, Luke.' The words tumbled out unexpectedly but they felt right.

His arms tightened around her and he smiled. 'I love you, too, Ellie J. With all my heart.'

Tears welled and a lone one spilled down her cheek. 'I have to tell you something that's going to upset you. I'd planned to tell you the night you told me about Miranda but it didn't belong there. It doesn't belong to us at all but it's part of me and—'

'Jesus, Ellie. Now you're scaring me. Just say it.'

She stomped on her rising panic and marshalled her thoughts. It would be okay—they loved each other. When she'd told Sarah, it had wrung her out, leaving her exhausted, and she didn't want to go there again. This time, she wouldn't allow the story to control her. If she told him quickly and cleanly she could deny it oxygen. She took a deep breath.

'Okay. When I was fourteen, my mother's lover sexually abused me in the dining room. That's why I stopped wearing bright coloured clothes. That's why I went to boarding school. That's why I never came back here.'

His body stiffened so fast it arched away from her. His nostrils flared and his face twisted into a terrifying grimace.

Gut-wrenching fear gripped her. 'Luke?'

Silently, he turned and walked out the back door and into the night.

Sarah was lying on the bed reading to Noah when she heard the thwack and crack of an axe on wood.

Noah wriggled out of bed and ran to the window. 'Why is Luke chopping wood?'

'To feed the Aga and keep the kitchen warm.' Except that wasn't the reason Luke was wielding an axe in the dark and the drizzle, but she completely understood why he was. She'd never forget the terrifying emotions that had assaulted her when Ellie told her story—that still did when she allowed herself to think about it. And it was obvious just by looking at Luke that he loved and adored her sister. At least chopping wood was a healthy way of working off his anger and devastation. She should suggest it to Gus.

'Come on, mate,' she said, patting the space beside her. 'Back to bed so we can finish the story.'

Two chapters later—Noah had the negotiating skills of a bush lawyer—Sarah made her way downstairs. She was about to walk into the kitchen when she heard great, hulking male sobs and then Ellie's voice, soothing and calm. Poor Ellie. She'd needed to do the same thing for Sarah when she'd told her, and it was inherently wrong; they should be helping her, not the other way around. It occurred to Sarah that she and Luke should form a support group so Ellie wasn't unfairly burdened by their responses to her trauma.

As she sat on the bottom stair waiting until things sounded calmer in the kitchen, she checked her phone. Alex had replied with a thumbs-up emoji to her text telling him Gus was spending the night with her. Gus had split his school suspension time seventy-thirty in her favour and she knew it disappointed Alex. He'd been hoping for fifty-fifty and Sarah had hoped for that too. About the only positive aspect of her leaving Riverbend was that her absence allowed Alex entry to the domestic sphere and she could see he'd benefitted. It was another brutal truth she'd had to swallow.

But right now they were too worried about Gus to push him on equal time. They accepted his decision, respecting his choice, and hoped that if he was comfortable with the arrangements he would tell them what had precipitated the fight with Mason Raith. So far, he'd given them squat and the mediation date was looming. It was challenging their parenting skills like nothing had before. They'd even given him permission to go to the party Finn threw before he returned to Melbourne in the hope he might tell his brother or his friends something. But all Finn reported back was that Gus hadn't got drunk and he'd spent the evening surrounded by the usual group of adoring girls. None of it gave Sarah and Alex anything they could pin their hopes on.

Meanwhile the situation between her and Alex could only be described as strange. Restrained politeness dominated every encounter, although there were a few odd occasions when they were chatting during a Gus pick-up and drop-off where they seemed to momentarily forget they were separated. Forget all the pain and heartache that sat between them like a brick wall. Sarah didn't know if she treasured the moments or disliked them; either way, they totally bewildered her.

Since the afternoon at the police station, their hostility and need to hurt each other had retreated—vanished even—and she sensed they were both equally ashamed of their behaviour, especially at how it had impacted on Gus. They'd searched his room together and found no traces of drugs or alcohol and not even a girly magazine, but as Alex had said, with the internet, sticky mags were old school and young men didn't need them anymore.

Neither she nor Alex had mentioned their conversation on the mountain or Alex's bolt-from-the-blue statement about Kelly. But that didn't mean Sarah had forgotten. She thought about it constantly.

Holy cow. So much for revenge sex. While she'd been screwing herself silly with Edmund, Alex had never even slept with Kelly. It confounded her—she'd seen the way he'd looked at Kelly and vice versa. He'd admitted his attraction to her, so why hadn't he acted on it? She couldn't deny part of her jumped with joy but when she thought about her own behaviour, she wondered if they could ever come back from it.

As if right on cue, a text arrived from Edmund apologising for not being able to get off the mountain yet again and lamenting the back-to-back functions for the ski games. The relief that filled her when she read it humiliated her. It was over a week since she'd seen him, nine days since the uncomfortable moment he'd kissed her in front of Alex, and she didn't know what she was going to say to him when they were finally face to face. He'd been so kind to her and she didn't want to hurt him, but she didn't love him the way he wanted to be loved.

God, she'd dug herself a hole the size of China.

The timbre of the conversation drifting from the kitchen changed. Luke's deep voice sounded steadier and Ellie was laughing, so Sarah pushed herself to her feet. Before she opened the door, she said in a loud voice, 'I hope you've opened that wine.'

'Luke and I were just discussing seeing a counsellor together.' Ellie handed Sarah a glass and gave her a pointed look. 'You know, so this old and nasty stuff doesn't get in the way of all the good stuff.'

Sarah's conversations with Alex on the mountain rang in her head and she dropped her gaze, turning her attention to the dip platter. 'Good for you.'

Luke's arm was firmly clamped around Ellie's waist as though he was worried he might lose her if he let go. 'We were also talking about doing some interior decorating and Ellie and Noah moving in with me.'

'You were talking about that, not me,' Ellie said evenly. 'I love you and Noah adores you, but it's early days and you've only played with him. You need to do more together. You need experience with tired and grumpy Noah, and he needs experience with stern Luke. I don't want us to rush into anything and spoil it.'

'Surely you agree with me that Ellie's got to move out of this house?' Luke appealed to Sarah.

'I've already tried. And I can't believe I'm about to say this, as I generally organise everyone who comes within my sphere, but she's got a plan and we have to respect it.'

'Thank you.' Ellie touched her lips with her fingers and blew her a kiss.

Sarah blinked, suddenly rushed by emotion. 'You're welcome.'

Luke slid the salmon into the oven. 'Ellie says you only found out about all this recently too. Did it knock you about as much as it's done me?'

'It gets in your head and it won't leave,' Sarah said with feeling. 'I've known Dan Horton all my life. He's the company lawyer and right now, I'm struggling to look him in the eye.'

Luke shot her a grateful smile. 'I don't know the family that well but I remember Max was friendly with Kathryn. Well, he was until the only relationship that was important to her was the one she had with ice.'

'Her death was such a waste of potential,' Sarah said, suppressing a shudder. 'I confess I quote her as the "don't do drugs" example to my kids, which is probably pointless, as they didn't know her. She must have died, what? Ten? Twelve years ago?'

Ellie sat down hard. 'I didn't know Kathryn died of a drug overdose.'

'Yeah. Max was pretty cut up about it.' Luke sat next to her. 'He tried to get her some help but there's not much you can do, is there, when someone's hell bent on destroying themselves.'

Ellie looked straight at Sarah. 'What about Megan?'

'What about Megan?' Sarah scooped more dip out of a ramekin.

'I mean is Megan okay?'

Sarah thought for a moment. 'I've got no idea. She left town years ago. I think Dan said she lives somewhere in Far North Queensland, in one of those off-the-grid communities.' She laughed. 'I've always thought it was funny how Dan and Michael are so boring and straight when their sisters were so—'

'Wild and out of control?' Ellie reached out and grabbed their hands, her face pale. 'You know what this probably means, don't you? That bastard abused his own daughters. It was bad enough he broke my trust but at least he wasn't my father.' She shuddered. 'That must be the worst betrayal of all. I don't think I could have recovered from that.'

Sarah squeezed Ellie's hand. 'Dad loved and adored us.'

'I know.' Ellie blinked rapidly. 'All the places I've lived over the years, I've always kept that photo of him with me on his lap close. It's got me through a lot of tough times.'

Luke opened his arms. 'You've got us now.'

'Yes,' Sarah said emphatically. 'You've got us now.'

So many things in Sarah's life were up in the air and out of her control but right then she knew there was one dilemma she could finally stop wrestling with. When Ellie had needed protection from Robert and Margaret, Sarah hadn't been there to give it. But she was here now and she'd move heaven and earth to protect her sister. The moment Gus left for school the next morning, she was burning her mother's letters—destroying the evidence and banishing the secret from her memory. She sent up a message to the universe: *I'm taking the secret of Ellie's paternity to my grave. Don't you dare let me develop dementia.*

Anita pulled up outside the newsagent. She was on her way home after spending the morning cooking at the Farrells' and she planned to eat her lunch while browsing through the latest fashion and cooking magazines. Len Gioffre always had her order set aside under the counter and teased her that she was his best customer. 'They're a business expense,' she'd always say with a sheepish smile, knowing full well the fashion mags were pure indulgence.

Her phone beeped with a text: *Get a babysitter & wear your LBD. I've booked Protea for 7. We're celebrating! Cam x*

Excitement zipped through her. Had the tribunal's final ruling for Mill House come through? She checked the date. No, it couldn't be that. And it wasn't going to be anything to do with the will because Rupert had told them nothing could be actioned until Margaret died. She assumed Dan Horton had told Sarah the same thing because her sister-in-law had gone very quiet about the wills. Not that they talked any more; Anita couldn't forgive Sarah for the things she'd said about Cameron.

Anita had studiously avoided Sarah since the argument in the Mill House kitchen, but two days earlier they'd run into each other in the hospital car park—Sarah departing and Anita arriving to sit with Margaret for ten minutes before driving to a job. Sarah's face had been strained and tired, but that was hardly surprising; her decision to move out of Riverbend and abandon Gus had come back to bite her. Not to mention the rumour that was flying all over town that she'd been sleeping with Edmund for weeks, a rumour Anita was convinced was fact; she'd seen the way the widower looked at Sarah. As much as she disapproved of Sarah's affair, it seemed wrong that there weren't rumours about Alex and Kelly, especially as he'd been the one to set the ball rolling. Poor Gus. His parents had completely lost the plot and their moral compass. No wonder he'd lashed out.

The news about Gus's school suspension had reached Anita via Phoebe, who'd phoned her. 'Mum, there's something horrible on Facebook about Gus.'

Anita didn't really understand how, if Phoebe wasn't 'friends' with the boy Gus hit, she'd been able to see a selfie of him in Urgent Care looking all beaten up. But apparently, he was 'friends' with a girl from pony club who was 'friends' with Phoebe.

'That's awful. Do you know what happened?'

'No, but Mason plays footy with Gus. Ami says Gus is a heaps better player than Mason.' Phoebe, like half the girls in town who had a crush on Gus, hotly defended her cousin.

'Which is unlikely to make Gus hit him. Unless he took Gus's place in the firsts?'

'As if. Gus is awesome and Mason is, like, not.'

None of it told Anita anything useful, but a reluctant part of her felt for Sarah, which is why she'd spoken to her briefly at the hospital.

'Sorry to hear about Gus.'

Sarah nodded briskly but then her brows rose sardonically at the bunch of cheery daffodils in Anita's hands. 'Good. This saves me a phone call. I assume Cameron's got medical power of attorney? Doctor

Kafi wants to discuss whether he treats our mother's pneumonia or just keeps her comfortable.'

Our mother? Anita caught the unfamiliar edge to Sarah's voice and wondered what was going on. She remembered Sarah on Mother's Day, almost three months earlier, busily organising the family and vehemently arguing that Margaret should move somewhere smaller. Medical power of attorney or not, *that* Sarah would be calling a family meeting, not handballing something this huge.

'Surely that's a joint decision between the three of you? I can get Cam to set up a—'

Sarah shook her head. 'Ellie and I want—think she should be allowed to die. Let Cameron know, okay?'

'Okay.' Taken aback, Anita had watched Sarah walk away and been left with the feeling that this version of Sarah was diametrically different from the sister-in-law she'd loved. Despite feeling ill-used by her over the Mill House situation, she missed their friendship and easy conversations. The PCM didn't fill the gap and Tam continued to be cool towards her at the school garden club. So much so that Anita had also skipped the last two yoga classes. The woman's attitude was really starting to piss her off.

Wanting to focus on happier things, she re-read Cameron's text and smiled. A night out at Protea was the perfect way to forget all the irritations caused by thoughtless people who let you down. It was also a time to focus on her sexy husband who adored her in her little black dress. *And stockings.* A flutter of anticipation twitched deliciously and she pressed her thighs together. New plan! She'd collect her magazines and then pop into the clothing and gift shop that carried a small range of intimate apparel.

Slipping out of the car, she stepped up onto the pavement and had just reached the top of the ramp at the newsagent's door when she was forced to step aside to allow Tam to exit. As with Sarah, Anita was determined to be polite and not give in to the temptation to be as rude as the other women.

'Hi, Tam.'

Wordlessly, the woman pushed past her.

Anita saw red. 'Hey! I said hello.'

Tam swung back, her bangles jangling. 'And I'm choosing to ignore you.'

Anita recoiled as if she'd been slapped and then resentment surged. 'With no good reason! Listen, I'm as sorry as anyone that your friends lost their house, but it isn't my fault. I don't know who's been whispering in your ear about Warrnbatt but I can assure you, everything was done legally and above board.'

'Hah!' Tam almost spat. 'Your husband couldn't lie straight in bed.'

Anita lifted her chin. 'That's slander.'

'No, it's the truth. Your husband screwed Chris on the selling price. That's why they lost their house.' Tam's usually calm and soft voice broke. 'And now he's dead.'

Despite the winter sunshine, a chill ran over Anita's skin. 'What? Dead? How?'

'He killed himself this morning.'

Anita's stomach dropped to her feet. She grabbed Tam's arm as much to steady herself as to offer her support. 'Oh my God. I'm so sorry.'

'Yeah, well, sorry isn't worth a flying fuck. Chris might have pulled the trigger but you and your husband loaded the gun. I hope that house gives you nightmares.' Tam stepped back and ran.

Dazed, Anita stood rooted to the spot until old Mr Davidson pulled up in his red scooter, the tall orange flag on the back waving in the breeze.

'Afternoon, Anita.'

Somehow, she managed to mumble her greetings, get her legs to move and walk back to the car. On the short drive home, she struggled to keep her breathing steady as the tragedy hammered her mind. *Dead. Dead. Dead.* A family was forever changed. Fatherless children, a bereft and grieving wife; it was all appallingly familiar.

Pulling into the drive, she was thankful to see Cameron's car. He was home for lunch and she needed the reassuring press of his arms around her.

'Hey, baby girl!' He lifted her off the ground, swinging her around. 'It's real champagne for us tonight. I just sold a property to a Chinese investor.'

The love and the security he gave her every day combined with the good news, sliding over her distress and soothing it. When her feet touched the kitchen tiles again, she kissed him.

'Congratulations.'

He grinned down at her. 'It gets better. I cleared three hundred K.'

'Th-three hundred thousand?' The figure spun her mind. It was the largest commission Cam had made to date.

'Do you know what this means, Annie? With Mill House, the education trust fund and now this, we're swimming in a completely different financial pond. Picture that luxury holiday you pinned to your dream board years ago. We can take it.'

'Oh my God!' She squealed and kissed him again. 'I'm so proud of you!'

'I told you coming to Mingunyah was the right decision. What's for lunch?'

'I'll heat up some soup.'

As she ladled out split pea and ham soup, the practical action penetrated her buzz of excitement. She only vaguely understood how Prestige Country Properties' commission rates worked. Depending on the sale price of the property, they usually started at around three percent for the first half million and rose in big jumps after that. 'Which property generated that size commission?'

'Oh, it wasn't a commission.' He grabbed soup spoons from the cutlery drawer. 'I sold Warrnbatt.'

'Warrnbatt? The Parrys' property?' Her legs turned to rubber and the kitchen suddenly swayed. 'But you couldn't sell it. That's why you bought it. To help them.'

'I did, but real estate's all about supply and demand. And timing.

Freaking amazing timing.' His eyes sparkled with self-satisfaction. 'I doubled the profit, Annie. The gods are smiling on us.'

'*No!*' She heard herself wailing. 'No, no, no, no.' She grabbed at him as her knees buckled.

'Annie! Jesus!' He caught her and carried her to the couch. 'What's going on?'

But she was breathing too fast and shaking too hard to speak. He picked up her hands and pushed them over her mouth.

'Slow breaths. I'll get a paper bag.'

She heard him rummaging through drawers and swearing but she didn't have any spare air to tell him where she kept the brown bags for the girls' lunch orders.

'Here.' He cupped the paper bag over her mouth and watched her through apprehensive eyes. 'Deep breath in ... and out. In ... and out. That's the way.'

She kept her eyes on his face and slowly the silver spots stopped dancing in front of them, the tingling in her hands receded and she felt air lingering longer in her lungs. Lowering the bag, her head fell back on the couch as she lacked the energy to keep it upright.

'Thank you.'

He was squatting down in front of her, his hands on her thighs and his expression worried. 'What was that?'

'I think it was a panic attack.'

'You get those?'

'Not since I met you.'

'So, why have one now? I just gave you fantastic news.'

'Oh, Cam. It's all wrong.' Tears trickled down her cheeks. 'Why couldn't you have got a deal like this for Warrnbatt two months ago?'

'I didn't own it two months ago.'

'Exactly!' She rubbed her runny rose on the back of her hand. 'The Parrys did. Oh, Cam, Chris killed himself this morning.'

'Yeah. I heard.'

He knew? She stared at him. 'When?'

'I dunno.' He blew out a contemplative breath. 'I think I was at the post office.'

'So you heard after you sent me the text?'

He scratched his head. 'Before I think. Why?'

She pushed his hands off her thighs, his touch suddenly burning her. 'You sent me a text suggesting we go out and celebrate our good fortune on the day the previous owner kills himself?'

Cameron looked taken aback. 'Annie, I'm sorry he's dead. I'm sorry that he didn't talk to someone and get the help he needed, but it's not like he was a close friend. I don't think you ever met him, did you?'

Her breathing quickened and she fought hard to slow it and stay cogent. 'It doesn't matter that I didn't know him. He was your client and now he's dead. If he'd got the Chinese deal, he'd be alive.'

'You don't know that.'

'I do.' Suddenly the memory of fish and chips filled her nostrils—the tang of salt and the seductive aroma of hot oil; the scent of her father—and twenty-eight years vanished in a heartbeat. 'I told you my father abandoned us, but he didn't just walk away. A month after he lost the shop and the bank forced us out of our home, he loaded his clothes with his diving weights and walked into the bay.'

'Jeez. I had no idea. Sorry.' Cameron pulled her into him, tucking her head under his chin.

She still remembered the first time he'd done that. Back then, all those years ago, a sense of calm would steal through her as she listened to the solid, rhythmic beat of his heart. 'He drowned himself and left Mum and me drowning in crippling debt. I've always believed that if he'd had other options, if he'd seen another way out, he'd have taken it. If Chris had got this deal, he'd still be alive for his wife and family.'

Cameron sat back, his expression sceptical. 'The thing is, Annie, nothing about a troubled mind is simple. I doubt it was just the money. Chris told me things with his wife were rocky and had been for a long time. She was the one who wanted the whole tree-change thing and dragged him out to live there. You haven't met her but she's one of those new age hippy greenies like Ellie. God, you should have seen all the bloody dream-catcher things on the veranda. The noise from constantly clanging wind chimes would drive a sane person batty.'

All Anita could visualise were three scared, snotty-nosed kids clinging to their mother's hemp skirt. A worn-out, grief-stricken woman with grey skin and a man driven to a desperate act. Lives forever changed by an irreversible decision. Flashes of her childhood hammered her and the panic returned. She gripped Cameron's arms, her nails digging into his skin.

'The Parry kids have lost their father. That's traumatic enough. They don't deserve a life of poverty too. Imagine if it was our girls. We have to give Jane Parry the money.'

Cameron stared at her as if she'd lost her mind. 'No way.'

'Why not? You said real estate was all about timing. This timing is appalling for them. If they'd hung on just a bit longer they'd be celebrating today instead of grieving.'

'They're not our responsibility.'

His lack of empathy rocked her. 'How can you say that? We've profited from their pain.'

'No,' he said firmly. 'We haven't. We helped. I bought the bloody place off Chris as a favour when no one else would. Hell, I had to extend the business loan to give him the quick sale he wanted and that cost me interest. I went out on a limb for the Parrys. It's not my fault my good Samaritan deed turned lucky.'

Her mouth filled with a bitter taste. A man was dead and Cameron was talking about luck? It didn't make sense. She breathed deeply, trying to push away emotions and focus on being rational.

'How did you double the profits in such a short time?'

'Christ, Anita, what's with the third degree? I did this for you. For *us*. I thought you'd be pleased. It's only the middle of the year and I've already earned three times what I ever did at Phillips and Hogan. It gives us the financial security you've always craved.

'Look at it this way. You had a tough time growing up and I was denied the family business that was rightfully mine. We've both weathered those experiences and they've made us stronger, fighters. I mean, hell, we deserve this.'

There was truth in all he said but instead of giving her peace of mind, it sent fraught ripples of unease skittering through her. He still hadn't answered her question. She suddenly remembered sitting at the kitchen table, asking him if he'd paid a fair price for Warrnbatt. Had he told her the amount then? He usually talked about numbers to the point where she tuned out. She wracked her memory for a number but drew a blank.

Tam's accusation slapped her. *Your husband couldn't lie straight in bed. He screwed Chris on the selling price.*

I doubled the profit, Annie. The gods are smiling on us.

The air in her lungs solidified and her skin itched. 'Oh my God! Are the rumours true? Did you undervalue Warrnbatt?'

'Fifteen years of marriage and you're asking me something like that? I haven't done anything wrong, Annie. This is business. The market is fluid. Supply and demand drive it. Timing is everything and, sadly for the Parrys, the timing didn't fall their way. But it doesn't lessen the fact that I worked bloody hard for them—and now for us—putting this deal together. I'm entitled to the profits.'

'A man is dead! You're entitled to the *commission*,' she spat. 'Not the profits. This is stealing. It's blood money. How can you sleep at night knowing you've profited from the Parrys' misfortune?'

Cameron's face suddenly twisted, stricken with remorse. 'I'm sorry this has triggered so many awful memories for you. You know how I hate it when you get upset, but you're right. Even though I've done everything above board, I should have handled it better and kept a lid on my excitement. I promise you I'll look at the figures again and work out a lump sum payment for Jane Parry.'

Unadulterated relief sank into her, shoring up all her doubts. *This* was the man she knew, loved and trusted.

'Thank you. It won't bring her husband back but it will buy her a house.'

He held out his arms. 'Sorry.'

'Me too.' She moved in, resting her chin on his chest. 'It's just too close to what happened to Mum and me and the thought of it happening to someone else ...'

Cameron patted her back sympathetically. The home phone rang and she lifted her head but he shook his. 'Let the machine get it. You need some time to regroup. I'll make us lunch.'

The thought of being looked after was too strong to resist. 'That would be love—'

'Cameron.' Sarah's terse voice blasted through the speaker. 'The hospital rang. Mum died fifteen minutes ago. I'm at Dan Horton's office and I've got her will in my hand. You know, the one you told me you'd never seen despite Anita telling me that you had?'

Cameron lurched to his feet. Anita, prickling all over, shot out her hand, grabbed his belt and halted his progress. Sarah kept talking.

'It makes for interesting reading, you deceitful, conniving prick. See you in court.'

The line went dead.

'Fuck, my sister's a cold-hearted bitch.' Cameron grabbed her hand, his eyes glassy with tears. 'What the hell sort of a way is that to tell me Mum's dead? Can you believe she went straight to the solicitor instead of the hospital?'

Anita disengaged her hand with a jerk; her heart hammering so fast she could barely hear over the pounding of the blood in her ears. 'To be honest, Cameron, I'm not sure what I believe anymore.'

CHAPTER TWENTY-THREE

When Ellie took the phone call from Sarah telling her that their mother was dead, she couldn't pinpoint exactly how she felt. Free? Regretful? Both came to mind along with other conflicting emotions, leaving her numb.

'Is it a relief?' Sarah asked.

'It will be once I get through the funeral. Dealing with people's sympathy will be the hard part.'

'I don't have a problem with you telling people you're glad she died,' Sarah said bitterly. 'People will interpret it as relief that she's no longer suffering and you get to tell the truth without the need to publicly hang out your story. It's what I plan to do.'

Sarah organised the funeral quickly and efficiently, modifying some of the instructions Margaret had prescribed. 'I don't care if she left money for a huge wake and an open bar so she can be the centre of attention yet again. I'm not organising it. Cameron and Anita can do it.'

'You mean Anita will do it.'

Ellie was forced to eat her words when her sister-in-law unexpectedly refused. Sarah chose the sandwiches, tea and cake option in the church hall after the service. Margaret would have hated it. If the guests at St Mary's noticed that Ellie and Sarah sat dry-eyed on one side of the church while a stiff-backed Anita sat next to a sobbing Cameron on the other, they waited until after they'd left the church before discussing it among themselves with gusto. When Edmund slipped into the back pew, his presence caused a ripple of sound but it was almost silent in comparison to the collective gasp that echoed around the red-brick church when Alex strode down the aisle and took his place next to Sarah. Ellie didn't know who was more surprised to see him—Sarah or the crowd.

After the service, Alex hugged Ellie so hard she had trouble breathing and he crushed Luke's hand in a long handshake. After Luke wrapped his bruised metacarpals in ice and checked Ellie was still travelling okay, he took a beer over to her estranged brother-in-law. Ellie watched the men across the food-laden trestle table, curious about their conversation. The moment Dan and Mary Horton walked over to give Ellie their condolences, Luke appeared by her side. She swore he had a sixth sense.

The four teenage cousins sat together, making a pointed statement about being united while the adults made a fractured mess of the family. Although Sarah chatted with her nieces, she didn't speak one word to Anita or Cameron, and Ellie found herself in the odd position of being the only sibling to converse with everyone. Not that she'd said more than hello to Cameron, but Anita had stuck to her like glue. When her elder nieces kissed her and their mother goodbye, Ellie was surprised they were returning to Melbourne so quickly.

'Aren't they staying for the weekend?'

Anita, elegant in a beautifully cut black dress that Ellie could imagine her mother wearing at the same age, said tightly, 'They've got school commitments.'

'Oh. Right.' Still, it felt like something was off, especially when Anita and Cameron had always made such a fuss of the girls spending time with their grandmother.

'Ellie, can the little girls have a sleepover with Noah tonight?'

Astonishment rendered her momentarily speechless. Then Noah and Chloe, who'd heard Anita's question, began squealing with delight and the deal was done.

Luke joined Ellie on the couch in the den and wearily rubbed his face. 'I've given Chloe a drink. I'm hoping I've defused Ava's hissy fit by substituting a Minion for her lost unicorn, but I wouldn't bet on it. And did someone sneak red lemonade into your mother's wake? Because Noah is bouncing off the walls. To keep him in bed, I pulled his mattress into the girls' room. I've read the riot act. I told them if I hear another peep from any of them, they'll be in separate rooms and no Nutella pancakes for breakfast.'

'Ooh, big bad Luke.'

'Too right. I feel like we're running a school camp.'

'Feeding them tonight felt a bit like that too. By the way, because you were under attack on the frontline doing teeth cleaning and stories, I've cleaned up that godawful mess you made in the kitchen.'

Luke gave her a sloppy grin, one that made him look slightly not quite right.

She gave him a gentle shove. 'What? Stop it. The wind might change and you'll be stuck looking like that.'

The grin widened. 'You love me.'

'Yes.' She gave a mock sigh. 'I believe I've mentioned that from time to time.'

'Yeah, but cleaning up the kitchen after I've cooked, *that* is cast-iron proof.' He kissed her. 'You're a keeper, Ellie J. I might have to marry you.'

She laughed at his teasing but it didn't lessen the happiness glowing inside her like a welcome lamp piercing thick fog. 'Before I marry you, I want a kitchen pre-nup and a promise you'll try mopping up spills as you go.'

His moronic smile vanished and his blue eyes sobered. 'Are you serious?'

'About you learning how to wield a sponge? Absolutely.'

'No, I mean about marrying me.' Hope burned in his eyes, underlined by trepidation.

Her heart rolled over. Oh God, he was serious. Of course he was—he'd happily made that sort of commitment before. She wanted to put him out of his misery and yet she needed to hold things at bay, stick with their plan of going slowly so she could savour it all and trust it completely.

'If we can survive days like today, I think me marrying you at some point is a lay down misère.' He opened his mouth but she shook her head and pressed two fingers against his lips. 'Not tonight. I don't want something this special to have any connection whatsoever with my mother.'

'Fair call.' He swung his legs up onto the couch. 'Want to wriggle in here?'

'Yes, please.' Sliding between his legs, she rested her back against his chest and welcomed his arms around her. She laced her fingers through his. 'Not that I ever want to go through today again, but I learned something.'

'Yeah? What's that?'

'You know how we talked at counselling about how I don't need protecting?'

'Hmm.' He sounded wary.

'Well, that stands. I could have got through today on my own or even just with Sarah's help but—' A lump formed in her throat and her voiced wavered. She turned to face him. 'It would have been a lot harder without you. You give me unconditional support and—' She gave a giant and undignified sniff. 'I know it doesn't sound like it, but because you were there, I wasn't the giant basket case that I might have been. Just a moderate one. Thank you.'

His expression mixed sadness and delight. Using his thumb, he wiped a tear from her cheek. 'Of course I was going to be there today. All I want is for you to be happy and feel loved.'

'I am happy.' More tears fell and she swiped at them, frustrated by their presence. 'I don't even know why I'm crying.'

'I have that effect on women,' he teased and dug into his pocket, producing a hankie. 'Here. I grabbed it this morning thinking you might need it at some point today.'

She accepted it, blew her nose and wiped her face. 'Most daughters would have needed it during their mother's funeral service.'

'Yeah. Well. Don't waste any time beating yourself up over that.'

'No.' She lay her head on his chest. 'I promise you, I won't.'

He stroked her hair. 'Do you know why Anita asked you to have the girls tonight, besides testing us to see if we can handle chaos?'

Her sister-in-law's out-of-the-blue request still stunned Ellie but there had been something frantic in her demeanour. 'She didn't say why and I didn't ask. All I knew was that I couldn't say no to her.'

'I guess she couldn't ask Sarah. Is this will thing upsetting you?'

'No. I've already told Sarah it's got nothing to do with me and I don't want anything to do with it. When she tried to talk to me about it, I maturely put my hands over my ears and said "la, la, la". She and Cameron can put on the gloves and duke it out. I don't want any money.'

'You could do with a new car.'

'Not if it costs me my peace of mind.'

'I worry you'll break down in the mobile dead zone between here and Valley View. Would you accept a loan from me?'

'Maybe. What are your terms?'

'Interest free and whatever you can afford to repay each week.'

His love and care circled her. 'You trying to make me cry again?'

'Nope. Like you, just looking after my own peace of mind. Talking peace of mind, my family are hassling me. They want to meet you and Noah. How do you feel about Sunday lunch sometime soon?'

The idea was more warmly inviting than terrifying. 'Just your parents or the full catastrophe of brothers, wives, nieces and nephews?'

'Either way. All of them want to meet you both.' He laughed. 'Poor Noah. Izzy is yet another little girl cousin who'll run rings around him.'

'Your family's normal, right?'

'What's normal? No family I know of, that's for sure. But I can tell you this. I grew up knowing I was loved and on the most part, we try to be respectful. Mum and Dad have turned themselves inside out to be fair to my brothers and me. When I didn't want to work in the family business, they gave me my share to start my own.'

'That's very fair.'

'Yeah. And they're hands-on grandparents. I know you're super protective of Noah and I get it, but just a heads-up, don't be surprised if they invite Noah for a sleepover. They do that with Max's and Henry's kids all the time.' A hopeful look entered his eyes, the same one that burned brightly when she said she'd marry him one day. 'Is the idea of us having a baby down the track something you'd be open to?'

'We're thirty-four.'

'So?'

'So sometime down the track should probably be next year.' She sat up fast, feeling wildly optimistic. 'But I better meet your parents first. Would this Sunday be too soon?'

He beamed. 'Sunday's perfect.'

She leaned in, loving the play of his muscles underneath her and the fact they were hers to explore. She kissed him, seeking his essential flavour and devouring it completely. It simmered in her veins, streaking exhilaration into every part of her and promising wonder, delight and unadulterated joy.

Panting, she broke the kiss. 'Stay the night?'

'Are you sure?'

'I've never been more sure of anything.'

After the wake and the few hours spent surrounded by Alex, Gus and Finn pretending her family was intact, Sarah returned to the old cheese factory and its ghosts, feeling more lost and alone than ever. She'd just changed into her comfort clothes—trackie daks, a long-sleeved T and a fleece-lined hoodie—when there was a knock on the door.

'Anita?' She knew her mouth was slack with surprise.

Spiky and confrontational, her petite but elegant sister-in-law stepped inside.

'The town's having a field day with the family. First it was Gus and now they're saying awful things about Cameron. Did you really have to add to it by having your lover at your mother's funeral?'

Furious, Sarah blew open the myth that was Margaret. 'Mum would have approved. After all, she did exactly the same thing at Dad's funeral.'

Anita sat down fast. 'What?'

'I've recently discovered the venerable Margaret, doyen of Mingunyah and professional widow, had a long affair with Robert Horton. It started years before Dad's death. I have no idea which came first, but piecing together some of her demented ravings, I think my father might have been gay.'

'Oh my God!' Anita breathed out, her eyes momentarily wide. They quickly turned flinty. 'You're not lying to me, are you?'

A grim laugh rumbled out of Sarah. 'I'm not imaginative enough to make this stuff up.'

Anita managed a small smile and the conciliatory moment hung briefly between them. Then her mouth stiffened. 'I want to see the original will.'

Sarah didn't hold back. 'I bet you do. Cameron sent you over to do his dirty work, did he? Scumbag.'

White faced, Anita read the will and then left without a word. Sarah screamed down the stairs after her that she'd fight the will until her last breath. The exterior door slammed. Feeling shaken and forlorn and embarrassed by her shrewish behaviour, she poured a drink. How had a close friendship become a pile of smouldering ashes?

Her phone buzzed with a text. *Thinking of you. Do you need me?*

Without a second thought, she texted, *Yes*.

Ten minutes later she was in Edmund's apartment above Protea with her back against the wall, her hands frantically tugging off his belt and nothing mattered except blocking out the awful day and the horrible weeks, and having his body driving into hers. Divesting each other of their clothes, the articles fell in a frenzied trail as, mad with lust, they made their way to the bed. When his weight settled over her and his mouth found her breast, she groaned in relief that oblivion was coming.

What are you doing?

What I need.

Shafts of pleasure shot from her breast to her vagina, tingling and tantalising, and she arched towards the promise.

Seriously, what the hell are you doing?

The words hooked her, taking hold and settling in. Like a hot north wind blasting over her throbbing and aching body, they shrivelled her libido, sucking it dry and leaving nothing but a hollow shell.

Swallowing a sob, her fingers dug into Edmund's scalp and she lifted his head. 'I'm sorry. This is a mistake.'

Confused, his lust-filled eyes took a moment to clear before understanding dawned. He rolled off her and tucked her in against him. 'It's okay. You buried your mother today. It's normal to feel confused.'

Stop being so nice to me. I don't deserve it.

She slowly moved his arm away from her belly and turned over to face him, propping herself on an elbow. 'I mean it's all been a mistake. Not just the sex right now.'

He frowned. 'I do not understand. From the start, the sex has been amazing. Electric. It was never like this with Catriona.'

She closed her eyes and breathed in deeply as if that would offer her some protection from hurting a good and decent man. 'It's been exhilarating.' *It's overpowered all rational thought.* 'But I think I've been using you.'

'Impossible.' He stroked her cheek. 'I wanted everything you offered me.'

She wrapped her hand around his finger and stalled the movement as her insides caved. 'And that's how I know that I've taken advantage of you. Alex's rejection left me hurt and bleeding and there you were with open arms and unstinting support. You made me feel loved and cherished and I needed that so much. But I've taken far more from you than I've given.'

'No.'

'Yes.' She closed her eyes for a moment, mustering strength. 'And now it has to stop. I'm sorry.'

He sat up, his face bleak. 'What brought this on? Are you telling me that you and Alex are getting back together?'

'No. We haven't talked about it and I doubt it's even a possibility. Right now, we're just trying to sort things out with Gus.'

'Then nothing has changed,' Edmund said firmly. 'There's no need for talk like this.'

You owe him the truth. 'I'm sorry, but there is. That afternoon on the mountain, the day Gus was arrested, you said, "When things are settled we'll tell the children together." It made me realise you see a future with me.'

'Of course I see a future for us. I have dreamed of it for a long time.'

'It's too soon, Edmund. I can't commit to anything when I can't see past tomorrow.'

He shrugged. 'I have waited eighteen years. I can wait a bit longer.'

Her heart lurched and she tasted salt as tears rolled across her lips. 'But I don't want you to wait. You deserve a woman who will worship you the way you worship me.'

He shook his head. 'You are just confused with everything that is going on in your life.'

'Oh, Edmund. I wish I could pretend I was confused but I can't. I'm sorry. I don't love you the way you deserve to be loved.'

He flinched and she hated herself.

Pulling the sheet up around her and covering her now shivering body, she said, 'I'm really sorry. I never wanted to hurt you.'

He stiffened and his sea-green eyes roiled in pain. 'That ship has sailed, Sarah.'

'I know and I'll always regret it. Your friendship means a lot.'

'But, sadly, I think more to me than to you.'

To her dying day, she would never forget his hurt and heartbreak or the awkwardness of knowing she needed to leave immediately, but was naked. Retrieving her scattered clothes from the embarrassing trail across the apartment, she dressed in the bathroom before returning to the bedroom. Edmund was up, dressed, and staring out the window. She automatically leaned in to kiss him goodbye.

He stopped her. 'I cannot do this, Sarah. Just like you cannot pretend to love me, I cannot pretend that the last two months didn't happen. It is impossible to return to a friendship I have always yearned would grow to be more. If we are over, then this is goodbye.'

The unexpected words punched her and she pressed her lips together, forcing herself to stay upright. What planet had she been living on these last weeks that she thought she could have sex with her best friend and still remain friends?

Somehow, she walked to the door and ran down the stairs to the street. As she stepped into a night dank with rain, she realised that for the first time in her life, she was truly alone.

Anita walked into the house, hearing the familiar sound of the television football commentator and then silence. She'd just put her handbag on the dresser when Cameron appeared in the kitchen. He still wore his black suit pants but his shirt was untucked and his tie askew. Holding a beer in one hand, he looked tired, forlorn and slightly bewildered. Three days earlier, she would have walked straight into his arms and hugged him. But three days earlier, she thought she knew and understood him. Now, she was struggling to make sense of anything—who he was, what he did, what he said. The truth was a chameleon and whenever she got a firm grasp on it, it slinked and slipped away only to resurface changed and equally confusing.

He smiled at her; a mixture of fondness and relief. 'Oh, good. You're back.'

'Yes.' She kicked off her heels, welcoming the touch of the floor against her aching arches.

'I thought you were just dropping the girls off at Jess's,' he said carefully as if he were stepping around a tripwire—one he'd been working hard to avoid for three days. 'Where have you been?'

'Out.'

'Well, I'm glad you're home. It's been a tough day saying goodbye to Mum, and I need a hug from my best girl.' He reached out to touch her but she ducked around him. 'Oh, come on, Annie. This is crazy. Remember what we promised each other when we got married? Never let the sun go down on a fight.'

'I'm sure we promised to never lie to each other either, but you've conveniently forgotten that.'

'I haven't lied to you.'

The tremble started at her toes and quickly reached her knees. 'That's not what the town's saying.'

'I don't know what else to say or how to explain it to you. If Chris thought the offer was too low he had every opportunity to walk away from it. It shatters me that you're choosing to believe unsubstantiated gossip instead of me.' A defeated sigh rumbled out of him.

It devastated her that he'd riddled her trust with more holes than an archery target. 'I want to believe you more than anything, but you're not making it easy. I've just spent the last hour with Sarah.'

Cameron's mouth predictably hardened and his face flushed. 'What the hell did you talk to Sarah for?'

'To try to work out why you told me you'd seen Margaret's old will but you told your sister you hadn't.'

'Jesus. My sister.' He slumped into a chair. 'Look, Sarah misunderstood what I said. Now she's letting forty-four years of petty jealousies take over and she's behaving like a bitch. The will clearly says Mill House was coming to me and Ellie wasn't getting a cent.'

'I've read the will, Cameron. It also clearly states Sarah was getting money.'

'And when Mum drafted her new will she changed her mind.' Cameron's tone was slow and deliberate, allowing no room for misunderstanding. 'I told you that after her meeting with Rupert.'

She remembered but the crows of doubt continued to peck at what was truth and what might be convenient fabrication. 'But was it Margaret's decision to cut Sarah out of the will or was it yours?'

His hands ploughed through his hair. 'Annie, if I could raise the dead, I'd do it to prove two things. One, to have Chris Parry tell you he was happy with the sale price of Warrnbatt, and two, to have Mum tell you she wanted us to have the money. You know I was her favourite. She knew the money would be more use to us than to Sarah. Surely what's important here is that Mum's been considerate enough to leave us comfortable.'

He opened the fridge and poured her a glass of wine. 'I know Mum never talked about her childhood but she grew up poor just like you. That's why she was better at handling money than Dad ever was. She understood being hungry. She understood what it's like to have far more month left at the end of the money and the fear of the debt collector. All the things you fear too. Is it so terrible that she wanted to lift the burden from your shoulders? I, for one, thanked her, because I know you still worry that one day you'll wake up and all this—' He threw out his arm to encompass their lovely home. '—will be gone. You've worked so hard to change your life and now you never need worry again. This is the universe righting the wrongs of the past.'

The siren call of security pulled at her with the strength of the tide. She ached to believe him. For life to return to what it had been when her faith in him was implicit and blissfully free of doubt. He was adamant he'd done nothing wrong yet she couldn't shift the feeling there was something in what the Parrys' friends were saying. Why else would they be baying for blood?

When she added the weight of Sarah's accusations, things got even more complicated. There was no doubt that Cameron was Margaret's favourite child. Nor was there a big argument for Sarah needing any inheritance money and everyone in the family knew that Princess Ellie created her own bed years ago and now she was lying in it. But the doubts gnawed at the long-held beliefs about Ellie as viciously as a rat's incisors. Tonight, her younger sister-in-law had taken the girls without questioning why Anita needed a babysitter on the night of her mother-in-law's funeral. For all that Cameron and Sarah said about Ellie, she worked hard, was raising Noah on her own and, right now, was the only Jamieson behaving fairly and reasonably.

Her thoughts diverted to Margaret. What sort of mother didn't forgive her wayward daughter when she finally got her life back on track? How would she react if her girls lost their way as badly as Ellie and committed the same sorts of dangerous acts? The reckless behaviour with no consideration of others? The drugs? The unprotected sex? Without a doubt, she'd be worried sick, but she'd fight for them; try to help them. Had Margaret done that? Family folklore said yes, but if that was the case, why, when Ellie returned to the valley and proved to everyone that she was a functioning member of the community, didn't Margaret change her will to acknowledge her? And Ellie was the one sibling whose life would change dramatically with a large cash injection, so why was she the only Jamieson calmly accepting the terms of the will? Why wasn't she slugging it out for her share of the inheritance, if not for her own sake, then for Noah's?

The questions joined the constantly moving veracity at the heart of her marriage and Anita craved to hold onto something reliable, solid and static. Thank God she had Cooked By a Friend. Cooking and planning for the business was real—what you saw was what you got.

Sarah's shrewish voice from half an hour earlier rushed back. *I don't care how much it costs, Anita. I'm fighting this. If you think the last few weeks have been ugly, think again.*

And there was so much ugly.

'Cam, I can't walk down the street without one of Jane Parry's friends almost spitting at me. When can we meet with her and discuss the financial settlement?'

'Settlement's in one hundred and fifty days so not before then.'

'Five months!'

He shrugged and opened his hands as if it to say, *What can I do? It's out of my control.*

'Can't we do something before then? The stress will kill me.' She gulped wine. 'And on top of all this nastiness, we've got months of a legal battle with Sarah before Mill House is legally ours.'

'Actually, I've got some good news on that front.'

Was this a blessed light in the dark, dark tunnel? 'Tell me fast.'

'Remember when I said Mum was tweaking tradition to help us out? Well, she signed the title deeds before her first stroke.'

The implications broke over Anita and her mind struggled to keep up. 'But if Margaret did that, why on earth have we put up with being locked out of the house?'

'Sarah,' he said portentously. 'She was already insane about me having power of attorney instead of her. It was better to keep it on the down low until after Mum died.'

But Anita wasn't really listening. Mill House was legally theirs. This was her escape from all the horrible stuff that was playing out around her and would continue to do so for months. When she collected the girls in the morning, she'd explain the situation to Ellie and quickly get back to running cooking classes, high teas, dinners; the possibilities were endless. She thrust her arm in the air in victory.

'Yay! We're back in business.'

He gave her an indulgent smile. 'Actually, Annie, the market's booming. We should take advantage of it and sell Mill House.'

Sell it? Her arm fell to her side. 'But your great-great-great-grandfather built it. It's been the tradition to hand it down through the generations. Why would you break that?'

'The tradition is to pass it to sons and we don't have a son.' He gently rested his hand on her thigh. 'And before you get upset, you know that not having a son doesn't bother me at all. I love you and the girls to bits. Besides, having daughters frees us from that tradition and the timing couldn't be better. The market's sky high and it's ripe to sell.'

He'd said the same thing about Warrnbatt. 'But it doesn't make any sense to sell when our plan's always been to use it for Cooked By a Friend. It was your idea. You said it suited the business to a T.'

'I said using the house for Cooked By a Friend would work in our favour in case Mum hadn't already decided to leave the house to us. As it turns out, we needn't have worried.' He smiled at her, half indulgent, half apologetic. 'I'm sorry you did all that work for nothing.'

For nothing?! The foundations of her already wobbly trust in her husband collapsed and a chill settled over her at odds with her burning rage. She had poured her heart and soul into Cooked By a Friend, working to create a business that, over time, would contribute to their income and he'd just dismissed it as *expendable*? The wriggling truth suddenly stilled and glowed fluorescent with clarity.

Cameron didn't care.

He didn't care that Chris Parry had money problems; all he saw was the financial opportunity Warrnbatt had represented. He didn't care about her business—the Melbourne version or this one—and what it meant to her. In Melbourne, it was expedient, giving him contacts. Here, it was a convenient ruse. All he cared about was money. Warrnbatt and Mill House held no sentiment for him, just profit. The Parry family had been surplus to requirements and now it was clear to Anita that she was too. She'd been a biddable pawn in his strategic game of family chess and his goal to take the king— one hundred per cent of Margaret's wealth.

He loved money more than he loved people.

Pain ripped through Anita and before she could catch her breath, the truth rained down, threatening to drown her. She was culpable too. She'd supported him in his quest to disinherit his sisters and his niece and nephews. What she'd naively thought was his love was manipulation. He'd used her fears and insecurities to control her and she'd unquestioningly believed they were more entitled to the spoils than anyone else. How could she have been so blind to his behaviour? Why did she fall so fast for the stories he'd told about Sarah, when she knew her sister-in-law was a good person?

If Cameron was prepared to throw his own flesh and blood under the bus for money then of course he'd have no qualms doing it to strangers. Despite her doubts and rigorous questions about the Warrnbatt deal, he'd cleverly convinced her of his regret by conceding to pay Jane Parry money—another amount he'd never specified to her. His money-grubbing heart was probably confident that, after the settlement in five months' time, he'd casually say, 'Oh, and I paid Jane,' and she'd kiss him on the cheek and thank him without question.

Anxiety skittered through Anita, making her light-headed, and she struggled against grasping panic. The man she loved and trusted more than anyone, the father of her children, was a master manipulator. Over the last few months, she'd accused Sarah of lacking a moral compass but she was just as bad. She'd unwittingly aided and abetted a thief. She'd allowed the love and security Cameron represented, the physical comforts of their life together and her paralysing fear of losing them, to erode her ethics. *Breathe!* It was time to take charge, hold tightly to the tattered shreds of her self-respect and live the life she wanted to model to her daughters. People and relationships always came ahead of money. The needs of others must be weighed up before acting. Greed was dangerous.

'I'm not selling Mill House.'

Sensing a shift, Cameron tilted his head, trying to assess exactly what was going on. 'We don't have to make any big decisions tonight, especially after the day we've had. We can talk about it in the morning.' He stretched out his hand. 'Let's take advantage of having the house to ourselves. Fancy putting on that turquoise ball-gown one more time before we post it to its new owner? I promise I'll take it off you very, very slowly.' His eyes glittered with desire.

It was like he'd slapped her. He'd probably never intended to give his mother the Vintage Glamour money either.

'I'm sleeping in the spare room tonight.'

He looked utterly flummoxed. 'What the hell for?'

Where to start? With his avarice and greed? With his cheating, lying and scheming? His total disregard for anyone except himself? All she knew was that it would be the hardest and most difficult conversation she'd ever have and tonight was not the night for it. When she told him she was leaving, she needed all her wits about her to stay one step ahead of his clever and conniving mind and ruthless exploitation.

'Like you said, it's been a tough few days. We're both exhausted and I need an uninterrupted night's sleep. We'll talk about it in the morning.'

It hurt to walk away from him—this man she'd loved for so long—and she felt the sting cleave the length of her body. But with each step, her new resolve firmed.

She was walking out of darkness and back towards the light. Her soul started to sing.

CHAPTER TWENTY-FOUR

SARAH HAD FAR TOO much time on her hands and not enough concentration to achieve much at all. Each day as she sorted through her mother's things, her thoughts circled from Alex to Gus to Edmund to Cameron to Margaret to Anita and back again, solving nothing and making matters murkier than ever. Her mother's death may have freed her from weeks of angst-inducing hospital visits spent hiding her fulminating anger with Margaret from the staff, but it didn't bring any relief. It was impossible to grieve for someone she'd never truly known—especially a woman who had inflicted so much pain on the people she supposedly loved. Sarah wasn't innocent from causing pain to loved ones either, but Margaret had taken it to a completely different level.

Reading up on narcissists had helped to explain some things but it didn't protect her from flailing in a sea of choppy emotions that threatened to pull her under. If anything, it increased her sadness for her father, Ellie and herself. Not Cameron—he'd been more sheltered from Margaret's self-centeredness, although not immune given the loss of the saw mill. His attempt to grab the lion's share of the inheritance gave truth to the saying that the apple doesn't fall far from the tree. Not that she was naive enough to believe her father was totally blameless in the inflicting pain and heartache stakes.

If she'd learned anything about marriage recently, it was that both partners played a role in the misery of the other. But when she thought about her childhood and her interactions with her parents she knew her father had always been the kinder, fairer and more loving adult in her life. The shock Margaret must have experienced on discovering Kevin was homosexual was a given, but it wasn't enough to join the dots and explain how Margaret had treated Ellie.

The narcissism also made the two wills harder to decipher— what were Margaret's intentions and what were Cameron's? Dan had offered to help with the legal battle but every time she looked at him, she saw Robert.

'I think it's easier if I use someone else. Can you suggest someone?'

Hurt had flickered across his face. 'If you're sure?'

'I am.' She quickly worked the conversation around to news of the family and to Megan. 'How long since she visited Mingunyah?'

'Too long. I offered to fly her home for Mum's eightieth but she's always got an excuse as to why she can't get away. In most families, it's the daughters who are the glue, but not in ours. My sisters ...' He sighed. 'I feel for Mum.'

Sarah felt for Megan and Kathryn. Although she couldn't say anything to Dan about his father and Ellie, she wanted to sow some seeds in case Ellie decided against contacting Megan. 'Maybe you could visit her in Queensland?'

Dan snorted. 'No point. Megan's always been all about Megan. Her life's far more important than anyone else's.'

She heard her old self in his words. 'There's always a point, Dan. It's too easy to make assumptions about people, especially family. We're invariably wrong. I'm starting to think I never knew my mother at all.' She picked up the satchel of paperwork. 'Although sadly, I've always known my brother. If I were you, I'd make time to ask Megan if there's a reason why she never comes back here.'

Sarah had driven to Valley View and engaged Derek Costiano as her solicitor. He, like Dan, told her that with scant evidence to prove her mother's failing mental status, it was going to be exceedingly difficult to prove Cameron had inflicted undue influence on Margaret's decision making. It was likely the court would rule in favour of the new will.

'We could lodge a testator's family maintenance claim,' Derek suggested. 'But with your income it would be hard to argue. On the other hand, your sister has a very strong case.'

But Ellie was adamant she wanted nothing to do with the will. As much as Sarah hated the thought of Cameron and Anita getting the lot, she couldn't ask Ellie to go through a protracted legal battle for something that might threaten her hard-earned but still fragile peace. No, this was a battle Sarah had to fight alone and right now, she was truly on her own.

Shame knotted her in self-loathing. *Edmund.*

'Ouch!' Sarah glanced down and saw a bloom of blood on the tip of her finger. She was preparing ingredients for tacos and she'd just grated her finger along with the cheese. She sucked the wound, welcoming the pain. It didn't come close to the misery she'd inflicted on Edmund.

She blamed herself, although not so much for tumbling into bed with Edmund the first time—everyone was allowed one mistake. No, the blame lay in being completely selfish and self-centred. For going back again and again and feeding her own needs without once considering his. She recognised that some elements of her own behaviour mirrored her mother's and it appalled her. She couldn't hide from what she'd done and as difficult and as uncomfortable as it was, she accepted she'd behaved atrociously. As a form of penance, she now volunteered at the neighbourhood house and asked Ellie to give her all the crap jobs no one wanted.

With the cheese grated, she diced lettuce. Mexican food was another of Gus's favourites and she was desperately trying anything to break her son's tight-lipped silence. With the mediation session two days away, the Raith family were making rumblings around town about wanting justice. The other day, when Sarah stepped into the butchers, the chattering customers fell silent—clear evidence they'd been talking about her, Alex and Gus. The Raiths' confidence that all the fault lay with Gus infuriated her and she'd ranted to Alex about it on Friday after he'd dropped Gus off at the flat. He'd cautioned her not to speak with the parents.

'I understand the mighty force of your mothering, Sarah and I get why you want to snot Craig Raith, but you risk making things worse for Gus.'

'How can you be so calm and rational about it all?'

His mouth had tweaked up on one side as if he recognised the switch in their parenting styles. 'I'm not, but I'm trying.'

The confident, father-knows-best Alex who'd flown off the handle when Gus told him about *Sweet Charity* and missing footy matches, and who sulked when Gus was dropped to the seconds, had disappeared. But despite their collaborative parenting efforts, they were out of ideas on how to get their younger son to talk.

Gus ambled out of his room. 'What time's dinner?'

'As soon as your dad arrives. He texted saying he's ten minutes away.'

'Jeez,' Gus said, opening the cutlery draw. 'That's a first.'

'Yes, well, we did reach an all-time low there for a bit. Now we're working on being polite and respectful.'

'It's weird watching the two of you together now you're ... you know ... not together.'

She knew what he meant. Touching Alex—hugging, kissing, caressing, tickling, nudging him—had once been as natural as breathing. Now they were stiff and formal with each other, studiously avoiding any inadvertent physical contact. Greeting him was a nightmare. A kiss was too intimate and a handshake too formal and ridiculous, so she was sticking with a cheery and breezy 'Hi' and 'Bye'.

'I'm sorry, Gus. I guess it's going to take some time for your dad and me to establish a new normal.'

He closed the drawer with his hip. 'A new normal?'

'Why not? One of the definitions of normal is "everyday" and "usual". We'll develop our own usual that's normal for this new us. Something we're all comfortable with, because you, me, Dad, Finn and Emma are all that matter.'

'What about Uncle Edmund?' Gus dropped spoons and forks on the table. 'Or when Dad meets someone else?'

Both scenarios made Sarah ache. 'Uncle Edmund isn't my someone else and neither is anyone else right now. To be honest, Gus, after everything that's happened with your dad and Gran, I need some time on my own.' She pasted a smile over her breaking heart. 'And if Dad meets someone then I guess we adjust the normal again. I'm hoping the new Hadfield normal can be flexible and inclusive and respectful. Or at least attempt to be.'

Gus stopped setting the table and hugged her.

Surprised and immensely grateful, she hugged him back. She'd desperately missed her affectionate son.

A knock sounded on the door and Gus opened it. 'Hey, Dad.'

'Hi, Gus.' Alex hesitated for a moment, clearly torn between hugging Gus or shaking his hand.

Gus made the decision for him and hugged his father. Sarah smiled, sharing Alex's look of relief over their son's shoulder.

'Do you mind if we sit down straight away and eat?'

'Suits me.' Alex handed her a six pack of beer and a sagging bunch of snowdrops from Riverbend's garden. 'The drive's white with them this year.'

She nodded, not sure she could speak without her voice giving too much away. Alex didn't do flowers; in fact, she was never sure if he really noticed them in the garden or inside the house. It was certainly rare for him to give her any and yet, here he was, having picked some. Taking in the wilt factor, he'd picked them a while ago but if this was Alex working at being thoughtful, polite and respectful, it was going to kill her.

Alex spun the top off a couple of beers and Gus got himself a Solo and they sat down. As they passed the bowls around the table and built their tacos, Alex asked Gus if he thought the seconds had a chance of winning next week and securing a place in the finals. Sarah listened to them discuss the players and the likely strategies the coach might use.

As the conversation reached its natural conclusion, she opened her mouth to ask Gus about the band but Alex said, 'I put your poster up in the break room, mate. Any news on the new amp?'

'Mr Montalto got it yesterday. We sounded awesome at practice today.'

Sarah sat in stunned surprise. Watching her estranged husband engaging with Gus on something outside of football, she celebrated the only positive thing their separation had engendered. The conversation flowed along without too many awkward silences. Alex didn't talk about work, which must have killed him, but she appreciated it, because that was a private conversation they must have soon and it would involve lawyers.

Eventually, Gus stood and cleared the table. When he looked like he was about to vanish into his room, Alex said, 'Mate, your mother and I aren't worried about you anymore. Now we're just scared.'

Gus's head snapped round, his face unreadable. 'You don't have to be.'

'Yeah, we do. The mediation process won't work if you won't talk. I don't want my talented and intelligent son carrying the legacy of a criminal charge. It sticks, Gus. Whatever you want to do in the future, whether it's playing footy with the AFL or doing something else that you love, it's going to stick to you like glue. Employers will hire someone without a record ahead of someone with one every single time. I know—I do it. So does your mother.'

Sarah patted Gus's chair. 'Darling, please talk to us.'

Gus stood, his jaw working, and Sarah steeled herself for a defensive outburst. But he pushed off the bench and reluctantly slid onto the chair, crossing his arms tightly over his chest.

'I've seen you deal with all sorts of crap playing footy and you're remarkable, the way you just block it out and get on with the game,'

Alex said. 'You've never slugged anyone before, so what was different with Mason?'

'I wasn't playing footy,' Gus quipped in the smartarse tone of a guilty teen.

'What did he say that made you so angry or hurt that you hit him?' Sarah asked.

Gus tore a strip off the label on his father's empty beer bottle, the damp paper clumping into balls around the base. Sarah glanced at Alex, reading worry and anxiety on his face and she knew he'd be seeing the same on hers. Pushing her hands under her thighs, she sat on them, focusing on the uncomfortable pressure instead of giving in to speaking. Hoping against hope that her and Alex's silence would drive Gus to break it.

The label was now completely off the bottle and Gus was levering the glue off with his thumbnail as if his life depended on it. 'He called me a poofter.'

Alex groaned. 'So, you hit a moron? Jeez, Gus. You know wankers like that are everywhere. Hell, you play footy against them every week and I've heard you called worse and react less.'

Gus's head was down and he mumbled something.

Sarah strained to listen. 'Sorry, I didn't hear what you said.'

'I said he's right!' Gus's head shot up. 'I'm gay.'

Sarah blinked as she stared at her son. Half-formed words bounced in her mind but she couldn't get her mouth to work to deliver them. Instead, she grabbed Gus's hand, holding it tightly.

Alex looked stupefied. 'But you're always surrounded by girls. It drives Finn nuts that you don't have to do anything to get their attention. And Ebony ... She's always at Riverbend. I thought you two were ...' He rubbed his forehead. 'You like girls.'

Gus shrugged. 'I like boys more.'

'Right,' Sarah heard herself saying inanely as her mind creaked and groaned, trying to absorb the news. 'Okay. Thank you for telling us.'

'Mum, you sound like you're talking to a customer.'

'I'm sorry, darling. I'm—it's—you've caught me by surprise. I wasn't expecting that. But sweetheart, you know it doesn't change a thing, right? You're my son. You're my Gus and I love you so much it hurts.'

'And you're sure you're gay?' Alex asked tentatively.

'Yeah, Dad.' Gus sighed. 'I've known for a while. At first it scared me and I just concentrated on playing footy. Then I met Jack and you know ... It wasn't scary any more.'

'And that's why you did *Sweet Charity* and joined the band?'

'Yeah. It makes it easier to see him. But I love footy. I want to keep playing and I want a shot at the Rangers and selection, but you know what the guys can be like. I didn't want to tell anyone. And I didn't have to. Everyone thinks Jack and me are just mates.'

His beautiful brown eyes implored them to understand. 'And then the band played a lunchtime concert and Jack and I stayed back to pack up. I made some dumb joke and he high-fived me, 'cept he held my hand for like a nanosecond. Mason walked past and saw it. He said he was going tell everyone we're fags.'

'He really is a cunt.' Alex's jaw tightened. 'It's not his story to tell.'

Gus visibly relaxed. 'Yeah, I know. That's why I hit him.'

Alex lurched to his feet and walked around the table to Gus, pulling him to his feet and hugging him. 'I don't love that you hit him, but I love you.'

Sarah blew her nose, stood up and went to the freezer for the ice-creams she'd bought for dessert. She lifted out the box and for one horrified moment she stared at it. A strangled sound escaped and then she giggled. It quickly morphed into a full-scale belly laugh until tears rolled down her cheeks, her ribs ached and she was left gasping for breath.

'You right there?' Alex asked, sounding mystified.

But every time she tried to speak, to explain, she laughed harder. Finally, sliding to the floor, she shoved the ice-creams at them.

'Golden Gaytimes.' Gus laughed and hugged her. 'Good one, Mum.'

Later, after they'd eaten their ice-creams, she and Alex flanked Gus on the couch.

'So about mediation ...'

Gus stared at his feet. 'I'm going to have to tell them I'm gay, aren't I?'

'Only if you want to,' Alex said. 'Listen, mate, I don't have a problem with you being gay, but I do have a problem with you being forced to come out earlier than you want to. You said you'd kept quiet because you want to play footy. If you want to play footy without coming out then you should be able to do that. If you want to play footy as a gay bloke, then you should be able to do that. Either way, we'll support you.'

'I can organise Mingunyah's first gay pride match,' Sarah said. 'I mean they've coped with sharing the club rooms with the women's footy, they can surely deal with this.' But even as she said it, she knew it was going to be a lot harder than it sounded.

'I don't know what to do. No one at school likes Mason much, so even if he tells people, I doubt they'd believe him. Jack hasn't told his parents about being gay or about me.'

'Does Jack want to come out?'

'Maybe. I dunno. It sucks that it's this hard. If I was dating Ebony, no one would care.'

'Darling, I think you have to do what feels best for you.'

'I don't want to hurt Jack.'

Sarah looked to Alex, who gave a 'fucked if I know' shrug. 'How about we prioritise? The first thing we need to deal with is the mediation. They're looking for an apology that you broke Mason's nose and signs of remorse. The fact that he was a prick won't make a lot of difference, because in a civilised society we're not supposed to hit people. I'm happy for you to blame me for upending your life. You can say the stress and worry your parents caused you by separating made you hit him. That takes the pressure off about making a decision whether or not to go public about being gay.'

'Yeah, I agree. Blame your parents,' Alex said with a wink before sobering. 'It gives you breathing space. I'm sure us yelling at each other didn't help. In fact, your mum and I got into trouble from Mrs

Darcas, so she's pretty much expecting you to say you were hurt and confused.'

'But if you want to say you're gay, that's fine too. It's your decision and we're guided by you. If you want to talk to Mrs Darcas about it, we've got that appointment on Tuesday before mediation.'

Gus was silent for a moment. 'I'll think about it. Thanks, Mum. Thanks, Dad.' He stood up. 'Don't tell Finn or Em, okay? I want to do that.'

'Of course,' Sarah said. 'But can you tell us when you've told them so we know?'

'Yeah.' He shuffled his feet. 'Can I go and see Jack?'

Sarah glanced at Alex, who nodded. 'Only if his parents are okay with it. Sunday night is often family time.'

'I'll find out.' Gus whipped out his phone. In less than a minute he said, 'All good.'

'It's a Riverbend night,' Alex said as Gus ran for the door. 'I'll pick you up from Jack's at nine, mate. No arguments.'

'Love you, Dad.' And he was out the door.

When the sounds of Gus's size eleven feet faded on the stairs, Alex asked, 'Do you want a cup of tea or something stronger?'

'I think I need the comfort of very rich and creamy hot chocolate.'

'Good idea.'

He frothed the milk while she melted the chocolate and for a few minutes they shared a companionable and contemplative silence.

'Did you have any idea at all?' Alex asked when they'd sat down at the table cupping their mugs with both hands, needing the soothing warmth.

'Not a clue. I read once somewhere that a mother's supposed to know. He's hardly flamboyant and as we've learned, he can pack a solid right hook.'

Alex smiled faintly. 'Yeah. Normally it's the gay kid who gets beaten up.'

'See, he's already breaking stereotypes,' she quipped, trying to work through her shock. 'I hate that his life is going to be harder.'

'I don't even want to think about gay sex,' Alex said with a shudder.

'Let's not jump the gun. So far, his first love sounds pretty sweet and innocent. We'll do what we did with Finn. Sit him down, embarrass the hell out of him by giving him the condom talk and a starter pack, then hope like hell he has sex later rather than sooner.'

'Yeah.' Alex still looked a bit green. 'I guess you're right.'

'And don't think about it. I mean, gay or straight, no one's ever comfortable thinking about other people having sex.' The words were out of her mouth before she realised their full significance.

Alex's resigned expression said it all.

Shame burned her and she rushed to change the subject. 'Mum said something before she had her big stroke. Actually, she said a lot of things I'd never heard before. I think my father might have been gay.'

'Christ, there's a lot of shit going down in your family.'

'You have no idea. But in the scheme of things, Dad being gay is on the more palatable end of the secrets scale. Oh, Alex.' She gripped her mug so tightly her knuckles gleamed white. 'Mum had a long-time affair with Robert Horton and they did terrible things to Ellie.'

The relief that flowed through her when she told him the whole sordid story—bar the one detail only she would ever know—was like a crane lifting a crushing weight off her. Suddenly, it was easier to breathe. She talked about her heartache for Ellie, her guilt at blaming her sister for her years of staying away, and her awe and pride at how Ellie had come through it, scarred but looking forward, not back.

'You've been dealing with all of this on your own? Shit. I'm sorry I haven't been there for you.' Guilt and contrition backlit his eyes and then he tensed. 'I suppose you've had Edmund.'

It was the first time he'd said Edmund's name without grinding his teeth and she appreciated how hard he was working to stay neutral. 'I didn't tell Edmund any of it.'

'I thought you told him everything.' A faint hint of bitterness rolled in under his incredulity.

'I did too.' She tried a small, wry smile. 'Partly, I couldn't tell him because of Ellie, but mostly I didn't want to tell him. It felt wrong. I've been wrong about a lot of things, Alex.'

'Like what?'

She blew out a breath. 'Where to start? When I left Riverbend I was angry and hurt and utterly poleaxed. Of all the things I might have imagined we could do to each other, you being unfaithful was never in the mix. But there was Kelly. I was reeling and Edmund was waiting in the wings just like you said. He was a balm to my battered self-esteem. He told me things I craved to hear and he offered me comfort. I didn't think or hesitate, I just took it with both hands. It was only later, after you told me he was my friend, not yours, that I started to examine our friendship.

'I didn't realise he'd loved me for years but if I'm honest—and that's been hard—I think I knew he's always made me feel special. I just never considered how that might make you feel. I'm sorry for that.' She cleared her throat. 'And I'm not proud of what I've done to Edmund either. He's a good man and I've used him to make myself feel better. I used him to try to forget you, us, this whole mess.'

She unwrapped a Lindt ball, needing the sweet solace of Swiss chocolate. 'How could I have done that to him when I know how much he's lost already?'

'We're human, Sarah. We make mistakes.'

'And I made a colossal one. He wants a future with me, but I can't give him that. I don't love him enough.'

Alex's dark eyes scanned her face intently, searching and seeking. 'So, it's over?'

'Definitely over. I ended the affair the night of the funeral. He ended the friendship.'

Alex was quiet for a moment. 'I was in the pasta aisle at the IGA the first time I overheard Stella talking to someone about you and Edmund. I was so full of rage I thought I'd explode in a ball of fire on the spot. I reckon, if I'd been the same age as Gus, I probably would have gone straight to Protea and king hit him. Instead I came at you. I regret that. I regret a lot of things.'

'So do I.'

'It was too easy to blame you, Sarah, for everything that wasn't working in my life. When you accused me of having a midlife crisis, I hated you. It felt too easy a label, too glib for what I was feeling and it was too bloody clichéd. But, label or not, I was having something and it had been going on for months. I don't know exactly when it happened but one day everything that excited me and got me up in the mornings stopped. Finn headed off to uni, Emma went to France and Gus was living and breathing footy and doing it well. They were all busy chasing their dreams and I assumed you were happy doing the whole juggling act with work, your mother, Gus.'

He smoothed the chocolate's foil wrapper. 'I thought I was the only one feeling disconnected from my life. It was like standing on the side-lines. I got overinvolved in Gus's footy and cycling but nothing was in sync. All of it left me numb. It scared me. I reached a point where I'd do just about anything to feel again. One Friday night you left work drinks early and Kelly stayed back to help clear up. She handed me a beer and said, "You look sad. Are you okay?"'

Sarah's heart twisted. 'I should have noticed.'

He shook his head. 'I should have told you. Instead I became the cliché I resented so much. I might have bought an Italian road bike instead of a red Ferrari but I still managed to detonate my marriage and my family.' He looked at his hands. 'I was stupid but when you're floundering, there's something incredibly powerful about having one person's exclusive attention.'

She thought about Edmund. 'Yes, there is.'

He looked up. 'And we had that once.'

'The halcyon days in France?'

'Yeah.' He looked desperately sad. 'What does it say about me that I still miss young us? I know it sounds selfish and juvenile and don't get me wrong, I love the kids. I'm just trying to explain where I was at the time ...'

His anxiety battered her but without anger on either side her thoughts allowed her to try to see things from his point of view. 'Kelly was there with her undivided attention. You didn't have to share her with anyone.'

'Yeah.' He looked taken aback by her perspicacity. 'Something like that. And I was less numb, so I thought she was the answer to fixing me. In my head, everything was clear. The three of us were going to be very adult about the whole thing. I'd move out, you'd stay at Riverbend, we'd all keep working.'

She couldn't prevent a hysterical laugh from escaping and he shrugged. 'I know. I was more screwed up than I thought. I believed Kelly when she said if we did things the right way it would be a civilised separation with minimal fallout. Her faith is important to her and she was turning herself inside out trying to do everything right, although God knows, what's right when she's part of a marriage break-up? When you moved out, she insisted we wait a few weeks before ... Anyway, I'll always be grateful to her for that.'

I never slept with Kelly. Sarah wondered if she might be grateful to the woman she'd vowed to hate as well. 'What happened?'

'Everything. You slept with Edmund less than a week after you left and all thoughts of civilised and amicable flew out the window. I spent days enraged. Kelly had always been able to offer me something but nothing she said touched me. When I finally cooled down, the truth was impossible to hide from. Sarah, even if you only felt half as jealous and betrayed about Kelly as I did about Edmund, then I know how much I hurt you.

'And work. Hell, after two weeks without you in the office, I felt like half of me was missing. Finn's right. *We're* the business. No one has ideas like you. We complement each other in ways I'd never appreciated before.' He rubbed the back of his neck. 'Actually, that's not true. I did know. The year after Emma was born I missed you just as much, but time suckers you into forgetting.'

'What about outside of work?' she asked, needing to know that their marriage was more than just a business arrangement.

'I miss you.' He tangled his thumbs with hers and his voice broke. 'I miss us.'

She blinked rapidly. 'I miss us too.'

'I'm sorry I broke us.'

'I did a lot of the breaking too.' Their shared pain eddied between them. 'Do you think we're irreparable?'

'I think what you said about us papering over the cracks was right. I want us to peel back the paper and use as much spackle as it takes to bring us back together. To accept our mistakes and forgive each other and find a new way to be together.' He cleared his throat and blinked rapidly. 'I love you, Sarah. I don't want to live the second half of my life without you in it.'

Her heart cramped and she squeezed his hands. 'Oh, Alex, I want this more than anything.'

'You don't sound absolutely certain.'

'I need to know how we're going to spackle.'

'I think we've already started. Don't you think since Gus's arrest we've functioned the best we have in a long time?'

'That's parenting.'

'Yeah, but you let me in to be part of it instead of expecting me to just follow your instructions. It's the first time we've truly coparented in a long time.'

'I've been trying. But what about us as a couple? You just told me how much you miss the early days when we were totally focused on us.'

'Yeah, and we can't leave the business and the kids and go back to France when we're hands-on parents for a few more years yet.'

'So we have to work on this. Maybe we need to regularly pretend we're newlyweds again and do something just for us. It could be as simple as booting the kids off the couch and reclaiming the TV or organising everyone so we can get away for the occasional weekend.'

'I picked up an application form for the film club. I thought if I plugged the dates into the calendar, then short of a disaster, we go. We could even do dinner first.' He glanced at her as if checking for her reaction. 'Although not at Protea.'

Remorse burned under her ribs. 'We're never going to be welcome there again.'

'And that's fine with me. Do either of us want to be reminded of how close we came to losing each other?'

She shivered. 'No, but are you going to be okay with …?'

He grimaced. 'Someone wise told me recently not to spend any time thinking about other people having sex.'

'Is that papering over?'

'I don't think so. I accept I played a role in what happened, but what's important to me is that you broke it off with Edmund when things were still unresolved with us. I trust you. I don't need to know anything more than you love me more than him. That's enough.'

'Thank you.' She wanted to kiss him but she knew if she did she wouldn't want to stop and they still had some important things to discuss.

'What about our bad habits? Me trying to do everything and you rarely telling me how you're feeling? I won't cope if they derail us again.'

Anguish pinched his handsome face. 'In the last few weeks I've told you more about how I've been feeling than I've ever told you or anyone in my life. I admit, it's not something that comes easy. I doubt either of my parents have ever talked about their emotions, but then again, they're hardly great role models for marriage. They've got the years but not the relationship. I can see the damage not talking to you does and I want to have a closer relationship with the kids than I've got with my old man.

'I'm determined to try to keep talking to you, but if you think we need professional help, then desperate times call for desperate measures.' His mouth tweaked up on one side. 'I'll go to couples counselling. I'll do whatever it takes for us to be happy.'

Joy rose in her. 'Me too.'

'Thank God.' Relief smoothed out his features and he suddenly looked less haggard—younger than he had in months. 'And I've been thinking about what you said about me needing a new challenge. When you're back at work, I want to bounce some ideas off you.'

'I'd like that.'

'Good.' He sighed, but it lacked the frustration that had dogged him for so long, and sounded more like freedom. 'What happens now? Do we do things in stages? Do you want to keep living here for a bit longer while you settle back into work first?'

'Are you okay with me moving home?'

'Hell, yeah.'

'I want to live at Riverbend but in a new way.'

'You want separate bedrooms for a while?'

'God, no. I mean I don't want to be that controlling superwoman. I want to share the load with you.'

'Fair enough. We'll draw up a list of jobs.' His smile was part regret, part triumph. 'I've learned how to use the washing machine and I've improved on ironing shirts but to be honest, I think we should just pay Rita to do it.'

She cupped his face—so very dear to her—and feeling his familiar stubble scraping against her palms, tried not to cry. 'I wasn't sure I'd ever be allowed to touch you again.'

'Aw, shit.' He stood, wrapping his arms around her to pull her in close, and kissed her.

His lips, as familiar to her as her own, warmed her and his quintessential flavour poured in, replacing heartache, shoring up the foundations of their love and taking her home.

She didn't know how long they stood there reacquainting themselves with each other's touch and taste, only that it felt right.

Alex finally lifted his head, his eyes dark with desire. 'Is sex on the first date out of the question?'

'Didn't we have sex on our first date?'

He grinned. 'Yeah.'

'I broke my five dates before sex rule for you then, and I can break it again now.' She caught his hand, turned towards the bedroom then saw the clock. 'Um, Alex?'

'Hmm?' His mouth was nuzzling the crook of her neck just like it had twenty-four years earlier at the party in the Carlton share house.

'It's five to nine.'

He groaned. 'Gus. I have to pick him up.'

'Sadly, you do.'

'What are you doing tomorrow?'

A zip of excitement raced up her spine. 'I thought I'd come back to work.'

'Can you start another day? I want to take you out to breakfast and spend the day with you. Just the two of us?'

'A day with no work, no kids, and no responsibilities?'

'Well, between the hours of nine and four, anyway. Gus has training.'

'I love it.' She stroked his hair. 'And I love you.'

He kissed her hard and fast before releasing her and racing out the door. She hugged herself tightly, squealing in delight just as she had the first time he'd kissed her goodnight all those years ago. Except now she wasn't an immature twenty-one-year-old with stars in her eyes, imagining life with Alex would be a golden road ringed in rainbows. This time she was forty-five years old, battle-scarred and a hell of a lot wiser. She knew the next twenty-two years of marriage would bring its own set of challenges, but this time they both knew the pitfalls. Even if they didn't know how to avoid them, at least they knew how to ask for help to navigate their way out of them.

Her phone beeped and she scooped it up off the bench, reading the text.

Love ya. Ax

She smiled. The x was back. Alex was back and in that glorious moment, she dared to dream.

EPILOGUE

'I've herded cats more easily than you lot.'

The photographer's frustration was palpable as Izzy moved yet again. Noah grabbed her hand just as Luke said, 'Stand still or there's no cake.' She instantly stiffened like a board.

'Okay, everyone look this way and say cheese.' The photographer took the photo and checked it on the camera's screen. 'Fantastic. You're free to go.'

The children scattered, the band started a new set and Luke leaned in and kissed his wife. 'How are you, Mrs Sorenson?'

'Happy, Mr Jamieson.'

'Did I tell you how beautiful you look in that dress? It's all floaty and soft and ...' He trailed off, seeking another word.

'Colourful.' She circled his waist with her arms. 'Because you brought the colour back into my life.'

'Oi!' Luke staggered slightly as Noah threw himself at him in a running jump. He reached behind him, hoisting the little boy up onto his back. 'Hey, buddy. Are you having a fun wedding?'

'Yeah.' Noah wrapped his arms around Luke's neck and rested his head on his shoulder. 'But when do I go to Gus's house? I wanna see the goats.'

Ellie laughed. 'When Luke and I leave.'

'Is that soon?' he asked hopefully before scrambling off Luke's back and racing after Gus.

'I see our honeymoon plans have traumatised him,' Luke said.

'You did bribe him with a new puppy and four nights at Riverbend.'

'I got the puppy to protect Hec. The poor old guy can't keep up with the kids. Remember Easter? He chased the ball so much the vet had to give him a cortisone injection. And Splotch is getting on in years.'

'Drinks for the bride and groom?' Ruby asked, appearing with a tray of mixed beverages.

Luke picked up a beer and Ellie selected a mineral water. 'Thanks, Ruby, but, please, you don't have to work. It's a casual garden wedding. Everyone can get their own drinks.'

'I know, but it's kinda weird being a guest when I'm normally working at Mum's events. I've got time to do one more round and then it's cousins' T-ball.'

'Cousins' T-ball?'

'Yeah, Emma's organised it.' Her eyes sparkled conspiratorially. 'I'm one of the captains and I've already got Gus on my team.'

Anita hurried over. 'Everything good?'

'Everything's great, Anita. The food's amazing, thank you.' Ellie kissed her. 'It's very handy having a caterer in the family.'

Anita smiled. 'I've enjoyed the challenge your wedding's given me. Thank goodness the weather's been kind. If it had rained ...' She glanced around and sighed. 'But I can see why you wanted to get married here. The garden's on fire with autumn colour and the mountains are awe-inspiring. You'll never tire of this view. You two got lucky finding this place.'

Ellie traded a smile with Luke. They had got lucky—*she'd* got lucky—and their purchase of Gerrigallop was just one example. She knew Anita was disappointed and didn't understand why she'd refused her offer to use the new wedding venue in the Mill House stables, but there wasn't anything Ellie could do about that. Over the last nine months, her admiration and love for her sister-in-law had grown, but she didn't feel the need to share her story beyond Luke and Sarah and, by default, Alex. Recently though, she'd been toying with the idea of writing to Megan Horton. The other reason she hadn't told Anita about the past was because she didn't want it to taint Anita's new home and new venture. After everything she'd been through with Cameron, Anita only deserved good karma.

Sarah sank into a chair, enjoying the relief of sitting after standing in high heels for a couple of hours. Across the garden, she watched Anita darting about checking that everything was perfect and she reflected on the transformation of her sister-in-law. It was *the* biggest surprise in the fallout of what she'd dubbed 'The Battle of the Wills'. Now, she and Ellie were Anita's biggest champions.

'Thought you might like this.' Alex set a few glasses and a bottle of champagne in an ice bucket on the table. He poured her a glass and took the seat next to her.

'You know me too well.' She dropped her hand on his thigh. 'Thanks.'

'You're welcome. By the way, you look amazing in that dress. You're as gorgeous as the bride.'

She laughed, knowing that Ellie's natural beauty, combined with today's radiance, put everyone in the shadows. 'You're just hoping flattery will get you what you want.'

'Well, I was hoping to get lucky tonight.' Grinning, he slung his left arm across the back of her chair and pointed to Anita with his right. 'She knows how to throw a wedding. Our investment's going to pay dividends sooner rather than later.'

'It's exciting watching her grow the business. Luke's finished the plumbing for the ensuite bathrooms and the tiler promised he'll be done by the end of the week. It's perfect timing for the harvest festival. She's already got her first booking for the Mill House B&B.'

'She's wise, doing it in stages.'

'She's working around the little girls. When they're older, she can manage all six rooms, but not right now.'

Sarah still got a very unfamilial kick every time she thought about how Cameron's manipulation, greed and grand plans had come completely unstuck when his previously compliant and biddable wife rediscovered her principles and sense of family. And Anita had done it in spectacular style by keeping Mill House, which was rightfully hers by law. Sarah had no qualms at all delighting in the fact that she'd lost Cameron from the family but she'd got to keep Anita and the girls. Not that she'd wish a divorce on anyone— except perhaps Cameron. While she admired Anita's strength of character, she felt keenly for her because she didn't deserve what had happened or the way Cameron had pulled the rug out from under her.

It rankled that, after all Cameron had done, the only real justice that came his way was at the expense of Anita and the girls. He'd lost his marriage and family. Sarah knew it had gutted him, but she didn't have any sympathy to waste on a conniving, avaricious man who'd schemed to disinherit his sisters as well as disadvantaging other people. The court's ruling had been a variation of both wills—a type of meeting in the middle. An education trust fund was established for all the grandchildren and Cameron technically got Mill House, but as he'd convinced Margaret to put the deed in Anita's name, he'd ended up losing it. It was about the only time his devious planning failed him. Sarah received seventy per cent of what had originally been left to her in the first will. Cameron got the third of Margaret's money he was entitled to along with the remaining thirty per cent of Sarah's, and all of what should have been Ellie's share—funds Margaret had denied her. Money Ellie refused to fight for. In the end, Sarah had given her own inheritance to Ellie, who had struggled to accept it.

'You're not making any sense, Ellie,' Sarah had said to her, frustration burning hot in her chest. 'You just told me that the sale of Luke's place is paying for three-quarters of Gerrigallop and you feel bad that you don't have any real money to contribute. Yet, you won't take money that is rightfully yours. Money Dad would have wanted you to have.'

'Dad didn't have any money to leave us.'

'He had some money separate from the business that got left to Mum.' Sarah told Ellie what Margaret had said about Kevin and her sister looked immensely sad.

'I hate the idea he was probably miserable for years. But I love him more for still managing to be our wonderful dad.'

'Then think of the money as an extension of his love for you.'

'That's a leap. You know why I don't want that money.'

'It isn't *that* money, Ellie. It's my money and I get to choose what I do with it. It will clear your mortgage and pay for Gerrigallop outright. Think about what life without debt means. It's a buffer for times when the building boom slows and Luke's business slows with it. It means you can have another baby and not rush straight back to work. It means holidays. It means a less stressful life and I want you to have that. If last year taught me anything, it's that sometimes you need to come out from under the blinding fog of your own issues and see the other person's point of view. You're my sister. I love you. I want you to have this money.'

Ellie stood firm. 'I'm not promising anything except that I'll talk to Luke.'

Sarah loved her new brother-in-law almost as much as she loved Ellie and she knew Luke would tell her sister that the decision to accept or reject the money was totally up to her. His love and respect were why Ellie finally accepted the funds and now Sarah got a thrill of satisfaction every time she thudded across the cattle grid and drove down Gerrigallop's glorious tree-lined drive. Ringed by mountains and overlooking the valley, Gerrigallop was her second favourite place—after Riverbend. It was the perfect setting for the wedding and not just because of the view, but because it represented a new start for Luke, Ellie and Noah.

She shielded her eyes with her hand and squinted. Ellie wasn't drinking champagne. Did that mean something wonderful?

'Wedding cake, Mother dearest.' Emma plonked herself down on Alex's lap. 'And Daddy dearest too.'

Alex laughed. 'What do you want?'

'You on my T-ball team.'

'Ruby and Phoebe bribed Gus with cake, did they?'

'And Finn!' Emma said indignantly. 'It's so not fair.'

'Life isn't, darling,' Sarah said sagely. 'Let's hope your brothers' betrayal is only limited to T-ball.'

'They're nothing like Uncle Cam,' Emma said stoutly. 'They said yes because they feel sorry for the cuzzies.' She studied her parents' faces intently, as she'd been doing on and off ever since she'd returned from France six months earlier; seeking reassurance they were happy together and not about to separate.

Sarah squirmed with guilt every time it happened; hating that she and Alex had traumatised their children and given rise to a level of anxiety that, although fading, still lingered.

'Thanks for not getting divorced,' Emma said finally, before shoving wedding cake in her mouth.

'We're thankful too.' Alex caressed the back of Sarah's neck. 'But our situation's a bit different. Some things are easier to forgive than others.'

'As much as your aunt may have wanted to, she couldn't trust or forgive your uncle for what happened to the Parrys and for changing your grandmother's will.'

Across the garden, Anita watched Alex's public display of affection for both Sarah and Emma. She tried not to let the ache of loss dent her happiness and pride at what she'd achieved, not just today, but during the last year. She loved Cooked By a Friend and now Mingunyah Country Weddings, but she missed sharing her life with a man who loved her. Of course, Cameron still loved her, but it wasn't in the way she needed to be loved. When she saw the respect that ran like a steel cable through Sarah and Alex's—and Ellie and Luke's—relationships, she realised the respect in her marriage had been an illusion. Cameron's needs and greed had always come first and she and the girls second.

Although they were a few months away from being officially divorced, their protracted and difficult financial negotiations had finally been settled. Cameron had begged Anita to reconsider the divorce, apparently distraught at the thought of losing her, but given everything she'd learned about him, she couldn't separate his claim to love her from his love for Mill House and the money. Even with Sarah receiving over two-thirds of her original share of Margaret's assets, Anita felt Cameron got more than he deserved from his mother's estate. She'd engaged Rebecca Chin, the family law specialist in Valley View, and instructed her to 'take him to the cleaners'. Neither Rupert Grimes nor Cameron knew what hit them.

All Anita had really wanted was Mill House and to be assured that the girls' education was taken care of. Ruby and Phoebe wanted to stay at boarding school and she conceded that Cameron had been good about that, especially when she heard tales of other divorced men pulling their kids out of expensive schools and refusing to pay the fees. The education trust helped, but even so, she cynically believed Cameron's support for the girls staying at their private school was more to do with his fear of losing a continuing source of clients if they left.

He was dividing his time between Melbourne and Mingunyah. Anita couldn't tell if Prestige Country Properties had survived the taint of scandal because Cameron was lucky or exceedingly talented in deception. Just like the lack of evidence to prove undue influence with Margaret's will, there was not enough evidence to prove any underquoting or price manipulation of Warrnbatt. During the investigation, reputable real estate agents stated that, given the limitations of the property, the price he'd paid for Warrnbatt, although at the lower end of the scale, was still within reasonable and fair limits. 'Fair' was arbitrary and many locals were leery of dealing with Cameron, but enough were tempted by 'offers on the table' from overseas investors to sell using him as the broker.

Anita had wanted a fifty-fifty custody arrangement but Cameron claimed his business didn't allow for this so she'd pitched for him to take the little girls each weekend. He'd insisted on every second weekend and as weekends were very busy for her, whether it be high teas, cooking classes or a wedding, Anita was confident this arrangement was to punish her for leaving him. Excluding the saw mill, she and Mill House were the only valuable possessions in his life that he'd lost.

She may have discarded a husband but thankfully she'd gained his family. She really didn't want to think about how her life might be without Sarah and Ellie's support. Even with it, there were still dark and miserable periods when she was tempted to forgive Cameron and get her old life back. Except that life was gone and with it, the needy woman she had once been. The morning after Cameron had told her he was selling Mill House, Anita had telephoned Sarah and said, 'I'm terrified you're right about Cameron.' From that moment, Sarah was unstintingly supportive of her; probably because Sarah hated Cameron more than Anita did.

At first the support was practical: stopgap childcare for the little girls when other arrangements fell apart and advice about lawyers. But one day, Sarah and Ellie arrived with Gus and while he took Noah and the girls to the park, the three of them sat drinking wine and talking as if they were old friends instead of strained in-laws.

Slowly, her friendship with Sarah not only resumed but changed into something deeper, more of a shared understanding rather than Anita being in awe of Sarah and Sarah being the wiser older woman.

If Sarah's brush with a marriage break-up had forged this closer bond, it was Ellie's experience as a single mother that provided the potting mix to grow their friendship. Although Ellie wasn't as open as

Sarah when it came to chatting about personal things, Anita knew that if she rang Ellie at three in the morning, the only question Ellie would ask was, 'How can I help?'

Her brothers-in-law had also adopted her and she appreciated Alex's business advice and Luke's mate's rates when he'd replaced all Mill House's aged plumbing. When the banks prevaricated on lending her the amount she needed to convert the stables into a function venue, Sarah and Alex's offer of a business loan was a godsend. Despite how busy Alex's massive sustainability project at Riverbend kept him—tree planting, the installation of solar hot-water systems and using renewable biofuel—he still found time to mentor her. Whenever she thought about how much he'd taught her, Anita almost cried with gratitude, but any time she tried to thank him, he'd shrug and say, 'Any questions you've got about the bloody financial software, ask Sarah.'

'Anita!' Sarah held up her champagne glass with one hand and pointed to it with the other.

She crossed the lawn and Alex stood as she arrived.

'Don't go on my account.'

'Come on, Dad.' Emma was tugging on Alex's hand.

'I'd love to stay and chat but Emma needs me on her T-ball team.'

'Sit, Anita,' Sarah said, pouring her a glass of champagne. 'We can watch this hotly contested game together, because I apparently lack the ball skills to be helpful.'

Ellie joined them, bringing her drink and a platter of nibbles with her. 'And as the bride, I've thankfully been spared. But Luke, Noah and the other Sorenson men can't resist the challenge, so they're in.'

'Plus, I paid a fortune for this dress.' Sarah handed the full flute to Anita. 'I'm not ruining it for T-ball glory.'

'It was worth every cent. You look fantastic. You both do.'

'Thank you. You should add personal stylist to your list of talents. With your advice and an eye for a bargain, both Ellie and I are better dressed now than we've ever been.'

'I'm just happy to help.'

'I love this ring.' Sarah picked up Ellie's left hand, tilting it back and forth, watching the many facets of the diamonds and the emerald-cut sapphire catching the light. 'Anita, have you decided what you're going to do with your diamonds from Grandma's brooch?'

Sarah had insisted that the diamonds in the Jamieson brooch be divided between the three of them. Each received four large diamonds and a ring made from up from the baguette diamonds. Ellie was using the baguette ring as her wedding band, two of the large diamonds in her engagement ring and the other two for diamond studs, which nestled in her earlobes.

'I'm keeping the big diamonds for the girls,' Anita said. 'When they each turn eighteen, they can decide if they want a ring or a necklace. What about you?'

Sarah had been pondering this question for the last few weeks. 'I was thinking of doing something similar.'

Anita frowned. 'I can see that working for Emma, but the boys?'

'We know the diamonds make a beautiful engagement ring,' Sarah said, thinking of Finn and wondering about Gus. She hoped the changes to the marriage act were only a matter of time but even if future Gus did meet a man he wanted to marry, did gay men have any use for diamonds? She guessed she'd learn, just like she and Alex were learning other things. Being the parent of a gay child was a lifelong learning curve. To be honest, being a parent of any child was.

Phoebe and Ruby suddenly squealed. Emma groaned loudly and everyone watched Gus dive and capture a high ball before loudly declaring his father, 'Out!'

Anita yelled, 'Go, Gus!'

He turned to the table, his handsome face alight with a broad smile and gave them all a big wave.

'He's done so well this year. What are his chances at the draft?'

'Apparently good,' Sarah said, 'but we have to wait and see. I worry he'll get drafted to WA or somewhere equally far away. I've got my fingers crossed for a Melbourne team, then he and Finn can share a house. That way I'll still worry, but I'll worry less.'

After a lot of thought, Gus had decided to limit his coming out to just his parents and siblings, joking that he was too young to be an AFL gay icon. If he got the chance of an AFL career, then he'd think about it. 'I just want to come out to people when I'm ready.' They couldn't argue with that.

Whether it was the relief of telling them he was gay or the relief that Sarah and Alex had reconciled, or a combination of the two, Gus had returned almost immediately to being his happier self. His life was full and busy doing Year 12, playing footy and being in the band. He'd cheerfully completed his mediation-mandated community service and continued helping at the nursing home long after his prescribed time was over.

'Mum, do you reckon if they knew I was having this much fun with the old dudes, they'd have made me do something else, like picking up rubbish?'

'They're just happy you're happy and unlikely to deck anyone again. So are we.'

He'd looked sheepish. 'Yeah. It was dumb. Sorry. Hey, did I tell you old Mr Prentice remembers Grandpa playing footy? He said he won best and fairest six years in a row.'

'Did he?' Sarah had told Gus her suspicions about her father's sexuality. 'I wonder if he remembers a man called Gary Longmuir?'

'Probably. His legs might not work but there's nothing wrong with his brain. He said he had some photos of Grandpa at his house. Maybe we could ask his daughter if we could look at them.'

'Do you think we could interview him and record him? I'd love to know all about my dad's football career and anything at all about the man I think he loved.'

'That'd be cool. I'll ask him.'

She and Gus had a date with Ron Prentice the following week and Sarah couldn't wait.

As she watched the T-ball players and listened to the good-natured sledging between Luke's brothers, she said to Ellie, 'Those Sorenson boys are competitive.'

Ellie laughed. 'Tell me about it. Whether it's cooking a barbecue, playing Trivial Pursuit or sport, they've elevated it to an art form.'

'One of the things I value most about the three of us is we're not competitive. Despite our occasional hiccoughs, we're always working on acceptance.' Sarah raised her glass. 'I love you both.'

'I love you both too,' Anita said. 'I couldn't do half of what I do without you two. Thank you.'

'I spent a lot of years thinking I didn't need either of you, but I was wrong. I wouldn't be without you now.' Ellie raised her glass. 'To always having back up.'

'To sisters,' Sarah said. 'Woman's best friend. Let's drink to that.'

ACKNOWLEDGEMENTS

This book could not have been written without the assistance and the support of many different people. Special thanks to writing mate and conference 'roomie' Jennifer Kloester for the laughs, the cheerleading and sharing her story with me, which sparked one thread in this book. Thanks to Jane Tierney for chatting about life in a big family and coping with ageing parents and to Kate Parsons for answering my questions about life in the high country, for sharing her mother's 1970s cookbook as well as making me fall down laughing with photos of party cuisine—frankfurters stuck 'stylishly' into a pineapple. Ah, the sophistication!

A friend and passionate sourdough bread enthusiast kindly shared her precious time and chatted with me about the challenges and highlights of running a successful business with a spouse, as well as giving me a tour of the bakery, feeding me amazing bread and promptly answering a bevy of frantic text messages as I wrote the book. Angus Cameron from Meredith Dairy filled me in on sheep, goats, cheese and sustainable farming practices, and kept me inspired with his Instagram feed. What's not to love about kids frolicking in spring pastures! Justin Hartnett, an estate lawyer, explained the basics of wills and power of attorney and helped me solve a plot problem that would not be thrown out of court. Kandy Shepherd filled me in on pony clubs as well as answering all my equestrian questions. Any and all mistakes are mine.

I was born on the edge of Victoria's high country, and as a keen snow-skier, the north east has long been a favourite part of the state for me. Just standing among the snow gums brings me peace. I try to visit each year and I am fortunate to have good friends in the district who are generous with their hospitality and will answer random questions such as, 'How much does a cup of coffee cost in Mansfield and Bright?' Thanks to Eryl and Keith Lowe for all the cycling stories and introducing me to 'turbo buns'.

On the publishing front, thanks to my agent Helen Breitwieser for her support and wise council. To editors Annabel Blay and Kylie Mason who have the hardest job. Thank you for putting up with my moaning as you challenge me not to rest on lazy writing laurels but to hone my skills to make each book the best it can be. Thanks to my publishers Sue Brockhoff and Rachael Donovan for their support and to the great team at Harlequin and HarperCollins who work tirelessly behind the scenes with cover design, marketing and getting the books onto the bookstore shelf so readers can buy it.

The writing life would be a lot harder without the support I receive from my family and writing friends. There are always deadlines when things are very intense and I hibernate in the office for weeks before coming back, blinking into the light to find the house still standing. Norm, I couldn't do it without you.

A huge thank you to my generous readers. I am heartened by your letters, emails and texts. I am very aware that the selection of books available to purchase is greater than most of our budgets and I very much appreciate your choice in purchasing this one. I hope you enjoyed it. If you did, please tell your friends and subscribe to my newsletter at fionalowe.com. Happy Reading!

ABOUT THE AUTHOR

FIONA LOWE has been a midwife, a sexual health counsellor and a family support worker; an ideal career for an author who writes novels about family and relationships. She spent her early years in Papua New Guinea where, without television, reading was the entertainment and it set up a lifelong love of books. Although she often re-wrote the endings of books in her head, it was the birth of her first child that prompted her to write her first novel.

Authentically Australian, her stories are often triggered by a secret or a mystery, and explore the themes of family, community and second chances. Described as gripping, thought-provoking, heart-warming and ultimately uplifting, Lowe's books have been praised for their emotional depth. She is the recipient of the prestigious USA RITA® award and two Australian RuBY awards.

When she's not writing stories, she's a distracted wife, mother of two "ginger" sons, a volunteer in her community, guardian of eighty rose bushes, a slave to a cat, and is often found collapsed on the couch with wine. You can find her at her website, fionalowe.com, and on Facebook, TikTok, Instagram and Goodreads.

BOOK CLUB DISCUSSION QUESTIONS

We're spending our children's inheritance is a popular bumper sticker. In the novel, Sarah says inheritance is a privilege not a right. Do adult children really believe this?

Experts say planning is important to avoid heir warfare but can emotion ever be taken out of a will?

With the Baby Boomers holding more than half of Australia's wealth, elder abuse is on the rise. Is there any way of preventing this within families?

Family inheritance traditions today can still disadvantage women. Discuss.

Sibling rivalry does not always stop in childhood and can adversely affect adult interactions. Think about your siblings. When you gather, are there moments of reversion to childhood roles?

Sarah was judged by Anita for leaving her son when she moved out of Riverbend. Do you think women are judged more harshly than men if they move out of the family home?

Secrets and lies morph over time to become family folklore. How hard is it to dismantle long-held beliefs?

Printed in Dunstable, United Kingdom

64998451R00255